Jane Linfoot writes fun, flirty, bestselling romantic fiction with feisty heroines and a bit of an edge. Writing romance is cool because she gets to wear pretty shoes instead of wellies. She lives in a mountain kingdom in Derbyshire, where her family and pets are kind enough to ignore the domestic chaos. Happily, they are in walking distance of a supermarket. Jane loves hearts, flowers, happy endings, all things vintage, most things French. When she's not on Facebook and can't find an excuse for shopping, she'll be walking or gardening. On days when she wants to be really scared, she rides a tandem.

🐦 @janelinfoot
f www.facebook.com/JaneLinfoot2
www.janelinfoot.co.uk

Praise for Jane Linfoot

'Jane Linfoot has got out the mixing bowl and whipped up a truly gorgeous story...A deliciously scrumptious treat'
Rebecca Pugh, bestselling author of
Return to Bluebell Hill

'Just like the perfect wedding cake, Cupcakes and Confetti is beautifully crafted and wrapped in romance'
Heidi Swain, bestselling author of
The Cherry Tree Cafe

'A pure delight...fabulous, fun and unforgettable'
Debbie Johnson, bestselling author of
Summer at the Comfort Food Café

'Simply stunning'   *A Spoonful of Happy Endings*

'Gorgeous book with characters full of heart, and an impassioned story to make you smile'   *Reviewed the Book*

'This author packs a punch'   *My Little Book Blog*

'Loved this book. The main characters are vividly drawn...the writing is fast and feisty'   *Contemporary Romance Reviews*

'With every book I read I fall more in love'
Booky Ramblings

Jane Linfoot

Christmas Promises at the Little Wedding Shop

A division of HarperCollins*Publishers*
www.harpercollins.co.uk

HarperImpulse
an imprint of HarperCollinsPublishers Ltd
1 London Bridge Street
London SE1 9GF

www.harpercollins.co.uk

A Paperback Original 2017

1

First published in Great Britain in ebook format by
HarperImpulse 2017

A catalogue record for this book
is available from the British Library

ISBN: 9780008260668

Typeset in Birka by Palimpsest Book Production Ltd,
Falkirk, Stirlingshire

Printed and bound in Great Britain.

For Anna and Jamie, Indi, Richard and Eric, Max and Caroline, M, and Phil. With love. xx

Author Note

Each of the stories abbot Poppy, Sera, Lily, Holly, Jess and their friends at Brides by the Sea can be read on its own. If you'd like to read consecutively, this is the order:

The Little Wedding Shop by the Sea
Christmas at the Little Wedding Shop
Summer at the Little Wedding Shop
Christmas Promises at the Little Wedding Shop

I hope you have as much fun reading the books as I have writing them, love Jane xx

Taking pictures is like tiptoeing into the kitchen late at night and stealing Oreo cookies

Diane Arbus

Chapter 1

Saturday, 2nd December
At St Aidan station: Sparkle all the way

'Could you possibly take me to Brides by the Sea?'

The whiskers I'm staring up at are curly, white and, at a guess, a hundred per cent acrylic. And let's be clear about this – hitching a ride on Santa's horse and carriage definitely isn't my first choice to get across town to the wedding shop, where I'm going to be staying for the next month.

When I got on the train this morning at St Pancras there was a seventy-five-foot tree in the departure hall, enough spangley lights to illuminate the northern hemisphere and choirs clustered around pianos singing carols. Christmas in London was rolled out in November. I can't tell you how blissful it was to leave it all behind and arrive in St Aidan to the sound of seagulls, and one wonky tree by the station exit that hadn't got its decorations on yet. And I know my mum and dad have let our family house in nearby Rose Hill village and gone off to Spain on a wild winter sun-seeking adventure in a motor caravan. But when I smell the salty air and catch

1

a glimpse of the jumble of white painted cottages and grey stone houses winding up the hill into the town here, even though my parents are away it still feels as if I'm coming home.

The bad news is, by the time I've jostled my way through the mass of travellers in their North Face jackets, and dragged my rucksack and a suitcase the size of a garden shed onto the pavement outside the station, the last of the line of waiting taxis is a disappearing dot on the horizon. So when a pony and trap driven by Santa Claus himself jingles to a halt in front of me, even though I've come to here to avoid Christmas, the offer of a lift into town is too tempting to turn down.

'Brides by the Sea, Jess's wedding shop?' Santa hitches his belt over a stomach so squishy it has to be hollowfill and raises one eyebrow archly. Then he nudges the huge elf in green beside him. 'Four floors of bridal gorgeousness, Cornwall's most fabulous wedding emporium. As advertised on Pirate Radio, and featured in *Hello!* and *OK!* magazines.'

'That's the one,' I say, mildly surprised that he's so word perfect. Although even that gushing description falls short of describing the delicious haven of white lace and prettiness that overlooks St Aidan bay. He's obviously heard about Seraphina East, known to us as Sera, the shop's dress designer, hitting the nationals last year, when she made a bespoke dress for a celebrity.

Santa beams as he rubs his belt. 'Brides by the Sea will always have a special place in our hearts. It's where we bought the suits for our very own wedding.' He and the elf exchange dreamy glances, a couple more nudges and some nose wrinkles. 'You know they're extending into the shop next door too?' Santa's sudden change of tone suggests he's impressed, yet possibly jealous.

'Do you know Jess well, then?' I've heard the news about the shop expanding, because I've been chatting to my bestie Poppy, who works there. But it always comes as a shock when I remember St Aidan's, the kind of town where everyone knows everybody, and everything about them too. Pretty much down to their bra size.

The elf jumps down and gives me a wink as he lands on the pavement next to me. 'We're Chamber of Commerce chums. Divorce was the making of Jess, you know. She's been turbo charged ever since. Any friend of Jess's is a friend of ours, so we're happy to go the extra mile for you, even if we're only out on a pre-season practice run. We're just getting our pony, Nutella – that's Nuttie for short – used to the bells again.' He gives the pony's chocolate brown rump a pat as he dips towards my luggage, groaning as he heaves my suitcase onto the back of the cart. 'Christmas crackers, how many wet suits have you got in there? You're down for the winter surf, I presume?'

The other thing I forget about when I've been away is the incessant questions.

I laugh. If anyone wants proof that you can grow up by the sea in Cornwall and end up with zero aptitude for water sports, just look my way. As for my heavy bags, I'm not admitting I've brought my boxed sets of *Friends*, every *Harry Potter* paperback I own, along with the *Princess Diaries*, and my entire *Sweet Valley High* collection. In case you're wondering, as far as my extended visit to Cornwall goes, I'm planning a big month in.

'Sorry, I should have warned you, my cameras weigh a ton. I'm here to take pictures for my friends' beach wedding.'

Choosing to get married at the seaside in December might sound bonkers, but when they asked me to do their photos I jumped at the chance to get away from London. In my real job I'm a food photographer, working for a product development company. I know taking pictures of burgers is a thousand miles away from capturing bridal parties. But this particular surfie wedding is so small and laid back I'm looking forward to the challenge of a change. I'm hoping it'll be more like fun than work. More importantly, the happy couple are my favourite friends of the ex I've spent the last year pining over. Not that I'm getting my hopes up in that area. But at least I might get to catch up on what he's doing and take some lovely wedding shots for my friends Becky and Nate along the way.

As I pull myself back to reality, Santa's hauling on my hand hard enough to pull my arm out of its socket. A second later my bottom crashes down next to his on the high seat of the carriage, and my own fake fur sleeve is crushed against his raspberry fleece. Then, as his yank turns into a vigorous handshake, my mouth goes onto autopilot.

'Hi, I'm Holly, lovely to meet you, Santa ... and your elf husband too ...' I usually have a rule never to tell people my name between November and January, so I brace myself for the wisecracks. Believe me, if it's December, they always come.

Santa nods and gives a little sniff. 'A Christmas wedding photographer called Holly. Very fitting.'

'Not too many pricks, I hope.' The elf widens his eyes at Santa, as he lands on my other side.

'Only my ex,' I say, pulling a face.

The elf takes in my groan and changes tack. 'Great, so how about a quick selfie with Santa before we set off?'

'I'll pass on that one, thanks.' If I sound appalled by the idea, I can't help it. Apart from the beach wedding, I'm here because I'm hell bent on escaping from Christmas. So running smack into my own dedicated Santa straight outside the station is a big backwards step. Ending up jammed between him and his chief elf is even more damned careless of me. A selfie would be the end of washday. In a launderette-burning-down kind of way.

The elf screws up his face and his whine is loud and startlingly theatrical. 'But *everyone* who rides in the Charity Christmas Special carriage takes a selfie with Santa, even if it's only a dress rehearsal.'

'Actually, I'm all good.' That's my polite way of saying I'd rather eat my own head than have my picture taken with Santa, when all I want to do is get to the shop, climb the stairs to Poppy's little attic kitchen and make myself a cup of tea.

The elf's nostrils flare. 'Be very careful. Santa can get a bit tetchy. In elf-speak what I'm saying is a refusal may offend.' His eyes take on a triumphant glint. 'Let's face it, you don't want cinders in your pillow case on Christmas morning do you?'

Ever heard of dressing up and getting right into character? And taking it *way* too far. Even if I'd be more than happy for

Santa to miss out my stocking this year, there are times when I know I'm beaten. 'Fine.' I grab my phone, jam my face up against Santa's, frown because he's wearing so much more eyeliner than I am and try for a smile. As I pull off a grimace, I'm resigning myself to a bad case of beard rash later.

'Brilliant.' Mr Elf – or should that be the second Mr Claus? – has reconnected with his happy self again. 'Hash tag St-Aidan-Santa-Special-Selfie underscore Kids-at-Christmas for every tweet please. Whenever you find some signal, that is. There isn't any here, obviously.'

Another of the joys of Cornwall I accidentally overlooked when Poppy suggested I use the little flat above the Brides by the Sea shop as a bolthole, and I agreed in a nanosecond. Poppy and I both grew up in Rose Hill village, a few miles inland from here. She was in the year above me at school and we both escaped to London and did the same food tech course at uni. And even though she's been back here a while, we've always kept in touch.

'Photograph your mad winter wedding then stay on for a fabulous low key Christmas above the wedding shop,' Poppy said one day when she was cheering me up on Facebook messenger. Reminding me straight afterwards that I still had my entire annual holiday allocation left. And offering to throw in as many cupcakes as I could eat, because Poppy is Brides by the Sea's cake baker. She also happens to be unexpectedly pregnant, with a whole load of Christmas wedding bookings to deal with as well as her bump. So all I had to promise in return for using the flat for the whole month was to lend a hand in the shop while Jess was away on a winter holiday and help Poppy with the weddings, at her partner, Rafe's, amazing wedding venue, Daisy Hill Farm.

I know, from when Poppy lived in the tiny top floor flat, that the views across St Aidan Bay from the little porthole windows are amazing. But that wasn't what swung it for me. The truth is, I'm not actually planning to make Christmas low key this year – I'm planning to erase it entirely. The idea of doing whatever work I had to, then locking the shop door and hiding away in the attic for the whole of Christmas is the perfect celebration-free scenario for me. This way I can watch back-to-back episodes of *Friends* all on my own, and come out again when it's all over. As an evasive plan of action, it's completely foolproof. And for someone like me, who's in Christmas denial, it couldn't be better. Once the wedding pictures are in the bag, it'll be plain sailing all the way to the New Year.

'Ready to go?' As Santa shakes the reins and Nuttie trots out into the road, the jingling from the harness bells is shockingly loud. And hideously festive. And it's not just who's driving the carriage. Thanks to the back being plastered with fake snow, dangling baubles, ivy garlands and a shitload of presents, not to mention huge banners proclaiming SANTA IS COMING YOUR WAY, *everyone* is staring at us. Pointing, even. The only way we'd be turning more heads is if we were being pulled along by an actual real-live reindeer. What's more, now we're speeding down the street, the wind is biting. On a good day in winter, much to my constant dismay, my nose is red enough to lend to Rudolf. And that's without the help of a hot, steaming coffee or a vodka cocktail. Both of which I try to avoid consuming in public, even if I don't always succeed. After a few minutes out in this arctic blast, my hooter is going to be positively luminous.

I let go of the seat and try to pull my collar of my trusty leopard-print jacket up over my ears so I can bury my nose in the fake fur. It's one of those coats that feels like a shield when you put it on. If you snuggle down into it, you're guaranteed to be warm and safe wherever you go. And pretty much invincible. Which is why I couldn't think of a month away without it, even if the rest of Cornwall are wearing on-trend down jackets, or gorgeous wool coats with humungous fur collars. Although faced with a Cornish westerly as stiff as today's, with me trying to make it double as an invisibility cloak, I'm asking a lot of my own small jacket.

'So, are we looking forward to Christmas?' It's a wonder Santa has time to chat as well as deal with the early afternoon traffic. His carriage driving technique consists of pointing his pony, then going for it. I reckon his costume must have gone to his head, because at every junction he assumes he's got priority. If he were driving a taxi this recklessly, they'd fine him and confiscate his license.

I blink as yet another car screeches to a halt, its driver open mouthed as we whoosh past, a snowflake's width away from his bumper. On balance, I decide it's easiest to bluff the reply to a tricky question.

'Christmas? I couldn't be any more excited, Santa.' Even without jolting along behind a pony's swishing tail, the truth is way too complicated to go into, even for Santa. Basically, the problem is, he's twelve months too late asking me the question.

For my whole life, Christmas has been my favourite time of year. When we were kids, my big sister Freya and I used to get so excited we'd hyperventilate from the moment we opened the first door on the Advent calendar until the last present had been opened. Freya embraced Christmas the same way she tackled everything – forging her way ahead with her amazing exuberance, dragging our younger brothers and me along on her wave of enthusiasm. Making hundreds of yards of paper chains, then hanging them in festoons all over the house, even in the bathroom. Spraying the windows along the entire street with fake snow late at night. Buying a bale of red fleece from the market and making the whole family Santa suits for her school textiles project. Then when I was twelve, the unthinkable happened and she died. It was the worst time ever. Fast growing brain tumours happened to other people, not girls like Freya, who was only fourteen and ripping through life like a tornado. Twenty years on, I've learned the best way to cope is to concentrate on the good bits. I've taught myself to love remembering all the happy times. And as my everlasting tribute to Freya, I go completely over the top with the festive thing. Because anything less would be wrong.

Which is why this time last December, I'd already decorated my boyfriend Luc's flat to within an inch of its life and I was holding my breath for a fabulous Christmas trip to his parents' place in the Highlands. I'd splurged to the max on presents. And bought at least a hundred rolls of paper to wrap them in, obviously. And yes, I was *aching* for Christmas to come. Then it did, and my entire life unwound.

I'll save the more desperate details for a time when I'm not careering round a corner at top speed on one wheel, like we are now. At least if we go super fast, we'll get there quicker, with less chance of anyone I know recognising me along the way. It's enough to say that entirely thanks to me, Luc's surprise Christmas proposal went all kinds of wrong. Okay, I admit that a woman running away at the speed of light isn't an ideal reaction when a guy waves a diamond ring under her nose. When you're as un-sporty as I am it's more than ridiculous. And I still don't completely understand why my legs reacted as they did. Or why, once I'd calmed down and come back, we couldn't work things out. But the upshot was that by January I was boyfriend-less. And eleven months on I'm still single, confused and way too sorry for myself. What's worse, my dream London life has completely lost its sparkle. And with my fifteen boxes of Christmas decorations still in storage and no proper home to put a tree up in anyway, I'm hardly going to be whooping it up on the twenty fifth this year. But thanks to Jess and Poppy's help, I've got that sorted. I just hope me telling Santa porkies isn't going to backfire on me, just when a tiny part of me is optimistic that things are about to get better.

'We'll take the scenic route along the sea front.' Santa's yell is a foot from my ear, as we suddenly veer away to the right. But the side winds off the bay are so vicious, I can barely catch what he's saying. 'It's a long way round, but easier for Nuttie and we get to see the lights.'

'Great.' I shrink further inside my coat, take in the dark grey swell, and a high tide pounding against the sea wall, sending foam splashing over the railings. When I look up at the unlit light strings thrashing horizontally, the flying sand stings my eyes. At this rate, by the time we reach the shop I'm going to look like a witch who's been on a broomstick ride in a hailstorm. I'm so busy trying to untangle my hair, I only look up to notice the huge rogue wave arching through the air across the road at the last moment. As we speed towards it I'm howling. 'Watch out ahead, Santa!'

'Whoa, Nuttie!'

Even a guy with Santa's powers can't easily stop a cart pulled by a ton of pony doing a twenty mile an hour extended trot. As the arc of water showers downwards, we clatter to a halt yards too late. The breaking wave smacks us full in our faces, then sluices down over our shoulders and legs.

'Holy mackerel! The hazards of sleigh riding!' Santa's letting out a choking squawk as he collects the reins again. 'We're lucky Nuttie didn't bolt there.'

'Jeez, bolting would be nothing.' The elf is gazing down in horror at his soaking green knees. 'My panty hose have gone entirely transparent. How about you, Holly?'

I'm scraping the icy drips out of my eyes, muttering as I squeeze streams of water out of my jacket. 'I couldn't be wetter if I'd been dipped in the ocean.' If this is payback for lying to Santa, it's come raining down on me scarily fast.

As the elf turns to Santa he's close to pleading. 'Let's call in the Surf Shack to dry off?'

Now he's talking. You have to admire an elf who knows his local cafés. So long as you don't mind walls made out of random planks, it's the best one on the beach. I'm already

11

warming up, mentally shovelling a ton of marshmallows into the top of my bucket-sized award-winning hot chocolate. But we've both overlooked the fact that Santa's on a mission.

'This isn't a jolly.' Santa's scolding is scornful *and* incensed. 'We're here to make deliveries. We need to get Holly to her wedding shop.' There's a jolt, and we're off again, this time even faster.

I spend approximately two minutes consoling myself for not getting the chance to visit the ladies' room so I could work on not looking so much like I'd crawled out of a shipwreck. Then the cliff side gives way to buildings again. As we whizz up the hill past significant and familiar landmarks, I'm getting involuntary flurries of excitement in my chest. Jaggers Bar, the Yellow Daisy Café, Hot Jack's, and Iron Maiden's Cleaners pass so fast they're a blur. We're yards away from Brides by the Sea, accelerating wildly as we make a turn into the mews, but by the time we get there, a four by four is already in the space we're heading for.

'Donna and Blitzen! What the hell happened to priority for the elderly? Can't he see the beard?' Santa's cursing bounces off shop windows shining warm light into the grim afternoon.

The whole point about Santa driving the carriage like a loon is that it only works when other road users give way. If you meet an 'eff-off' driver head on in these narrow streets, you're likely to end up in big trouble. Even dealing with any driver who doesn't jump on the brakes a hundred yards away, you might end up with the carriage and the car wedged between the buildings. Which is exactly how we are now. Don't ask me whose fault it is, because even though it happened right under my nose, I really can't tell.

Enough to say, the vehicle we're jammed up against is plastered from one oversized bumper to the other in an expensive paint job. I can see some local artist has had a great time painting beer bottles bobbing on exceptionally realistic airbrushed breakers. And the signage on the door is conveniently at knee level. *Huntley and Handsome's Roaring Waves Brewery – St Aidan in a Bottle.* That pretty much says it all. Aren't the current rash of microbreweries all run by overgrown boys with too much disposable income, staving off their midlife crises? I shiver as the car window slides down, and realise mournfully that we could be stuck here for ages arguing when I'm freezing my butt off.

But as I stare past the elf to the car driver, heat sears through me. It's the kind of hot flash under the collar I haven't felt since I used to blush on the school bus every morning as a teenager. My face bursting into flames at the slightest provocation was why sixth-form bad boy, Rory Sanderson, singled thirteen-year-old me out for my own personal conversation as he made his way down the gangway to his seat at the back. Every *single* morning. By the time he left for uni, one tweak of his eyebrow from a hundred yards was enough to turn me scarlet. I just wasn't prepared to meet him today. Especially with me jammed between Santa and an elf, doing an impression of the old woman who crawled out of the sea.

I shudder inwardly as I stare into the car. The rock-star long hair might have been trimmed back, but the broad grin I'm staring straight into is unmistakable. And it hasn't lost an ounce of the kind of insanely inflated self-belief that I suspect came from having his own personal tractor from the age of ten. There are crinkles around the kind of come-to-bed eyes that were only one of the reasons for his legendary status. Rumour had it he also burned down the school music room due to a fault on his guitar amp. What's more, he was the only pupil with the cheek to call Mrs Wilson, the deputy head, 'darling', and the charm to live to brag about it. Although thinking back, I reckon it was him driving a car off an actual cliff top that fast forwarded him to the top of *every* mother's banned boyfriend list.

'Holly-berry-red-cheeks? What the hell are you doing here, dripping all over Santa's sleigh? Did you take up swimming? I thought you always hated water?'

If it's divine payback for me lying earlier that's hurled him into my path here, let's be clear. I'd rather have a hundred rogue waves crashing down on my head than come face to face with the awful Mr Sanderson again. Since I last heard of him light years ago, storming the world of corporate law in Bristol, I've stupidly let him drop off my 'worry about and avoid at all costs' radar. And this is him all over. Straight in there, claiming to remember a person's intimate details. Familiar as if I only saw him yesterday.

For a second I'm wishing he'd caught me at some do I'd made a big effort for. That I'd had a shit-hot professional blow dry, got my long lasting lippy on, squeezed into some killer dress I probably don't even own. At least then I'd be coming from a position of strength. The thing is, right now my hair is in rats' tails, I have half the beach in my fake fur, but I'm so bright red from the wind and the cold, no blush on earth is going to make it any worse. That particular scenario might never happen ever again. This is my one chance to lay the ghosts and wipe the floor with him. It's one of those iconic now-or-never moments. I shove my hands deep into my pockets, drag my coat closer around me and launch.

'Actually, you know what I hate more than water?' I've barely been here half an hour and I'm already talking in questions. 'It *is* Rory, isn't it?'

'It was last time I looked.' He taps his fingers on the steering wheel and nods. 'And? I'm all ears here. And I'm sure Santa and his elf can't wait to hear either.'

That back chat is only what I know to expect. If there's a confused frown overlaying that laid- back smile of his, it's probably because I'm coming on so kick-ass here. Believe me, I'm actually shocking myself too. You wouldn't believe how liberating it is, when for one time only you don't have to worry about blushing.

'Well ...' I pause to drag in a breath and my chest ends up expanding so much I feel like a cat with its fur standing on end. 'I hate inconsiderate drivers who force their way into spaces that don't even exist.'

He pulls a face and his voice rises in protest. 'Excuse me, but *I'm* the injured party here. Your friend Santa's the one who cut *me* up.'

So likely. 'You always were a knob head. For one time only you're going to have to grow some balls, give in and back up. It's obviously escaped you, but ponies don't have reverse gear.' Even though I'm on a roll here, I actually just meant to tell him to grow up. But whatever. I ramp up my scowl. 'You wouldn't want ashes instead of presents in your Christmas stocking, would you? Seeing as you're still behaving like a kid.' I know it's the elf's line, but it's too good not to borrow.

As Santa leans past me, his voice is conciliatory. 'Sorry she's so prickly, Rory. You'll have to forgive her, she's just come all the way from London.'

Rory's actually laughing, damn him. 'Don't worry, Gaz, I haven't had a tongue lashing like that in years and I'm loving every second.'

My jaw freezes. For every reason. 'You two know each other too?'

Santa gives me a strange stare. 'Of course we do. This is Rory Sanderson, a.k.a. *the* Mr Huntley and Handsome, our eminent local wine supplier.' He pauses to cock an eyebrow at me. 'He's a *lovely* boy. I'm sure this unfortunate squeeze here wasn't deliberate.'

The elf purses his lips. 'Rory's solely responsible for keeping the fizz flowing in St Aidan, and our own personal Adonis in the Chamber of Commerce. I can't think of anyone we'd rather be wedged in a crack with.'

The disgustingly attractive Sanderson body is obviously still working its magic then, despite it being twenty years older. It wasn't that any one bit was particularly spectacular. But working as a whole, the effect was apparently knock-out. Not that I was ever a public fan. I made damned sure I never admitted to any of my misplaced teenage lusting.

'No need to be quite such a tart, Ken.' Santa's looking daggers at the elf.

Rory looks like he's choking back his laugh. 'Great, we all

know I like to claim that most of the upmarket hangovers in St Aidan are down to me. Anyway, if you hang onto the pony, Gaz, I'll get out of your hair –' He leans forward and eyeballs me, '– definitely not implying you look like a haystack, Holly. Or a witch who rode through a hurricane.' He leans back again, and it's obvious when he lets his smile go, that's exactly what he means. 'Then you can all get on with your day.'

Clamping my hands on my head, I try to find a snappy last word to hurl, but my wisecrack stream has totally dried. Instead I'm left, mouth sagging, staring at his manoeuvres. It's only at the very end of his six point turn that I see past the Bad Ass Santa Brew transfers on the window and spot the two baby seats in the back of the car. I swallow hard and hang on to my deflating stomach as the engine purrs away. Rory Sanderson with *kids*? I did not see that one coming. Though why I should give a damn, I have no idea.

'Holleeeeeeeeee ...'

I turn as I hear my name. A shriek like that can only mean one person. 'Poppy?'

She's haring down the mews, blonde pigtails shining in a sudden shaft of afternoon sun, her Barbour coat flapping. 'Great transport, Hols! Here's me searching for you everywhere and you've been hijacked by Santa. How wild is that?' Her forehead wrinkles into an appalled frown as she comes close. 'Jeez, what happened here? Did you drive through a car wash?'

Frankly I'm relieved it's not worse. 'We collided with an early Christmas wave.' Now I'm climbing down and shaking the sand out of my hair, it's easier to laugh it off. 'But thanks for the lift, Santa, it was way more exciting than a taxi. Take this for your charity box.' I grab a tenner out of my pocket and push it into his hand.

Poppy leaps backwards as I land next to her. 'No hugs for you when you're this wet, even if you do look like an adorable baby seal.' Poppy's great, because she always sees the good side. Even from a distance, the air kisses she tosses a foot from my cheek smell of warm vanilla, icing sugar and waxed jacket. She turns to Santa and the elf, who's grappling with my suitcase. 'I've just made some Christmas pudding muffins if you'd like to come in and try some?' That's another good thing about her. Poppy's always looking for testers for her baking.

The elf grimaces at his thighs as he hands me my rucksack. 'Sorry, not today. I'm struggling with a see-through tights situation.'

Poppy glances at the elf's tiny tunic as it rides up, then looks away quickly. 'Eeek, I completely get where you're coming from on that. Wait here, I'll bring the cakes out.' She jostles my arm excitedly and makes a lunge for my case. For someone pregnant who needs my help, she's incredibly energetic. 'Come on, Hols, I'm *so* pleased you're here, and I promise we're all going to have the most *amazing* Christmas.'

'Great.' There's no time to remind her I won't be doing Christmas. A second later, she's dragging me and my case on wheels down the cobbled street towards the shop door.

Chapter 2

Saturday, 2nd December
At Brides by the Sea: Small talk and straight lines

Later that evening, as Poppy clears away the papers from the fish and chip supper we've just had in the tiny kitchen in the attic flat, she's doing her best to talk me into what sounds suspiciously like a party.

'There's no Brides by the Sea Christmas bash this year because Jess is away. So tonight's her consolation prize. It's just a few friends for drinks. You'll know everyone, you *have* to come down.' She pushes the cake box towards me. 'Another?'

Even though there's a huge kitchen at Daisy Hill Farm, Poppy still does a lot of her cooking here in the flat above the shop. Blaming her boyfriend Rafe for eating the cakes is probably only half the story. Every time I come through to the blue-painted cupboard fronts and shelves of brightly coloured, mismatched crockery, crammed with bowls and baking trays of every size, I can see it's not a place you'd give up easily. Which is probably why she keeps working here and has as many friends to stay as she can find excuses for.

If Poppy's trying to soften me up with sugar, I'm confident I can fit in a second Christmas pudding muffin and still resist the invitation. 'I was planning a quiet evening, listening to the roar of the wind and the crash of the sea. Googling hot tips on wedding photography and getting ready for my practice shoot with Nate and Becky tomorrow.' In case she's forgotten, I'm here to hide not go out on the razz. Peeling my holly leaf off the muffin top, I bite through the white dribbled icing. Then my teeth sink into that familiar dark chocolate sponge heaven.

Poppy's cakes take me all the way back to the cosy kitchen at her mum's house, with its table covered in cake crumbs and icing sugar. The warmth and the smell of baking, and the house always full of Poppy's friends, including me and Freya. It reminds me of how as teenagers, when we dribbled icing onto buns and made feathery patterns with a knife, I didn't have to think about my big sister never coming back again. They were happy times.

She tidies up a stack of mixing bowls and grins at me as I get up from my stool. 'Your shirt and trousers look great. You showered earlier, your hair's fab. A bit of lippy, you'll be good to go for the get-together.'

As I scrunch up my muffin cases and head for the bin, I'm still holding out. Then I peep out through one of the porthole windows. Even on winter days, the postcard views across St Aidan bay will have some kind of sparkle about them. Tonight as I look down on the shimmering light reflections bouncing off the inky water, I'm so grateful to Poppy for bringing me here. However much I'd rather avoid a crowd, I have to go with her to the shop's Christmas 'do'. 'Okay, let me find my bag.'

She's already passing it to me. 'Right answer. Jess said she wanted a word too.' Dipping into her own bag, she takes long enough to wave her mascara wand at her reflection in the kettle. Then she's hurrying me towards the landing. 'Great, there's champagne cocktails down there, we don't want to be late. Mine will be a virgin one, of course, but I like to pretend.'

Considering the size of Poppy's bump, we clatter down the stairs alarmingly fast. As we arrive in the ground-floor hallway the tree we pass is on the large side of stonking, but the all-white colour scheme means it blends perfectly into the background, and doesn't set my Christmas alarm bells jangling too loudly.

Bracing myself for my first evening out in ages, I peer gingerly into the White Room, with its rails of white and cream dresses, and drifts of tulle and chiffon. The shop windows beyond are studded with a thousand tiny fairy lights that spark off the beading, where white-glittered ivy falls in cascades behind slinky satin skirts. I turn to Poppy. 'It's very quiet. Where is everyone?'

Poppy wiggles her eyebrows. 'We're going all the way down to Lily's new department in the basement. It's way more practical when you don't have to worry about spilling drinks on the dresses.' Lily is another friend from Rose Hill who we grew up with. She was always flower-crazy and worked here when we were all younger. Now, thanks to one of Jess's career-building schemes, she's extended her florist's skills and moved onto styling.

As we get to the bottom of the next flight of stairs and edge our way into the white-painted brick rooms of the lowest floor of the shop, the crowd of people in sparkly clothes waving cocktail glasses around is the first clue. The table groaning under the weight of champagne bottles and ice buckets, which Poppy steers me towards is the final giveaway.

'Right, Hols, I give in, it is a party. But it's only small, and I promise it'll look better through an alcoholic haze.' She's looking very guilty as she rams a fruit-filled glass at me. 'Kick off with a Christmosa, which is grape juice and Champagne. Here's a Tickled Pink, which is pomegranate and Prosecco.' A glass of pink liquid lands in my other hand. 'And try not to miss the Christmas Margaritas.'

I shiver as the Champagne bubbles prick my nose. 'Are you trying to get me drunk?' It's so long since I last went out, it won't take much.

She picks up a tumbler for herself. 'Not at all. But I'm stuck on pomegranate juice and fizzy water, so think of it as drinking for me.' The grin she flashes at me is triumphant. 'Cheers, Hols, and well done for coming. Truly, it's time you learned how to have fun again. Come on, let's see who's here.'

But before we move off Jess comes towards us, her chiffon blouse billowing. 'Holly, lovely you've made it. First, I must apologise for our local Horsemen of the Apocalypse. They might be St Aidan's answer to Boy George and the late, great Pete Burns, but Gary and Ken get well out of hand at times.'

'No worries.' I'm smiling because my ride in Santa's cart seems so long ago. Then I scan the room hurriedly to check no one else from this afternoon is about to creep up on me unexpectedly. When I was doing my best to avoid the non-party, the waking nightmare of Rory Sanderson being here hadn't actually crossed my mind. But then neither had Ken and Gary.

Poppy sees my head swiveling. 'Don't worry. There's Lip Sync Karaoke at the Hungry Shark. Ken and Gary won't miss a second of that. They'll probably catch us up when we move on to Jaggers' *Warm up for Christmas* night later.'

I let out a silent groan. Jaggers is the local bar dedicated to happy hours and teenage drinkers. I can't personally think of many things worse than necking cocktails by the jugful and falling into bed at three a.m. so that's one after-party I'll be wriggling out of. But once I've gazed round the whole room without anyone giving me heart failure, I give Sera and Lily from the shop a little wave. Then I turn back to find Jess is staring at me hard.

'So, Holly, we're both about to hurl ourselves off cliffs. Do you have any tips to offer me?'

'Tips?' I'm blinking at her blankly, because Jess doesn't usually ask for advice. Being that bit older and having built up her empire from one room in the basement selling flowers, she's pretty much seen it all. Let's face it, this fabulous department is only a fraction of the shop, especially now she's bought next door too.

Even after another sip of Christmosa, and one more slug of Tickled Pink I'm still confused. 'Which cliffs are you talking about, exactly?'

That makes her smile. 'The cliffs are proverbial, Holly. The unnerving bit is I'm about to go on holiday with a man I barely know and you're here to be a wedding photographer when you haven't got the first clue how to be one.' She pauses long enough for that to sink in. 'I always tell people to feel the fear and do it anyway but now it comes to me, it's not that easy.'

As party talk goes this is a bit deep. And whereas my little surfie wedding isn't quite the big deal for me she's making out, it's true Jess is about to dive out of her comfort zone. After years of being defiantly single, she's taken everyone by surprise and got together with a guy called Bart, who she first met as a teenager. Bart's main claims to fame are an all-year-round tan and being loaded. As well as owning the fabulous Rose Hill Manor just outside the village where I grew up, he's got places in the Caribbean and Switzerland. He lets out the Manor for occasional weddings, which are now run by Poppy and Rafe's wedding team, from nearby Daisy Hill Farm. With a couple of December bookings coming up, he's decided to go away, and has persuaded Jess to go with him. But as Jess hasn't had a day away from the shop in ten years, being whisked off to the Alps by Bart is a huge deal for her. So I can completely see why she's feeling less in control than usual.

'To be honest, Jess, I'm hoping we'll iron out any problems for the wedding when we do our practice shoot tomorrow.'

She gives a disbelieving sniff. 'Well, I'm glad you feel so chipper. But that still leaves me with two weeks at Bart's mountain hideaway in Klosters. I'll be going mad worrying about the shop. And all that time alone with Bart, too.' The corners of her mouth couldn't be pulled any further down. 'I don't even *like* snow.'

The note of panic in her voice sweeps me back to my first time away with Luc. That was when I saw his passport said Luke, and found out he'd swapped the 'ke' for a 'c' in a bid to look less geeky. We went for two weeks in Madeira with his parents, because that's what he'd done every year before he met me. Although holidaying with his mum wasn't a great idea for someone trying to look cool. I swear I only stayed sane getting sloshed on cane rum cocktails and eating my own weight in honey cake. Then the ticking time bomb of all-inclusive caught up with me. By the second week the only holiday clothes I could get into were my travel leggings. You wouldn't believe how badly fleecy joggers chafe at thirty degrees. Not that Jess will have that problem, with her wide-leg linen trousers in sub-zero Klosters.

'Some time apart every day might help?' I'm remembering how burying myself in a book got me through. 'And take thermal leggings.'

Jess knocks back her Margarita in one go and reaches for another. 'Good thinking. My trouble is, Bart can be *such* a wind-up merchant.'

Poppy laughs as she joins in. 'You know we'll be fine here, Jess. And even though Bart loves to tease you, you always give as good as you get. Don't forget, you two love birds have been pretty much joined at the hip since September.'

That was when Jess and Bart finally went public, after a summer of secret assignations on a secluded island at the Manor. Although, if they really are as close as Poppy says, it hits me that maybe there is a piece of valuable advice I can pass onto Jess, after all. If they're trying to make up for lost time, it's completely possible that in a backdrop as picturesque as Klosters, Bart might pop the question. In which case, it will pay Jess to be prepared.

I take a deep breath, and given what I'm about to throw into the mix, I drop my voice. 'There is one very important tip – if Bart does happen to get out a ring and ask you to marry him, for goodness sake ram your finger into it and nod madly. Then decide how you really feel about it later.' This one's right from the heart. My downfall last Christmas is a well shared secret among our friends in St Aidan. I'm completely resigned to people knowing every last detail. 'If you panic, like I did, and go skiing off into the distance, there's a chance you'll blow it forever.' I've spent the last year pining for my lost life. I wouldn't wish that on anyone.

For a second Jess looks as if she's going to explode. 'Me ski? I'm not a bloody snow bunny.' As her voice rises to a shriek, everyone turns to listen. 'Bart knows, I will *not* be going anywhere near *any* slopes, kindergarten or otherwise. And salopettes are completely out of the question.' As her tone softens, a smile spreads across her face. 'Although I'll make an exception for the après ski, obviously.' That thought puts the purr back into her voice. As tonight proves, no one loves a party like Jess does.

'Good point, Hols.' Poppy and I exchange glances over our three glasses. It's significant that Jess has chosen to go ape at the mention of skiing, not the proposal.

'Thank you, Holly. I had a feeling you'd set me straight. It's exactly why I asked the question.' Jess's nostrils flare and her smile warms. 'When our resident wedding photographer, Jules, gets here I'll introduce you. He'll be delighted to help *you*, in return for the absolute gems you've given me.'

I get in fast to jump on that idea. 'Thanks, but there's really no need.' Super pro Jules is someone else I was hoping to avoid. I definitely don't want him thinking I'm treading on his toes here.

'I absolutely insist.' Jess is beaming now. 'And the forecast for tomorrow is abysmal. You've heard we've taken over the building next door and the first floor's still empty. It will be perfect for you to use for indoor shots with your lovely couple.'

Over the years Poppy's told me about Jess's legendary rail-roading. I just wasn't expecting to be flattened by the runaway train myself. 'Nate and Becky want us to go to the beach, whatever the weather.' Even though I say it in my firmest voice, I get the feeling no one's listening.

'So where were we?' As far as Jess is concerned, I haven't said a thing. 'Ah yes, waiting for Jules to arrive. Meanwhile, Lily's over there, she'll be looking after the shop with you, Poppy and Sera while I'm away. Hasn't she done wonders down here?'

'It's brilliant.' As I check the room again, this time I'm taking in the decor and the beautifully arranged stock too. Even if the silver stars-all-over theme is way too Christmassy for me this time around, it's obvious Lily's a natural with the styling. The space is bursting with everything from vintage cake tables, to signs, to place settings to four-foot-high illu-minated letters spelling LOVE.

That's the funny thing. A snap shot of any corner of this showroom might have come from my food photographs at work, because the props we use are exactly like the pretty things here. The cleverest people at our company, like Poppy in her previous career, develop the tasty new food products. Then it's my job to photograph them so they look so delicious that people rush to buy them.

The first time someone put a camera in my hand it was for a student project, photographing a bread range. We were all collapsing with giggles as the lecturer kept telling us to arrange our baps so there was a spiral in the picture. None of us could see any spirals at all, but apparently all my pictures had them anyway. Which was lucky in a way, because when it came to taste innovation, I turned out to be hopeless. My spinach and toffee pudding scored the lowest mark in the history of the course. But once I'd accidentally hit on those invisible spirals, everyone overlooked my strawberry and cauliflower tart disasters. So what began with those seeded buns ended up for me as a career taking food pictures.

Jess's eyes are shining with pride as she beams at the fabulous place settings and the fairy lights overhead. 'Every couple needs to make their wedding unique to them, and Lily brings those dreams to life. And talking of making dreams come true, I can't wait for you to see the studio space next door.' Note that in two minutes, Jess has changed an empty floor into a studio. But that's Jess all over, from what Poppy's told me. 'Oh, and here's Jules now. Ju-u-ules!' As she yells and practically knocks us over with her wave, a guy who could have strolled straight off the pages of GQ magazine is heading our way. With his trademark pink, blue and green-striped scarf muffled around his stubble, he's exactly as Poppy has described him.

Jess couldn't be looking more pleased with herself. 'Holly, meet Jules, our very own photographic wizard. You two are going to have *so* much to talk about. I'm hoping you'll be able to give Holly some pointers, Jules.'

I'm wanting the ground to open up and swallow me. 'Lovely to meet you, Jules, but forget the pointers. My wedding's so low key it's almost not happening.' I force out a smile and, thankfully, I'm saved having to shake hands, because his are buried deep in his pockets.

As he turns to scrutinise me, his eyes are so blue and startling they could have been painted in on Photoshop. 'I take it you've brought a camera with you. What do you use?'

From what Poppy says, Jules is as legendary for his ecstatic hugs as he is for his fantastic pictures and extravagant wardrobe. But his famously floppy fringe is suddenly stationary. And in place of the gush, I'm sensing an ice flow.

I push on, ignoring how awkward this is. 'Most of my stuff is Nikon.' You've no idea how many arms and legs it's cost me to get the best there is. Although my memory cards are tiny rather then the true pro ones. And how many clothes I haven't bought over the years, to save up so I can afford it. Some of the lenses alone cost a month's salary. Which is why I'm wearing a New Look top from four seasons ago rather than designer cashmere, and a four figure price tag jacket like Jules.

Jules's nose pinches and he flips back his hair with what almost could be a head toss. 'You do realise it's not the camera that makes good pictures. It's actually down to the person behind the lens.' He says it like it's going to come as news.

I nod. 'Right.'

He's straight back at me. 'A successful wedding photographer needs to be a great communicator.' The slight curl of his lip has nothing to do with a smile. 'Ordering a hundred guests around takes skill. Not to mention bucket loads of charisma.'

I'm letting this wash over me, exchanging 'what the hell' glances with Poppy, because it's got so little to do with a few friends having an informal beach party.

Jess is swishing the ice round in her glass, looking slightly bemused. 'So am I sensing there's a problem, Jules?'

Jules draws himself up looks at a spot four feet to my left. 'From where I'm standing, I'm just not feeling it with Holly. Not one iota.'

I force my cheeks into a smile. 'Well, thanks for sharing, that's very ...' I can't bring myself to say helpful, '... illuminating. Always fab to have insight from an expert.' Although now he's mentioned it, he's probably spot on. At work I always hide behind my camera. In a crowd I'm actually a bit of a mouse. In our family Freya was the 'out there' one, with enough pazazz to grab the spotlight for both of us. Meanwhile I made the most of her shadow, and hid in it. And even though I lost her, that's how I always stayed. At least it's good to realise that to handle a proper wedding I'd actually need a personality transplant.

Jules flips his scarf and turns his gaze onto Jess. 'And while we're here talking pictures, my answer is "yes".' Tight lipped doesn't begin to cover it.

Jess's eyes widen. 'Answer? Was there a question?'

Jules sniffs. 'Thanks for giving me first refusal. I'll definitely take the first floor space next door. Congratulations, Jess, you've just added a fully in-house photographer to your Brides by the Sea portfolio.'

Jess shakes her head. 'You're spectacularly missing every point, Jules. We're talking camaraderie here, not contracts.' She pauses to roll her eyes at Poppy and me. 'As for that first floor, I'm leaving my options open for the moment.'

'Great.' Jules's snap says it's anything but. 'Let me know the minute you come to your senses. My offer won't be here forever. And now I've got somewhere else to be.' There's a draught from his well-cut jacket as he whirls round and pushes past people towards the door.

Poppy pulls a face. 'Someone's in a rush to get to Lip Syncing.'

Jess shakes her head. 'Sorry, Holly, I don't know what got into him there.'

Even if Jess is mystified, I can see why Jules hasn't put me straight on his air-kiss list. So I'm happy to leap in with an excuse for him. 'Maybe he's not in a party mood?' I can sympathise with him on that one. Although, seriously, I don't blame Jules for being appalled to be forced to give tips to someone who could be here to nick his clients. He doesn't know that's the last thing on my mind.

'Poor boy.' Jess sounds more sympathetic than cross. 'He's an only child, living at home. If he doesn't get his own way, he get his tripod in a twist every time. Apart from that, he's usually second to none.'

He might have sounded objectionable, but at least he reminded me why I work with objects not people. What's more, I'm secretly glad there's someone else my age who hasn't got their independent accommodation a hundred per cent sorted. And I'm inwardly cheering that he's left so fast. All in all, if I had to meet Jules at all, it couldn't have gone better.

I knock back both my drinks to celebrate, and beam at Poppy. 'Time for a Festive Margarita, then?'

She grins at me. 'That's more like it. Rafe and Bart and Immie will be here soon. Let's see who we can find to introduce you to in the meantime.'

Considering I wasn't up for a party, the next few hours fly by. And the funny thing about Champagne cocktails is, they slip down so easily it's hard to keep count. By the time I head off up the stairs, with the excuse that I can't go to Jaggers *and* keep a clear head for the shoot tomorrow, my legs are feeling strangely wobbly. As I cross the hallway, I decide to run my own sobriety test. I'm staring so hard at my leopard print pumps as I try to walk in a straight line along a floorboard, I completely miss that there's someone hurrying towards me. The first I know is when I canon into a denim-shirted torso.

'Shit, I'm sorry ...' Seeing how fast that came out, I can't be *so* drunk.

The jeans I'm staring down at are soft and worn, and run down to scuffed boots. Then I spot the poppers stretched tight across a pretty ripped chest. However well I was sticking to my floorboard, the way I'm wanting to rip open those poppers has to be a sign of too much fizz. Then I take in a fist full of mistletoe. As I blink and breathe in a guy who smells fab, half of me thinks I'm dreaming. The other is almost ready to swoon and take advantage.

'Holly Berry Pink Cheeks? Why aren't you at the party?'

I jolt and lurch away. 'Rory?' If I'd had another freezing wave crash over me, I couldn't have sobered up any faster. As it is, from the jangling of sleigh bells and the white pine twigs sticking in my ear, I seem to have landed mostly in the Christmas tree. 'What the hell are you doing here?'

His lips are twitching. 'I get invitations to all the best parties. I like to drop by and check my Champagne's going down okay.' Then he lets his smile go. 'If you're typical, it looks like everyone's had plenty tonight.'

Now I'm sober *and* indignant. 'What the hell kind of player walks round parties clutching a handful of mistletoe?' I'm dying inside because I even *thought* of leaning in back there.

His face creases as he laughs again. 'One who makes sure Jess has every detail in place in the shop before she leaves for her holiday.' He looks at the bundle in his hand. 'I'm not so much a player, more her mistletoe supplier.'

What's mistletoe got to do with a wine and beer seller? If I'm not keeping up here, it's nothing to do with the booze. 'So you're not ...'

'Out to snog you in the stairwell?' His laugh is very low this time. 'Not unless you order that specifically. We like to go the extra mile for our customers, wherever it takes us.' His face splits into the broadest grin yet.

'As if ...' I'm shaking my head hard enough to rubbish that reply and fan my burning face at the same time. 'Great, I'm delighted for you. I imagine you'll have lots of very happy customers.' I'm not only talking bollocks, but I'm also sinking backwards into the tree branches. They're springy like a cushion, but any minute now I'm going to reach the point of no return and topple over. And probably take the tree with me.

'We import the mistletoe from Normandy along with our festive cider, to give away with our Christmas orders. That's the kind of detail Huntley and Handsome customers appreciate.' Rory suspends his mission statement for long enough to frown at me. 'Are you sure you're okay there, Holly Red?'

Before I have time to answer, an arm slides round my back. Next thing, I'm out of the tree and vertical enough to protest loudly as I push him away. 'Hey, no need to wade in. I was totally fine there. Thanks all the same.'

He blinks and shakes his head. 'Sure. So how about the stairs? It's a long way up to the attic.' And bugger that his dimples are there now too. 'If you need a hand, I'm always happy to help. After throwing barrels of beer around, carrying you will be a doddle.'

I'm skimming over how he knows where I'm heading, because I'm desperate to cut him off before he gets to point out it's happened before. I make a lunge towards the stairs, and once I grasp the handrail I feel much steadier.

'Only a few flights up.' And thank Christmas I'm in flats, not heels. Getting carried home by Rory isn't something I want to remember, or repeat.

There's that laugh again. 'It wouldn't be the first time. Just saying.'

Forget kicking myself for knocking back so many

Christmosas, I'm actually cursing for having come down at all. As for Rory raking up the past, I'm furious enough to want to wring his neck. Which in the end is good, because suddenly my legs spring to life. Before I know it, I'm looking down at him from the enviable position of the first landing. There should be some snappy last word I could come out with, but in the end all I manage is a wave.

His voice comes floating up the stairs after me. 'Take care up there. See you later, Red Cheeks.'

I'm crawling into bed when I finally mumble a reply. 'Not if I see you first, mate.'

I had every reason to stay in my attic flat before. But Rory Sanderson just gave me a hundred more.

Chapter 3

'Sorry, there's no leopard ones, but you can have a monkey, a zebra, a lion or a cat.'

It's Poppy, and she's talking about the cupcakes she's been making while Jess and I have been busy downstairs. It's no surprise that Jess doesn't do hangovers. So we started early and moved straight on from helping the crack team clearing up in the basement to poring over the appointments book in the White Room. Jess talking me through every bride booked in for December is ideal displacement activity for both of us, because, realistically, Sera, Poppy and Lily are going to be in charge at the shop. But it keeps my mind off the engagement shoot – or more specifically Luc – and hers off her impending departure.

As I pore over the box Poppy pushes towards me and see the perfectly iced cake tops, my mouth waters. 'I'll have an orange cat, please. Which lucky person's ordered these?'

'A lion for me.' From the way Jess strides across the room to take one, she's momentarily forgotten her holiday wobbles. And Poppy still hasn't answered my question.

'Mmmm, totally delish, there's zest in the icing too.' It's only when I open my eyes again, after peeling back my paper case and taking a bite, then letting the tangy icing melt on my tongue, that I realise Poppy's hesitating. 'Aren't you having one, Pops?' She eats for England, even when she's not pregnant. I'd have put money on her going for a chocolate monkey first. Then a zebra.

She wrinkles her nose and looks down at her cropped sweatshirt, which is hiding a neat, yet surprisingly sizable, bump. 'I didn't have a muffin yesterday either. Midwife's orders. I've cut back on carbs, and taken up Pregnancy Pilates, and Yoga for Mums.'

'That's *harsh*.' I don't mean to sound negative. It's just hard to think of *nine* low-sugar months, with *that* much exercise.

'It's not for long.' Poppy's frown deepens as she shrugs it off. 'Although there is something else I've been meaning to mention. About who the cakes are for.'

As the sound of the shop door opening echoes along the hallway, Jess beams at me over the top of her lion. 'You've got a complete treat in store here, Holly. Poppy's been baking for the owner of Huntley and Handsome. A lovely boy, he gives us the most fabulous deal on our Prosecco ...' Those words sound like a horribly familiar echo of what Santa said yesterday.

My mouth drops open midbite as her words sink in. Surely she can't mean ... *Rory?* As I gasp in disbelief, a lump of sponge goes straight down my windpipe, and a second later I'm coughing into my fist, eyes watering as I struggle to breathe. If you've ever had a violent choking fit that turns into a humungous sneeze, you'll know what I'm going through. Even as I'm fighting for air, I'm desperate not to expel a throat full of chewed up cupcake, and spatter the entire rail of exquisite bridal dresses with bright orange cake crumbs.

Through my half closed eyes, I see Poppy, launching herself across the room. Then there's a noise like flapping angel wings and she's thrusting a handful of tissues into my hands to catch my sneeze. By the time I look up from blowing my nose, the dresses are saved. And Jess's beam is wide enough to stretch from one chandelier to the other.

Poppy's voice is a low murmur as her hand lands on my shoulder. 'Sorry, Hols, there's a blast from the past coming that I know you're going to hate. Rory Sanderson's come for his cupcakes horribly early. I promise I'll explain it all later.'

It's my own fault. If I'd had the guts to admit about bumping into him twice before, no doubt Poppy would have told me. At least this time I get to watch him walk in from the high ground of the mother-of-the-bride throne where I'm sitting. And I'm already a hundred per cent scarlet due to choking. Even so, his footfalls on the floorboards send prickles up the back of my neck. Whoever said attack is the best form of defence, I'm going to take their advice.

As I see the first, horribly familiar, weathered brown Timberland come through the doorway, I jam my mouth into a smile, scrape the last stray cake crumbs off my mouth, look up at the approximate place where his head is about to appear, and fire.

'Rory Sanderson, one more time. Just when I thought I'd waved goodbye to you for another twenty years, too.' I sink back against the cushions, but the hurtling retort I'm bracing myself for doesn't come.

Instead of storming in, tearing up the the White Room with his super-confident swagger, Rory's coming in at a shuffle. Leaning over to one side, so he can reach down to hold the hand of a small girl.

'Wow.' I'm not sure if I say that in my head or out loud.

At a guess, looking at his daughter's pale silky hair, Rory's partner's a blonde. As if a rock god would settle for anything less. If her disagreeable pout came from her mum, it's obvious he's chosen looks over personality. Although for once Rory's incessant grin has given way to a frown too as he clasps a rather over-sized baby tightly against the folds of his Superdry windcheater.

He pulls a 'holy crap' face at me over the top of the baby's head and blinks. 'Holly, right, great, hi.' It's a big change to see Mr Sanderson looking less than delighted with himself. Although the bad side is that when his dimples disappear, it makes the hollows under his cheekbones look even deeper.

Now I've seen who's actually arriving here, I'm regretting my over-explosive 'hello'. Somehow, even though I saw the car seats, the small people come as a complete shock. If I'd hoped for something to wipe Nate and Becky and Luc out of my mind, it definitely wasn't this. Kids have that strange effect of making everyone around them more gentle. And although Rory doesn't exactly look like a relaxed dad, having children hanging off him has certainly taken the fire power out of his smart-arse replies. As for Jess, she isn't hanging round for an air kiss with her favourite Huntley and Handsome hunk either. Her expression is equal parts terror and horror as she shoots behind the desk. I'm not sure I've ever seen anything make Jess recoil this fast backwards before. Retreating isn't her style.

Poppy is the one person in the room who looks delighted, as she clasps her hands and moves towards them. 'So are you going to introduce us, Rory?' Her eyes are shining as she smiles down at the girl. Which might well be down to her baby hormones. 'We don't often have visitors as exciting as you in the wedding shop. Although we do have lots of children at our farm. And I think you're going to like the animals there too.'

I wonder where the hell she's going with this, because the frown she's sending me is equal parts worry and guilt.

Rory shakes his head, as if he's trying to wake himself up. 'Er, right ladies, this is Gracie. And Eddie.'

The girl pats his arm with her free hand and mumbles into his sleeve. 'No, it's Teddie.'

Rory gives a sheepish grin. 'Oh shit, fine, okay. What she said.' Even for a prat like Rory, this is taking disinterested fatherhood to a new level.

'We've got some mini cupcakes here for you.' Poppy holds out the box to the child.

Gracie hangs back. 'Teddie isn't allowed icing ... he's too small. And Mummy doesn't let me say shit. Plops is gooder.' She sounds like she's channelling her inner disapproving head-mistress.

Poppy, undeterred, flips up the box lid to reveal a whole miniature set of what we were tucking into. 'They're animals. Holly just ate a cat and Jess had a lion.'

Gracie wrinkles her nose. 'I mainly have Frozen cupcakes ... blue ones with snowflakes ... and pictures of Anna and Elsa.'

Poppy's holding back her amusement. 'Maybe you'd better take these for later, then.'

Rory lets out an exasperated sigh. 'Well, this *is* going well. Not.' He looks at the baby in the crook of his arm, then down at the girl squirming behind his knee. Then at me. 'C'mon Gracie, I'm running out of hands here, the least you can do is hold the box.' A second later, the weight of a large baby lands in my lap, and he's picked Gracie up with both hands and dumped her down in front of Poppy.

'Eeeek!' When it comes to babies this near, I'm with Jess. Although as I close my fingers round Teddie's hoodie, and the scent of fabric conditioner drifts my nose, I can't believe how soft and squishy he feels. Or how heavy he is. 'You do know I might drop him?' I'm not sure I ever held a baby before. One of Rory's is making me extra shaky. My cheeks burning up are only to be expected.

Poppy's biting her lip. 'When did you pick them up, Rory? Even Rafe thought you'd last more than ten minutes before you tried to pass them on.'

Jess is mellowing. 'You'll have to do better than this, Uncle Rory.'

I'm trying to work out what's going on here. 'So they're not yours, then?'

For the first time since he walked in, the corners of Rory's eyes crinkle. '*Hell* no! Jeez, Holly North, how would I end up with two of *these*?' At least that explains the name blunder. 'On second thoughts, given there are children here, don't answer that.'

I know not meeting his eye isn't the best way forward. I'm staring down, marvelling at how warm the baby feels when I notice a dark splodge spreading across my left thigh. What is it about me and water? 'Is Teddie leaking?' If I carry on at this rate I'll have run out of clothes by teatime. Lucky for me we had guinea pigs when we were kids, so wee on my knee is no big deal. Whereas judging by Jess's apoplectic expression five yards away, if these had been her chinos, she might have exploded.

Rory's voice rises. 'You're joking? He *can't* need changing. Not *already*.'

Poppy wanders over to give a second opinion. 'Something here's very wet. That's babies for you, they pee and eat and … plop.'

Gracie's expression is solemn. 'Teddie's got clean joggers in his nappy bag.'

Poppy laughs. 'You're right, Gracie. I knew something was missing when you walked in.' She turns to Rory. 'Lesson one – wherever the baby goes, the changing bag goes too.'

Rory prises the cake box from Gracie's hands, and as he shakes his car keys the miniature beer bottles on his key ring jiggle. 'Jeez, the good news keeps on coming today. I'll be two minutes. And no accusing me of child desertion, either.'

I turn to Poppy, keeping my voice low. 'Rory *babysitting*?

Isn't that like hiring Edward Cullen as a childminder? And when did you two get so friendly, anyway?'

Poppy raises her eyebrows. 'He's one of Rafe's besties from way back. He's a lot better for knowing. He's also our main wine and beer supplier for weddings at the farm. Rory's sister Erin's gone in for an emergency heart op, and their mum's in Australia. As there's no one else, the poor guy's had to step in at short notice and look after the small ones.' She lets out a sigh. 'They're staying in one of the holiday cottages at the farm, so we can all help out. I'm sorry if it's awkward for you, but it's all happened at the last minute.'

Worse and worse. My heart sinks. Not that I'll be involved. But I could do without the thought of Rory popping up around every barn corner when I'm at the farm helping Poppy. Who knew industrial quantities of concealer foundation would be top of my shopping list? Although, even if I live to be a hundred, Rory will never fit into any 'poor guy' box in my head.

'Edward Scissorhands might have been safer.' As I mutter to myself, Rory's stomping back along the hallway so hard his footfalls are making the sleigh bells on the Christmas tree jangle. If he looked uncomfortable dragging two children in, that's nothing to how incongruous he looks with a peony-print Cath Kidston holdall slung over his shoulder.

Gracie waits until Rory swings back into the room, then she eyeballs him. 'Who's Edward Scissors?'

Poppy's straight in there. 'Edward has scissors for hands, and he's my favourite character from a film, in the same way you like Elsa. He's great at cutting up paper, and trimming garden plants.' She's certainly going the extra mile here. For all of us.

I seize baby Teddie around the waist and hold him at arm's length. 'Okay, who's doing the honours?' Obviously not Jess. 'Rory? Poppy?' I look from one to the other, as Teddie sags back down onto my knee.

Rory hands Poppy the bag. 'Be my guest. The bag's flowery, it has to be you.'

Poppy shakes her head. 'Sorry, but the antenatal classes haven't got that far yet. Didn't Erin show you what to do? Are you using terries or disposables?'

'No idea.'

Dropping to his knees in the middle of the White Room might not be the ideal place, judging by Jess's eyebrows hitting the ceiling. But he's flipped out the changing mat before we can stop him.

'You're looking like a pro there, Sanderson.' I've no idea why I'm being so mouthy either. Unless I'm unconsciously limbering up for my wedding work. Or hitting back for yesterday evening.

He shrugs. 'Sorry, that's as far as it goes. Erin wrote me a hundred page Operating Manual, but she showed me the nappy change, and it looked easy. But I'm damned if I can remember any of it.' Baby clothes, plastic bags, creams, bottles, nappies, potions and muslin squares are skidding across the floor as he tosses them out of the bag.

Jess gives a groan. 'This is our second best bridal area. You're making a terrible mess down there, Rory.' It's lucky for Rory that Jess thinks the sun shines out of his butt. She's run people out of town for less.'

He lets out a grunt. 'I thought it might jog my memory if I saw the equipment. But I'm none the wiser. Anyone got any bright ideas?'

It's in my interest for me to rack my brains, as I'm the one whose knees are getting soggier by the second. 'We could ask at the chemists. Or Google it. Or find someone with a baby out on the street and drag them in to show us. Or Gracie might know?' As I try to catch her eye, her scowl tells me what she thinks of that idea.

'Jeez, I was hoping for suggestions that *weren't* going to embarrass the shit out of me. And why would a three-year-old know when I don't?' Typical Rory. Still the same straight A-star student, with a gaping hole when it comes to common sense. Probably why he ends up letting cars fall off cliffs and being entirely unsuitable for childcare. I mean, he's said shit so many times even Gracie's picking him up on it. At this rate she's going to go home swearing like a trooper.

Poppy's got a smile lilting about her lips as she peers out of the window. 'Or maybe Immie might be able to help? It's our lucky day, she's on her way down the mews now.'

Immie grew up with us all in Rose Hill village. She may only be five foot nothing in her high- heeled Doccies, but she's queen of spiky hair, belly laughs and straight talking. Back when we were kids she was the one tough enough and loyal enough to fight all our battles, single-handed, from the age of three onwards. Thinking about it, Rory was the one guy she failed to bring into line. When Immie squared up to him for embarrassing me, he took no notice whatsoever. And although she never did give the reason, she had to admit defeat. Which says a lot about how impossible and out of hand Rory is.

She and Poppy see each other every day now, because Immie looks after the holiday lets at Daisy Hill Farm. And Immie and her hunky new husband, Chas the fireman, live in one of Rafe's cottages in the village, along with her son Morgan.

I laugh. 'Brainwave. Immie's got a teenager, she'll definitely know about nappies.' The one thing I assume about baby changing is it's like riding a bike. However long it's been, you never forget how to do it. So long as you knew in the first place. I can't believe that there are four adults in the room and we're all clueless.

From the way Immie's hammering along the hall, she can't wait to see this either. 'Rory Sanderson, what the eff? And, hello, Holly too.' Her husky laugh sets the chandelier jangling as she bursts in, then takes my breath away with a bear hug as she passes. 'I spotted the beer-mobile parked up in the mews with a baby-on-board sticker.' She pauses long enough to make an 'OMG!' face. 'So I thought I'd call in and see how you were all getting on. Lovely to meet you, Gracie and Teddie. Anyone like a gender-neutral fluffy snowman to play with? Or should that be snow person?' Immie, who's still wearing her sparkly *I'm getting married at Daisy Hill Farm* t-shirt, four months after the event, hands one incredibly cute cuddly toy to Gracie and drops another on the floor next to the changing mat. Obviously bought specially. With a ton of thought and insight, seeing as Immie is studying psychology part time at uni. Then she retreats with her hands on her hips to take in the scene.

'Isn't there a snowman for me?' Rory sounds like he's used to joshing with Immie.

Immie sniffs. 'They're suitable for under-threes, Rory. You'll have to grow up a bit before you have yours.' And given she's name perfect with the kids, she's well briefed, as well as having Rory down to a T.

'You two know each other too?' There's a lot I've missed out on since I was last home.

Immie pulls a face. 'Not only does he hang round the farm incessantly with Rafe but since he got his own bottling plant, he's always at the Goose and Duck too.' For anyone who's not local, that's the pub in Rose Hill, where Immie does glass collecting in return for pints and other favours. Like catering at her wedding reception.

Poppy sends Immie and Rory a warning frown. 'Are you going to say thank you to Immie, Gracie?'

Gracie's pout deepens. 'Actually, mostly I like *proper* snowmen ... like Olaf.'

Poppy makes her voice bright. 'Another *Frozen* fangirl moment there, I'm afraid, Immie. My cupcakes got the thumbs-down too. We clearly can't win them all with a three-year-old.'

As for Rory, I'm quietly delighted to witness him being brought to his knees by two kids so fast. It's heartening to know Rory Sanderson has an Achilles heel after all.

Rory gives a grunt. 'From where I'm kneeling, I'd say we haven't won *any* yet. But it's very early days.' Now he's coming head to head with the same headstrong genes he's got himself, he sounds less than delighted. 'I might be temporarily troubled by the technicalities of nappy changing. But give me a couple of hours to read the manual, I'm hoping to be across the whole game.'

'*Which* game's that?' I can't believe I actually said that out loud either. My mouthy side is certainly working overtime today. I might have zero experience looking after children, but I'm still incredulous he can sound so sure of himself, and that he thinks this is going to be easy.

Rory gives a snort. 'I've overseen billion pound corporate contracts. I'm the South West's biggest quality wine importer. I brew barrels of magnificent pints every day. Throwing a couple of kids into the mix for a week should be child's play.' He stares around the circle of disbelieving expressions. 'What? How hard can it be? It's great you women are all crowding around to help, but I'll be coming at this from a no-nonsense male perspective. Just watch me. I'll crack it in no time.'

Immie makes a choking sound. 'Snorting toad bottoms, now I've heard it all.' She catches sight of Gracie's wide-eyed surprise and grins down at her. 'There's nothing wrong with a woman speaking her mind. It's important to say what you think, Gracie.' A second later she's picked up the mat, scooped up Teddie and plonked herself down on the grey striped bridesmaids' chaise longue.

Rory's jaw is sagging. 'Whatever happened to showing *me* what to do?'

'Gracie, pass me the wipes, please, a nappy and the scented bags.' Immie shakes her head at Rory as she peels off Teddie's wet joggers. She raises her voice over Teddie's sudden howls. 'In the interest of not turning Jess's lovely shop into any more of a disaster area than you've already made it, you can have your tutorial back at the cottage. Meantime, get that lot folded up and back in the hold-all.'

Rory still hasn't moved, but he's grinning back at her. 'A "please" might be nice. Just saying. If we're teaching little people to be polite.' This is exactly why he drove the teachers round the bend at school.

Immie ignores him, then turns to Gracie, who's bobbing backwards and forwards. 'Cream, please. Then clean trousers and hand sanitiser.'

Poppy and I have got the strewn bag contents collected and packed. Rory's still standing where he was, as Immie shoves first the changed baby, then the snowman, into his arms.

He staggers backwards. 'Great. Thanks for that. It looks like we're ready to hit the road, then.'

As Teddie's screams of protest subside, Immie gives Gracie a play punch on the arm. 'Yay, well done, we're Team Teddie.'

As I hook the changing bag over Rory's shoulder, another comment slips out. 'If you're going to be *completely manly* about this you might want to get a changing bag with stripes on, or beer labels.' I can only blame my spontaneous banter on Immie's influence. A moment later, I'm hooking the bag of wet clothes over his finger. 'And don't forget this. Thirty degree wash. Cool tumble. I take it anyone who can make fabulous home brew also knows how to use a washing machine?'

From the mystified look on his face, as he backs towards the door, that's not necessarily true. 'Never heard of a service wash, Holly Berry? You should try them. For an extra tenner, they iron for you too.'

Which just goes to remind me – Luc did all his own ironing. And washing. Once you've lived with it, it's a great quality in a guy, especially one who regularly got through four shirts a day. Although he did once go overboard and spend three hours taking every single crease out of one of my favourite crinkle silk dresses.

We're all waving at Teddie and Gracie, who's managed to overcome her disapproval enough to be clutching both snowmen.

Poppy shakes her head as they finally edge out into the hallway. 'See you all soon, up at the farm.'

'Did someone mention cupcakes?' Immie's rubbing sanitiser into her hands. 'In which case I may need a couple to keep me going on the drive back.'

Poppy opens the box. 'One more for you, Hols, too, to keep your strength up for this afternoon's shoot?'

I flip out my phone to check the time. 'It's only an hour away.' Now it's hurtling towards me so fast, I'm getting twitchy. 'I need a large injection of instant courage.' It's not that I'm stalking Luc, and I've no hopes of getting him back. But when someone you love walks out of your life so abruptly, it's hard to turn those feelings off. When you don't quite understand what went wrong, it's very difficult to let go.

Immie dives in and grabs a monkey, then shoves a cake into my hand too. 'Have a lion. That should do the trick.'

But it could take a lot more than butter cream to save me this afternoon.

Chapter 4

'Okay, let's go for a shot by the window. Maybe with your arms around each other this time?'

It comes as a bit of a shock to hear my own instructions to Nate and Becky echoing around the empty upstairs room. Although they live in London, St Aidan's one of their favourite surfing destinations. Meeting up here with them always made it easier to persuade Luc to come to visit my parents.

As for the location, in the end Jess was proved right. Given the choice between horizontal rain on the beach, or a studio flooded with natural light, Nate and Becky took pity on me and opted to stay inside. Today is meant to help them relax in front of the camera, but it's great for me to have a dummy run with moving targets too. Although, when I suggested a casual dress code, with accessories to ring the changes, I didn't bank on them turning up in wet suits and immediately adding in Santa hats and sunglasses. It's no surprise that every shot I've taken so far looks like a surfie selfie from Christmas Day

51

at Bondi.

'Is this a good pose?' Becky, bless her neoprene socks, isn't stinting on the effort as she stares out to sea through a window and coils herself around Nate's neck.

'Brill.' I can overlook that she's entwined like a contortionist. The trouble is, whenever she takes up a pose she goes rigid. 'Remember to let Nate breathe, though.'

I was confident it would be easy to get some fabulous results in this space. But with Nate and Becky so tense it's proving harder than I thought. I've been concentrating so hard on snippets of news I might get from them, I've completely overlooked how strange it was going to feel coming face to face with Nate and Becky without Luc. Or that seeing them again would give me quite so many pangs for the life and the boyfriend I don't have any more. What's worse, within a few minutes of Nate and Becky arriving, I'm getting flashbacks. And I thought I'd left those behind months ago.

There's no way to put this tactfully. 'Can we lose the hats and sunnies this time?' I beam to show them how well they're doing. Even if this is turning into a total photographic disaster, I absolutely can't let them know.

'Without shades?' Nate couldn't sound more horrified if I'd asked him to get naked and pose in the buff. 'I'm going to feel *way* too self-conscious staring straight into that lens.'

Just my luck to hit a wedding couple like this, but I know exactly how he feels. I might as well 'fess up. 'I'm just the same. I hate having my photo taken.'

Becky gives a guilty shrug. 'It's why we *had* to have you to do the wedding. I knew you'd understand. We couldn't possibly have a *real* wedding photographer.'

Now they tell me. And all this is before we get to the not smiling thing. I have to say Luc's friends are a lot more intense than mine. You'd at least expect surfers to be relaxed, but Nate and Becky surf so hard it's more like work than fun. It goes without saying that jobs in insurance and finance involve a lot more responsibility than laughs. It's understandable that a banker will be more weighed down than a cake maker or a dress designer. And Luc couldn't have taken his own career in health and safety any more seriously. But then, as he always pointed out, it's a life and death area. Whereas making food look pretty totally isn't. I have this vague idea that when I accidentally gate-crashed the party at the shared house where he lived five years ago, we both got the wrong end of the proverbial stick. I thought he was an easy going, student accommodation kind of guy, whereas he was only there on the way from one massive loft apartment to another. The fact I was working on a one-off job, snapping champagne for Fortnum and Mason, gave him the entirely wrong impression about my gravitas. If we'd met up a month later when I was styling basic chicken nuggets for a cut price supermarket, he'd never have let me eat every toad-in-the-hole canapé on the plate he was circulating with. He'd have whooshed his platter further around the room until he found someone more suitable. I think more than my hunger for sausages, that night I hung on in there because he was a dead ringer for Ashton Kutcher. Although that could have been down to too many WKD's on my part. Even if he did still go on holiday with his parents, he was hunky enough for women to give me envious glances when we were out together.

As for his mates branding me as 'a Cameron Diaz', really, there's no resemblance. I'll admit to the odd ditsy moment. But implying I'm out there, blonde and sexy? Mainly I hide in corners, and obviously my hair's dark and usually messy. So they're totally wrong on every count with that comparison. Although I will admit I was Luc's fun side.

One last try and I'm throwing it all in. 'Forget I'm here ... talk between yourselves ... think happy thoughts ... try humming *Heaven is a halfpipe* ...' If I can't even get one decent photo when it's just the three of us, I'm starting to wonder how I'll get *any* at their wedding.

From the way Nate's lips twist, he's halfway to amused disgust. 'Wrong sport. Halfpipes are skaters, not surfers.' And the moment's over and he's back to looking like an undertaker.

'Okay, take a breather, I'll see what we've got so far.' Truly, wild accessories aside, as I flick through the camera roll, if you overlook that Becky's got a single teensy blue streak in her hair, these two wouldn't look out of place on the front of a funeral plan brochure. Thinking back to yesterday afternoon, the ride from hell with Santa was bliss compared to this. Although it gives me an idea. 'How about you get your hoodies on and we'll pop for a walk round town. It'll be more authentic. And much more like being at the wedding than this.' I'm bullshitting here, but I'm desperate. So long as we don't bump into Santa, things can't get any worse than they are now.

'Great.' It's strange how these men respond to big words and office speak. From the way Nate almost smiles again, I had him the second I said 'authentic'.

In no time at all, they're changed and we're out on the street. As I do up the top button on my jacket and hang on tight to my camera strap, I'm wishing I'd bought some fingerless gloves.

'So, you two wander and look in the shop windows, and I'll follow you with my zoom,' I say. Then I retreat a few feet across the mews and start snapping. Becky and Nate, holding hands, ambling down the cobbles, Becky and Nate laughing – really! – Becky pulling Nate back to look at the sparkle in the Brides by the Sea window. And we're away. Three shops along, they stumble across the Riptide surfie shop winter sale and we all troop in. Cue more cute pics. Looking at sweatshirts. Becky in a Christmas tree hat. Nate holding up a *Have a Swell Christmas* t-shirt. By the time we leave they're both swinging handfuls of brightly coloured carrier bags and Nate's carrying a body board. And I snap them spilling out onto the street.

An hour later, after a trawl all round town and down to the harbour and back, I've taken what feels like a thousand shots. The light's fading and my fingers have turned to ice. As we stagger past the window at the Hungry Shark, even though the hot drinks aren't as delicious as the Surf Shack's, the yellow light inside is warm and inviting.

Once I've checked there isn't a Lipsyncer anywhere in sight, I can't resist. 'Hot chocolate anyone?'

Nate hesitates and looks longingly at the Sundowner Bay window further along the street. 'There's still one surf shop we haven't been in yet.'

'Phew, I thought you'd never ask' Becky blows with relief.

'Shopaholic Nate can catch us up later.' She's through the door and ordering faster than you can say salt caramel swirl.

As we sit on high stools, scooping whipped cream off the top of cups the size of plant pots, Becky's blinking happily. I can't resist one last close up. And best of all, she doesn't even flinch.

'Well, I think we've found a way of making you relax in front of the camera.' When I push the mini screen towards her, with a lovely dusk shot of the two of them silhouetted against the masts in the harbour, her delighted smile makes me glow inside. 'Less than three weeks to the big day now.' I know the stress on the day will make it adrenaline filled. But after this afternoon, it feels like we're as prepared as we can be.

She sighs as she runs her fingers through hair that's surprisingly tidy for a surfie. 'You know, I think you did the right thing running away when Luc brought your engagement ring out.'

My spoon of cream stops in mid-air, halfway to my mouth. 'What?' She has to be joking, doesn't she? 'Are you okay, Becky?'

She pulls a face. 'A lot of days lately I wish I'd run when I caught sight of mine.'

I give a rueful sigh. 'For what it's worth, if I could turn the clock back, I wouldn't run a second time around. I'd definitely handle it differently.' In a way that didn't wreck my relationship, for starters.

She scrapes the grated chocolate off the top of her cream. 'When I dreamed of Nate proposing, I had no idea getting married would be so draining.' The sigh she lets out is long and weary.

Poor Becky. I give her hand a squeeze. 'Don't worry, you'll feel better when you've drunk your chocolate.' Wedding fatigue hitting the woman who has the stamina to ride the waves from dawn until bedtime comes as a surprise. Whereas when I legged it, the wedding itself hadn't even crossed my mind.

If we hadn't been staying with Luc's parents it might have all panned out differently. In Madeira they would have been in the holiday mood due to downing vast quantities of Poncha. As it was, three days into our stay in the Highlands, when his dad's dour expression hadn't lifted and his mum's mouth was still the same hard line, it finally dawned on me. Luc's serious side was probably an inbuilt part of his gene pool that was only going to get worse as he got older. Down the line, I might not be able to tease it out of him.

My family lost a child and still manage to be jokey, so permanently long faces are an alien concept to me. I mean, who, faced with Prosecco popcorn says, 'Sparkling white gives Keith heartburn'? And all my cute reindeer crisps got was a resounding, 'We don't do wild game.' In the split second when Luc went down on one kilted knee in front of the Christmas tree and his entire, unsmiling, extended family all that flashed in front of me was a lifetime without laughing. Although, to be fair, I haven't exactly been splitting my sides since then. And I suspect it was a complete overreaction. When I look back on our times in London, Luc did smile. Just not as much as me.

'Today is the first fun we've had for ages.' Becky's meticulously sinking every marshmallow with the back of her spoon.

Somehow, I feel I need to share more here. Make it clear our cases aren't the same at all. 'My trouble was, Luc made his proposal sound like we'd only be getting married so I could get a US visa.' Announcing he was leaving for a fabulous new job and life in the States, then popping the question in the next breath. What's worse, it was like my whole world being hit by an earthquake. I wasn't even aware he was up for promotion, let alone a leap across the Atlantic. If we'd discussed it in advance, I might have been more ready for it. I can see now, it was only natural that someone so work orientated would be super-excited about saving his news for a big reveal. For someone like me, who hates surprises, it couldn't have been worse. It was my fault too. I should have made my phobia about surprises clearer. And the size of the audience made the outcome all the more cataclysmic. Had it just been the two of us, Luc might have forgiven me for taking fright. But so many cousins and aunties seeing me vote with my feet was the ultimate in public humiliation. Everyone understood that. A proud man like Luc couldn't marry a person who'd done that to him. Even if I was mortified afterwards, there was no clawing my way back, no matter how much apologising and begging I did.

Becky shrugs. 'Luc's doing well over there.' This is just the kind of snippet I've been aching for. Now it's come without prompting I'm not sure I like it.

'He would be.' Most days I try not to think about it. I pick up my cup to cover up that one tiny fragment of news about him has my pulse racing. 'Although, actually, I'd rather not talk about him.' A deep draught of dark cocoa is just what I need to slow my heart rate again. Who knew I'd feel *this* uncomfortable?

'He's still on his own, too.' She tilts her head to gauge my reaction. 'It's a shame he can't come to the wedding. Second chances and all that?'

If spluttering with my face in my mug is a bad move, sloshing hot chocolate right down my coat is worse. The amount of drink I've lost, it's a good thing I'm cold rather than thirsty. But at least the wipe-up gives me time to regroup. Leopard print is so forgiving, that's why you have to love it every time. I'm frantically dabbing my soggy fake fur with serviettes, racking my brain to move on to an easier topic. 'So how are the wedding plans going?'

Becky rolls her eyes. 'There are so many decisions to make. Nachos or tacos for the burger van. Do we want hog roast or fish and chips for the main. We even need council permission to erect our own beachside marquee.' She gives a guilty squirm on her stool. 'We haven't even begun to choose groups for the photos from the lists on Pinterest.'

'Absolutely no worries on that one.' Although organised group photos don't fit with the kind of informal wedding she's talked about before.

She lets out another sigh. 'The only thing Nate's looking forward to is getting his hands on our own Roaring Waves beer, with Mr and Mrs Croft labels on.'

'No surprise there.' Another reason for my heart to sink. Let's just hope the brewer's not on the guest list. 'So how many people have you invited?' As Becky's repeatedly using the word 'small', I'm confident this won't be an issue.

'Not many. Although weddings have this awful tendency to grow.' She thinks for a second, then looks up brightly. 'A hundred and forty-seven, tops.'

The way that number makes me lurch, it's a good thing I've already tipped most of my drink away. What's that expression? Three steps forward, two steps back? Or in my case, fifteen steps back, ending up with falling off a cliff top.

Which just goes to show, your blindsides don't always come from where you expect them. Here I was, assuming I'd be thrown off track by hearing about Luc, when all along I should have been worried about an out of control guest list. I was expecting twenty, tops. Add in an extra hundred and twenty, I'll be needing to find a lens with a wider angle.

Chapter 5

Sunday, 3rd December
At Brides by the Sea: Hidden cameras and flash photographers

'So how did it go?' Jess asks, as I come down into the half light of the White Room later, clutching my laptop. If I wasn't blanking Christmas this year, the fairy lights playing on the lace, making the wedding dresses in the window glisten against the night outside would make my heart flutter.

Jess turning up again and calling me downstairs to show her my pictures isn't quite what I'm expecting on a Sunday evening. But as this is her shop, I can hardly argue.

'It was a bit stiff to start with.' I've had time to up load the pictures and sort a few of the better ones into their own folder, so at least I know they aren't *too* awful to show her. 'And the wedding party's going to be a bit bigger than I'd first thought.' I'm understating this to play it down. There's no point panicking about something I can't change.

'That's exactly what I'd heard. A hundred and forty guests is a lot for a photographer to take on for a first time. It's lucky

I'm on hand to get you the extra support you need.' Her nostrils are flaring. 'So did the shooting get any better once you took Nate and Becky out?' From her prompting smile, it almost feels like I'm her latest project.

How did I forget? There are no secrets in St Aidan. Everyone, including Jess, will know every last detail of Nate and Becky's local wedding orders, as well as our exact route around town this afternoon. I put my MacBook Pro on the table and open it up. 'Have a look, see what you think.' There's silence as I flick through the first few photos. 'Once we got into town they relaxed a lot.' I look round for Jess's reaction.

'Oh my.' Her mouth is open as she murmurs, then she snaps it shut. 'Keep going, then.'

I'm flicking through, trying to find a picture she'll like. I get through the first fifty, then pause for her reaction.

'Well, well, well.' Her loafers clatter towards the winding staircase up to Sera's dress design studio and she calls up the stairs. 'Okay, Jules, you can come down now.' As she turns to me, at last, she drops her voice to a husky whisper. 'Poppy was right, your pictures are *wonderful*. Now we need to persuade Jules to give you a helping hand, so you get to know your way around weddings enough to tackle your expanded one. And I'm going to lean as hard as it takes to make him cooperate.'

'Jules?' My voice comes out as a squeak. 'Is that *really* necessary?' From the aftershave cloud that suddenly wafts up my nose, I don't have to look round to know he's behind me. I can tell by his disparaging sniffs that he's giving me the evils.

'Go ahead, show us a few more, Holly.' Jess's purr is so

proud, I don't dare to do anything else.

There's a choking noise coming from Jules's throat. When he finally forms words, he sounds like he can't get them out for yawning. 'Very bland, very reportage. And I'm really missing the drama here.'

As I turn to Jess, she's giving an incredulous headshake. 'They're shots of a windy walk in St Aidan, not the bloody coronation.' Her voice rises to a shriek. 'For goodness sake, Jules, stop being so *silly*. They're incredible.'

I have to butt in here. 'Really, I wouldn't go that far.'

Jess is growling. 'Come on, Jules, even *you* have to admit they're good.'

Jules gives a kind of shiver. 'Okay, technically, they aren't the disaster I was expecting.'

'Bloody hell, Jules, the last thing I expected was prima donna behaviour from you.' Jess is shouting now. 'There's only one reason you're playing the diva here, and that's because you're *jealous!*'

Jules obviously isn't the kind of good looking hunk who smoulders when he's angry, because he's gone pale and very snappy. 'Well, you're the one who's brought in the competition right under my nose. You bill her as someone who snaps quiches for Lidl and then bring on bloody Annie Leibovitz. What am I supposed to do? Cheer?'

I'm sitting with them shouting over the top of my head, wanting to yell, 'excuse me, I am here,' but I'm so shocked at how wrong they've got it, the words won't come out.

Jess's cheeks are scarlet. 'After *all* the support Brides by the Sea has given you, Jules, we deserve better than this.'

Jules sticks out his chin like a petulant three-year-old. 'And my point is, ditto. From where I stand, I'm the one with the talent. And I'm the one who's lost count of the times I've hauled *you* out of the shit.'

Jess drags in a breath, and at a guess she's speaking through clenched teeth. 'Holly is a fellow professional who needs a tiny bit of support from you so she can come through for her friends when their wedding has unexpectedly expanded to whopping proportions. It's for one time only, she's not trying to steal your clients. We put a huge amount of business your way, Jules. If you won't oblige on this, I promise I'll run you out of town.'

'Fighting talk. You're really getting your salopettes in a twist over this, aren't you?' Jules's nostrils are flaring.

Jess's voice becomes a roar. 'If I'm about to disappear off up a bloody mountain pass, the last thing I'm going to leave behind me is you two up to your zoom lenses in bloody wedding photographer warfare.'

I'm waving both my hands frantically, trying to get my squeaks heard. 'I'm definitely not fighting. And *definitely* nothing to do with weddings.' Other than a surfie party that accidentally expanded, obviously. Although hearing how loud she shouts, I'm just pleased Jess is sticking up for me and not going against me here.

Jules gives a sneer. 'Don't take it out on me because you've got holiday jitters, Jessica. If you've got polar bear toes at the thought of jetting off to Switzerland, seriously, you need to tell Uncle Bart.'

Ouch. This man is mean.

'That's enough from you, Blue Eyes.' The blood has drained from Jess's face now. But despite her cheeks being the colour of wedding dress lace, her voice is booming louder than ever. 'Jules. You're going to let Holly second shoot your next wedding, on Tuesday. I know Zoe and Aidan will be up for it. What's more, you're going to give her *all* the benefit of your vast experience, without any of the temperamental star crap.' Thunderous doesn't begin to cover it. 'That's non-negotiable. Understood?'

I have to stand up for myself here. 'No! It's not necessary, and not happening.' A whole day following Jules around? Even if I would learn a lot, I'd rather eat my own Nikon. But they're both ignoring me.

Jules's mouth is all bunched up. 'And?'

Jess's expression is steely. 'In return I'll give your suggestion for the studio serious consideration. Although you do understand, I'll be asking top price for that space.' Her eyes glint. 'Agreed?'

As Jules unwinds his scarf to wipe the sweat off his brow, the sound he lets out is almost a whimper. 'Okay.' His naked Adam's apple does a lurch as he swallows. 'I'll be round tomorrow at two to brief you, Holly. You'd better charge up your battery packs.'

'Lovely.' Jess is suddenly beaming again, 'Well, that went well. Anyone for a Winter Warmer while we look at the rest of Holly's photos?'

But no one replies, because Jules is already out of the door and I'm busy working out what the hell I can do to get out of Tuesday's wedding.

Chapter 6

Tuesday 5th December
In the Bride's dressing room at Daisy Hill Farm House:
Drain pipes and perfect shots

'So, Holly, the dress and the girls are all yours now.' Jules flips his scarf so high it bangs on the brides' dressing room chandelier, and sends it jumping wildly. 'I'm off to catch Aidan and the boys having breakfast at the Goose and Duck.' As he flounces towards the door there a brief flash of sapphire as he glances at his watch. 'I'll be back at twelve, for Zoe's "bride gets buttoned up" pics.' As yet, he's still avoiding eye contact with me, and he hasn't cracked even a fake smile in my direction either. This far, his lips are as zipped up as his next shot with Zoe.

Another day, another couple. First Nate and Becky. And now Zoe and Aidan. What started as a favour to some friends has somehow got right out of hand. And this pair couldn't be more different from Nate and Becky and the huge 'let it all hang out' beach bash they've ended up with. Today's couple are trying the knot in Rafe and Poppy's amazing Georgian farmhouse at Daisy Hill Farm, in front of a mere forty guests. And having their reception and evening party here too. Although technically, given there's chamber music rather than a disco, that part sounds more like a soiree than a wild party. As weddings go, this one's teensy according to Poppy. And so far, I've managed to get some gorgeous shots of the flowers. So whatever happens, I haven't scored a complete fail.

To be honest, I'm still picking my jaw off the floor at the idea of complete strangers welcoming me into their getting-ready room at all. We're in the newly converted bridal suite, downstairs in the Old Farmhouse venue, where Poppy and Rafe have done a brilliant job with their renovations. It's wall-to-wall luxury, with white carved chairs, whisper-grey velvet cushions and huge mirrors. And enough space to be hit by the explosion of a bride's party complete with hair and make-up entourage and all the props, and still look elegant. According to Jess, who phoned from the first class lounge yesterday, as she waited to take off for Zurich, Zoe was – and I'm quoting here – 'completely delighted to have an award-winning London photographer on board to add another dimension to her wedding album'. Jess might be the queen of spin, but when I see the curly hand- painted wooden sign hanging on the door, saying *The dressing room*, it leaves me feeling someone should hang one around my neck saying *Fraud*. And that's the only point Jules and I would ever agree on.

When he whooshed through the shop yesterday afternoon to give me my briefing, it was a flying visit. However hard his mouth was working, his feet didn't appear to touch the floor.

'Fuel up in advance ... prepare to be crushed by the weight of your cameras ... your people skills will be pushed way beyond their limits ...' He was rapping like a machine gun, only pausing to give Jess's desk a once-over. 'You *will* be ready here for an eight thirty pick up?'

'Yep.' I was shrinking back against the wall as he nosied at the piles of papers on the table. 'Absolutely.' Despite only being an apprentice assistant, I managed to whisk the appointment book away from him just before he opened it to snoop.

Then he started again. 'The bride and the groom will be jangling with so many nerves they won't know which way's up. You are the voice of reason they look to in their day of craziness. The sober one, when the rest of the room are off their faces. It's high octane, high expectation and a lightweight won't last two frames.' He delivered his entire manifesto in the time he took to do a circuit of the White Room. 'Oh, and no flashes, unless they're off-camera.'

'Great.' No idea how I managed even a grim smile after that lot. This is exactly why I'd take pictures of a biryani rather than a bride every time. It's a doddle in comparison. 'Got you.'

Except he wasn't quite done. He paused by the mannequin for one last sideswipe on his way to the hall. 'If you think you can mosey in from Oxford Street and swan all over this, prepare yourself for an epic fail, Holly. If the only thing you learn is to stay the hell away from weddings in future, it will not have been a wasted day. For either of us.'

I was completely in agreement with him on that. But I never got the chance to tell him. Next thing, the hallway Christmas tree jingled as he bolted past. And before I got my words out the shop door slammed.

I'd heard that Jules is big on playlists for setting the mood. But more fool me for expecting *Now That's What I Call Love* tunes on the way to the farm this morning. Instead it was *Music To Go To War To*. Rather than being lulled by the Coors and Adele, we left St Aidan to the battle music from *Star Wars* and hit Rose Hill to *The Ride of the Valkyries*, with the volume at 16. As far as subliminal messages go, it couldn't have been more in my face. But whatever my preconceptions, I'm determined to give this opportunity everything I've got. After all Jules's animosity, it's a massive relief when he closes the door behind him again this morning. Now it's just me, Zoe, her bridesmaids and the make-up ladies.

I warm up with a few shots of the jars spilling out of the make-up team's boxes. I even dare to take a few reflections of the girls in the mirror. Then I walk across to where the dress is hanging and turn to Zoe. 'Is it okay if I move this to where the light's better?' I'm feeling so guilty for being here, my apologetic plea couldn't be further from Jules's masterful orders.

Zoe peers past the hairdresser pulling rollers the size of drainpipes out of her hair. 'Of course, help yourself.'

The champagne silk drifts as I move it across the room to a hook on the other side of the room. 'Is this one of Sera's designs?' Even after only being in the shop for a couple of days, I can spot her trademarks. Fabulous flowing satin. The exquisite embroidery winding across the straps, the slight flare of skirt.

Zoe looks delighted that I'd know. 'That's right. It's very

light for December, but I fell in love with the way it moves. I've got a little fur jacket to go over it.'

'I'll try to capture how amazing the beading is.' I hang on to the one useful thought Jules threw at me this morning. *Never rush. Take your time for that perfect shot.* A few minutes later, all thanks to Sera's lovely work, I have some fabulous close ups.

Despite the hairdresser dragging her hair through the tongs, Zoe carries on, with a wistful look in her eyes. 'We got engaged on Christmas Day last year, so we wanted to get married in winter too.'

I swallow my gulp at the coincidence and force my face into a smile. 'Lovely.' It comes out a lot too brightly. Although, truly, it's good to know that *someone's* festive proposal worked out well, even if mine crashed and burned. And if I'm silently groaning, *this could have been me,* I need to stop.

Zoe frowns at me as I put the dress back. 'Are you sure you're okay there?' She dodges the hairdresser's comb and nods at the ice bucket and champagne flutes. 'Would you like some bubbly? You look even paler than I feel.'

And damn that it's that obvious. 'I'm fine.' I'm lying. And dying of embarrassment too, because everyone knows the bride should have the monopoly on wobbles on her wedding day. I smother the shock waves and concentrate on how I was before. 'Actually, I'm a bit nervous.' It's the ideal way to cover up that the moment I heard about her Christmas Day proposal I felt like passing out. 'Whatever Jess told you about me, this is actually my first wedding.' I can see the make-up girl's eyebrows hitting the ceiling as I blurt out the truth. But I can't help it. Now they've noticed, I have to come clean.

'So what about the *awards*?' The bridesmaid in the baby-pink Team Bride dressing gown is looking daggers.

I'm ready to take my camera and go. 'I have won stuff, but for pictures of food, not brides. Things like ...' I rack my brain for anything to block out Luc and his engagement ring. 'Country Living Food Campaign of 2016 for my sausage casse-role shots?' *Sausages?* That sounds worse than nothing now it's out.

'Right.' Six faces are giving me bemused stares.

'I'm really sorry. I started off in food design, but I moved across to photography after a massive roast beef and meringue debacle.' I take in the bridesmaids' expressions getting more horrified by the second. I know this isn't the moment to babble my entire life story, but I can't stop. If my feet weren't welded to the spot, I'd already be out of here.

'One moment.' Zoe lifts up the hair tong wire. 'It's good you're not on the catering team. Show me what you've got so far.'

As I move in and flick through the frames, she's nodding. Then she pushes back a stray hair grip and grins up at me. 'For an assistant, I'd say you're acing it. Don't forget, it's my first wedding too.'

I can't help but smile back at that. 'So you don't mind if I stay?'

Zoe laughs. 'I'll throw a bridezilla fit if you *don't*. Jules is lovely, but it's nice to have a woman around too. Especially if you're taking pictures like those. How about you go and beg some leftover cupcakes from Poppy before you expire?' From the way Zoe's taken command from her hairdressing chair, I suspect she might be an army general in her day job. 'We'll all feel better after some of those. Better still, bring back some pictures of what's going on outside.' She nods beyond the door.

'Brill, back soon, then.' I don't need to be asked twice to escape. As I yank my camera bag onto my shoulder and dash out into the hallway I can see Poppy amidst a sea of tables and chairs. She's deep in discussion with Lily from the shop, who is here sorting the styling and the flowers.

Poppy grins as I skid to a halt on ancient floorboards, polished to a sheen. 'How's it going?'

I give a shrug. 'Getting there.' It's not ideal to be *this* anxious to leave the wedding venue when I've barely been here half an hour. 'What are you doing here anyway? I was coming to find you in the kitchen.'

Now her bump's getting bigger, Bart's nephew Kip, who is Lily's new boyfriend, is supposed to be taking over Poppy's wedding work here. And since Kip started work as wedding manager, and Poppy's got more pregnant, she's supposed to stay in the part of the farmhouse where she and Rafe live, for at least some of the time.

Poppy wrinkles her nose. 'Kip and I are still in the hand-over phase. I've been working with Zoe all year to make today perfect. It's hard to let go.'

Lily pulls a face. 'We'd have to tether Poppy to the Aga to keep her away today.'

I sense I'm treading on proverbial eggshells here. 'Zoe's asking for spare cupcakes. Does that help at all?'

Poppy sighs and rubs her tummy. 'Okay, we'll have to go back to the kitchen for those. But remember, I'm not broken, I'm simply growing a small person.' Poppy and Rafe have only known about their surprise baby for a couple of months, and it seems like they're still catching up.

From the ease with which Lily chimes in, it's an ongoing problem. 'Eighteen hours on your feet at a wedding isn't ideal when you're this far pregnant, though.'

'I'm fine. Most pregnant women these days go straight from work to the labour ward.' Poppy brushes away Lily's concern and nudges me towards the front door. 'Come on, Holly, let's get those cupcakes. The first rule of weddings – if the bride's hungry, feed her. Otherwise she may explode.'

'Great.' I store that nugget for when Becky gets married. And make a mental note to forget it the day after.

As I follow Poppy outside and along to the part of the house she and Rafe live in, Immie is ahead of us in the court-yard, showing a group of early wedding guests towards the holiday cottages. It's great to see so many of our friends all pulling together in such a brilliant team. The people where I work are more colleagues than friends, and we rarely go out after hours. I'm asking myself when Rose Hill became so buzzy? Or when my fabulous life in London became so quiet in comparison? Although even if it's temporarily shrunk to nothing, I definitely wouldn't swap it.

After the cold breeze that blasts us as we hurry up the cobbled yard, the farm kitchen is deliciously warm. Jules wasn't joking about the cameras weighing a ton. As for me being a lightweight, I'm holding my hands up to that already.

I slide my bag onto the table, rub my cramping shoulder, push the kettle onto the Aga and reach for a mug. 'I'll make you some tea while I'm here, Pops.' At least then she'll have to stay to drink it.

Poppy shuffles a stack of cake containers. 'I'll give you vanilla ones. We can't risk chocolate smudges before the ceremony.' She frowns at me as she hands me a box. 'You look like you could do with one now.'

I'm already regretting skipping breakfast. 'Chocolate stains won't show on leopard print, will they?' It's worth a try.

Poppy answers that with a beam. 'That's my girl. How many?'

'No more than two.' I'm feeling mean that I'm only passing her ginger tea in return. 'I don't want to spoil my appetite for the vanilla ones.' Now I'm back in the normality of the kitchen, sinking my teeth into soft chocolate butter cream, I'm reluctant to leave.

Poppy squeezes my arm as she sinks onto the bench. 'It's lovely to have you home, Hols. We've all been hoping we might tempt you into coming back here full time.' By the time she drops that bombshell, she's looking innocently out of the window. 'To live, I mean.'

'What, and leave London?' If I sound shocked, it's because a move back is in the wrong direction entirely. We spent all our time at school plotting how to get away. For Poppy, it was all about the lure of the bright lights. Whereas for me, I was desperate to get to a place where I could be anonymous. Where I wouldn't always be the girl whose much more popular sister died.

She laughs. 'I did it and I survived. It's different when you get a bit older.' From the way she bites her lip and looks guilty, she's going to push it. 'It isn't as if London's brilliant for you right now.'

I sigh and try to shut out that I just had the same fleeting thought. Then I make sure I get the right tone of bouncy. 'I might be back in my old flat share, in a room the size of a shower cubicle. But I'm at the hub of the action. What's not to like?' The worst thing is that my social life dematerialised when Luc left. And a year on, it's not looking up. All enrolling at woodwork classes and zumba did for me was give me splinters and a pulled hamstring. But coming back to live here isn't an option. I try to sound jokey, yet firm. 'Me moving in with the oldies and working in an ice- cream kiosk? That would go down a storm when my parents are doing their best to leave home themselves.' So happily, it's not a choice I'll need to address.

Poppy leans towards me. 'This is why we've all got our fingers crossed for you today, Hols. Strictly between us, now we've expanded, there are too many weddings at Daisy Hill for Jules to handle on his own.'

Originally Daisy Hill Farm held summer weddings in the fields, but they've now added in the main farmhouse and converted a barn. There are also the weddings at Bart's Manor too. And it looks like I might have been completely set up here. As Poppy wiggles her eyebrows expectantly, my heart sinks.

I let out a sigh, because it's all so impossible. 'It's really sweet of you to think of me.' But leave London *and* become a wedding photographer? How the hell do I express that those are the two last things I'd do – in the world, ever – without sounding ungrateful? 'I'll do my best today. And get back to you on that one.'

'There is another thing.' The way Poppy's screwing up her mouth tells me I may need to brace myself for bad news.

'Yes?' I've got no idea what's coming, but it can't be any worse than the last suggestion.

'You'd be way more likely to find a new partner here than in London. Especially given who's staying in the cottages.' She wiggles her eyebrows madly.

What the hell is she hinting at? 'Surely you can't mean ... ?'

She grins. 'Yes, I'm talking about Rory. Truly, once you get past the joking around he's all heart, and way too nice to be on his own. You two always had the hots for each other. Twenty years on might be a good time to finally check that out?'

I let out a shriek. 'We *TOTALLY* did not!' However much I want to stamp on this, I can't bring myself to say the word 'hots'. 'The guy drives me round the bend. If we were stranded on a desert island together, I swear I'd swim to get away from him. And you know how much I hate water.'

Poppy's making no effort to hide her laughter as she looks down at her bump. 'They don't call me elephant memory just because I'm huge, you know. Deny it as much as you like, but I remember the way you two always had your heads together, back in the day. And he always looked out for you too. That time you got off your face on cider punch at Hannah Peveril's birthday because you thought it was lemonade with colouring in, he was the one who insisted on walking you round until you sobered up, then driving you home.'

I stifle a shudder. 'Trust you to rake that up. That night was so awful, it still makes me groan with embarrassment even now.' And moving neatly on from Mr Sanderson ... 'My mum went ape about that, and Hannah's dad never forgave me for throwing up all over his Gertrude Jekyll prize roses.'

But Poppy's seen what I've done there and she's not having it. 'Better still, Rory delivered you home in one piece, without driving into any ditches or off any precipices. He might have been older, but he was wonderfully protective of you. Pretty besotted, if you ask me.'

I have to close this down. 'Which I *definitely* didn't.' She's sounding like she's teasing, but we both know she's not.

As her laughter fades, she gives me one of her stern stares. 'You broke up with Luc almost a year ago now, though. It's definitely time you moved on.'

'That's the problem, Pops. I haven't even begun to think of myself as free.' Saying it out loud now, I'm realising it's totally true. My heart hasn't actually let go yet. Although I'm not sure I can admit that to anyone.

Her smile is sympathetic. 'What's that old phrase? You're still holding a candle for Luc, even though it's over.'

My shrug is as noncommittal as I can make it. 'Maybe.' In truth it's probably more like a bloody great beacon flare than a candle. Which is yet another reason why it's best to push on here. 'Anyway, I'd better get these cakes to Zoe. Before she spontaneously combusts. Or whatever it is brides do.'

If Poppy's on the matchmaking warpath, I need to get the hell out of here. If I hang around with her in this mood, she's so determined that I'm quite likely to get bumped into an arranged marriage before Zoe and Aidan even get to theirs. And if Poppy's got Rory in her sights for me, all I can say is, her taste in other people's men is appalling.

I hadn't counted on bolting back down the yard so soon, or so fast. Although since I left the wedding venue a huge and fabulous winter wreath has appeared on the front door. The heavy twines of ivy and pale eucalyptus in a circle the size of a hoola hoop have me skidding to a halt on the flag path. How many ways are there to photograph a wreath this awesome? At least it takes my mind off Poppy's shudderingly awful suggestion. It's a perfect expression of winter against the warm sandstone, untinged by the negative overlay of Christmas. A broad hessian bow which trails to the floor. White frosted mistletoe berries against the dove grey paint-work. I admit I'm so lost in the prettiness of the moment I barely hear the car engine thrumming down the yard. And when I hear a shout, I jolt so hard I nearly drop my battery pack.

'Holly Berry, what the hell? When did you join the paparazzi?'

Rory? I've been so busy worrying about being a wedding crasher and putting Poppy right, I've overlooked this particular pitfall in my day. And completely failed to have a contingency plan for it. Which is beyond stupid, given the guy's staying in a holiday cottage barely a hundred yards away. I drag in a deep breath and repeat my mantra. *Never rush. Take your time for that perfect shot.*

'Rory. And your beer-mobile. Great to see you too.' I don't need to look. Right now I can guarantee my cheeks are blazing red instead of deathly pale. 'Haven't you got some fizz to sell, or a brewery to go to?'

I don't hang around to enjoy the moment my words hit his ears. Instead I fling open the front door, hurtle to the safety of the bustling venue interior and slam the door behind me. And even though the door is monumental, hand hewn from oak planks in the seventeen hundreds, when I lean my back against it, it's still not thick enough to keep out the echo of Rory Sanderson's laugh.

Chapter 7

'Awesome transformation or what?' Lily's beaming at me as I come back in from the hallway.

And it's true. She and the catering team have been working miracles while I've been away. By the time I wind my way through the area where the wedding breakfast will be held, the tables have been laid with snowy linen cloths and decorated with an array of lanterns, with buckets of gypsophila, vintage lilac roses and pheasant feathers, and hessian bows to match the outside wreath. Through the line of sash windows along one wall I can see across the garden, to where Kip and Rafe are walking across the back lawn. They've both swapped their jeans for dark suits. One note for fashion slaves, Rafe's still wearing his Barbour too, for now. Although Poppy assured me earlier, it's his best one. Definitely not the one he feeds the cows in then.

As I dip here and there clicking my shutter, the crystal ware and cutlery on the tables are sparkling in the light from the chandeliers above. Then I hurry through to the fabulous orangery, with its ancient black and white tiles and floor-to-ceiling windows, which is where the ceremony chairs are arranged. Each has its own hessian bow on the side, holding a bunch of gyp like a miniature snowstorm. There's a fabulous grand piano in the room where the evening dancing will be, and that makes a lovely picture too. And for the sake of completion, I snap the Ladies, with its deep-blue painted walls and massive mirrors. Then I hurry along to the Dressing Room with my cake box, knock and tiptoe in.

I brace myself, then make the announcement. 'I have cakes, ladies.' I put down the box, and open the lid. 'Obviously I need pictures first.' Although, to be honest, any view of swirly icing, topped with silver balls was knocked out of the park by the sight of four bridesmaids in their ice cream-coloured robes, wrestling the cakes out of the box straight afterwards. I take it from the long line of empty fizz bottles in front of the mirror, which I also snap, that they've been binge drinking. Which might explain the no-holding-back cupcake rush. Then I whoosh in and deliver a cupcake to Zoe.

'Thanks for bringing those, Holly. How's my messy up-do?' She points to her hair and pauses for my admiring glance. 'It's the only relaxed bit of the whole day I got past my mum.' So that explains the string quartet tuning up outside. Also ridiculously photogenic. Jules doesn't know what he's missing here. But in addition to a chamber orchestra for later? From where I'm standing, still very much on the outside of the wedding scene, it all sounds like over-kill.

Although I mustn't let my mind wander. That's another cue

for me there. 'Gorgeous hair, Zoe. The diamond strands in there look amazing. If you hold still, I'll just get those.' And they're done.

By the time I've taken shots of the girls right along the hair and make-up line, all the way into their bridesmaid's dresses, I'm staring at the big clock on the wall and wondering where this morning went. And then Jules is here, arm in arm with Zoe's mum, looking every inch her new 'best friend forever', as he marches her in to help Zoe into her dress.

One bark from him. 'Okay, I've got this, now, Holly.' I'm back to hovering in the background like a hawk, mopping up the leftover shots. Jules only broke his silence in the car to give a rundown of the occasions where he wanted me to shadow his shots. And to drum into me that for the rest of the time I had to be on high alert, every single second of the whole day, to cover the relaxed angle. It's the candid shots that make the day, apparently, and they're over in an instant. I need to anticipate each bridesmaid finally sinking into a chair and kicking off her shoes. The moment the hard man groomsman cracks and wipes away a tear. Every toddler yawning.

And then Kip's at the door, calling. 'Time for the brides-maids, please.' As he sweeps them away, Jules marches Zoe's mum out too.

And now it's just me, Zoe, and the hair and make-up ladies, unplugging their hair tongs, and packing up the lippy. Four empty chairs. And the rest of the room that looks like every suitcase on an entire luggage carousel just exploded.

Zoe's standing, tugging at the satin of her dress, wagging

her small bouquet, having the last pale brushstrokes added to her lips. 'What happened to the last four hours?' Her voice is rustling like tissue paper. And despite enough contouring and blusher to make her look like a supermodel, her skin looks the colour of parchment. 'How can it be time? Am I even ready?'

'You have to be more ready than I am.' As I mouth the words silently, my stomach feels like there's an iron hand gripping it. How ridiculous. I couldn't feel more nervous if *I* was the one getting married. It's as if I'm living the moment I'm never going to have with Luc.

It starts as the iron hand tightening on my guts, and it ends with me making a dash to the bride's bathroom and hurling my non-existent breakfast down the luxury toilet bowl. It's all over in a few seconds. Then I'm pulling the flush, washing my hands and face, throwing down a glass of water. A minute later I'm out again, grasping my camera in one hand and grappling my camera bag onto my shoulder with the other.

Kip's back at the door. 'Okay, we're ready for you, Zoe.' I know he's Lily's man, and apparently his wedding skills weren't always this well-honed. But Kip has definitely found the bucket-loads of charm it takes for a job like this now.

I don't even have time to say sorry for my hugely embarrassing bathroom dash. I give Zoe's hand a little squeeze and she's off. But as she hesitates to drag in a breath in the doorway, a shaft of sunlight illuminates the hallway ahead of her. And the stark lines of her neck are silhouetted against the light. The diamond strands in her hair are glinting. From somewhere

I scrape my voice together. 'Hold it there, Zoe, just for a moment, please.' I don't rush. I press to adjust for the back lighting. I capture Zoe's last terrified second as a single woman. 'Okay, all done.'

Kip grins over his shoulder at me as he ushers Zoe out of the room. 'Watch out for the oldies falling asleep during the speeches, Holly. Happens every time.'

And as they glide off down the hallway, I shoot back into the bathroom.

Chapter 8

'So, you can head off now, Holly. We're pretty much done here.'

It's Jules, and if he's finally called a halt to hostilities, it's probably because it's nine in the evening and he's completely knackered. We've seen his famous bounding all day, but for the first time at this wedding he's come to a complete stand-still, by the front door.

To be honest, I can't remember a day this action packed, ever. Even the year we all went to Glastonbury after A levels, there was time to flop. And today has been one of those weird days that has whizzed by, but it still feels like at least a century since I first wriggled out from under the duvet this morning.

'If you're sure?' I say, hoping that he won't change his mind. Aidan and Zoe have swayed to their *Wonderful World* first dance and we've spent another half hour taking pictures of other couples, also swaying. As we're assured there definitely won't be any *Macarena* action this evening, apparently this is traditionally the time we photographers disappear. While Jules is going to hang on to do a couple of his signature illuminated outdoor shots with Aidan and Zoe, I'm getting a taxi back to town. 'If I wasn't so tired, I'd shout woohoo.' And phew to me finally getting out of his hair.

Jules can't hold back his 'I told you so' grin as he flips back his fringe. 'Bad as that, is it?' All day on his feet and the guy still looks flawless.

I pull a face. 'One of the most full-on days of my life to date.' I'm being honest, not ungrateful. And if I'm sounding cheery, it's probably because it's finally over. 'Thanks for letting me tag along. I've picked up enough to know that my beach wedding will definitely be my last.' When it comes to photographic subjects, give me pizza every time. High octane wedding stress has gone straight to the top of my avoid-at-all-costs list. My one lucky break today is that Jules didn't find out about my pre-wedding puke.

He's beaming at me now. 'Great to hear you've come to terms with your limitations. I knew weddings weren't your bag.' No one gloats quite as much as a man who's just been proved right, even though I was with him all along. 'Although you might have a shot or two for me to put in the album?'

'There's a couple of a snoring grandma.' That was all thanks to Kip's tip. I caught her nodding off, then jolting when the person next to her woke her up. Cruel, but if you look at it from the humorous side, it's a nice sequence. To be honest, I think that'll be the sum total of my contribution. Jules really did have this entire day covered. More than that, he seemed to be under the impression he was personally in charge of the whole damned shebang.

'I'll call by the shop very soon and we'll whizz through what you've got.' Despite the hint of a smile, Jules deals in orders not requests. 'Well if you want to say "bye" to Zoe and Aidan, they're here now.' What was I saying about him being in charge?

And that's it. I grab a quick hug with Zoe, who, despite the all-day make-up, looks as done in as I feel. Then I'm out into the night, rushing off up the cobbles to Poppy's kitchen, to say goodnight and ring for my ride.

As I hurry out into the frosty night I'm so relieved to be free that I punch the air, obviously being careful not to drop my camera bag. As I stare up at the dusky-blue sky, the star specks are so amazingly bright and wonderful, I almost feel like singing.

The weird thing is, as I go up the courtyard, the tune in my head – Poppy's favourite, *Don't Stop Me Now* – seems to be echoing off the walls of the barns. When I stop and hold my breath to listen, the sound's still there. But it's more of a yell now, overlaid with a scuffling of feet. A moment later, a small figure comes hurtling down from the cottages, arms waving wildly. There's a moment to take it in. From the spangles on the sweatshirt that are sparking off the floodlights in the yard, it's a girl. Before I know it, she's banged straight into me and she's burying her howls in my leopard fur. As I put out a hand to steady her, I hear heavier footsteps thumping down the yard.

'Gracie, Gracie! Jeez, people are trying to sleep round here.' The voice is urgent and low. It takes approximately a nanosecond to work out it's Rory.

I try to ignore the fact that Gracie's clinging to my leg. 'Everything okay?' For nine at night, after a very long day, having just bumped into the person at the top of my 'best avoided' list, I'm astonished how breezy I sound.

'Brilliant, thanks for asking, Holly Berry.' Rory gives me a 'what the eff' look as he shakes back his hair. 'One's yelling, the other's bailing. Life doesn't get much better.' He's got Teddie under one arm, bundled in a Barbour, and he blows as he hitches him up.

'Sorry, I just mean ...' I don't want to sound judgemental. '*Someone* doesn't seem very happy, that's all.' Given Gracie's wellies are cannoning into my shins and her fists are pummelling my thighs, it's an understatement. I look down for a bit to pat, and when my hand lands on her shoulder it's bony under the soft jersey of her pyjama top.

'The feeling's mutual, okay?' Rory's reply comes through gritted teeth. 'They get me up at four a.m., then run me ragged all day doing kiddie stuff that lasts two minutes max. If I refuse to end the day singing songs from *Frozen*, that's too bad.' As he says the 'F' word, Gracie stiffens and pricks up her ears.

'What's wrong with songs from *Frozen*?' I'm sensing he's a long way from cracking looking after the kids. But however much I'd like to cut him down to size, I hold back on pointing that out.

He shakes his head. 'It's still no reason to leg it at a hundred miles an hour.' Then he gives a sniff. 'In a hundred pages of Erin's descriptions about how to keep her children happy, there's nothing about singing at bedtime. And no mention of *Frozen* songs either.'

I stare down at Gracie. 'How many songs do you want?'

'One.' Her voice is small and husky now the yells have subsided. '*Let it go*.'

'Great song choice.' I can't hold in my smile. 'That's all?'

Gracie nods. 'To go to sleep with.'

I'm squeaking with indignation. 'How's *that* unreasonable, Rory? *Everybody* loves *Let it go*.' Okay, it's maybe not worth leaving home over. But a girl has to have principles. I'm with Gracie on this one. And after what Poppy said earlier, it's also vital that I fully express my disagreement with Rory on every point.

Rory gives a dismissive shrug. 'I don't sing. End of.'

Not strictly true. I'm sure he used to hurl a mike stand around when he played with his teen band. Not that belting Bon Jovi songs at the top of his voice ever counted as tuneful.

'You'll have to man up and try, Rory. For the sake of a peace deal.' As Gracie shudders against me, I put my hand out to steady her. 'It's freezing out here. You'd better all get back into the warm.'

'Unless ...' Rory's holding Teddie in front of his t-shirt like a sack of potatoes, apparently impervious to the bite of the wind. When I finally tear my eyes away from the sculpted shadows on his forearms, he's staring at me expectantly.

'What?' Shovelling hops into vats must work wonders for your biceps. When I finally re-divert my mind to sensible stuff, my instinct is yelling at me to do a runner of my own.

The floodlights are bright enough to light up the curl of

his try-it-on smile. 'If it's *that* easy, then I'm sure *you* won't mind doing the honours. Bedtime serenade here we come.' It isn't even a question. It's like he's been taking lessons from Jules-the-dictator.

I'm opening and closing my mouth, and my 'Er-er-er ...' is stuck on repeat. I feel like I'm about to be sucked in by a giant vacuum cleaner. And being spat out in the heart of Rory's home is my number one nightmare scenario. Even if it is only a temporary holiday let, it still counts as the full-blown dragon's lair. It's horribly close to this dead-of-night fantasy I had as a very misguided teenager, where Rory would take me back to his house for tea and worse. It probably grew from the night he took me home. Although whatever I said to Poppy, I don't actually have much recollection of that bit, other than what people have told me. But I'd die of embarrassment if I admitted any of this, even to myself. Even transmitting the thought waves this close to Poppy, I could be dead meat.

'Okay, Gracie. Panic over. Holly's going to sing you to sleep. So what are we waiting for?' That inscrutable smile is as infuriating as ever. 'As you just said, it's too damned cold out here to hang around.'

Except from where I'm standing, with Gracie tugging on my sleeve, suddenly the inside of my fur jacket feels like a sauna.

He's striding ahead. 'Straight on up the yard. It's the cottage with the grey door.' It takes a self-important guy like Rory to miss that all the cottage doors are grey. Luckily for the neighbours who might otherwise have been accidentally gate-crashed, Rory's door is ajar.

Despite the open door, as I follow him into the hallway, the warmth hits me in the face, then envelops me. Gazing past Gracie to the wide white-painted room beyond, I spot a log burner in the corner, blazing behind a fireguard. In the time it takes to drop my camera bags onto the tiled floor by the entrance and shed my leopard, my cheeks have flushed from crimson to burning beetroot.

I scan the sofas and table for an empty space to put down my coat, and fail. 'Good to see you aren't a tidy obsessive.' If were talking mess explosions, this is on a par with the brides-maids' room. Whereas I'm still used to Luc, who liked everything in its place. Although that insistence on order is something I never properly appreciated until I lost it.

Rory clears a space with his boat shoe, slides Teddie onto the rug and throws the Barbour he was wrapped in behind a tub chair. 'The mess is the downside of having a three-year-old for a housemate.' As he rubs his forehead with his fist, there's a disgusting flash of tanned stomach. 'You wouldn't believe it but Immie had this place looking impeccable this morning.'

Actually I would. Him leaving the dirty work to someone else sounds exactly right. Which is why I need to get in and out of here like a lightning strike. 'Okay, time for bed?' If I wasn't purple already, I would be after how that came out.

'Sounds like a plan, Holly Berry Red Cheeks.' There's the lowest chuckle in his throat. 'Bedrooms are straight through, past the kitchen.'

I'm not even going to bother about his jibes. It's bad enough being in his living room. If I stop to think about being near his bedroom, I might vomit again. From sheer distaste.

As I clamp my eyes onto the sparkly snowflakes on Gracie's top and march her across the rug, I can't help noticing. She's rocking the 'Courtney Love walking out of a wind tunnel with a hangover' look. Complete with dark shadows under her eyes and cheeks so white I'd swap with her in a heartbeat. I'm puzzling at how this fits with the super-uncle care package. 'Have you brushed your hair today?'

There's another low laugh from across the room, as Rory picks Teddie up and tosses his own hair out of his eyes. 'You already *know* I'm allergic to hairbrushes. Fingers work every time for me.'

I can't quite believe what I'm hearing. 'It might come as a surprise, but there are other people here apart from you, Rory.' I smile down at Gracie. 'Maybe ask Uncle Rory if you can have your hair done tomorrow.' I turn and look daggers at Rory. '*Before* the tangles get too bad. A week like this and she'll have dreadlocks.'

He shrugs. 'It's all about priorities. There's no time to sweat the boring stuff here.'

I sniff. 'I can see that.' As I pick my way over the mayhem and pass the bathroom, on balance I decide not to mention teeth-cleaning.

Rory's swagger at his mantra takes us all the way to the kid's room, where he rolls Teddie down into a travelling cot, muttering as he drops in a soft toy. 'Instructions page two, cat stays with baby at all times.'

Blocking out his self-congratulatory expression, I step over a tangle of t-shirts and towels as Gracie clambers into bed. Then I get out my phone and I try to sound businesslike. 'Right, time for *Let it go?* We'll have the YouTube version – with lyrics.' It's not strictly necessary, seeing as *Frozen* is one of our go-to films when we have girly nights with Poppy and the crew. Singalong? You bet we do. But there's no way I'm about to claim I'm word perfect without accompaniment. I'm so tempted to say 'watch and learn' but I bite my tongue. 'Thanks Rory, I'll take it from here.' Hopefully he'll take that as a dismissal. The last thing I need is an audience.

'I can't watch?' His disappointed wail sounds a lot like Gracie's.

'Absolutely not.' I wait for him to move, but he's still standing smirking, shoulder against the wall. 'It's a deal breaker.'

I ignore his disgruntled sigh and wait until he's shuffled well out of view. Then I perch on the blue-striped duvet and grin down at Gracie. 'Ready?' From somewhere in amongst the mess, she's found both Immie's snowmen and a teddy, and tucked them under the covers next to her.

As she nods back, her hair's like a haystack on the pillow, but her eyes are glistening. I grab her hand, press play and we go for it.

'*Let it go, let it go …*' I love this song. It's the kind that lifts you up and makes your heart burst, all at the same time. '*I am one with the wind and sky …*' It's very easy to lose yourself in the moment. After the fourth time through – or maybe the fifth – I suddenly crash back into the room and two things hit me. First, I'm singing at the top of my voice. And second,

Gracie's hand is limp in mine. What's more, despite my bellowing, her eyes are tightly shut and she's breathing deeply. When I gently turn down my volume and peer over into the cot, Teddie's the same. As I turn off my phone and tiptoe back to the living room I'm already missing the noise.

As I make my announcement, I can't help feeling pleased. 'Two kids, both sparked out.' Although, at a guess, they were exhausted. When the pause for his profuse gratitude doesn't get filled, I carry on. 'You're welcome.' Luckily I bite my tongue before I get to the 'any time' bit.

Somehow I'm expecting to find Rory sprawled, beer in hand, looking exhausted enough to have been at a wedding. Instead he's on the sofa, poring intently over his laptop. It's only when I clear my throat loudly that he finally looks up from his screen.

'Great. I've got a mountain of Huntley and Handsome orders and dispatches to check. I hope you don't mind, I made a start.'

I have no idea why I'm opening and closing my mouth. It's not as if I was secretly hoping he'd be eavesdropping on the singing, hanging around outside the bedroom door. 'Fine by me. And the clearing up will still be here when you've finished.' More fool me for thinking he'd do that first.

He rubs his fingers through his hair and holds up an unopened bottle. 'There's a beer if you'd like one, Pink Cheeks?'

There we go. I knew he'd push it. 'No thanks, I was already hurrying home when you grabbed me.' At least this way I have the satisfaction of turning him down.

He sighs and drums his fingers on the keyboard. 'It's one

of the first-ever bottles of this year's Bad Ass Santa Christmas brew. I thought you might like to take it with you. You can't turn down an offer that special, can you?'

My eyes are wide because he's just wrongfooted me again. 'Watch me, I just did. Thanks all the same, but I don't do beer.' There's a certain satisfaction in seeing his jaw drop, even if I'm getting the feeling he can't wait to get rid of me. Although, seriously, I doubt I'd be this sassy if I hadn't just sung *Let it go* so many times.

For a guy in shock, he picks himself up surprisingly fast. 'So, Holly Berry, what are you doing tomorrow? With the pre-Christmas rush at Huntley and Handsome, I've got to go into work. But you and Gracie seem to get on so well, I'm sure Immie would appreciate a hand with the kids if you're at a loose end.' He holds a bottle up to the light and scrutinises it. 'These beauties don't happen all on their own, you know.'

I pull a face. 'You don't say.' As for this 'hand with the kids', read a full day's free child care, without appreciation. Whatever happened to Rory having it sorted? 'Sorry, I'm tied up all day tomorrow.'

Rory frowns. 'Aren't you on holiday?'

Not that it's any of his business, but I try to sound nonchalant. 'I'm actually snowed under with computer work.' That covers editing a few thousand pictures. But he doesn't need to know that. I dive into my coat and haul my camera bag over my shoulder. 'No time to lose. I'd better run.' And no idea why I didn't just say I'm covering at the shop.

'Careful you don't die of boredom.' Rory's fleeting grin

fades as I move towards the door. 'You do know I wouldn't have dragged you up here if it hadn't been an emergency, Berry.'

It takes a moment for his words to sink in. 'It was a panic not a crisis.' If I'm sounding snappy it's because it couldn't be clearer. Not only is he desperate to get rid of me, but it's also obvious he'd rather I hadn't come at all. 'Once you crack the childcare, you'll know the difference.' No doubt Poppy and Immie will keep him right on that. Because from now on I'll be making damned sure I stay well away. From Rory, and his kids.

He lets out a long sigh as he rakes his fingers through his hair. 'Thanks anyway. For hauling me out of the ...'

However much I'm dying to know if he's about to say 'plop' or 'shit', I don't wait to hear. A second later, I'm hurrying down the yard, kicking myself for the way my stomach just descended like a highspeed lift when I saw him rub his thumb across his jaw and give that pained look.

I was fourteen when my insides last did that. What you can excuse as very bad judgement from a clueless teenager is totally unacceptable when you're well past thirty. Especially when I'm in love with someone else. One thing is certain. It definitely won't be happening again.

Chapter 9

Tuesday 5th December
In the kitchen at Daisy Hill Farm: Mental pictures and
wind-down tipples

'Are you there, Poppy? I'm just coming to say bye and ring
for a taxi. I met Rafe and he told me to come on in.'

As I knock and crack Poppy's kitchen door open, Jet, the
black farm dog is there to welcome me with a thump of his
tail on my leg. After the heat and mess of Rory's cottage,
Poppy's place feels like a haven of calm. Apart from a few
notes of violin music drifting up from the main house and
the occasional slam of a car door, it's hard to believe there's
a wedding party going on a few yards away. As I walk into
the gentle light, Poppy looks up from where she's curled on
the sofa.

'Rafe keeps popping in. He's a lot more twitchy about all
this than I am.' She gives her tummy a rueful glance. As she
checks her phone, she stifles a yawn. 'Hey, you stayed late,
Hols.'

'I bumped into Gracie running off as I left, so I took her

back to Home Brew Cottage on my way here.' My name for the Rory residence, not Poppy's. And we both know it's a lot further up the yard. I'm hoping we can skip over the aching embarrassment of the last twenty minutes and that I'm still smarting at the speed of my ejection. Which is ridiculous, when staying was the last thing on my mind.

'How are they doing in there?' From Poppy's wince she already knows.

Hopefully my huge eye roll will cover it, because my cheeks are already lighting up again. 'He's a long way from Uncle of the Year, but at least the smalls are asleep now. And, for the record, he couldn't get rid of me fast enough. Just saying, so you know where *he* stands on this.' Seeing she's looking so tired, I won't push it further now.

Poppy grins and thankfully moves on. 'So, well done, you survived your first wedding. It's always a milestone.' She's looking at me searchingly. 'And I'm sorry if I didn't pick up quite *how* wobbly you were earlier.'

'It was a great day, I learned loads, my batteries lasted, nothing broke.' Apparently dying power packs and failing equipment are a wedding photographer's worst nightmares. And I know *exactly* what she's getting at with the last part, so I might as well explain. 'The puking wasn't about nerves, though. I just got a horrible shock when Zoe told me Aidan proposed last Christmas, and it suddenly hit me that it could have been me getting married today.'

Her face wrinkles into a worried frown. 'Poor Hols.'

'I'm okay again now. But there's something else I've been puzzling over too.' Probably all brought on because I don't come face to face with bridal couples that often. 'I've just spent a whole year pinning my hopes on patching things up with Luc. Then today, as I watched Zoe and Aidan signing the marriage register, I realised – I've never had a mental picture of me in a wedding dress, standing next to him.'

Poppy pushes her finger on her lips as she ponders. 'And is that good or bad?' It's a measure of the kind of friend Poppy is, that she isn't jumping in with her opinion too early.

'It's a surprise. That's all.' Not that I know what to make of it.

She laughs. 'A lot of women have their weddings worked out on Pinterest, down to the last detail, before they've even got a boyfriend. Maybe you're at the other extreme. Because you're a photographer, you prefer real images to imagined ones.'

Now I'm the one who's smiling at the skill of that reply. 'That's one way of looking at it.' We're neatly skipping over that I had a boyfriend and was careless enough to lose him at the vital moment. Seeing as I haven't got a clue what the explanation really is, I try to move on. 'Today was the most exhausting day ever. How the hell do you do it on a regular basis?' At her busiest times, Poppy will have several weddings a week. For someone who's wilting after one, that's a mind blowing thought.

Poppy laughs. 'Believe me, I was a wreck for my first few too. But now I get this huge buzz from helping couples to have a wonderful day. When I'm there, that is.' She gives a wistful sigh.

I'm picking up her frustration. 'Not quite the same when

you're viewing it from the sofa?'

She pulls a face. 'Being stuck in here makes me feel so useless.'

I try to find a bright side. 'It gives you time to catch up on your pram ordering. And your baking.' From the piles of full cake containers on the work surface, she could be cooking for Cornwall.

Her nostrils flare. 'If I see one more Christmas Pudding cupcake, I might just scream.'

'Fine.' If she wasn't off alcohol, I'd already be making her a Winter Warmer. If ever I saw a girl in need of a wind-down tipple, it's Poppy.

As she sits up, her chin's doing a strange kind of wobble. 'The trouble is, even though Rafe pops in, I'm actually really lonely. Stuck in here all on my own makes me feel excluded. Daisy Hill Farm weddings were so much my thing, and suddenly they aren't any more. Feeling shut out is horrible.'

When I look closely, it's only the dim light that's masking the shadows under her eyes. 'But don't you get tired by the weddings?' I hesitate. 'Extra tired, I mean, with your bump?' I'm sure Rafe is only being protective, suggesting she stays here.

She gives a rueful shrug. 'I *am* tired. And grumpy. But actually, most of all, I hate that it's all going fine without me.' As she bites her lip, her face crumples.

'Babe.' I cross to her sofa, put my arm round her shuddering shoulders, and push a tissue into her hand. 'We're all here to help you. No one's trying take over. It'll all be here waiting for you as soon as you're ready to come back once the baby's here.' Poppy's been so strong since she came to work at the farm. What's more, she's been storming around as if her bump wasn't there. So it's unnerving to see her upset, just when she seemed to be coping so well. But I know it's more than my life's worth to mention pregnancy hormones.

After a few more gasps, her shivers subside and she gives a gulp. 'I know it's silly. And irrational. But I can't bear that I'm not going to be there any more when the bride says what a lovely day she's had.'

My heart goes out to anyone whose nose is redder than mine. 'Let's have some hot chocolate.' Poppy and Rafe's fridge is the size of a small barn and they have a herd of dairy cows, so hopefully they'll have enough milk. I grab a pan and open up the Aga top.

Poppy sniffs. 'I'd like that. I'm sorry, I feel so mean for grumbling.'

I can completely understand why she feels awful. 'It's the change that's the hardest part. And handing over what you've built up.' As I wait for the milk to warm, I find a soft throw and tuck it around her. As I bustle around, I'm throwing out random thoughts. 'But you need to think of the guys as looking after weddings while you're away. And it's only for a while.' I'm whisking the chocolate powder into the frothy milk, adding squirty cream, grating on some dark chocolate. 'You're close enough to keep an eye on things. And you can always pop in for a guest appearance ...' I'm searching the baking shelf, locating the marshmallows, when a gentle snore floats over from the sofa.

'Poppy, are you ... ?'

I tiptoe over to check. Eyes closed. Fair ponytail spread across the grey wool sofa. A hundred per cent asleep. And this time I wasn't even singing.

If I didn't love her so much, I'd drink her hot chocolate as well as mine. Seeing as I do, I leave her full mug next to her on the side table, just in case she wakes from her nap. And give Jet the kind of stern stare that Jules would be proud of when I retreat to the other sofa and tell him not to snaffle the cream.

But in the end, Poppy doesn't move. By the time my taxi arrives half an hour later, she's drifted into a deep sleep.

Chapter 10

Wednesday 6th December
At Brides by the Sea: Drop-ins and blind spots

'Have you heard from Jess today?'

It's Poppy, arriving at the shop late the next afternoon, in time to help with what, from the appointments book, looks like a mass collection of groomsmen's suits.

I look up from the desk, where I've been sorting through my pictures since early this morning, and nod at the phone. 'Jess has rung every half hour. If not more.' How can I spend all day shuffling pictures? Discarding the rubbish ones is easy, but it's amazing how long it takes to sort the rest. If you're a ditherer like me, faced with a couple of thousand shots from the day, the tweaking could go on forever.

Poppy's brow wrinkles. 'That bad? And Jess has barely been away a couple of days. I knew we should have installed webcams in every room.'

I shake my head. 'If she had more signal, she'd be on Skype full time. Lucky for us, halfway up a mountain, she's got problems with her buffering.'

'So is there any *news?*' Poppy's eyebrow wiggle tells me exactly the kind she's asking about.

I laugh. 'She's found Kaffee Klatsch, which sounds exactly like Jaggers Bar, but with gluhwein and an upper level.

Poppy's eyes go wide. 'Jeez, these skiers must be hardcore. There's no way Jaggers' customers could negotiate stairs after Happy Hour.'

I carry on. 'The chalet's got a fabulous balcony. There are six bathrooms, but they're all on the small side.'

Poppy's listening intently as she slips off her Barbour and hangs it in the kitchen. 'That's the trouble with living at the Manor. Everywhere else will feel like a doll's house afterwards. Is there any sign of a ring?'

'Not yet.' I have a feeling we'll be asking the same question every hour for the next two weeks. 'If he hasn't done it already, he might leave it until the last day? Unless he's planning to take her somewhere special.' It's ironic. After making a complete wreck of my own proposal, I've become the expert on them.

Poppy's flicking through the rail of suits that Sera brought out earlier. 'And how are the pictures?'

Now it's my turn to frown. I hesitate. 'The food ones are fine. Your cake looks as amazing in the photos as it did in real life.' I love taking pictures of oysters at any time. And Poppy's simple three tier cake, with a silver-leaf bottom layer and delicate lace icing, was a gift to photograph.

'And can I peep at the rest?'

I stand up and sigh as I give her my chair. 'Help yourself. Lucky for me, the first dance was very slow.' As I stare at the close up of Zoe and Aidan on the dance floor, I've lost all sense of whether they're good or bad.

Poppy sighs as she flicks through. 'Zoe looks gorgeous. You've really captured how in love they are. And the house is looking fabulous too.' Her face lights up. 'And these are all the bits I missed.' She flicks through some more. 'Seeing it all here and filling in the gaps from the day, I mind much less about not being there.'

'In that case, I'm pleased I took them.' Poppy looking at them in that light makes it easier for me to write off my awkward day with Jules.

She grasps my hand and squeezes tightly. 'Truly, I'm all good again today. But thanks for helping last night.' She's already sent me about a hundred texts saying the same thing. And telling me not to worry.

But there are times like yesterday when I know all she needs is a hug from her lovely mum. As huggers go she was a world champion. When we were younger I had my fair share from her. Especially as she was the one who stepped in and had me round a lot after Freya died. There was nothing quite like having your cheek pressed up against one of her flowery, icing-sugar covered pinnies in that kitchen that always smelled of warm baking. When she died suddenly from cancer a few years ago, it felt as if the sun had gone out in the village. It's the saddest thing that she isn't here to see Poppy's baby.

'Any time, Pops. That's what I'm here for, remember.' There's a jingle of bells as the shop door opens. 'And obviously I don't mind helping a few groomsmen into their suits either.'

She grins. 'That's good to hear, seeing as there are ten of

them.'

'That'll be five each, then.'

We're both looking towards the doorway, stifling our guilty giggles, expecting to see a crowd. So when it's Jules who appears instead, we can be excused for exchanging puzzled glances.

Poppy gets her act together first. 'Jules, lovely to see you, how can we help?' You can tell from the way she thinks on her feet she's a seasoned wedding pro.

Me standing in front of Poppy seems to have nipped the usual air kiss fest in the bud.

'I said I'd pop round. So here I am.' As Jules clears his throat, I sense there's something different about him, but I can't pinpoint what.

Poppy and I are both grinning like loons. 'And?'

'You're going to show me your wedding album, Holly.' Another of Jules's trademark steam- roller statements, where a question would have been way more appropriate.

'Right.' I'm croaking because my voice has dematerialised. When he said he'd drop by soon, I assumed he'd give me a couple of days. Not come leaping in next afternoon. 'They're not quite ready.' It's a massive understatement. Maybe he expected me to stay up all night on Photoshop? Looking at his grey complexion he might well have done that himself. Now I focus more closely, his eyes are so bleary I wouldn't be out of line offering him some matchsticks to prop them open. What's more, his sparkle is totally – well, what can I say other than 'not sparkling'. It's like today we've got Jules, the totally wrecked, matt version.

'Not ready? And you call yourself a professional?' His voice is high with disbelief. Even his hair is lank as he tosses it back. Wrestling a laptop from a pregnant person isn't polite either, but he does it anyway. And if we were craving questions, they weren't ones like those.

Poppy pulls out her phone and starts texting madly. A second later my own phone pings. It's a one-word text from her.

Pimples

She points to her cheek and forehead, then swizzles her eyes towards Jules. Sure enough, when I look again, yesterday's flawless complexion is breaking out. Okay, I know it's shallow and mean. But when I zoom in on the two giant zits on his forehead I can't help feeling a teensy bit pleased that he's not quite so perfect after all. Absolutely bloody delighted, even. In the same way seeing Kate Middleton with a spot makes you feel better knowing she's human too. There's another ping.

Your pics are so great you've brought him out in a nervous rash lol

Let's be clear. We wouldn't text literally behind Jules's back if he hadn't forced his way in so rudely. At least smirking at Poppy makes me feel less as if my soul is under the microscope here, with Jules sniffing and snorting and coughing his way through my wedding files. One more ping.

Sorry, he is well out of order. Defo no cupcakes for him

By the time he clears his throat again, I'm almost past caring about the scrutiny. He leans back, shuffles in his parka pocket and pulls out a memory stick. I'm still smiling at the Lilo and Stitch key ring it's attached to, which seems way too cute for serious old him, when he starts talking.

'I like to post a best moments mini-album for my wedding couples within twenty four hours. There are a couple of shots here I know they'll love. If you don't mind, I'll take copies.'

It takes me so long to pick my jaw up off the floor, I don't reply.

'Hello, anyone home?' He dangles Lilo in front of my nose. 'Some of us haven't got all day, you know. A quick yes or no will do.'

Poppy steps in. 'Yes – so long as we see what you've chosen.'

He's straight back at her. 'All in the file I've created here. *Jules for Zoe and Aidan's First Album.*' His memory stick is in and out of my computer in a flash. 'I may edit a teensy bit more. Get the rest to me by Friday. Okay. That's me done.'

I finally get my gaping jaw into gear. 'You want *my* pictures?' If I'm behind here, it's because after everything he's said, I can't believe he's even asking.

'Obviously.' Jules's look of disgust couldn't be huger. 'No point keeping a dog and barking myself, is there? Some of them are …' He hesitates as if he's searching for the right phrase.

And that's when I spot what's wrong. A ping three seconds

later tells me Poppy's seen it too. Except it's so obvious once I've noticed, there's no need to read the text.

One of Jules's startling blue eyes is brown!!!!

Where Jules should be rolling two deep-turquoise eyes, the colour of St Aidan Bay on a summer's day, complete with shimmer, instead there's only one. The other's a murky greyish brown. More like a puddle after a rainstorm.

'... not too bad at all.' Jules frowns at us. 'Is something wrong?' As he blinks at us we get an uninterrupted view.

Poppy and I stare at each other as though we're about to burst. I'm aching for her to jump in, when there's the sound of the shop door. From the excited voices and clatter of feet, it sounds like the start of a stampede. From the speed of Poppy's reaction, however big her bump, she isn't suffering from baby brain.

Pushing past Jules, she dives in the desk drawer and pulls out a pair of sunnies. 'Quick, pop these on before the boys arrive.' She's hissing at him. 'You've got a wardrobe malfunction. One of your contacts is missing.'

Jules stutters. 'Contacts? *What* contacts?' He gives a wince of disgust as the specs hit his hand. 'Don't you have Ray-bans? Or some with less bling?'

Poppy shakes her head at me. 'Jeez, Jules, we're a wedding shop not an opticians. They're unclaimed lost property, not prescription lenses. Just put them on or these guys will eat you for breakfast.'

'Who's here?' The flyaway cat's eye frames he's peering

through give him a curiously androgynous air. But at least the mismatch is hidden.

This one I know. 'The groomsmen's party, from the upcoming Manor wedding.' Probably the reason poor Jess is stuck up a mountain as we speak.

'Shite, if they see me like this I'm done for.' Jules groan is heartfelt.

Poppy nods. 'On every count. So move it. Lie low in Sera's studio.'

He pushes his sunnies up and wrinkles his nose. 'My head's hammering, I've got what I came for, so I might choose my moment and make a run for it.'

'As you like.' Poppy's already got her welcoming face on and she's crossed the room to usher in the group. 'Hello Paul, Brett, Gus ...' She's talking to them through the doorway. 'Gary and Ken, you two already met Holly.'

As Gary laughs it's obvious he's Santa from last Saturday. 'Without the pony and tights this time.' Although he's clean shaven, he's still got a sizable paunch. What's more, I can completely see how he nailed the local karaoke championships with his *Karma Chameleon*.

'Not to mention the beard, and the ho ho ho's.' As if they weren't enough clues for me, Ken gives an elfie skip. Just to be sure.

'Harry, Travis, Tom, Taylor and another Tom.' As Poppy waves in the last man, there's a blur of a stripy scarf as Jules bolts across from the desk.

As he pauses momentarily in mid-dash, the chandelier reflections flash off his glasses. 'I'm going to say, "hi and bye".

I'll catch up with you all very soon.'

As Jules whooshes away down the hall, Gary gives a chortle. 'Now there's a man with a twinkle in his shades. I'm liking Julian in blue mirror glasses.'

Ken's purses his lips and he arches one neatly plucked brow. 'My gaydar's on overdrive. Do spill, has pin-up boy Jules finally come over to the dark side? I always knew he'd make a fabulous pixie.'

I surprise myself by leaping to defend Jules's manhood. 'Absolutely not. Those are borrowed sunnies. To ward off a headache. That's absolutely all.'

'Whatever.' Ken gives a smirk. 'We might change his mind at St Aidan's wedding of the year.'

Poppy's taken up her station at the end of the rail of suits. 'So, who's for trying on?'

Aware I'm supposed to be helping here and knowing I need to get my wedding muscles into shape, I decide to chip in. I look down the line-up of friendly faces. 'So, which one's the groom?'

I can see Poppy's lips twitching as a sandy haired guy steps forward.

'That's me.'

I'm opening my mouth to congratulate him, when another voice chimes in.

'And me.' Blond number two steps next to him.

It's out before I can stop it. 'What?' From the way my eyes are popping, I'm entirely giving away that my customer service skills are zero. After Mr and Mr Claus, two grooms shouldn't come as a surprise. I make up for it by racking my brains to remember their names. 'W-w-w-well, great. That's brilliant, T-travis and T-taylor. You two are going to make a lovely couple.'

I'm standing back, mentally patting myself on the back for the way I picked myself up there, when I hear a ripple of laughter. Small at first. Then it rises to a room full of hearty guffaws. From the way Poppy's smile is splitting her face in two, there has to be something not right.

'Two lovely guys are tying the knot. Which explains why there are so many groomsmen. What's so funny?'

Travis takes pity on me first. 'We *are* both getting married – just not to each other.'

I'm bemused. 'Keep going.'

Taylor joins in. 'Travis and I are twin brothers. And we're getting married to twin sisters.

'Double trouble,' Ken chimes in.

Obviously not happy to be outdone by an elf, so does Gary. 'Two for the price of one.' He grins. 'Like all your Christmases coming at once.'

'Right.' Twins marrying twins. If I'd done every combination, I doubt I'd have got to that. Ever.

Although, just for a second I get a stab. Not that I get flashbacks a lot. But when I do they're as clear as if they happened yesterday. Playing weddings with Freya. Not that we did it often. We were way more likely to be shipwrecked, or dressage instructors, with our little brothers as horses. Or on safari using a cut up dustbin for a jeep. She was the strong one, the wild outdoor one, always the one who decided. But on the days when we wore those long dresses handed down from our cousins and paraded around with tea towel veils, we always promised each other when we grew up we'd get married on the same day. Which just goes to prove how little we knew about real life. And how much we were taking the future for granted.

Lucky that one of us is on the ball here instead of drifting off. Poppy's already back by her hanging rail. 'So, all the alterations have been done, boys. We're using the bigger fitting rooms down here today. I hope no one's put on too much weight the last couple of weeks.'

As fast as Poppy locates the name tags, I'm handing out the suits. Once everyone's safely tucked behind the fitting room curtains, she comes over and hisses into my ear.

'So Jules's big secret is that he wears coloured contact lenses.' Her tone is dramatic.

'So *that's* why his eyes look like he got them enhanced on Photoshop?' I've heard of them, I've just never met anyone who was a regular user. 'And why he looked so lopsided with one missing?' And all this time I assumed it was because he was extraordinary. Not just the spots, then. He's less super-human in all departments.

Poppy nods. 'I found out by accident when I woke him up one night when he was staying in a camper van at the farm. He'd taken them out to sleep.'

'But otherwise people don't talk about it?'

'It's St Aidan's best kept secret.' She grins. 'If anyone mentions his startling eyes, he claims it's all down to his mum's blueberry smoothies. She smiles. 'Mesmerising blue eyes are a great way of holding people's attention when he's taking pictures. And women love them too – mostly.'

I suspect she's pulling a face because he had a crush on her a while ago, but she knocked him back. 'Like Jess, you mean?'

'Jess is ninety per cent immune. But she still has a soft spot for Jules. Although she gets very cross when he won't do as he's told.'

As the fitting room curtain moves and the first guy comes out Poppy moves to enthuse.

'Hey, transformation, or what, Brett?'

He runs his fingers through not much hair. 'Once my new haircut's grown a bit, it'll be perfect.'

I nod as he grins at his reflection in the huge White Room mirror. 'Grey tweed. That's very easy on the eye.' Especially on a hottie like Brett.

As the line of hunky guys files out, they're all looking stunning in their own way. But the sad thing is, although I can appreciate the lookers, none of them raise even a tiny flutter. Not that getting Luc back would ever happen. I'm resigned to that. But even this far down the line, I'm still a million miles away from moving on. And anyone reminding me of my lift shaft tummy at Home Brew Cottage the other night, forget it. Because I have. That didn't count for anything at all.

Refolding ten suits, sliding them into their smart Brides by the Sea travelling covers, sorting the payments, I can see why Poppy needs an extra pair of hands. It's the best part of an hour later by the time the guys file out past the Christmas tree.

'Have a fabulous day on the 15th,' Poppy calls after them, as we stand together waving.

After yesterday I can't help musing. A double wedding in the most upmarket venue in the county? What the hell kind of nightmare would that be for a photographer? Even Superman Jules will have his work cut out with that one. In skiing terms, it makes my two-person ceremony on the beach seem like the nursery slopes. But on the upside, it's not something I'll ever have to worry about. After Nate and Becky, I'll be full speed back to quiches, casseroles and my easy life. And for me, it can't come soon enough.

Chapter 11

Thursday 7th December
At Brides by the Sea: Gobstoppers and disappointments

'So how did it go with the midwife?'

I've been in the White Room all day, helping Sera with bridal appointments and working on my pictures in between. By the time Poppy comes in and flops in the mother-of-the-bride's chair, it's late afternoon, and through the shop windows the mews outside is yellow in the street lights' glow.

Poppy wrinkles her nose. 'My blood pressure's a teensy bit up, but still completely normal. Baby Rafe is absolutely fine. But I'd rather not worry Big Rafe with this just at the moment.'

It's completely confidential, for all kinds of reasons. But Rafe and his previous girlfriend lost a baby a long time ago. Since she's been pregnant, Poppy has shared this with her closest friends, if only to explain why Rafe's reluctant to leave her side for a second. And this is why every medical appointment is extra tense for Poppy.

She gives a low moan. 'Rafe's trying *so* hard to be relaxed and positive.'

I shrug. 'You being pregnant is bound to bring it all back. It's completely understandable that he's anxious.' I'm sympathising despite being completely clueless.

She puffs out her lips. 'No, anxious was before. Since we went past the dates when it all went wrong last time, he's totally bricking it.' Her sigh is heartfelt. 'And the other need-to-know yet completely off-the-record news today is, Immie *isn't* pregnant. She told me when I met her in town on my way back from the surgery.'

I let out a groan. 'Oh bummer. That's a shame.' Immie's never one to keep things to herself. When she got married last summer she didn't throw her bouquet, because she wanted to keep it for the grandchildren. That, and leaving pregnancy test boxes scattered all around the farm office, mean it's common knowledge she and Chas are trying. 'With so many brides moving on to have families, Jess needs to scrap the studio idea and open Babies by the Sea instead.'

'Sera's sister Alice has a little girl now too.' Poppy laughs. 'Jess is great with brides. Children not so much.'

As the phone rings the call comes up as out of area. 'Speaking of Jess, this is her eighth call today.' I fill Poppy in as I pick up the handset. 'Still no sign of a ring. But she's on first name terms with all the bar staff in Kaffee Klatsch.'

Poppy puts out her hand. 'Let me take it.'

'Thanks.' As I peep past the fairy lights in the window down the shadowy mews, my heart sinks. 'Although, we may have visitors.' Rory, swinging Teddie in a car seat from one hand and Gracie from the other, is heading straight for the door.

I grab one of Jules's flyers and I'm fanning myself, wildly trying for a pre-chill before the heat hits, when Immie strides in, thumping her head with both fists.

'Hols, we need a toilet for Gracie and a gobstopper for Rory. That man's doing my head in.'

Poppy's backing away into the kitchen, shaking her head. Although that may be more because she hasn't got a word in with Jess yet, than because of who's arriving.

'I'm with you on that one.' I grin at Immie. 'What's he done now?'

She tugs at her spikes of hair. 'Two kids in tow, and he still goes on endlessly about wine recommendations and mashes and labels. If I hear one more word about Mad Elf or Santa's Little Helper, when he should be focusing on baby milk, I might just bottle Rory Sanderson himself.'

I take it she's talking about beers there. And seeing Immie is one of the world's greatest sinkers of pints, with a spectacular interest in any hop-related liquid, this is a big turnaround indeed.

There's an outsized jangle going on in the hallway, then Rory bursts in. Teddie's car seat slides along the floor as he puts it down, and then he releases Gracie.

'Baby carrier in collision with the Christmas tree back there. You guys really need to work on your parent and baby access.'

'Hi Gracie,' I say, making a point of ignoring Rory. 'Remind me to brush your hair before you go.' If she was rocking the haystack look the other day, today she's moved onto fourth day festival chic.

Immie's holding her hand out to Gracie, who's clutching

both furry snowmen to her chest. 'Toilet's this way.'

I'm inwardly cursing for not jumping in on the bathroom run, because now I'm stuck facing Rory. 'Dropping by with the kids isn't the best idea. All this white lace isn't exactly a child friendly environment.' If I'm fierce enough, with any luck next time Gracie's bursting he'll drop into the Hungry Shark instead and save me the bother of tensing my muscles so hard to keep my stomach in place, they feel like they're cramping.

He shakes his head. 'You do know you're still just as hilarious when you're up yourself, Holly North? Don't get your trousseau in a twist. Good thing for you we're only here to use the facilities, not rate your welcome on Trip Advisor.'

Seeing as we're in the shop, I'm feeling the pressure to be professional. Ignoring his taunt, I jam my mouth into a smile. 'So how has your day been?' It comes out sweet to the point of sickly. Chocolate brownie, with double toffee sauce would be less cloying.

He folds his arms. 'Great, so long as screaming and sulking are your bag.'

'That bad?' If my smile gives way to a frown of concern, it's for Gracie, not him. 'Can't you make an effort? Take them out somewhere? Kids usually like to chat. And most of them will eat vegetables too if you chop them into sticks.' Not that I'm an expert, but I seem to have more idea than he does.

'Thank you to St Aidan's latest childcare guru.' His shrug is dismissive. 'There's no common ground. Gracie's not interested in pubs and I'm well out of touch with my childish side.'

'Really?' If my voice is a disbelieving squeak, it's because that claim would be more credible if it didn't come from the same sixth-form joker who left the school skeleton sunbathing in a deck chair on the roof of the science block, in full view of hundreds of drivers passing in the rush hour. What's more, he apparently threw in a successful job in law to make home brew and flog champers. Rejections of adulting don't come much bigger than that. He's pushing forty and swanning around with zero responsibilities and no visible ties. Apart from having to stir the odd vat occasionally, this guy has the life of Riley. From where I'm standing, Rory is the original teenager who refused to grow up. 'So you're not going to try at all?'

He saunters over to the desk and throws himself down into the Louis Quatorze chair. 'This is a holding exercise now. As Gracie puts it, three more sleeps and they'll be gone. Roll on Sunday, so we can all get our lives back.' He puts his hands behind his head and starts to extend his legs. 'Let's face it, it's as bad for them as it is for me. This has to be the longest week ever.'

I'm about to point out it's only half over. And however long it's seemed for him, being stuck with a bad-tempered beer obsessive, who doesn't know the words to *Let It Go*, has probably seemed even longer for Gracie. But as he kicks the table, there's a flicker as my laptop screen bursts into life. 'Careful there.' I leap forward to slam it shut, but I'm too late. His hand shoots out and stops me.

'Wait a minute.' As he leans forward, tilts back the screen and squints at it there's the start of a smile playing around his lips. 'Well, I never. So, Holly Berry, you weren't just a poseur with a camera case. You really *were* taking pictures at the farm.' Then a low chuckle comes from his throat as he scrolls down. 'You're a dark horse. When did *you* become a wedding photographer?' There's delight on his face that he's blown my secret.

Anyone else would have been bad enough. With Rory peering at my photos, I'm so confused the words won't come out. 'It's ... I'm not ... big mistake ... complicated ...' As usual Mr Sanderson's put two and two together and made sixty six. Not hard for an idiot like him.

All these years on, it's times like this when I miss Freya most. Actually, that's not true. I'll never get over not having her there to talk to at night. Or sitting around the family table, coming out with all the clever stuff. And lounging on the sofa, always ready with a cushion for when her wimpy younger sister bottled at scary films. That Child Catcher in *Chitty Chitty Bang Bang* who gave us nightmares for years still makes me shiver even now. But she was always the one who dared to creep into my bed and talk until I fell asleep. Without her, I was out of my teens before I dared to watch the headless horseman in *Sleepy Hollow*, even though everyone else had seen it years before.

But if she were here now, even though it's years on, I know she'd jump in with a fitting put- down. Squish Rory to the size and significance of a pea. Make me come up roses, looking bloody brilliant. She had the ability to whip out something more eloquent in a second than I could think of if I sat and pondered for a week.

I'm halfway through failing to explain myself when Poppy reappears from the kitchen. Then Immie and Gracie come galloping back from the loo. A bit like buses. I've been sitting so long opening and closing my mouth like I've got no brain cells at all, and now the two of them are here to save me at once.

'You were quick. Everything okay?' Funny how the words come out fine when I'm speaking to Poppy. The way she's staring back at me like a guppie, it's almost like I was with Rory. And, come to think of it, she's galloped through the phone call with Jess. I've been pushed to get Jess to hang up inside thirty minutes. In the end I have to ask. 'Is there a problem?'

Immie's thinking the same, but expressing it differently. 'Come on, Pops, spit it out. You're dithering like a lily-livered walrus.'

Poppy blinks. 'Okay, so here's a thing. Zoe totally loves your pictures, Hols. See, I told you she would.'

'Jess rang to tell you that?' It's great to know, but somehow it's coming from the wrong place entirely.

From Poppy's grimace, she's agonising. 'The other news is less good. Basically ...' She hesitates, then it comes out in a rush. '... Jess rang to tell me we're a man down.'

Immie's hands are on her hips. 'Sorry, you're going to have to do better than that. We're still none the wiser.' As her coat opens, there's a flash of her *Don't f**k with me* t-shirt slogan.

Poppy groans at her. 'Zip up Immie, thank Christmas Gracie can't read.'

'What?' Immie's expression is inscrutable. 'For frig sake.

This is my "going out when I'm cross" t-shirt. It's only fair to warn people.'

As Rory leans towards her, for once he's not joking around. 'Don't take it too hard, Immie. You and Chas are bound to get lucky soon. Fingers crossed for next month, eh?' If it's a shock that Rory can sound that sincere, it's also a shock he's in the inner circle of people in the loop about Immie's baby disappointment. Although that's St Aidan for you. It's the only place in the world where a wine merchant would be commenting on your menstrual cycles and publicly cheering you on to fertilisation. What's more astounding still, he's getting full appreciation for his input.

'Thanks, mate. I hope you're right. Give us a couple of days, and we'll be less gutted.' Immie pulls the corners of her mouth down, then moves on. 'So, who the hell's dropped out of the team?'

The way Poppy's stalling, maybe she has got baby brain after all. 'It's Jules. Jess rang to say he's housebound.' She drags in a breath. 'So he's asking if Hols could go out to a wedding venue up near Port Giles tomorrow. Check out a few angles and shots. Take a few pictures in advance of a wedding he's booked for on Sunday. Nothing too difficult. If we can get someone to take you, do you think you could manage that?' She raises an eyebrow at me.

I'm blinking, because I'm doubtful. 'He wants me to finish the edits on Zoe's pictures tomorrow.'

Poppy's looking anxious. 'Actually, Jules has offered to do a job swap on that. As he and Jess say, the pictures from the Port Giles venue will be great for your portfolio. It's a converted lifeboat station an hour and a half up the coast. A fabulous place.'

I'm puzzled. 'How come Jess is the one sorting this out?'

Poppy shrugs. 'Just because Jess is in Switzerland, it doesn't mean she's not in control. She's everyone's go-to person if they have a problem, because she'll always find an answer.'

From nowhere, Immie chimes in. 'Why doesn't Rory take you up to Port Giles, Hols. It'll be a good way to get the kids out.' From the way she catches Poppy's eye, I suspect they could be colluding on this. Although when Poppy mentioned Rory as partner material the day of Zoe's wedding, I had no idea they'd be this proactive.

Luckily for me, Rory couldn't look more horrified as he jumps in with his own protest. 'Even if I'd love to see how Supernanny stands up to a day of screaming from the back seat, I don't think so.'

As I frown at Poppy and Immie, I can't help my whine. 'Why do I feel like you're ganging up on me?'

Poppy sends me a soothing smile. 'Not at all, Hols. We're just over-stretched, due to unforeseen circumstances. Rory's not working tomorrow, so he's the most available of all of the team to take you. Immie's completely right to suggest him.'

This is such a bad idea, for every reason. Although the kids are the least of the problems. 'Actually I'd rather walk than spend two hours in a car with Rory.' That would be on hot coals, by the way. 'What's more, he obviously feels the same way. And for the record, I only put edible stuff in my portfolio.'

Poppy's straight in. 'In which case you could pull in lunch too. If you're wanting food pictures, you could find an award-winning real ale pub that does posh nosh.' The triumphant smile she sends Rory is simply because he's anyone's for a mention of beer.

I'm going to close this down straight away. 'Everyone, please. What part of "no" do you not understand?'

Rory's tilting his head and narrowing his eyes. 'It's obvious Holly Pink Cheeks can't take a day with the kids. We should all respect that.'

I'm glaring at him for ducking out and not taking the blame fair and square himself. Growling through clenched teeth. 'Gracie and Teddie aren't the problem here.'

Immie's holding her hands in the air. 'Stop guys! I'm up to my ears with cottage changeovers, Poppy's very pregnant and needs to rest. It's a few hours tops.' Her voice rises from reasonable to a roar. 'Whatever's going on with you two, man up and get over it!'

I have to jump on this. 'There's absolutely *nothing* going on.' I turn to Rory, who's staring somewhere out in the mews. 'Back me up on this, Rory.'

He turns and blinks as he hears his name. 'What's that? I've got no idea what the hell … but I'm damned if …'

Immie's roaring again. 'Language, Rory.' Then she drops her voice to a hiss. 'By the sound of it, we're in a shit hole here. Poppy's helping both of you out massively with your accommodation, so the least you can do is put your differences to one side for half a day and go with this. Okay?' Faced with a scowl that fierce, there's nothing else for it.

I can hardly believe what I'm agreeing to with my squeak. 'Okay. I'll go.'

Rory snorts like a bull. 'Fine.' If there's one consolation, it's that he's as unwilling as I am.

Poppy's eyes are wide and a lot less relaxed than her voice. 'Great, so that's the first hurdle sorted.'

I'm back to opening and closing my mouth, because on reflection, I'm not sure it is at all. Right now I've been lined up for a day out with the last person in the world I want to spend time with, taking pictures of a wedding venue as a favour. A favour for a guy who, to be honest, has been pretty hostile to me up till now. What's more, I'm moving further and further away from my sausage casserole comfort zone with every second.

Immie's moved on. 'But what's wrong with Jules?'

I'm momentarily putting my immediate problems aside and thinking back to his hammering head. 'Is this because of his nervous rash?'

Immie's straight in there. 'Rash?'

'He had a couple of pimples on his forehead yesterday.'

Immie's voice soars. 'Refusing to leave the house just because he's got a spot? Jeez, I know Jules is faddy and vain in spades, but this takes the biscuit. What's wrong with a blob of concealer? That wimp needs to grow some balls, slap on the *Hide the Blemish*, and show his zit to the world, like the rest of us mere mortals do every day.' Sounds like the full brunt of Immie's baby angst has moved on from us to Jules.

From the way Poppy's face crumples, she could be sucking on a sour lemon. 'Jess said to break it to you bit by bit, Hols. But maybe it's best to tell you the truth, all at once.'

I'm frowning. 'You mean there's worse to come?' From where

I'm standing a day out with Rory is as bad as it gets. Worse isn't possible.

Poppy's voice is soft. 'Jules has got more spots since yesterday. A lot more. They think he's probably got chickenpox. And that can be really serious in adults.'

Immie's chortling. 'So you won't be in any danger from that, Rory. That's one advantage to being an eternal child.'

Rory says nothing, but the way he's waving his middle finger at her confirms she's right anyway.

Gracie's twiddling with her fingers so quietly we'd almost forgotten she was there. 'Rory showed me and Teddie the loose sign.' As she sticks up her middle finger and waves it around everyone except Rory exchanges horrified glances.

Immie grabs her hand and closes her fingers around Gracie's. 'Snowmen don't do the hang loose sign, because their fingers are too stumpy. So you and Teddie need to forget the hand signals, right now, okay?' She rolls her eyes at me, but Poppy's words are slowly sinking in. Like dumplings into stew. Checking out camera angles in Port Giles sounds like the start, not the end of this nightmare.

'So what's happening to all of Jules's wedding bookings?'

Poppy's eyes are very bright. 'Jess thought ... and Jules thought ... as your pictures from Zoe's wedding were so fab ... that *you* might like to ... help out ...'

Despite my iron muscle control my stomach lurches, and this time it's nothing to do with Mr Sanderson. 'Me step in?' It's almost a yell. Although why I'm clutching my waist when my gut's already left the building, I have no idea. 'Absolutely not. That's NO with the caps lock on.' Seeing Poppy isn't reacting, I might need to suggest my own solution. 'Isn't there someone local to do it? Doesn't he have any friends in the business?'

She sighs. 'His two besties are grabbing some winter sun in Fuerteventura, so they can't help. It's lucky this happened in the off season.' Poppy's got her pleading look on. 'After Port Giles, all the weddings are with us. If you could take over ... just until he's back on his feet again ... we all know you'll nail it ...'

I might as well throw it in. '*Actually* Jules agrees with me on this. He *actually* told me weddings weren't my bag.'

Poppy's eyebrows lift. 'According to Jess, he's had a radical rethink on that. Nothing like chickenpox to change a man's mind. You're his best hope here, because you've got the technical skill and the flare to come through with the kind of shots he likes to do. Don't worry, we'll pull together for the rest.'

Worry doesn't begin to cover what I'm feeling here. My throat is dry, but I have to explain. 'Becky and Nate are understanding friends, who know what they're getting, and would excuse me for less than perfect pictures.' They're completely ready to take a chance I might screw up on their big day, in other words. Which let's face, it is quite possible given how complex weddings are these days. 'But Jules's couples will be clients demanding a top notch job. And deserving it too. There's a world of difference.'

Poppy's got her pleading face on. 'You have no idea how much work goes into putting a wedding together. And the photographs are what the couple have to remember the day forever.'

'That's my point entirely.' At least we're agreeing on something here. The pressure to deliver perfection is immense.

'But that's also why all those weddings happening without a photographer would be unthinkable. Please, Hols. I know it's hard, but you've *got* to help us out here.'

I'm thinking back to how much Poppy's helped me over the last year. How she's messaged me every day. Agonised and sympathised. When she let me borrow her flat, it was purely to help me through Christmas. If this is how things are accidentally working out, given there really isn't anyone else, maybe I need to dig deep. I give a huge sigh. 'Maybe I can try.' My main reason for helping out Nate and Becky was because I was desperate to grab a last lifeline to Luc. And get myself out of my rut. If it wasn't for that, I wouldn't even be here at all.

Poppy pulls in a breath. 'Jess thinks you're going to surprise yourself. And I think she's right.'

Talking of which, it's no surprise that Immie's joining in. 'We'll all be here to help you. With the Daisy Hill team behind you, you can do this, Hols.'

'So that's all settled.' Poppy's grinning at me. 'Brides by the Sea just got a shiny new stand in wedding photographer. Complete with back-up team.'

'Great.' It comes out as a whisper. Except it's really not. As for Rory Sanderson having *any* part of this, that is nothing short of a disaster waiting to happen.

Chapter 12

Friday 8th December
At Brides by the Sea: Ready and unwilling

'**O**pening up at nine?' As I lug my camera stuff down
four flights of stairs and into the shop next morning,
Poppy's already behind the desk. 'I thought you were supposed
to be taking it easy?'

She looks up from checking through a stack of parcels.
'With some clients it's worth going the extra mile.' The corners
of her mouth droop. 'It's damage limitation. Stave off the
problems before they happen and everything will be fine.'

I'm getting the message. 'So you're expecting a difficult
customer?'

Her grin is rueful. 'Let's just say, if Marilyn had told me to
be here at dawn, I wouldn't have argued.' She laughs. 'But at
least coming in early meant I was here at eight to talk Jess
down.'

'What did Jess want at that time?' Usually she waits until
the shop opens at ten.

Poppy raises her eyebrows. 'Last night Bart took her on a

moonlight ride in a pony and trap, followed by a five star fondue on a private balcony at the smartest local restaurant.'

I'm impressed. 'He's not stinting on the romance, is he?'

'Poor Jess spent all evening convinced she was about to dip into the melted cheese and pull a ring out. So much Gruyère and nothing at the end of it. Reading between the pauses, I think she was devastated.'

Oh my. 'I wish I'd never mentioned proposals.' I'm feeling very guilty for raising her expectations.

Poppy shakes her head. 'Engagement must have been on her mind or she wouldn't have cornered you. And I'm sure she'll be back with a diamond on her left hand. I just wish he'd get on with it and then we can *all* relax and enjoy their holiday.' She peers at me more closely. 'Are you sure you're feeling okay? You're very pale this morning.'

Result! As I put my fingers to my cheek, despite the cakey feel, I'm mentally punching the air. 'Probably just my late night. It's hard to stop watching *Friends* once you start.' It's too embarrassing to admit I've splashed out on some Red Alert blush hider. At forty quid for a teensy tube, I'm pleased she's noticed because, to be honest, miracles come cheaper.

'You aren't going to puke again are you?' Her frown deepens. 'It's just you look a bit crusty.'

I hadn't anticipated an inquisition. 'Really, I'm all good.' Which is a complete lie, seeing what's ahead. But as it might stretch to an entire morning with Rory, I went for four layers. Then just to be doubly sure, I added a layer or two of talc I found in the bathroom cabinet. Crusts are a minor drawback, if it means I stay pale.

She glances at her phone. 'Is Rory late?'

Me hopping from one foot to the other is probably the giveaway. I'm twitching the chiffon layers of the wedding dress in the window display so I can get a better view down the mews. Although it's only to be expected. He doesn't exactly come across as Mr Reliable. 'He's probably still struggling to get the kids up and dressed. Although there's someone coming now. She's blonde, powering down the street like she's going into battle.'

Poppy pulls a face. 'Damn. Our nine o'clock must be early.'

From the sheer confidence in her stride, she's already making me want to find a corner to hide in. 'I'll stay out of your way. Unless you need me to help, that is.' I dive and perch on the end of the bridesmaids' chaise longue furthest away from the desk.

'Marilyn! How are we doing with the spreadsheet?' Poppy's welcome couldn't sound warmer, considering Marilyn's arriving in the White Room like a force-ten gale, cape flying. If her hair was less mayonnaisey she could stand in as a body double for Theresa May. As she storms to the desk it's obvious from her jingling wrist chains she's got a serious Tiffany habit.

'I'm here to talk cakes, Poppy.' Hands on hips, and she's not holding back. 'I know Seth and Katie asked you to make theirs. But honestly, chocolate sponge at a wedding?'

Poppy purses her lips. 'They took a long time to decide. And they did take your wishes into account and hold back on the complete alpine scene. But they loved the idea of the white drip icing looking like snow on top of a chocolate mountain.'

Marilyn makes a choking noise. 'That doesn't count as a wedding cake in my book. Which is why I've had to overrule them and make my own. Square, dark fruit, glycerin icing, five tiers. All I need now is a miniature bride and groom to top it off. Preferably with a blond haired groom, as I said on the phone.'

'We've got three here.' Poppy widens her eyes as she fiddles to open the boxes. 'Although Katie did want winter berries and skis to top er – whichever cake she'd chosen. To go with the bouquets?' This is Poppy treading super carefully.

Marilyn's eyebrows shoot up so fast they almost collide with the chandelier. 'Berries?' Her voice has shot up an octave. 'No one mentioned berries when I spoke to the florist yesterday. How do berries fit with glittered classic white-rose posies?' She picks over the bride and groom ornaments. 'This one will do. Now *please* tell me the favours are here.'

Poppy's looking bemused. 'They are. A hundred and three personalised silver keepsake boxes. Lily and I checked them personally, the names and the hallmarks are all perfect. Is that everything for this morning?'

Marilyn dives into her bag. 'One last item, because I won't be backing down on the headgear issue. I need a veil to attach to this.' The heavy, diamond encrusted tiara she pulls out would be more at home in a safe in the Tower of London than being dragged around St Aidan in a Longchamp Le Pliage bag. 'We need to try this. The girl in the corner will do.' A second later she's sprung across the floor and rammed it onto my head. Then she grabs a veil from a display and impales that on me too.

By the time I wail 'ouch' she's snatched them both off again and she's pushing the veil across the desk to Poppy. Along with half my messy topknot too.

Poppy winces as she teases the hairs off the soft tulle. 'Would you like that in a bag?'

'So long as you're quick.' Marilyn scoops up the box of favours. 'I'm on double yellows and I'm already hours late for the caterers. I'll take these out and come back for the veil.' Hours? So maybe she does make dawn appointments.

As she sprints away, Poppy's blowing her fringe up.

'So that's what a fully stressed-out mother of the bride looks like?' I ask as the shop door slams. It's almost as if I'm spotting rarities for a wedding version of those *I Spy* books we had in the holidays as kids. Mother of the bride, five points. Add two more points if she's in a bridal shop, and ten more if she's pulling her hair out. Make that fifty if she pulls out someone else's. Freya filled in every line. On hers and mine. She had *The Seaside*, which was a bit of a gift, given we came to St Aidan so often. Mine was *Pets*, but even though we lived in pirate country, I never did find a parrot.

'Not quite.' Poppy's expression is pained. 'Katie and Seth are the sweetest couple, organising their own fabulous alpine-themed wedding in the converted barn at the farm.' She shakes her head. 'Marilyn is Seth's mum, and her vision for Seth getting married couldn't be more different from Seth and Katie's.'

'Mother of the groom on an uninvited takeover mission, then?'

Poppy screws up her face. 'Pretty much. Hijacking the cake

is minor compared to the rest. The favour order is entirely without consultation. A while back she tried to change the colours of the bridesmaids' dresses from brights to pastels. She wanted to line the barn with silk to make it look less stoney. Katie's more likely to get married in ski goggles than in a veil *or* the family tiara. No doubt Marilyn's on her way to the caterers to re-do the menus.'

'Oh my days.' I can completely see why Poppy came in to handle this client personally. I just hope it doesn't push her blood pressure through the roof.

'I'm sure she's coming from the best of places. Lily has worked so hard with them and the ski-lodge styling is going to be amazing, regardless of Marilyn. But it's impossible to second guess where she's going to strike next.' Poppy rolls her eyes and laughs.

I laugh too. 'If you're a wedding manager, she's a total loose cannon.' So long as you aren't involved, there's definitely a funny side.

As Marilyn comes back in, I make sure to wedge my cheeks in place so my smile is appropriately wide. Although this time round I'm ready to dodge any more tiara moves. And this is not being two-faced. It's simply taking a leaf out of the customer service survival guide. As weddings go, Marilyn sounds like she's at the nightmare end of the spectrum.

Marilyn takes her carrier bag from Poppy. 'Just put everything on my account. Jess found me the most *wonderful* fuchsia fascinator before she left.'

'Lovely.' Poppy's trying for a soothing croon. 'So only the final dress appointment left now, then it's downhill all the way to the big day.'

Marilyn holds up her hands dramatically. 'And I'll be full speed ahead to Christmas straight after. For my sins. As if getting married on a farm and pretending it's a mountain wasn't awful enough.'

Despite my smile I give a gulp. 'Christmas? Which Christmas would that be, then?'

Marilyn glowers down at me as if I've got an IQ the size of an apple pip. 'The one in nineteen days' time. Why, is there another one?' As she backs towards the door, for the first time since she walked in, there's an uncertain look in her eyes.

Meanwhile Poppy's doing her best to examine the plaster-work on the ceiling. She waits until the shop door slams before she speaks. 'You managed to baffle her there with that Christmas question of yours. Well done on that, it takes a lot to knock Marilyn off her stride.'

Except I'm the one who's confused here. 'So if this wedding's at the farm before Christmas, who's doing the photos?'

Poppy blows out her lips. 'A Christmas ski-themed wedding is going to be an absolute gift in terms of pictures. You should see what Lily's got lined up. There'll be a roaring log fire and a ski lift gondola for selfies, and fairy lights and fake snow and antlers and red gingham cushions. And signs and vintage ski posters.'

I'm talking over her. 'Frig the snow and soft furnishings. Who's the photographer?'

'There's a hot-chocolate bar and frosty cocktails, the brides-maids are wearing tulle mini skirts and knee-high fake-fur boots.' Now she's in full flow, she's unstoppable. As her list comes to an abrupt halt, she couldn't look more guilty. 'Actually, it's Jules.'

This I can't believe. 'Jules?' I'm struggling to get this straight in my head. 'That's Jules, meaning me?'

'Yep.' As she nods her expression is pained. 'I was holding back, because I didn't want to load too much onto you all at once.'

I can't hold in my wail. 'That means Marilyn's going to be at one of Jules's weddings ... that *I'm* doing?' If she's hell bent on taking over the rest of the wedding, she's hardly going to hold back with the photographer.

'I'm sorry. You weren't meant to meet her today.' Poppy's face crumples. 'Really, we'll handle her. I promise, she won't be a problem to you on the day.'

'And I'm a snowman,' I say. What's more, I can't help wondering how many more hidden Marilyns and alpine ski weddings are going to jump out of the snowdrifts at me in the next few weeks.

'Snowman?' There's an echo along the hall and a second later Gracie comes pelting in, followed by Rory swinging Teddie.

'Jeez, where the hell have you been Holly Berry? We've been stuck out there for hours behind some car parked on the double yellows.'

However huge a problem looming in the future, a current one will dwarf it. And as current problems go they don't come any bigger than a day out with Rory Sanderson that should have started ten minutes ago. At least he won't be calling me Red Cheeks today.

Chapter 13

Friday 8th December
On the way to Port Giles: Tidemarks and burst bubbles

'Are you wearing your pyjamas, Gracie?' As I finally clamber up into the beer-mobile, a few drops of rain are spotting the windscreen. Which is a shame, seeing I was hoping for some sun. But as I turn and grin at the backseat passengers, I can't help recognising the spangly star top from the other evening.

Rory shrugs. 'That's what happens when people refuse to put their clothes on. Unfortunately your helpful serving suggestion blew up into an almighty showdown. It turns out Gracie goes ape-plops if her cucumber arrives in sticks instead of circles.'

I'm screwing up my face. 'Jeez, I didn't mean you to give them veggie sticks for breakfast.' What kind of numbskull would get that so wrong?

'No worries, we're here now.' He stares across as I do up my seatbelt. 'Holly, have you got white stuff on your face?'

Damn. 'Probably Poppy's icing sugar.' It's the first thing I think of. I sniff and make a big play of wiping my cheek. 'All those cupcakes, it gets everywhere. Or toothpaste maybe?' So long as it hides the red, I don't give a damn what it looks like.

For some reason he seems to find that funny. Then he drags in a breath and goes all serious again. 'You need to understand about Gracie. She's a three-year-old who travels with her own iPad and a whole heap of attitude. She's like one of those pets that think they have staff not owners. Although I reckon a cat would be more friendly.'

I turn to look at her. 'If we sing along to some *Frozen* songs, we'll soon get you smiling, Gracie.' However much we'd both rather not be here, I'm not letting the children see that.

As Rory eases the monster truck out of the mews, he's straight in there. 'Absolutely not.' He throws his phone across to me. 'Find some festive tunes on there and stick them on.'

If he can veto, so can I. 'Sorry, I'm not doing Christmas this year.'

'Fine. So what else do you suggest? And don't even think about girlie love songs.'

I'm wishing I'd taken Poppy up on her offer of *Five Tracks to Fight the Fear (It's only a wedding! Dammit)*. That was the Spotify list she had to boost her courage, when she was new to the business and bricking it as much as I am. Although flicking through Rory's playlist is like looking into a teenager's head. 'Green Day?' It slips out because I'm gobsmacked to see it.

Rory grins. 'Good choice, that'll do.'

'It was an exclamation of horror at your taste, not a suggestion.' I let out a groan. Then put it on anyway in the hope that it'll shut him up.

As the first few bars fill the car, he's tapping on the steering wheel. 'High energy, loud guitars, what's not to like? Although I can see you might want something more wedding-y, given you're such a novice. There's a lot to learn in two days, which is why it's a great move on Immie's part to send me along to advise.'

As we roar out of town and take the road to the north, if the twangy rock and the whirr of the wipers wasn't bad enough, now I'm drowning under the latest rush of Sanderson bullshit. 'And when exactly did *you* become the expert on weddings?'

He laughs. 'Definitely not by getting married, that's for sure. But I must have been to forty or more in the last few years. When you're a perennial wedding guest you get to know how the days roll out. Don't knock it, I could be useful.'

'You have *that* many friends?' Somehow I've managed to miss most of the weddings I've been invited to. And Nate and Becky are the first of Luc's friend group to take the plunge since I've been around. Which is why I'm clueless.

'A lot of my friends are in the marrying demographic. And a wine merchant with a brewery is a natural choice for a guest. Who wouldn't want a crate of personalised Mr and Mrs beer and ten per cent off and sale-or-return on vintage Champagne?' He pushes back the sleeve of his tartan shirt. 'When I checked in my diary, I actually went to a wedding at this venue a couple of years back. So if you're looking for information, I'm your man.'

'Brilliant.' Mr Know-it-all strikes again. As I glance into the back for some light relief, Gracie is already busy tapping her iPad and Teddie is kicking his bare foot in time to the music. 'What are you playing, Gracie?' I make a mental note to find the baby a pair of socks before we get out of the car.

She looks up for a second. 'Popping balloons.'

'Is it fun?'

'Yep.' Then as she cuts me off and looks back down straight afterwards, I'm kind of getting how she might be hard to get through to.

Rory clears his throat. 'So, no Christmas for you, then?'

'Nope.' I swallow hard and decide to deal with this before trying Gracie again. More fool me for thinking I'd got away with that one.

He sends me a sideways glance. 'I can still see you staggering onto the bus at Christmas with your schoolbag covered in battery-operated fairy lights. Wasn't that your way of remembering Freya?'

Alongside the surprise that his memory's that clear, it's lovely to hear someone call Freya by her name when most people seem to have forgotten she was ever here. 'We always try to make Christmas a special time to celebrate her life. She'd understand why I'm toning it down this time around, though.'

He rubs the steering wheel for a few seconds before he carries on. 'I heard all about you legging it when you got proposed to last year. Bit insensitive with the timing there, wasn't he?'

I sigh and decide it's easier to deal with the second bit than the first. 'He probably missed the significance.' Although Luc

141

knew about Freya, it was more that I'd lost my sister a long time ago than something he ever asked me about in depth.

Rory's frowning as if he can't believe my last answer. 'So what was so bad you had to run?'

I suppose the question had to crop up sooner or later. And me breaking out into a sticky sweat isn't half so bad when I know my cheeks are going to stay one colour. I can't believe this is what it's like permanently for most of the rest of the population. As I rub the perspiration off the inside of my shirt collar, I'm praying there isn't a tidemark on my neck where the concealer runs out and the flushing skin begins. And if it comes as a shock that Rory knows every last detail of my embarrassing romantic past, it's only a sign of how healthy the damned St Aidan community grapevine is.

Sometimes it's easier to reply than to resist. 'Getting proposed to took me by surprise, that's all.'

He shoots a glance at me. 'Still a scaredy cat, then? Although I don't blame you for taking fright. The idea of committing to someone for the rest of my life would make *me* want to run too. Especially someone who had no idea a Christmas proposal should have been off limits for you.' This is just how he is. He needles and digs, and pretends he understands when he doesn't have the first clue.

'Running was a gut reaction. By the time I warmed to the idea, it was too late.'

He's chuckling to himself. 'Poor Holly Pink Cheeks. It sounds like he barely knew you, but it must have been serious if he got around to proposing. So what was he like?'

I stick out my chin. 'If I wasn't stuck in the passenger seat,

I wouldn't be doing this.' And my answer wasn't meant to bring out the sympathy violins either. I try to think of a way to describe Luc. 'Good looking, amazing job, fabulous flat, great taste in rings.' Actually, I have a feeling the ring might have been his dead grandmother's because, despite the sparkle, it looked ancient rather than new. But the diamonds were very chunky, even if it wasn't really my first choice of style.

'Which makes your break for freedom even more astonishing.' His eyes narrow. 'Although I'm not hearing anything there about how much he loved you.'

My voice is high because he's so damned presumptuous. 'What is this, marriage guidance?' And if I'm extra jumpy it's probably because we weren't ever one of those lovey dovey couples. Luc was more of a matter-of-fact kind of guy. It definitely suited him to have me around to come back to those times he wasn't away with work, but he wasn't the sort to go on about it.

His eyebrows close into a frown. 'It is over, *isn't it*? Please tell me you aren't still aching for the chance to say yes a second time around?'

'Jeez, Rory, I'd go back to him in a heartbeat, if he asked me, okay? But he's not going to, and a year down the line I'm *completely* fine with that.'

There's more tapping of fingers on the steering wheel, and luckily for all of us, more staring at the road. '*So* fine, you still can't face *anything* to do with Christmas? That sounds like you're *definitely* over him, then.' His tone is strangely serious when he might have been jokey. 'Personally I reckon you should *always* trust your first instincts. If you ask me, you were probably right to run.' Except no one did ask him.

'To be honest, I'd rather the kids were screaming than listen to this.'

He shrugs. 'Sorry, but sometimes it hurts to face the truth. If he'd been the right guy for you, you wouldn't have run and you'd still be together. I reckon you had a lucky escape. That was why you stood out at school all those years ago. You were quiet, but you could always cut through the crap and see the bigger picture. That's why I liked talking to you.'

Bugging me, more like. I'd wondered when we'd get onto this. If we're talking crap, there's a shitload there. 'You talked to me on the bus so I'd go red. End of.' Obviously I'm only free to say this today because I've got my face armour on. And you've no idea how bloody liberating it feels.

'Maybe at the start. After a while I kind of forgot about that.' He sounds wistful. 'The other girls had been warned off. Whereas you were mature enough to see past my mishaps and treat me as a person.'

'Mishaps' is a mild way of describing his disaster catalogue. But I suppose my mum and dad had more on their mind. Boys who sent cars into ravines and over cliffs were a small threat to daughters compared to fast growing brain tumours that strike you down in a couple of months. The only thing in his favour was he was never usually in the cars he totalled. I have to push this. 'But asking me out *every* morning?' The frequency didn't make it any less mortifying. Worse still, I was always rigid in case my inner voice accidentally got out of control and accepted, and made me the laughing stock of the entire school.

His laugh is low enough to hear under the driving drum beats. 'Back then I wouldn't have minded if you'd said yes.'

I somehow gulp down my appalled gasp. Years later and he still talks bollocks. 'As if that would have happened.' Incredulous doesn't begin to cover it. I was years younger than him. Still am, come to that. And still sensible enough to know to keep as far away as I can. Today being an unfortunate blip that I'll avoid at all costs in future. I sense that I need to move this on while I'm ahead, so I turn to look behind me. 'Hey, Gracie, shall I tell you a story about snowmen?'

Before she looks up, Rory's cut in. 'No point disturbing her if she's quiet. Leave that stuff to her mum. She'll be home soon enough.'

'How's Erin doing?' Seeing the latest signpost, showing that Port Giles is still miles away, I need a surefire way to steer the subject away from me.

Rory gives a disgruntled snort. 'She might be doing better if Gracie didn't catalogue the disasters every time they talk on the phone. Anyone can put hand cream in the bath instead of bubbles. And who knew you could get the right number of legs and arms into sleeves and legs on a babygrow, and it would still end up upside down and back to front? And fine, Gracie hated the lamb pasanda, but I'd gone to a lot of trouble with that saffron rice.' He's set off on a rant now. 'As for having a hissy fit about four marshmallows in the hot chocolate instead of five – how can a three-year-old tell the difference when they can't even count?'

I can't help but laugh. 'Sounds like Gracie's on your case.'

He shakes his head. 'Don't I know it. Her and her mum.

Erin's been having some heart procedure in London, but she's due home tomorrow.' He takes his hands off the wheel to do a silent cheer. 'It was a minor defect she was born with, but having the kids made it worse. By the time they investigated it was urgent.' Luckily the road is straight and he takes hold again.

'And her partner's working?' Another space-filler question to counteract the desolate winter landscape beyond the car windows.

He gives me an incredulous glance. 'What rock have you been hiding under, HB? No way these poor proverbial babes would be stuck with an incompetent like me if their dad was around. Everyone knows, at thirty-eight Erin decided to go it alone using the sperm-donor route.' He pulls a face. 'She's strong and very independent. Getting ill really wasn't in her life plan. Or mine.'

I can't resist reminding him. 'Gracie and Teddie are actually real, not proverbial.' And right on cue, Teddie begins to whinge.

There are better ways to spend an hour than waggling a snowman over the back of the seat to keep a six-month-old's howls at bay, while Green Day pulsates on your eardrums. But on balance it's better than talking to Rory. And by the time we arrive at Port Giles it means I've spent an entire sixty minutes without worrying about dying batteries or backing up data. As the road veers closer to the coast, the hedges open up to give a view of the sea being lashed by the rain. And then we're winding between the neat white and grey cottages of the village, coming into Port Giles, and making our way along the stretch of road that leads to where the Old Lifeboat

Station stands stark against the washed-out sky.

But as the neatly raked gravel of the car park scrunches under the tyres and we pull in further along next to two picturesque upturned boats, there's a hand-painted blue and white sign. And the words *Wedding Venue* jerk me back into the room with a bang.

Chapter 14

'You didn't want to use the car park, then?'
  Rory couldn't have parked further from the building if he'd tried. I'm tempted to use the 'don't worry, we can walk to the kerb from here' line. It's only after we've suffered Teddie's roaring as we changed a nappy – Rory's job – found missing silver wellies – Gracie's – and checked our cheeks – me, and they couldn't be more floury if they were baps from the bakers, but on the upside at least they're not pink – that we set off. As I duck into the horizontal rain, pushing Teddie's buggy towards the venue, my smallest waterproof camera bag slung on my shoulder, I realise the beer-mobile is actually up on a hump between the car park and the beach.

  Rory gives me a doubtful stare. 'What's the point hiding away in car parks? Every outing is a Roaring Waves publicity opportunity. After the trouble I went to with that paint job, I go for maximum exposure.' He's back to laughing again. 'Whatever you think, I didn't *only* agree to come so I could spend a day winding you up. I'm hoping I might get some orders out of today's foray into northern territory.'

Two hours in, I'm resigned to the fact that these badly aimed side swipes are the best we're going to get. 'It'll serve you right if your four by four gets swept out to sea.' Just saying. It wouldn't be the first time.

He gives me a dirty look for that. 'The good news is, the rain's stopping tomorrow and the wind's set to drop. Sunday should be a balmy six degrees, with enough sun for photos on the terrace deck in front of the ceremony room. The tide will be on its way out when they get married at one, so you should be good for beach shots too. Low tide's at four twenty, high tide again at eleven.'

'Show off.' I seem to be travelling with my own personal weather and tide geek. As for the lifeboat station, I wasn't expecting it could have been converted to anything so stylish. Today the grey blue frames of the floor-to-ceiling windows along the single storey extension exactly match the diesel colour of the sea. The tall stone building, with its dark slate roof, stands proud against the racing clouds, with the old boat slipway sliding down to the beach.

Rory ignores that snipe. 'My mate's manager here, he's expecting us to help ourselves. It's actually a virtual offshoot of the local pub business in the village.' He nods at the long row of windows as he pushes through the massive blue-painted entrance door. 'The ceremonies are held in there, with a view straight out to sea. Then, so long as it's fine, the guests spill out onto the terraces either side for drinks, depending which way the wind is blowing. If the sun's out, there should be plenty of natural light for your photos.'

'Great.' I hide my surprise by fiddling with the pushchair cover and grinning at Teddie as I push him down the ramp. For a bonehead, Rory seems to be completely across this job. And more. If we weren't dancing round each other locking horns, I'd almost be grateful to Immie for sending him.

He can't hide his enthusiasm as we move through into the high space of the main building, where an elliptical staircase sweeps to the upper level that sits below the sloping roof. 'It's a brilliant place for wedding parties. And there are fabulous hanging deck balconies on the seaward side, too.'

Inside the light has the soft luminous quality you only get by the sea. It's splashing off the white-painted walls in a way you'd never find in London. And although it looks sparse, I can see it will leap into life once the wedding gear and the guests arrive.

'So who gets married here, then?' I've got as far as finding out that Sunday's couple are sailing school owners, Scott and Nancy, and they're having thirty for their buffet wedding breakfast, and forty more to their evening party. I'm still waiting for Jules to forward the rest of their instructions.

Rory rubs his nose as he thinks. 'Beachy people having smaller weddings who like things quirky and simple.' He lets go of Gracie's hand, squats on the edge of an immensely long cream leather sofa and pulls an iPad out of his jacket pocket.

I wrinkle my nose. As I run my hand along the soft leather of the sofa back, it feels jarringly familiar.

Rory narrows his eyes at me. 'And?'

I wasn't intending to mention it, but seeing as he's asked.

'These are the kind of couches Luc used to have in his loft.' The open plan living area of his flat wasn't so much huge as epic. Anything less than ten feet long would have been dwarfed.

Rory looks up from his screen. 'If I didn't already hate him, I do now.' He gives a disparaging sniff, presumably to show he's joking. 'Here, I uploaded some of the pictures from the wedding I came to. I don't know if they'll help. I'm sure you'll find great shots of your own, but in case you don't have time ...'

I get the subtext. In case I'm too nervous to think straight. Although I'm not offended. Seeing how far up this particular shit creek I am, I'm happy to grab all the help I can get, even if it comes from a Sanderson direction. So I perch as far away from him as I can, suspend hostilities for a moment and crane my neck to see as he flicks through. 'That's a good angle to make the most of the staircase. Nice backdrop of the sea with all the bridesmaids along the balcony rail. Groomsmen standing on the sofas. So where do *you* usually live, then?' That came out all on its own, when it wasn't meant to. Which is exactly what used to worry me every day on the school bus. That I'd make an even bigger fool of myself and accidentally say yes to him.

He moves onto the next one without answering. 'The way that cluster of umbrellas looks on the terrace, it's almost a shame it's not going to rain on Sunday.'

As I look at the fabulous shot of guests with their brollies taken from above, it suddenly strikes me. 'That's the difference between taking pictures of burgers and pictures of weddings.

With the food, I set it all up in advance and I'm in total control. Right down to faking the steam coming off a stew with a carefully hidden tampon soaked in boiling water.'

'Really?' A look of delight spreads across Rory's face as that sinks in. 'Cheating like that? I'm surprised at you, Holly Berry.'

I don't even bother to reply to that comment. 'Whereas with weddings it's all about reacting to the moment. You can plan a certain amount, but the rest is pure spontaneity. It's an adrenalin junkie's dream. But for someone like me who likes certainty, it's the stuff of nightmares.'

He pulls down the corners of his mouth. 'Sounds like you'll be feeling the pain, big time.'

I sigh, because the more I think about it, the more hopeless it feels. 'Even if the venue is the same, everything else changes every time. The dress, the weather, the guests, the styling.' As I say it, the enormity of what I'm taking on is sinking in. 'And *I'm* the one who's got to capture and maximise all those possibilities. That's *so* much responsibility. There's *so* much potential to fail.'

He flicks through a few more photos then turns to me. 'Although as Poppy said – or was it Jess – if they're anything like these, you'll be getting some great pictures.'

I take a moment to consider. 'In my day job, it's all about making the product look its best.' At Zoe and Aidan's wedding, I wasn't even considering if I might like the pictures. But looking at the photos on Rory's iPad that are nothing to do with me, it's different. 'Capturing the prettiness and creating lovely pictures is a whole side I've overlooked.' I'm surprised that a shiver zings up and down my spine when I think about that.

Rory smiles. 'If you concentrate on the pretty bits, who knows, you might even start to enjoy it? You are a girl, after all.'

'Highly unlikely,' I say, with the most conviction I've felt all day.

His face crumples. 'Me going on about pretty stuff. I can't even believe I said that, either.' He gives a groan. 'Anyway, are you and the twelve-foot sofas still in the penthouse, then?'

I'm surprised he's flicked back to that. '*I* wish.' Although, as I say it, I know that's not true. I'd hate to be there on my own. 'Actually, I live in a room the size of a cupboard in a not very nice flat.' It was the obvious way forward – or in my case back. Luc was fully committed to the American dream and we both knew I couldn't stay in his apartment. He was moving on and I went back to the old room I'd always kept. Realistically flats like Luc's are out of my stratosphere. I probably wouldn't even earn enough to cover the service charges.

Rory laughs. 'A London cupboard sounds well upmarket. I share some barns with some brewing tanks and an owl or two.' Lucky for everyone local he hasn't ended up on an estate. House prices would take a serious dive if this wild boy landed in any respectable neighbourhood.

Despite myself, I'm grinning. 'Weddings might be the only chance we'll ever get of flopping on a decent sofa, then.'

He stares at me. 'What, are you crazy? There won't be any time for sitting down.' He laughs again. 'Not for you, anyway. In fact, you'd better get to work now, or we won't get lunch till tea time. Go and check out your viewfinder angles and leave me to enjoy my comfy seat.'

There's no point telling him I've no intention of staying out for lunch. It's only when I come to stand up, I feel a weight and find that Gracie's crawled onto my knee. As I ease her gently down next to me, I see a chest on wheels over in the corner. 'Come on Mrs, I think there might be a toy box.'

She stretches her hand towards Rory's tablet. 'I like the iPad best.'

Rory's too fast for her. 'Mitts off, mongrel, this one's mine.'

I'm staring at them, shaking my head. 'Either of you two heard of sharing?' If it wasn't so sad it would be funny. 'You could play ten green bottles together? Or watch *The Little Mermaid*?'

'Or not.' Rory's pout is almost as big as Gracie's. 'That could cause more trouble than cucumber sticks.'

Gracie's joining in. 'Actually, I only like *Frozen*.'

With a sigh, I peer into the toy box, pull out some brightly coloured skittles and push them towards them. 'Try these. They're a pub game.' That should tempt Rory, if nothing else does.

'Actually we might come and make ourselves useful instead. Model for you, open doors, that kind of thing.' He pushes himself to standing and hitches up his jeans.

'Congratulations, Rory, that's a first. You used a pronoun that included Gracie there.' Progress like that can't go without a mention.

He ignores the praise and springs towards the staircase. 'Grab your camera, see if you can get me coming down.'

What follows is the exact negative of Jules in action. Because in our case – read nothing into the inclusive pronoun this time around, obviously – the photographer is totally getting ordered around by the subject. 'Try one against the balcony rail ... leaning on the door frame ... upside down, legs over the back of the sofa ...' *Yes, really.* Portrait, distance, close up. Jacket on, jacket off. Drenched by the rain, towelled dry. Back against the wall, knee up ... next to Gracie ... looking out to sea ... looking in through the window from outside ... light playing on stubble ... shadows sculpting the hollows under cheekbones...

The next hour is a whirl. Back lit, front lit. Blurring the background, blurring the foreground. In the end, I'm the one who gives in first and collapses back onto the sofa. As I begin to flick through what I've taken, I'm surprised. 'Hmmmm, some of them aren't too bad.'

Rory nods. 'You've relaxed, you're familiar with the venue now, I reckon you're as prepared as you can be.' He's looking particularly pleased with himself as he rubs his hands. 'Anyone hungry?'

That's my cue to jump in. I'm about to say my bit, then I think about a two-hour drive home with ravenous kids and a hungry driver, and do a fast U-turn. 'So before we go for lunch, we need to agree some ground rules.' I've got this. And I'm right on it, because I can just imagine where we'll end up if I leave it to Rory. 'Ideally it'll have high chairs as well as bar stools. And a kids' menu.' I'm not asking for miracles. I know if he went within a country mile of a place with a play area the beer-mobile might spontaneously decompose.

'Whatever you say, Holly Berry.' He dives into the nappy

bag and whips out a packet. 'But before we go, it's your turn for the baby wipes.'

'Nice try. I don't think so.' Then I think again. 'Teddie needs changing again already?'

He pulls a face as he hesitates. 'No, but you might like to check out the – ahem – toothpaste situation.'

I squint at him. 'The what?'

'When you said about icing before, I couldn't see it. But since you came in from the rain on the balcony, I'm getting the full drip cake thing.'

'How the *hell* do *you* know about drip cakes, Rory?' I have to ask.

He looks sheepish. 'They're very popular lately. I told you, I go to *a lot* of weddings.' His face crinkles. 'Although this is the first strawberry base with white drips I've seen.' He's holding up his phone like he's taking my picture.

'Still not getting you?'

'That whole icing on your face thing? It's running.' As he flashes his phone screen at me and my own face looks back at me, my eyes practically pop.

'Aaaaaaaaaaaaaagghhhhh ... !' I'm looking at everything he said and more. Bright pink cheeks, streaked with dripping white paste doesn't begin to cover it. 'Jeez, Rory, why the hell didn't you say?'

He stifles a cough. 'So maybe you will be taking those baby wipes after all?' He slips them into my hand along with a plastic bottle and a disgustingly smug laugh.

'Baby bottom moisturiser?' Now I've seen it all.

He pulls a face. 'It's the best we have in the bag. From where

I'm standing, you need all the help you can get.'

There's no answer to that. But it's a measure of the situation. And if I'm relying on Rory for help, truly, the trouble I'm in couldn't be bigger.

Chapter 15

Friday 8th December
In the kitchen at Daisy Hill Farm: Seahorses and cockle shells

It turns out that Gracie's gourmet tastes are more in line with her uncle's than I've given her credit for. She might turn her nose up at Rory's lamb pasanda, but while Teddie kicked away in his borrowed designer high chair in the bar at the Salty Fish pub in Port Giles, Gracie tucked into dough balls, cucumber-free crudités, dips and pizza served on a slate. Then, when I discovered my appetite had mostly been whittled away due to the wedding racing towards me at a hundred miles an hour, and my newly crimson complexion, Gracie went on to demolish most of my smoked salmon, dill and quinoa. If Rory hadn't guarded them so closely, I suspect she'd have wolfed his triple-cooked hand cut chips too. By the time we roll into the courtyard back at the farm at dusk, it's bliss to wave goodbye to Rory and the kids, and pull up a chair next to Immie at Poppy's kitchen table.

'Cupcake to go with your hot chocolate, Hols? I'm trying

out beachy ones for Nate and Becky. Thanks for sending them my way.' Poppy's waving a piping bag and curling waves of blue- green buttercream onto a tray of mini sponge cakes.

'What happened to putting your feet up rather than working?' Not meaning to nag, but the rest of us have agreed we'll keep her on track where we can.

Her voice rises in complaint. 'This is my way of relaxing.'

Immie rolls her eyes. 'I've persuaded her to sit on a stool and I'm doing my bit by eating as many as I can.' She gives a gruff chortle. From the pile of bun cases in front of her, she's not joking.

After today's concealer trauma, it had struck me I might never face icing again. So as I watch Poppy working it's a relief to find my mouth's watering. 'Maybe I could manage one.' Funny. In the pub I felt as if I'd never be hungry again. Whereas now one cupcake won't even touch the sides.

'Add your own decorations.' Poppy hands me a cake and pushes a plate of pearly yellow shells and starfish across to me. 'It's good to see you've got your colour back again. Are you feeling better now you've seen the venue?'

I take a large bite through a mountain of buttercream and into the cupcake, and let the sweetness dissolve onto my tongue. 'The old lifeboat station is fabulous.' I say through the crumbs, leapfrogging the cheek issue and going straight for the important stuff. 'But how the hell am I going to learn to handle crowds between now and Sunday?'

Poppy's brow wrinkles as she thinks. 'I'm free, so I've decided I'll drive you over and stay to give you a hand.'

Immie chimes in. 'Or if I jiggle a bit, I could make time

too.'

'Thanks for that. It will be a huge help having either of you there.' Even though it's really kind, I'm not sure Poppy should be offering, so I go back to my main problem. 'The thing is, Jules's bright blue eyes keep people mesmerised, especially when he's organising the formal groups.'

Immie guffaws. 'Aren't you forgetting his famous dictator tactics?'

Poppy sends Immie a warning frown. 'What you need is something to grab people's attention, Hols, and I may have the answer.' She dips into the table drawer. 'I know it's a bit Christmassy, but how about this?' As she holds up her hand and shakes it, there's a serious jingling.

'A heart made from bells?' I help myself to another two cupcakes to celebrate. 'That's brilliant.'

She nods. 'I found it in with the tree decorations. Every photographer has their own unique method and this can be yours.' She holds up a silver whistle, then blows a blast. 'And this can be your second line of defence.'

Immie's grinning. 'Whistles and bells? I like your thinking, Pops.'

I'm almost excited. 'It might just work.'

Poppy's smiling at me. 'If you use the head groomsman to round up the guests, I reckon you'll crack it.'

'Holy crap, beer-mobile alert!' Immie's cry comes through a mouthful of cupcake, as she peers at the window. 'What is it with Rory? He won't stay away.'

As Poppy catches my eye I leap into denial. 'Today was every bit as awful as we both anticipated. Worse, even. So he's definitely not coming to see me. One more day, then he'll be free of the kids, and with any luck he'll beetle off back to his brewery.' Fingers *and* toes crossed on that one.

It's getting to be a familiar sight. Rory, staggering in with Teddie clamped against his stomach, Gracie hanging off his finger. As they clatter into the kitchen, a burst of cold air comes in with them. Before I know it, Gracie's elbowing her way up onto my knee, ramming a fluffy snowman into my hand and eyeing up my buns.

'Cupcake, Gracie?' As I pass her my spare, she takes it and shoves it straight in her mouth. 'Would you like a starfish to go on that?'

She's very serious as she licks her fingers. 'I don't like fish.'

I can't help grinning. 'You didn't say that when you ate my smoked salmon.'

'You've made a friend for life there, Gracie,' Immie says.

Rory blows out a long breath. 'Which might be a good thing. Given the circumstances.'

Poppy's keeping her voice light, but her tone is concerned. 'Is everything okay?'

'It could be better.' Rory shakes his head. 'Apparently they aren't going to discharge Erin tomorrow after all. So we're stuck here till Monday. At least.'

'Well, the cottage is there as long as you need it.' Poppy's got her comforting voice on. 'Would a cupcake help?'

Immie's straight in there. 'Or there's a crate of Bad Ass Santa in the office?' She's obviously got more of a measure of Rory's state of mind with her offer. 'Any plans for Sunday, then? I've heard Bizzy Bouncers is good at the weekends. Or you could go to Crazy Kids, or Fun World.' Or maybe she hasn't got him at all, given these suggestions.

'Fun? For who?' Rory looks as though he's about to vomit.

There's a glint in Poppy's eye. 'Or maybe Immie and I could manage here with the kids, and you could help Holly with the wedding in Port Giles. That could be a better distribution of labour.'

Hell no. Not this again. I let out a low moan. '*Please* let it be someone else.'

Immie joins in. 'As Cornwall's most popular guest you certainly know your way around weddings, Rorers. You've probably been to more ceremonies than Rafe and Kip put together.'

Poppy sighs. 'A day here would be way less tiring for me, even with the kids here.' Her eyes light up as she grins at Gracie. 'We could do baking. Hey, how about we make snowman cupcakes?'

Rory's face is a picture. 'Or ...' Considering Fun World, or St Giles with me, he looks as if he's been told to choose between having his nails pulled out or his teeth. Without anaesthetic. 'Maybe I could help Poppy with the baking and Immie could do St Giles.' His face crinkles into a smile as the thought takes shape.

For a few seconds we women all stare at each other.

'So what do you think, Hols? Who would you like to take you, me or Rory?' Immie's up, hands on her hips, her *Forget the truck, ride the firefighter* t-shirt stretched tight across her boobs. If we were going for a fun night out in town, I wouldn't be hesitating.

Poppy props her chin on her hands. 'You know, Immie, you do a fabulous job here with the holiday cottages. But, you'd be the first to admit, you're not strictly a front of house person.'

Rory's laughing now. 'Yes, Immie, with your colourful vocabulary and your knack for telling it how it is, you might easily lose it and end up telling the mother of the bride to stuff her ass hats and toad bollocks up her jacksy.' He doesn't seem to realise, if he carries on like this, he's talking himself into a job here.

Immie's suddenly indignant and the gloves are off. 'Frig off, Sanderson. You might bribe your way into weddings with crates of beer, but losing count of the cars you've lost at sea is not a good look.' She rolls her eyes, then gives a cough and flexes her biceps. 'And don't forget, I'm Arm Wrestling Champion of the Goose and Duck. My muscles are just right for lugging around equipment *and* sorting out trouble.'

I jump in, clutching at straws *and* clichés here. 'Maybe Rafe or Kip could help me? Rory and I can't bear to be in the same county, remember.' If he had his own t-shirt, it would probably say *Walking disaster area … with issues*. Although, on second thoughts, of course it wouldn't. We all know it would just say *Dickhead*. Plain and simple. 'Actually, I'll toss this back to Poppy to choose.' I can't possibly tell her how much I want *her* to be the one who comes.

Poppy folds her arms. 'Sorry Hols, but you and Rory have both been to the venue. He's got charm by the bucket load to use on the guests. And he does have a camera too.'

My stomach collapses. 'You do?' The camera came from left field. As for the charm, we all know I've yet to experience

163

that personally.

Rory's scowl is a lot bigger than his nod, so at a guess he's regretting being the local Patrick Lichfield.

Immie shakes her head. 'Flaming elephant balls, I'm out. In that case, Teddie's mine.'

'So that's settled, then. Last call for jobs for Sunday?' As Poppy looks around, beaming, I can't quite believe what just happened.

As I pull down the corners of my mouth, I'm thinking I might have to do this on my own. 'Tough luck, Rory. It's a lose-lose situation.'

'Back at you, Holly Berry.'

Which is great. Except when he comes across and gives me a conciliatory punch on the arm, the sudden blast of his body spray I get sends my stomach into freefall. Again.

Chapter 16

Sunday 10th December
In the attic kitchen at Brides by the Sea: With bells on

When I wake on Sunday morning, it's to the sound of the landline ringing and the smell of toast and bacon. When I finally find the phone under my folded shirt and capri pants, it's Poppy.

'Hols, an early call to warn you that Rory's on his way.' Which sadly rubbishes the idea that she's the one in the kitchen, making the fry-up.

My groan is loud and long. 'Brilliant, thanks for that.' Two seconds later, I'm out of bed, jumping at the sound of clashing crockery in the distance. 'Actually, I think he's already here.'

I stagger through to the kitchen, cursing that I've lost my opportunity to use the sticky cleansing strip on my nose to clean the last of Friday's gunk out of my pores. As I rub my eyes into focus, Rory is clattering around by the cooker. 'Is this an excuse to dump the kids off extra early? And do you know that's Poppy's second-best apron you're wearing there?' If I'm extra tetchy, it's because he's totally invaded my space.

And also because as I take in a kitchen with so much mess it looks like Masterchef just happened, I'm thinking ahead to the washing up.

As he turns to me he's grinning. 'Lovely to see you too, Holly. I'm sure Poppy won't mind lending her pinny to keep the photographer's assistant's chinos clean.'

'But what are you *doing*? Apart from digging out every pan in the building.' Poppy's new maternity aprons are extra large. If I were trying to size up his bum in smart trousers, which I'm definitely not, I'd be limited to a couple of inches of dark fabric between the pink stripes.

'Don't worry, Holly B. I've got your back here, just like in the old days.'

'Excuse me?'

'I've always looked out for you. We're social pariahs who stuck together, and I'll never forget that. Today might be tough, but we'll tough it out together. For one day only.' He's waving a spoon like he's been taking lessons from Jamie Oliver. 'As for the cooking, I decided it's sensible to have a precautionary breakfast.'

We both know he's exaggerating the significance of our acquaintance here. And when was rational *ever* in his mind-set? 'So how did the guy who was stupid enough to let his car float away on the tide suddenly become wise?' I'm asking because it's a valid question. Most clueless people stay that way for their whole life.

He narrows his eyes. 'Let's put you straight on a few things. My *dad's* car got swept out to sea, not mine. And it definitely wasn't accidental, it was *deliberate* payback. Me hitting him where it hurt most.'

Being let in on this direct action has me flinching. 'Jeez, Rory, that's a bit harsh.' If people steered clear of me because Freya died and they didn't know what to say to me, I never minded. As for his family feuds, I knew his parents weren't together, but I had no idea it was so acrimonious.

He snaps back. 'It was no less than he deserved. I'll tell you about it sometime.'

'I'll take your word on that.' I'm already struggling with the concept of baked beans this early. I can't cope with any more spilled secrets. 'At least the weather's good.' As I peep through the porthole, desperate to find something else to talk about, far below the sun is sparkling off the sea. Although I'm not about to give him credit for being right about the better weather today.

'Scrambled eggs, wholemeal bagels, mushrooms and tomatoes okay for you?' He's already pulling out two stools and pouring coffee with the other hand.

'Great.' I blink, trying to wake up my appetite, as he slides two full plates across the tabletop. 'Thanks.'

'Bacon rashers? They're chestnut smoked sweetcure. Fried bread, waffles.' As he swings them over, he couldn't be scrutinising my face any more closely if he were looking for blackheads. 'You aren't going to throw up with wedding jitters again are you?'

Again? That one word's the giveaway. 'You heard about the last time at Zoe's wedding?'

At least he has the decency to look guilty. 'Hasn't everyone?'

That's what I was afraid of. 'Is there *no* privacy around

here?' Even as it comes out, in a foot- stamping rush, I know it's a ridiculous question. In fact, it's one I've known the answer to practically my whole life. And if that's slipped my mind, it's only because I've been away so long. 'For the record, it wasn't a nervous puke, it was something else entirely.'

He gives a rueful shrug. 'Why else would we be sitting down to a decent, stomach-settling breakfast? Chucking up at a wedding is never good.'

As I hold up my hand, my stomach's already squelching. 'Enough, okay?'

His nostrils are twitching as he sits down and piles egg onto his fork. 'At least I finally get to see what kind of pyjamas you wear. You always refused to tell me, back in the day.' He's holding back his laughter.

'Quite bloody right too.' Not that I remember him asking that specifically.

His brow wrinkles. 'Whenever I imagined it, you were in a Wonder Woman onesie.'

I almost snort my coffee out of my nose at that. 'Total bollocks. Onesies weren't even invented then. And I'd never choose to wear that, because I'm not that kind of "zippy" or "out there".' I brush a crumb off my pyjama trousers and study the Eiffel Tower print.

He's straight back. 'That's always been your problem. You could be zippy, if you'd only put the effort in.'

I completely sympathise with his frustration. Sometimes I even feel it myself. 'But that's just *me*. I like to think about things and *then* do them. Freya would have been more your kind of person. She'd have been fine zooming round in a

Superman flying suit.' What's more, she wouldn't have been fazed by anything as minor as wedding pictures. She'd have been gutsy enough to have been a war photographer, although in reality she probably wouldn't have been free to do a job that minor, because she'd have been too busy ruling the world.

Rory gives a shudder. 'Freya could be downright scary. You should have seen the way she laid into me when you first started getting the bus to senior school and she thought I might upset you. She was like a she-wolf protecting her cub.' The way he's talking about her so openly is lovely. Nothing can bring her back, but it's great to be with someone who knew her well enough to remember her telling him off.

I laugh. 'Feisty and fearless – that's just how she was. It was awful once she wasn't there to fight my battles for me.' I don't have to say it was awful in every other way too, because he was there. He already knows.

He's looking thoughtful. 'It's a shame the "oomph" didn't get shared out more equally. That way it would have saved her whipping my ass. I mean, look at your top ...'

As I stare down at my boobs, I'm wishing we weren't. 'Don't knock my *Meet me in Paris* jersey, it's my favourite.' It was damned hard to find *any* winter PJ's that weren't covered in reindeers or festive robins.

He puts down his fork, rests his elbow on the table and his chin on his hand and stares at me hard. 'But would you really be up for meeting me in Paris?'

For a second my stomach flips. Then, as I crash back to earth and remember who the hell I'm talking to, my mind finally engages with my mouth. 'Eff off, Rory. You *know* I wouldn't.'

He smiles. 'Exactly what I'm getting at. If you were a tiny bit wilder, you might start to enjoy life more. If you're always scared and sensible you're going to miss out on so much.'

'Crap, Rory, I'm a stay-at-home person getting over a failed relationship. I'm not going to go running off with the first chancer who reads my pyjama top.' It's bad enough us going to Port Giles together. If Rory were the last available guy in Cornwall, I seriously doubt if I'd go as far as Plymouth with him, let alone Paris.

'Why wear it, if you don't mean it, Berry?' He gives another of those challenging stares he's so great at.

For crying out loud. 'Get real, Rory, it's a meaningless printed slogan, not a manifesto. If I hadn't been avoiding Christmas it would most probably have been a snowflake, okay? And given it's on my sleepwear, most people wouldn't get to see it anyway.' Good points well made. It's not exactly like I'm parading it around Jaggers.

From his superior expression he could be thinking he's back in his lawyer's office. 'In fact, Paris would be the last place I'd offer to go to with you anyway. For the record, dating and commitment aren't actually in my remit. I should have said before.' Up himself doesn't begin to cover it.

My voice rises to a screech because I'm gobsmacked. 'Your *what*? You grumble about my pyjamas and then come out with crap like that?'

'What I'm saying is, we're being thrown together a lot lately, but I can't be around afterwards. So long as you're clear on that.' Now he's found his calming tone, he's backpedalling for

England. 'I'm sorry, mentioning meeting me in Paris was a mistake. It was only a hypothetical way of pointing out you'll have to be more daring if you want to get your happy face back.'

And when exactly did he step in as my bloody well-being coach? He'll be lecturing me on hygge next. As for the teensiest twinge of disappointment that he's turned this round from real to pretend faster than you can say fairy godmother, that definitely wasn't any twinge of mine.

I drag in a breath. 'So now we know *neither* of us wants to go to Paris, can we please finish breakfast and get on with the day?' I might have been stalling over my buttered bagel before. But if chewing mushrooms is the best excuse I can find not to talk, right now I'm keen to do it. As for a day that's shaping up to be the nightmare from hell, Rory Sanderson in my kitchen is awful enough to make me rush on to even that.

'Fine by me. It's what I'm here for.' If he were Gracie, she'd be pouting.

I wait until I get most of the way through my food, then I wave my phone at him, while he's still eating. 'So a few rules for the road. We had your tunes on Friday, so today we'll be having mine.' Poppy's loaded me a special *No need to call the lifeboat, you're going to smash this wedding!* selection onto my phone. My fave eighties tracks, interspersed with her personal 'power up the courage' tracks. With *Don't Stop Me Now!* a few extra times for good measure. I'm already secretly whooping at the thought of what Rory's about to sit through.

There's not much else he can do other than agree. 'Whatever.'

'And have you brought your camera?'

He shakes his head like I'm the idiot. 'What do you think?' I mutter. 'Exactly as I thought.'

He looks at his phone. 'Are you going to get ready? Or is your photographer's attention- seeking gimmick going to be *Hey, look at me, I forgot to get dressed*?' However long he laughs for, the joke really isn't *that* funny. Eventually he stops and begins to wipe up the last of his bean juice with his toast. 'Time's getting on. Maybe we'd better leave the washing up?'

I didn't need to be a clairvoyant to know that was coming.

As we set off down the four flights of stairs twenty minutes later, despite a nutritionally balanced breakfast with enough calories to sustain a lumberjack, after the best part of an hour with Rory, I'm already exhausted. And I've still got a wedding to face.

Chapter 17

Sunday 10th December
Scott and Nancy's wedding at the Old Lifeboat Station,
Port Giles: Sponsors and driftwood

'Breakfast still on board, Holly B?'
This is Rory, his breathless shout pursuing me as we rush towards the Old Lifeboat Station. If he's checked the state of my jitters once, he's checked it at least as many times in the last hour as we've heard *Don't Stop Me Now!* And as soon as he'd got his 'I'm not available' speech out of the way, he went straight back to hostilities as normal. As we drew level with the coast, he said if he had to sit through *Bat Out Of Hell* one more time he'd leave the car. So as we drove along the last few miles gasping at the views across the beach to the glittering sea, he put *Titanium* on repeat, at the same volume Jules played his *Going to War* Collection. Just to be clear, we're talking serious loudness here. Decibel levels that made my cheeks shudder and the door panels vibrate. Then, as we arrived at the car park and he manoeuvred the beer-mobile into his preferred, inappropriately conspicuous

beach-edge space, I was still yelling 'I'm bulletproof, no time to lose' at the top of my voice all the way to the end of the song. So by the time we begin our hike to the venue, I'm feeling pretty damned unstoppable. Put it this way, if I were about to cycle a hundred mile stage in the Tour de France with Chris Froome, I'd put money on me getting a podium place. Add in the sunshine, and the fact Rory let me sing along to *Let It Go* three times too, I'm crossing the gravel with the exuberance of a manic lemming haring towards a proverbial cliff edge. In fact, I'm zooming so fast, Rory is having to do a leap every third step to keep up.

'I'm all good ... so far,' I try to say, but as fast as I open my mouth to form the words, from somewhere deep inside me a breath comes and whooshes the words out to sea. So instead I'm nodding, wildly. As Rory sweeps in front of me to open the diesel-blue door of the Old Lifeboat Station, my knees give a sudden, unexpected creak. When I try to move forward, it's as if every bit of 'unstoppable me' has pooled in the soles of my feet and turned to glue. That's the trouble with a spontaneous, totally unplanned stop. Rory has no idea it's happened, so he carries on and bowls right on in, straight into the path of – according to what it says on her sweatshirt – the mother of the bride. He glances over his shoulder, clocks me, rooted to the spot in the doorway, doing my best guppie impersonation. Then makes a typically Rory Sanderson kind of executive decision and bashes on regardless.

He shoots out his hand and grabs the woman by the wrist. 'Hello there, we're Rory and Holly, the photographers standing in for Jules. And it's *great* to meet you.' His voice takes on this irresistible low resonance. In the split second it takes for him to grasp her hand and grin, it's obvious he's already got her.

She softens, then gives a giggle. 'What a total hero you are, Rory. We're *so* grateful to you for coming to our rescue.' Despite being almost old enough to be his mother, from the way she's leaning in, she's definitely flirting. As for her totally over-looking that I'm here, given I've signed the 'no publicity' clause, I can hardly complain. In fact, it couldn't be better.

He's wiggling his eyebrows at her. 'We're sponsored by Roaring Waves Brewery, by the way. The car's right outside and there's a complementary crate of Bad Ass Santa coming your way later.'

Even if I'm rooted in the doorway, my own eyebrows are mobile enough to go skywards in horror.

He's calling to me, walking backwards into the venue. 'Come on, Holly, time to find the bride.'

Somehow, as I shuffle after him, I force out an incredulous croak. 'Sponsorship?'

His shrug is inscrutable. 'Obviously I'm not rude enough to crash their big day without compensation. Once they see the paint job, most grooms want pictures with it anyway. It's win-win for everyone.'

If he hadn't made such an effort to look smart, I'd tackle him on that. As it is, under his windcheater, his white shirt is expensive and ironed. Any other chin and I'd admit it looked fabulous against the stubble. So fabulous there are flutters where there shouldn't be any. It's obviously because it's a year since I had sex and crisp white shirts remind me so much of

Luc. Let's face it, I'm a beggar not a chooser here. So to calm myself down, I focus on the decorations that have appeared since Friday.

'Wow, this place is looking fab.' As we hurry across the wide-open space I'm dazzled by the stunning driftwood Christmas trees and enough white fairy lights to illuminate most of Lapland.

As we arrive at the dressing room, Rory taps on the door, waits for the word from inside, then eases it open. 'Rory and Holly, photographers coming to the rescue.' If he's rushing around, acting like he's the responsible adult here, for once I'm happy to let that go.

The room we're walking into is a lot smaller and more simple than Poppy's. Three girls in pale-grey fleecy robes are clustered by a long mirror next to a kettle. The one with the *Bride* embroidered on her chest steps forward.

'Hey, I'm Nancy ...'

I dive into my camera bag. 'Great, bride in hair rollers, with a cup of tea. That's a brilliant first picture. And it's lovely to meet you too, Nancy.' There's no time to lose. The sooner I start, the more chance there is of me salvaging anything for any of us.

It seems a bit abrupt, not to say bizarre, air-kissing literally three seconds before I start taking pictures of the most important day in Nancy's life.

'Brilliant. And another of the champagne bucket, then the make-up bags.' I'm mentally ticking the shots off the prompt list Jules emailed me yesterday, along with the list of groups he'd agreed with the bride and groom. We've got those on paper, and Rory, being a guy who has an iPad permanently in his jacket pocket, put them on there too.

Rory gives me a nudge. 'So, if you're all settled in, Hols, I'll just grab a camera and head off to meet the guys at the pub.' He glances into my open bag for a second, then grabs one of my spares and slings the strap over his shoulder. 'Catch you later then.'

What can I say? Rory's never one to stay away when there's beer to be sampled. And that camera of his must be as non-existent as I thought all along. I'm left shaking my head, and looking around the room, because compared to Zoe's day, it feels like there's something missing. Then it suddenly strikes me. 'So where's your hair and make-over team?'

Nancy laughs. 'Emily's fabulous with plaiting and we're doing our own make-up.' She nods at the bridesmaid without rollers. 'This is more of a low-input kind of wedding than a biggie. We want everything to be understated and natural.'

I nod. 'I noticed the driftwood decorations. They look amazing.'

Nancy smiles and wanders across the room. 'The brides-maids are in short scarlet dresses, for a splash of winter colour.' She nods at them hanging on the wall. And this is my wedding dress. Bought on eBay.' She slides off the cover and the mass of tulle and muslin layers she shakes out seem lighter than air.'

I can't help gasping. 'Wow, so simple, yet so beautiful. It's what I'd imagine a mermaid might wear.'

Her eyes light up. 'That's *exactly* what I thought. I love that it's almost ragged, as if the wind's torn it. It seems so right when we're getting married by the beach.'

'I'll take some pictures.' Although I'm not sure I'll be able to do it justice. 'Is it okay if I borrow your hair strand?' Pearls trailing across make the fabric seem softer than ever. If the day carries on like this, I might just pull it off.

'I've got a chunky grey hand-knitted wrap for when we're outside.' She gives a rueful grin. 'The dress really goes with the lovely venue. I can't believe we only stumbled on this place by accident. We were struggling, because there weren't many places that accepted dogs.'

'There's a dog?' I'm almost swallowing my tongue.

She nods. 'Two, actually. They're like our babies. We couldn't get married without them.'

'B-b-but …' My mind's racing. Humans that do as they're told are bad enough. I'm totally unprepared for the randomness of dogs. I'm trying hard to sound less thrown than I am, so I yank my voice down back to where it should be. 'There weren't any dogs on the group lists … were there?'

Nancy looks mildly ashamed. 'Hetty and Hannah? I know we might be overdoing it. They're in pretty much every picture.'

I hesitate for a minute, to get this right, because I've seen the names. 'I'm *so* sorry. I thought Hetty and Hannah were bridesmaids.'

Nancy giggles. 'They'd like to think that. And they have got red satin collars to match the bridesmaids and the flowers.'

Talking of crimson, as I catch a glimpse of my hot cheeks in the mirror, it's bloody obvious today's concealer foundation isn't totally up to the job without the added talc crust. It could be worse. Some people have pet tigers or alligators. Hopefully these dog babies will be the kind people keep in their hand-bags. The sort that only emerge for the odd cuddle and pee stop. One time when I was in Paris when Luc was on business, I saw a woman with three in one Gucci carrier. I make my voice bright, scour the room for doggy holdalls and force myself to ask. 'So are they here now?'

Nancy rolls her eyes. 'Oh my, if you knew how out of control they are in new situations, you would *not* be asking that. We're bringing them in just before the ceremony, otherwise they might demolish the Christmas trees. And they're horrors with food. If they were here, they'd definitely steal our cupcakes.'

Worse and worse. 'What kind are they?' I once saw a Scottie dog skittle a toddler, so I'm throwing out the handbag idea and adjusting my expectations upwards.

Nancy's clasping her hands. 'You mustn't panic. Truly, they don't eat photographers. Jules met them and they all got on fabulously.'

'Okay ... tell me ...' My hands are waving, and I try to imagine the biggest dogs I can. As I get to Labradors I've a feeling I might be hyperventilating.

'They're Great Danes.'

Shit. 'But aren't they like ... *really* huge?' Compared to the sausages and individual trifles I'm used to taking pictures of, they might as well be racehorses.

'Don't worry, once they stop jumping around, they're complete sweeties.' One of the bridesmaids passes her a mug and she pushes it into my hand. 'Sit down, have some tea. Then we thought you could do us a few "mad girls in dressing gown" poses. We can nip out onto the balcony before the guys and the dogs get here?'

The bride talking me down from my ledge again. How does this keep happening? Two gulps of tea later the fun begins and we spend the next hour chasing around the venue. We start with the girls jumping on the extra-long sofas waving their arms in the air and end with them flopped on the tub chairs back in the dressing room. In between we visit most points, including the beach where I snap them leaping in front of the sea and jumping out of the way of the waves. Then we head back for another round of pictures as they take out their rollers and move onto make-up.

Nancy's smoothing cream onto her cheeks. 'That was such a laugh, Holly. You could hire yourself out for hen parties too. I wish you'd been at mine.'

And I'm wishing I *was*. When they were messing around with balloons, we were having so much fun, I almost forgot this was a wedding. Now we're back, I crash back to earth with a bump. Here's me laughing with the bridesmaids, when there's a thousand other images to capture. I should be out, making the most of the empty venue, to get views of the decorations and the table flowers, and the ceremony room, with its rows of chairs, and twig and rosemary posies. A couple of hundred shots later, I'm hurtling back to the dressing room again to make the most of the lovely moment when Nancy's mum helps her into her dress.

Once Nancy loses her bulky fleece, there's very little of her left underneath. If the dress looked amazing on the hanger, on Nancy's slender frame, it looks out of this world, even before it's done up. She slips her shoes on, and stands, hands on her waist, as her mum does up her zip. Then as she gently tweaks the big bow, the enormity of what's about to happen to Nancy finally hits her mum. As her chin starts to wobble, I'm feeling like a guilty intruder in their private moment. But as I catch the actual first tear rolling down her cheek, I'm mentally punching the air because I've got at least one decent shot of the day. Then cringing because I've been so crass.

Then her mum's gone and her dad comes in, and it's tears all over again. I'm so busy catching every minute, I barely have time to breathe, let alone worry. When Rory rushes in, even though it's been hours, I'm surprised he's back so soon.

He gives me a hard stare. 'Still holding up, Berry?'

I suddenly remember there's something way more important than my stomach somersaulting. Which is obviously down to the adrenalin rush. 'Have you seen the dogs?'

He laughs. 'We met at the pub. They're totally adorable, just like those big stone dog statues people have outside their stately homes. Only bigger.' As he gives my arm a squeeze, he seems to be missing the point that statues don't move. 'Okay, come on, we need to get to the ceremony room. I've got your bells here for later, but don't worry, I've got the list ready. I'll get everyone to their places. You're going to nail this, okay? You can count on me. I'll be a hundred per cent here for you. All the way.'

Seeing who's talking, that's a lot more worrying than reassuring. If my heart wasn't lurching before, it is now. Although as I tiptoe into the ceremony room and make my way to the front, and the registrars smile at me, it's more the feeling of a gaping hole in my chest, as if my heart has left my body entirely.

'Here they come.' Rory's next to me, breathing in my ear, reminding me I meant to ask what his aftershave is. On anyone other than him, it would smell pretty damned impressive.

'Who's coming?' There's another huge lurch, as though I've been thumped in the chest. He can't mean Nancy and her dad, yet.

Rory's laugh is low. 'Hetty and Hannah, of course.' No surprise that he's on first name terms already. 'Dark grey, very photogenic. Aren't they perfect with the suits?'

There's a scrabbling of paws and panting, and two dogs dash up to the front, each hauling a groomsman behind them. Then they launch themselves at Scott, who jackknifes onto a chair.

Rory hisses at me, 'Quick, over there, get the groom being trampled by his hounds.'

If I shudder, it's because there's so much slobber involved. I hiss back, hardly daring to lower my camera. 'All done.' As I pan around and zoom in on the people taking their seats, and the registrars, I can't help noticing Rory's got my spare camera up, looking through the viewfinder, pretending to take pictures. So if I'm a fake photographer, pretending to be a real one, jeez knows what that makes him.

And then the registrar is clearing his throat and the processional music is beginning. 'Please be upstanding for the bride.'

As the first few bars of *Truly Madly Deeply* drift into the room, the goose pimples pebble up on my arms, just because the sentiment's so beautiful. For a nanosecond I forget my knees are wobbling and think what a great choice of song it is. Then I stop hearing the words at all, because I'm concentrating so hard. Then there's the red blur of the bridesmaids, and then Nancy and her dad are heading down the aisle, and this really is *all* down to me.

Chapter 18

Sunday 10th December
Scott and Nancy's wedding at the Old Lifeboat Station,
Port Giles: Tasty snacks and sticky fingers

'If I ever grumble about my day job *ever* again, you have my full permission to pour soup over my head.'

This is me talking to Rory. We're sitting in tub chairs in the quiet corner where we're taking our first break of the day. Although for me, it's more about backing up all the memory cards than any kind of rest. As Jules says, backing up the data is the first rule of weddings. But the last five hours have been so full on, this is the first chance I've had to do it. So while Rory's making his way through the big tray of food in front of us, with the dedication of a truly hungry guy, I've got my laptop and memory sticks out, making multiple copies of all the day's pictures. And the day is still a long way from over. Even if the end is way closer than it was at ten this morning, there are still some crucial shots left to do now it's fully dark, and the fairy lights are twinkling in their full glory. Then we're onto the last lap and it's full steam ahead to the first dance and the disco. And finally home time. If someone had told me ten days ago I'd be this anxious to get into the beer-mobile and head off into the night with Rory Sanderson, I'd have thought they were bonkers. Which only goes to show how fast circumstances can change and how quickly life can change you too.

Rory perks up. 'Would that be homemade soup, then? From where I'm sitting, that sounds a lot like a dinner invitation.' Only Rory could twist it to that. Although obviously, from what he said this morning, he wouldn't be up for it even if he got one.

Despite the day being peppered with food servings, until now I've only seen it through my lens. If I wasn't so tired I'd sigh. 'In case you'd forgotten, mate, dinner dates aren't in your portfolio or whatever it is you call it. I'm just flagging up how hard today's been, and that I'm *really* not in tune with weddings, okay? End of message.' I unplug the lead from my last camera and move onto the pile of memory cards I've carefully arranged on a plate.

He looks at me like he thinks I'm mad. 'What's not to like about today? It's had all the fun of a party, with none of the social demands of being a guest. It's scored pretty close to a perfect ten for me.'

I'm snorting because it's fine for him to say that. 'You haven't had the responsibility. Or the worry of failing. Hell, you're not even taking real pictures.'

He looks affronted. 'I've had *my* camera out too.'

'Sure.' That claim is so ridiculous, it's barely worth the effort of a headshake. He's been carrying it around like a theatrical prop. End of story.

He frowns. 'So which bit did you object to? You had a good time with the girls before, judging by the screams coming out of the dressing room. The ceremony was great, the fake snow confetti shot couldn't have been more of a blizzard. Thanks to my dictator tactics, we rattled through the group lists. You nailed the crowd shot from the balcony, neither of us fell asleep in the speeches. With my expert advice to keep you on track, why wouldn't the day go like a dream?'

I admit some bits weren't so bad. 'Taking Nancy and Scott's couple pics on the beach was okay.' Her dress flying in the wind by the sea was phenomenal. When Scott wrapped her in her chunky wool cardi and hugged her, they looked so much in love they could have walked straight out of a magazine ad. And the cake and the flowers were great too.

Rory's pondering. 'Those mini fish and chips on the buffet were one of my high points.'

I shake my head, despairing because he has so little idea. 'You do know, the photographers aren't supposed to graze?'

He shrugs. 'If it's the bride's mum offering, it's rude to refuse.' No doubt he's milked that relationship to the max. 'My wedding radar tells me we'll be off again soon. You need to stop playing with your cameras and eat something.' He drops two mini quiches and a large vol au vent on the plate next to my two remaining memory cards.

I let out a squawk. 'Careful, I haven't done those yet.'

'Stop panicking. It's the only way I'll get you to notice food.' He looks unrepentant, then his face breaks into a smile as he spots a hound wandering our way. 'All that freaking out about the dogs and they've been lovely. This one's Hetty, she's got diamonds on her collar.'

I hate to be agreeing with him. 'They're very photogenic.' If you can overlook how huge they are, they're dark grey, elegant *and* well behaved. 'This one's greeting you like a long lost friend.' Her head's at table level and I watch her snuffling round Rory as he fondles her ears for few seconds, then look back to my computer.

'Hetty's the hungry one, I've been feeding her titbits all day.' Rory laughs as she makes a lunge for his sandwich. 'No, this one's mine, girl. Oh, shit!'

'What's the matter?' As I look up and see the last of my vol au vent disappearing into the dog's chops, I let out a groan. 'She took my quiches too. Nancy said if there's food around, they're like doggy Hoovers.'

'Jeez, just listen to those teeth crunching.' Rory's obviously impressed that a dog can fit that much food in its mouth all at one time.

Then, as I stare at the crumbs and the memory card left on the plate there's a tiny lurch in my chest. 'Where's the card gone?'

Rory frowns. 'It's there, on the plate. Next to the pastry flake.'

My stomach deflates like a popped balloon. 'No, there were two. Definitely two.' As I hear my high-pitched squeal rising, I haul it down to a hissed whisper so people don't hear. 'They were there next to the food. Waiting to be backed up and *full* of wedding pictures. If the card's gone, they've gone too.' If my heart was racing earlier, it's nothing to the way it's thundering now.

His face crumples. 'Crap, crap, crap.' He thumps his fist on his thigh. 'Has Hetty just eaten the wedding photos? If it was the card she was crunching on, whatever was on it is gone forever.'

'Noooooo.' I'm already on my hands and knees, patting the floor in the hope it's somehow down here. As I come nose to nose with Rory under the table, he's shaking his head.

'Vol au vents and quiches just aren't that crunchy. I think we have to face that it might be gone, Holly Berry.' If this is breaking it gently, it's hurting way too much.

I'm about to let out the biggest howl of my life when he holds up his hand and I swallow it back in again.

'Wait. We need to take our time and have a sensible plan here.'

I'm whimpering. 'As said by the guy who was so sensible he put the vol au vent next to the memory cards, then called the food-inhaling dog over.'

His voice is low and very measured. 'There's no point saying anything now and spoiling the day for Nancy and Scott. Other than mentioning that Hetty ate a piece of plastic, obviously.'

Even if I get where he's coming from on that, he's missing the point. 'But what about the *pictures*?' It's a full-on banshee scream, funnelled straight into his ear.

He winces and rubs the side of his head. 'Whatever we do, it won't bring those photos back. So we need to concentrate on making the rest the best they can possibly be.'

I'm still screeching in his ear. 'But I need to see what's been lost.' It might only be a small fraction. If it's random shots of people eating wedding cake it's bad enough. If it's the cake cutting picture, it's horrendous. But if I've lost the only pictures of the ceremony, what the hell am I going to do then? This is like being awake in a nightmare. I want the ground to open up and swallow me.

'No, we'll check what's missing later. Right now, you need to get out there and carry on.' His mouth is a straight line and his jaw's set. He nudges me and points out from under the table. 'Look, everyone's getting their coats on. It's time to go outside to do sparklers.' He may be right. If I discover I've trashed the family groups, the meltdown I'm having now would be minor in comparison to the one I'd have then.

I crawl out from under the table, then sink down on the floor with my back against the chair and my hands over my head. 'I've screwed up. I can't go out and face them knowing I've fed their photos to the dog. This is exactly why I'm not a bloody wedding photographer.'

He's glaring at me. '*You* didn't screw up. This one's down to me and Hetty. No one will blame *you* for it. But they will if you don't get your butt onto that balcony this second and take the sparkler shots. So you get out there and take the pictures of your life, okay? And we'll sort the rest as soon as we leave.'

I'm not going to argue when he's growling through gritted teeth. 'Okay.' As okays go, it's pathetic. If there's one good thing about this total wimp-out, it's that he's seeing me as I truly am. Any mental image he has of me in Wonder Woman pyjamas will be blasted forever. If I wasn't so gutted about losing the pictures, I'd be whooping about that. As it is, I'm going to have to screw every bit of courage together and see if I can make the tiniest amends for letting Nancy and Scott down so badly. Although how I'm going to do that, I have no idea, when my heart is lurching like a car with three wheels, my knees have turned to mush. My hands are faltering so much I have no idea how I'm going to hold the camera, let alone press the right buttons. I push my arms into the sleeves of my fake leopard, but even my lovely snuggle-in coat can't save me from this stuff-up. I'm almost through the door going out onto the balcony when Rory's fist hits my arm.

'What?' I turn to see what he wants.

His arm comes round and he squeezes my shoulder. 'Don't worry, HB. Really, I've got this.' He's swinging my spare camera in his other hand.

'Thanks.' In terms of watery smiles, mine is fully diluted. However overinflated his sense of self-importance is, he can't have 'got' anything. Nothing he can do will help me out of this.

He's staring again, this time at the hair straggles, blowing horizontally across my nose. 'It's freezing out there. Don't you have a hat?'

As the wind slices off the sea, I pull my coat closer and listen to the sound of the breakers crashing up the beach. I shiver and stick my chin up, and say the first bullshit that comes into my head. 'Hats are for wimps.' I know as the biggest wuss here I should be a fully paid-up member of the hat wearers' club. Although everyone knows with my hair, hats give me helmet head every time. In my normal, proper, balanced everyday existence, mostly there's central heating anyway. And talking of normal life, I can't wait to get back to it.

Beside us, guests are spilling out into the night, with unlit sparklers and lighters, jostling shoulders, as the strings of lights fly above our heads.

As Rory eases back across the deck, he's still swinging my spare camera. 'Remind me, I'll get you a hat for next time.' He has to be joking.

Next time? 'Seriously, I'm not sure I'll be doing this again.' The great thing is, when word gets out on a stuff up this huge, no one will want me within a mile of their wedding. They'll definitely make other arrangements.

'Rubbish. You can't give up on anything this much fun.' As he raises the camera to eye level, his finger is on the shutter button. 'Okay, one for the archives, to celebrate a mostly fabulous day. Big smile, Holly Berry.'

But I'm not smiling because my face is screwed into a ball as I'm trying to get my head around this. 'What the heck are you playing at, Rory?'

He gives a shrug. 'Same as I've been doing all day. Following you around with your camera, second shooting for you. With luck I should have caught something to patch over your – er – gap.' He grins. 'The photos might not be perfect, but so far I haven't fed mine to the dog. How have you not seen?'

I could say 'How have you not told me?' but I don't. I'm torn between fury that he didn't think to mention it and relief that the lost card disaster might just be fixable. Instead I say, 'Maybe because I've had all my attention on my first solo shooting? Just saying.'

That goes straight over his head, but he's right back anyway. 'Talking of which, have you seen the moonshine on the water?' Whereas some of us have been dumbstruck ever since the dog trauma, Rory won't shut up. 'You couldn't have a better backdrop for a newlywed pose, so we'll work that in before the first dance. Although we'll have to watch the waves. Have you brought your wellies?' Even if his enthusiasm is getting right up my nose, he's right about the reflections off the sea. And annoyingly unstressed enough to have had time to notice.

'I left my gumboots at Glastonbury in 2005.' There's not much call for them in lovely London. And ideally, that's the way I'd like to keep it.

He's not listening because he's gone onto crowd-control mode. 'Okay, two lines either side, bride and groom in the centre, stand by to light those sparklers everyone ...' If he wasn't so annoying, you'd have to say he was a natural at this. Maybe even better than Jules. Somehow due to his sheer enthusiasm, he manages to give his orders without people feeling bossed around. For a second he stops waving his arms, drops his voice and looks down at me. 'In that case we'll put wellies on the shopping list too. Snow's coming in for next weekend. Looks like we'll be shooting a white white wedding at the Manor.'

The good news just keeps coming, then, and for once I let the royal 'we' flow over me. With any luck, by next week Rory should be safely back in his very own Brewer's Yard. What everyone's forgetting is, I came here for a quiet time. Snow has to be the last complication on the horizon. Doesn't it?

Chapter 19

Sunday 10th December
In the attic kitchen at Brides by the Sea: Pension schemes
and home improvements

'You hit the laptop and I'll get the hot chocolate, Berry.'
As we finally arrive in the little attic kitchen on our
way back from the Old Lifeboat Station, I'm still panting from
rushing up four flights of stairs with a bag of cameras on my
shoulder. But Rory is already over by the hob, clanking sauce-
pans with surprising gusto given how late it is. Although that
might have something to do with the fact he just picked up
Immie's message saying the kids were fast asleep and she and
Chas were hunkering in at Home Brew Cottage for a night
of baby-sitting and Bond movies.

A cosy nightcap with Rory wouldn't have been my first
choice. In fact, it would be pretty high up on my to-be-avoided
list. And I'd usually prefer to argue a bit more, rather than
doing just what he says. But right now, seeing that finding
out which pictures are missing is my first priority, I'm happy
to agree to all of the above. It's hard to believe that we were

having breakfast at this same table only a matter of hours ago. Because after the day we've had this morning seems like light years away.

'I didn't want to stop for pizza, but now we're back, I'm glad we did.' As I pull out a stool and push up my screen, however much I grumbled outside the restaurant, I know now I'll concentrate much better with a delicious meal inside me. Despite Trattoria Remo being *yet another* place, owned by *yet another* of Rory's numerous mates, Remo turned out to be entirely lovely. With a Cornish accent rather than an Italian one, he was a welcome distraction from what was sitting across the table from me. It's the weirdest feeling to suddenly be living out my most secret teenage fantasies. Back then being whisked away to eat pizza by Rory seemed so out of reach I only allowed myself to picture it occasionally, in the darkest part of the night, with my head completely buried under the duvet. Luckily the goats' cheese and caramelised onion pizza I had with the crispest green salad drizzled with virgin olive oil was beyond yummy. Concentrating on that stopped me cringing at the memories. Let's face it, there's no rational explanation for dodgy taste in guys as a teenager. And when I think about the crinkles at the corners of his eyes when he smiled at me as he topped up my low-alcohol wine, I can kind of forgive myself.

Surprisingly Rory dipped out of the 'boy's usual' of every single hot topping, plus extra chili, and instead went for prosciutto, olives and buffalo mozzarella. Then he let me eat a lot of his as well as mine.

'Although I still say it was mean of you not to let me scroll through my pictures in the café or the car.' The arguments over that pretty much obliterated my current favourite relaxing playlist for the entire journey. Seeing I was allowed to play my music all the way home, Rory has to be feeling guilty about something. Although the arguing might have been a deliberate ploy on Rory's part to shut out Lana Del Rey and Christina Perri and what he calls my 'vommy love songs'.

He swings open the fridge and pulls out the milk. 'Be honest, if you'd been looking through pictures, would you have eaten *any* of your pizza?' His grin over his shoulder tells me he's not expecting an answer to that. 'Remo would have been mortally offended if you'd left it. And anyway, it's way better to do the work back here where you can concentrate properly.' All shockingly logical, considering who's talking. I've also noticed he's letting his grin go much more freely since he talked about Paris and ring fenced himself in that place he calls 'unavailable'. Which is hilarious, given he's the last guy in the area I'd touch with a long stick, even if he does have really lovely teeth. And the kind of mouth it's hard to take your eyes off. Especially when he's biting it. In fact, all things considered, it's good that Luc's taking up all my emotional energy.

'Right, here goes ...' I screw up my courage, open the first file and begin to scroll through. 'Sheesh, the bridesmaids on the beach are safe. And some of the photos are okay too.' In fact they're so much better than I could have hoped for. My heart does a kick as I take in how alive and vibrant they are. Somehow they completely capture the exuberance and poignancy of the morning. I must have got hooked on looking through them, because I'm still on the same file when a flowery mug of frothing hot chocolate arrives at my elbow.

'Squirty cream, baby marshmallows, grated chocolate?' Rory couldn't be more attentive if he were working at the Surf Shack.

'Please. Five marshmallows not four, though, remember.' I smile, but carry on without looking up. Just this once I'll trust him to add the embellishments. Then as I open the next file I let out a scream. 'Oh my, the ceremony's here.' I'm so relieved I want to get up, fling my arms around Rory and squeeze him until he shrieks as loudly as me. But luckily for me, I hang on tightly to my stool instead and slurp hot chocolate all over the tabletop, due to me jumping so violently.

He's moving around behind me, reaching over to mop up with kitchen roll. 'Careful, HB. Not that I'm being a lightweight here. But I'm not up to dealing with a cocoa flood on your keyboard at midnight.'

I'm with him on that, so I scrape off a few fingerfuls of cream and take a long drink of thick, delicious chocolate. By the time I open my eyes, after licking my lips, there's already a tray there to put it on.

I put down my mug. 'Thanks for the tray.'

'No worries, best to be safe, all part of the service.'

I brace myself to go in again. 'Yay! The groups seem to be here too.' I do a mini air punch. 'Speeches ... cake cutting ... the beach ... guests relaxing ...' As I work through, I'm almost in a trance. If the kitchen cupboard doors are banging behind me and the plates are rattling on the shelves, it's all happening a long way away from me. When I murmur, it's as if I'm talking to myself. 'These food pictures are making me feel hungry all over again.' I flinch as I come to a platter of vol au vents. But I'm also beginning to puzzle, because I can't work out what isn't here.

'You're frowning. What's wrong, Berry?' For some weird reason, Rory's got a tea towel in his hand.

I hesitate. 'I can't see what's missing.'

He's right over my shoulder, leaning past me, finger on my track pad. 'Shall I look?' Slightly late with the question there, because he already is.

And what the hell happened to respecting my personal space or asking me to move? He's so close I can tell whatever body spray it is he's wearing has lasted all day, and it's still just as ... Heady is not a word I'd ever use in the same sentence as Rory, so definitely not that. Let's just say, if Poppy or Jess were asking for ideas for Rafe or Bart's Christmas present, this particular scent would get five stars on Phwoar Advisor.

I sigh, then reach for my mug as he scrolls down the screen. I'm scraping the last of the froth onto my spoon when I realise he's stopped at the picture of two little boys on the floor, playing with the same skittles he and Gracie had ignored the other day. I'm about to mention that, but he cuts in first.

'So were you and Runaway Luc planning to have kids, then?'

I spend a minute picking my jaw up off the floor at the question, then dive in to put him right. 'I was the one who ran. So technically, it's Runaway Holly, not the other way around, okay?'

His sniff is dismissive. 'Seeing as you're here and he's in the

States, I'd disagree on that one.' He gives me one of his significant, know-it-all looks. 'So did you? Think about kids, I
mean?' He's not backing down on the interrogation, but at
least he starts scrolling again.

'It wasn't that kind of relationship. We were more in the
moment, both busy with our work.' Even if it's true, I suspect
that's not going to be enough. Luc wasn't that preoccupied
with the future, beyond his next meeting and his projected
career trajectory. Apart from his personal pension scheme, of
course, which did seem to occupy an extra large part of his
leisure time thinking. But that caution and care was part of
who he was, and the reason he was so good at his job. It
never particularly bothered me that we didn't have long term
plans. The loft apartment was like a cloud I'd hitched a very
comfortable ride on. I hadn't got as far as looking beyond
that.

From the way his nose wrinkles, Rory's not buying into
this. 'Surely Luc didn't just produce a ring, like pulling a rabbit
out of a hat? Didn't you ever talk about your hopes and
dreams when you were chilling on those ten foot sofas of
his?' If there's the slightest bitter twang in his voice there, I'm
probably imagining it.

Actually the magician analogy is close to what it felt like,
watching Luc as he whipped out his surprise ring. On the
day it happened I was frozen with that same wide-eyed, startled astonishment and disbelief magicians get in response to
their tricks. But I'm not going to admit that now. 'Mostly
when he was home we went out. We didn't spend that much
time at the flat.' However luxurious Luc's sofas looked, they

weren't anything like as comfy to sit on as the ones at the Lifeboat Station. As for Luc, he was usually racing around the flat, on his phone, working out his appointment itinerary. He rarely sat down at all, unless he was out with clients. That was just part of how conscientious he was. He used to explain he had until he was forty to get where he was going and, understandably, he had to give it everything.

Looking back, however much I personally enjoyed slurping round in my pj's, Luc didn't join in, because he always had too much work on. Watching my boxed sets was alone-time for me. Done on last season's couch next to an abandoned cross trainer, in the surprisingly small and cosy fourth bedroom. To be honest, I'm not that sure Luc even knew the room existed. He certainly never visited when I was in there. But that wasn't a bad thing. At least it meant I could watch what I wanted.

Rory pulls down the corners of his mouth. 'So you weren't that close, then?' Why the hell is he still pushing this? As he rubs his thumb across his jaw he gives a sigh. 'Do you remember that party where you drank too much punch and chucked up?'

'What's that got to do with anything?' I can't help my wail, but I surprise myself by moving on so fast to close it down. It might be great to look back and talk about Freya, but Rory dragging up my most embarrassing moments is the flipside of our reminiscing. 'I didn't know it was cider. Lucky for me I have a memory blank for the whole evening. Why?'

He gives a wry smile. 'Maybe you're wilder than you think. Back then I was damned impressed by a girl who pebbledashed an entire row of prize roses. You were so warm and chatty and spontaneous, it's impossible to understand how you'd end up with someone cold and clinical. Harder still to see why you're desperate to get back with someone who sounds like they don't understand you at all.'

My voice is shrill because I'm so indignant. I'd rather he'd made me relive the puking and the shame than come out with that damning condemnation. 'Crap, Rory, relationships come in all shapes and sizes. And they certainly aren't meant for other people to stick their noses in.' One way to shut him up is to turn this back onto him. 'So how about you? How are your plans for kids shaping up? Have you got it all worked out?' I already know the answer. Anyone as child-unfriendly as he is couldn't possibly be contemplating them. When you're as self-absorbed as Rory is, there's definitely no room for other people in your life. If what he says is true, he hasn't even got the space for a girlfriend, let alone kids. Which is probably a good thing, seeing he's hanging round the attic kitchen this late.

His face twists. 'I *was* planning lots of things. First the Audi TT. Making the boardroom as a corporate lawyer. The four storey Georgian house complete with a huge family, all haring up and down the stairs yelling at each other. A big basement kitchen, tiles from Fired Earth, massive Sunday barbies in the garden cooked on volcanic rock, rugby kits strewn across the landing ...' His bottom lip pulls into the familiar Gracie pout. 'Sometimes life doesn't play out quite as you expect.'

I'm blinking at the detail. 'In London on-trend people mostly get their tiles from Bert and May.' And I only know this because after their jobs, Luc's friends' main obsession was their homes. 'If you're wanting flashy ceramics, they're definitely worth a look.'

Rory's shaking his head. 'My whole point is, I'm *not* needing tiles, Berry. They belong to the lives my mates are living, not me. I got as far as the car.' He frowned. 'Then other stuff got in the way.'

'Stuff, what stuff?' It's a squeal of frustration. Because, if I'm honest, he lost me at 'volcano'.

His sigh is so long and deep, I feel it on my cheek. 'Nothing I'm going to go into after a full day at a wedding where the dog mashed the memory card, that's for sure.' He's leaning forward. 'Actually, it's the bride walking down the aisle shots.'

Here we go again. 'Sorry?' Still no idea what the hell he's talking about.

The smile that spreads across his face is so broad, he actually gets dimples in his cheeks. 'The aisle ones are the pictures that are missing. I remember now, you swapped to a different camera for those.'

'I did?' I'm busy swallowing back the whoosh that swept through my chest when I saw those slices in his face. But I'll take his word for it. For me the day is all a blur. Then it sinks in. 'Shit, Nancy walking down the aisle is pretty significant.' Even if the aisle was only a gap between rows of bleached wood chairs and twiggy lavender posies. *Shit, shit shit.* And I used that camera for the confetti shots too.

He's already pulling his camera out of the bag. 'If I've got them, they'll be quite near the start of mine, after the pub, and the guys messing around outside when they arrived.'

My voice is like an echo. 'You took pictures of the groomsmen on the beach too?'

He shakes back his hair and grins. 'Of course. All the best wedding albums have pics of the guys before. I might look like a washed-up rock star, but I'm not *purely* decorative.'

'Or modest.' I have to mutter it. He might be about to save me, but I still need to counteract his eye-watering big headedness. However short his life-plan plans have fallen, he still comes over as mighty pleased with himself. As I watch him, poring over the screen on the back of the camera, I'm clutching my arms round my ribs, willing him to find the pictures to fill my gaps. If he comes through on this one, I might just have to...

'Here you go. Am I superhuman, or what?' He pushes the camera into my hand, then raises his fists in a silent cheer. 'How's that for a result?'

On the first shot he's wobbled the camera, the next has someone's head in the way, but the third is passable. Nancy is clinging onto her dad's arm, biting her lip. No idea how it's possible to look terrified and blissfully happy at the same time, but she does. 'Wow, I think you just saved me.' Definitely useable, with a bit of cropping. And the fourth is ... 'Totally bloody brilliant.' I know the risks of bigging him up. But just this second I couldn't give a damn.

His grin is rueful. 'I might be totally shit at nappy changing. But, like I told you, for weddings and parties, I'm a good bet.'

Whizzing through the camera roll, I can see he's got some good confetti shots too. 'Brilliant. Thank you *so, so* much, Rory.' How the hell can I thank him for this? 'And thanks so much for taking me, and everything. Another hot chocolate?'

But he's already looking at his watch, then towards the landing. 'Thanks for the offer. But if you're sure you're completely sorted, I'd better get back for Chas and Immie.'

'Absolutely.' Definitely the right answer from Rory. The sooner he gets out of this kitchen and down those stairs, the better, really. As he hesitates by the door my stomach flips.

He gives a low laugh. 'No need to look so scared. I am leaving.' Although he's actually come all the way back into the kitchen and his hand is on my shoulder. The one firm squeeze he gives me sends a seismic wave through my torso. 'Well done for today, Holly Berry. You definitely nailed it. Carry on like this and you might be needing those Super Woman pyjamas after all.' Although he's totally glossing over that a lot of it was down to him.

This time round he's grabbed his windcheater from the table end. And then he's gone.

As I listen to the echo of his footsteps as he winds all the way down to the street, I'm bracing myself. 'Okay, clearing up, and then bed.' If Poppy's back here to cook tomorrow, she can't come in to the devastation of today's breakfast.

And it's only when I stand up and brace myself to stagger to the washing-up pile that I look around and see that everything is clean. Sink shining. Hob buffed to Poppy's exacting standards. Apart from my hot chocolate mug, there's not a dish out of place.

Chapter 20

At the Fun Palace at the Crab and Pilchard: Rock bottom
and other happy places

Piped music with a kids' choir singing *Jingle Bells*. Tinsel garlands strung across the room. Dangling fold-out bells strategically placed to hit you in the face. A ten foot tree, groaning under the weight of decorations, complete with multi-coloured chaser lights. Last December, I admit, I'd have gasped at the ombré rainbow effect they've created by zoning the bauble colours in bands on the tree and rushed home to create a mini version of my own. If I'd seen this brave berry palette last year, with additions of lime, Tiffany blue, and shrimp, it would have been snapped and posted on my Pinterest pages and Insta within seconds of me arriving. But as I stand this year, if I'd asked the elf interior decorators from hell to create my 'worst-case scenario' festive backdrop, the Fun Palace at the Crab and Pilchard pub has gone one better. It really is a case of not being able to see the ball cage or the soft play area for the baubles. Add in a mechanical Santa, riding on a humungous sleigh of toys, pulled by eight animated reindeer, and it's top of the pole so far for my personal nightmare environment this December.

On the other hand, I can completely understand why the Christmas explosion and singing reindeer are striking a chord with the kids. Gracie's standing transfixed at the edge of a small group, joggling both Immie's snowmen.

Poppy wheels Teddie's pushchair to a halt, puts their apple juices down on the table next to the bouncy castle and sinks into a chair. '*How* cute is that? Gracie's singing along and Rudolf's actually dancing in time to the music.'

She was *never* this mushy or susceptible before she fell in love and got pregnant. Her eyes widen as she catches sight of Immie's soft drink. 'Not having a beer today?'

She's right to be surprised. The Crab and Pilchard's real ale selection is the main reason we're in this particular beach-side bar. Not that we usually hit the alcohol this early in the afternoon. But once Immie mentioned a play area attached to a pub, suddenly Rory couldn't wait to visit. Although, true to form, as soon as he'd roped the three of us into coming along as well, he delivered us to the door, then remembered an urgent errand he had to dash off on. We all know he's got a lot on, running the wine business and the brewery at arm's length, and we all sympathise. As a rule of thumb, the second he hands the changing bag to someone else, you know he's about to make a break for freedom. Not that any of us mind, but we still laugh about it all the same. At least if Poppy's away from the farm and the shop she's more likely to have a sit down. And Immie's overseen all her cottage changeovers for the day. As for me, I picked out some pictures for Nancy and Scott's Best Moments Mini-Album and sent them to Jules to forward yesterday. Since then I've been messing with the rest pretty much non-stop. After all that screen work, Poppy's offer of an hour in a play zone, complete with chat, sounded like bliss. In fact, Rory buggering off and leaving us on our own is the icing on my own personal afternoon cupcake.

Immie takes a sip of her raspberry coloured drink and pulls a face. 'However bleugh they taste, I'm sticking to the J2Os, at least until the boys arrive.' Rafe's supposed to be dropping in too. As she turns to me she seems anxious to move the conversation on. 'What's the news from the Alps today, Hols?'

As I push the nappy bag under the table and put down my coffee I can't help smiling. 'Poor Jess. Bart hauled her out of bed so early this morning, it was practically the middle of the night. Then they went trekking across this mountainside to see the dawn breaking before breakfast. She froze her butt off and marched for an hour, all to see a peachy sunrise over the snowcapped peaks.'

Poppy chimes in. 'And she *still* didn't get her ring. It's driving her wild. But she has given in on one thing – she's wearing her salopettes now. And swapped her linen slacks for ski leggings.'

Immie gives a chortle. 'If I know Kip's Uncle Bart, he'll be loving this. Although he's definitely right with his tactics. Prolonging the anticipation has been scientifically proved to increase levels of eventual happiness.' It's always useful to have a psychologist's view. Even if she hasn't done many modules of her degree yet, Immie's always great for her insights.'

I laugh. 'If that's true, Jess is going to be beside herself by the time he does pop the question. So long as she doesn't snap and push him off the mountain first.' I was the one talking to her this morning, so I know how wound up she is.

Poppy shakes her head. 'Bart's so naughty. You should have seen him last summer. He literally teased Jess into submission to make her go out with him.' She gives Immie a nod. 'She's also managed to talk to Jules on Skype.'

Immie dives forward as she hears this. 'Really. How did he look?'

'Still very spotty.' If Poppy's laughing, it's only because she knows how delighted Immie's going to be because Mr Perfect Complexion has tumbled off his pedestal.

I'm fumbling with my phone, hesitating to spill the beans. 'She did send us the secret screen shot she took of him. She was very proud to have pulled that one off.'

'Make my day, why don't you?' Immie's punching the air, then an anxious look passes across her face. 'You *are* going to show me?'

I pass my phone across. 'Just a quick flash.' Despite sitting back in the shadows, Jules is still looking very peaky.

Immie lets out a whoop. 'Trumping frog bollocks, now *that's* what I call *spotty*. At this rate he won't be coming out of the house again till spring.'

Poppy's already seen it, but she still comes back for seconds. 'He has got it badly. But the good news is he was over the moon with the pictures his stand-in delivered from Port Giles.'

Thankfully she's moved Immie on before she had time to demand a copy of her own. 'And the bride and groom love the rushes too. So well done for that, Hols.'

Immie's nudge on my arm is so forceful I nearly fall off my chair. 'There, what did we tell you? We knew you'd do brilliantly. With Jules's spots as they are, you might have got a job for life, Hols.'

'Totally not.' I can't help jumping straight in, because I can't make this clear enough. 'Once my beach wedding's done I'm never going near another one again. When I agreed to that one, it was like a challenge to stretch myself. But now I'm landed with the others, truly, I already know I'm not cut out for the stress.'

Immie lets out another chortle. 'There won't be *that* many brides out there with camera-eating dogs, you know. Mind, you have to watch out for pigs around here too. When the porkers we had as our ring bearers got loose they nearly totalled the wedding down the yard.' In fact, before they went on the rampage Immie's piggie ring bearers were so cute their pictures went viral and that brought in a lot of business for Rafe and Poppy.

Poppy gives a shudder. 'Never work with animals. Two pigs almost running riot through the farmhouse when it was all set out for a wedding was *such* a near miss. By the way, is Gracie okay?'

Immie gives a nod. 'Fine, I've got my eye on her, she's still singing with Santa. When she moves on we can all go with her.' Immie takes another swig from her bottle and chokes. 'Jeez, bat piss would taste better than this.'

Poppy sends her a puzzled glance. 'So why not have a bitter? It's not as if you're driving.'

Immie's frown is so intense, her eyebrows end up somewhere near her top lip. 'Don't tempt me.' The sigh she lets out couldn't be deeper. 'Chas and I have made a pact. We're both cutting back on the booze.'

Poppy's jaw drops. 'Frigging heck, what happened there? You have remembered Christmas party time's coming up?'

Immie grunts. 'We've gone alcohol free to help our fertility. But I had no idea it would be this hard.'

It must be tough for someone who enjoys her beer as much as Immie does. Especially when she works at a pub. 'So how long since you started?' I ask, ready to jump in with congratulations for how long it's been.

Immie gives a groan. 'About twelve hours.'

'That long?' Poppy and I exchange hopeless shrugs behind Immie's head.

Poppy makes her tone bright. 'It's really good practice for when you get lucky. You'll *have* to give up then.' She didn't go through any of this, because she was already quite a few months pregnant by the time she found out.

'If cutting out the alcohol helps it to be sooner rather than later, I'm happy to make the sacrifice.' Immie forces a smile. 'We're giving up getting stressed too. It's statistically proven – conceiving is easier if you're relaxed.'

There's a supervisor dressed in a dirndl dress walking past our table, and from the way her eyebrows shoot upwards, it's obvious she's heard. She leans towards us, speaking in a loud whisper. 'Very true. The minute you stop worrying about them, that's when babies show up. Just ask Jenny-on-pots.' Then she waltzes away.

Due to having a voice like a foghorn, Immie's comments often resonate beyond our group. Her loud cough of complaint is very restrained, considering it's Immie. 'Who the eff does she think she is, joining in our conversation? And what the jeez is she wearing?'

I jump in to smooth things over. 'She's meant to be Snow White. There's a matching set of dwarves too, but they're mostly in the other bar.'

Before her struggle to find a dress for her wedding last summer, Immie *never* noticed what people wore. She gives a snort. 'In that case, I'll let her off, then.' For once Immie's guffawing voice goes so small we have to lean in to hear. 'I'm really lucky, because I've already got Morgan. But it was different with him, because he was a happy accident. And I know Chas and I have only been trying to get pregnant since August. But every time I'm a day late, I can't help thinking we're on our way. For that one day, in my head I've already had the baby and got it as far as school. Then when it doesn't happen there's this crushing disappointment. And I know it's early days, and it's nothing compared to what a lot of people go through trying to have kids, but it kills me every time.'

'Poor Immie.' I'm aching for her. I squeeze her hand, because I know exactly what she means. 'It's true. As soon as you're late, it's like your whole world perspective changes. By the time it's a week, you feel like you're practically ready to give birth.' As I hear the words come out, and both Immie and Poppy turn to me, my face goes hot. And damn for oversharing here. At least Snow White isn't joining in this time.

Poppy leans forward and puts her hand on mine. 'You know that feeling?' Her voice is a low whisper.

I sigh. 'It happened after Luc left. Looking back, it was probably the shock of the break-up. I emailed him to warn him I was late and going to do a test, but he didn't ever get back to me. I spent ten days trying to get up the courage to pee on that stick. In the end my period came before I did it.' I blow out a long breath. Even now the disappointment makes me strangely raw inside. Like my heart is being twisted in my chest. 'Those ten days were the longest of my life. Waiting to hear back from Luc, then when I didn't, planning how I was going to manage on my own. But then I didn't need to anyway. It was something and nothing. But I *do* know how you feel, Immie.'

Immie blows out her cheeks. 'Maybe he didn't get the email, if he was between countries?' We both know she's only making excuses for him to make me feel better.

I pull down the corners of my mouth. 'It had to be a mix-up with the emails. But when you've sent one with news like that, you don't want to send another to check the first arrived.' Somehow I couldn't get over the feeling he'd made his new start, and he wasn't turning back whatever happened. 'It doesn't matter now. There wasn't a baby, and Luc is a hundred per cent in the past. We've both moved on.' Poppy's the only one I've told I haven't completely let go.

'Yeah, right.' Immie purses her lips in obvious disbelief.

'I wish we'd been there with you.' Poppy leans over to give me a hug. When she eventually lets me go, she's straight in with her bright voice. 'You certainly *have* moved on with your weddings, though. From Jules's reaction, it sounds like you've cracked them. Which is exactly what I was hoping.' She gives me an eyebrow wiggle.

I screw up my face, glad to change the subject. Although somewhere other than here would have been better. 'Cracked *up*, more like. They're *so* high pressure.' I consider for a moment. 'I hate to admit it, but if it hadn't been for Rory, I don't think I'd have managed to take any pictures at all at the Old Lifeboat Station. You know what he's like with that mix of charm, enthusiasm and genuine friendliness. He just smoothed everyone into the right places, including me. All I had to do was point the camera and press the button.' It crosses my mind that now might be a good time to ask. 'So why did Rory stop going out with women?'

Immie narrows her eyes as she thinks. 'There was some kind of accident back in Bristol. Way before he came back here and took over Huntley and Handsome. Can you remember what happened to Rory, Pops?'

I'm on the edge of my seat, when Poppy cuts in.

'Maybe that needs to wait, given Rory and Rafe are coming now.' Although however enthusiastic her wave is, it might not be enough of a cover-up for Immie's foghorn voice.

I watch as they pick their way past the happy crowd of kids singing along to *Rudolf the Red Nosed Reindeer*. Whereas Rafe's obviously a hundred per cent the hunky farmer, with his hollow cheeks and his Barbour, Rory's looking for all the world like he raided Kurt Kobain's charity shop bag to find something to wear to come out in.

Rafe swoops in to give Poppy a kiss on the cheek, as Rory finds a beer mat for his bottle of Coke, and shrugs under the rags that are passing for a t-shirt. 'Someone talking about me, then?'

If I'd managed to keep my cool by doing long, slow breaths, I lose it at that, but luckily Poppy jumps in. 'We were discussing your great crowd-control tactics at the wedding, Rory.'

He takes that on board with a smile. 'Berry and I definitely smashed it. Best day I've had for ages.' This is Rory all over. He takes the compliment in his stride, then expands it. 'When's the next one? I'm definitely up for it if you want me.'

If my sweaty neck wasn't enough, now my stomach's imploding. The twins are marrying twins later this week and I know I need help. I just hadn't thought as far ahead as that help possibly coming from Rory.

Poppy steps in. 'Travis and Taylor are getting married on Friday at the Manor. Aren't you invited to that?'

Rory scratches his head. 'Jeez, you could be right.'

Immie's straight in. 'If you're there as a guest anyway, it makes sense to help Hols while you're there, then.'

I butt in. 'If Rory's a guest, maybe someone else could come along with me?' It's a long shot, but anyone else would do.

From the way Rory's looking at me, it's like he's taking pity on me. 'If the kids are still here, I'd obviously need someone to look after them.' He turns to Poppy and Immie. 'How are you two fixed?'

'Maybe if you ask very nicely.' Poppy's grinning at him. 'Seeing as you're helping Hols and the team, you're on.'

'That's not definite.' I'm still fighting them. 'Jules's friends might be back from holiday.' I might be able to get my dad back from Spain. Or persuade one of Rafe's workers from the farm. Or I could even borrow a dwarf from the Crab and Pilchard.

'It'll cost you.' Immie laughs at Rory. 'Depends how many cases of Bad Ass Santa you're offering?'

As he turns, Gracie is approaching, a snowman trailing from each hand. 'Would you like to make some more snowman cakes, Gracie?' Rory talking to Gracie directly has to be a first, even if she won't have a clue what he's on about.

Gracie looks almost as bemused as he does, but she manages a solemn reply. 'Actually ... I want to go on the slide next.'

All us adults look across the room to where the slide sweeps down and lands in the ball cage, but I'm the first to seize my chance to get away.

I hold out my hand to her. 'I'll take you.' Obviously no one else is listening to me *here*.

She thinks for a few seconds then her hand slides into mine. 'I had snowman cakes at Poppy's house. We put carrots on for noses. And chocolate buttons.'

Rory cuts in. 'It's fine, we can all come over to the slide.'

I have to argue. 'Really, it doesn't take five adults to look after one child.' However ridiculous it sounds, they're all traipsing after me in a line, Rafe coming up the rear, pushing Teddie.

'Have you been in a ball cage before, Gracie?' Poppy sounds concerned as we reach the netting enclosure with literally thousands – if not millions – of brightly coloured balls inside.

Gracie nods back at her. 'All the time. Mummy lets me.' She drops her snowmen at the bottom of the slide steps, then begins to scramble up.

Immie's laughing. 'At Morgan's fourth birthday, we had to evacuate the area when some kid from another party did a poo in the ball pit.'

Rory pulls a face. 'Gross.'

Rafe laughs. 'Sounds more like a House of Horrors than a Fun Palace.'

Gracie looks down from where she's poised at the top of the slide. 'My snowmans want to come too.'

Rory picks them up and delivers them to her lap. 'Jeez, anything else?'

Gracie stares down at him. 'Mummy says "one two three go".'

'Christmas crackers.' Rory's muttering under his breath. 'Is that all, your majesty?'

'She does clapping too.'

'What?' Rory groans. 'It's a slide, not the frigging Cresta Run.'

'Maybe just do it, Rory.' From where I'm standing the slide looks pretty high for a three-year-old. I remember one time when Freya queued with me all the way to the top of this huge slide in the park. And when I got to the top it looked such a long way down, I lost my bottle. The entire queue behind me had to go back down the steps to let me climb off. It might have been the ultimate humiliation for me *and* Freya, but for once I didn't care. I'd have happily suffered the embarrassment ten times over if it meant I didn't have to whoosh down that polished stainless-steel channel. As Gracie pushes off, I shout, 'One two three, go!' By the time she whizzes round and flops into the ball pile, *most* of us are clapping. As I glare at Rory, he joins in too.

Gracie flounders around, then struggles the length of the cage and clambers out of the hole in the netting. 'Again.'

'Great,' I say, catching Poppy's eye. 'Why not?'

Half an hour later, Gracie's still doing her circuits, cheered on by her own personal fan club. Even the single kids with their grandparents in tow don't have quite as many supporters in their crowd as Gracie does.

'So are you free tomorrow afternoon, Berry?' Rory breaking the cycle of clapping and sliding takes me by surprise.

I exchange glances with Immie, who's spooning food into Teddie from a jar, and give Rory a superior 'told you so' smirk. 'See, we knew once you came to a play zone you wouldn't be able to stay away.' Even if Gracie hasn't smiled yet, I'm sure I've caught the occasional twitching at the corner of Rory's mouth. Who knows, his face might even crack into a beam before we trundle back out past Santa and his bobbing rein- deer. 'Coming again might be fun. Maybe Gracie'll try the bouncy castle tomorrow, for a variation.' An hour by the ball cage, surrounded by whooping kids might be noisy. But even though it's horribly Christmassy, it's relaxing enough for me to be tempted to come again.

Rory looks at me as if I'm totally crazy. 'Jeez, I don't mean we're coming here. If I hear *Frosty The Snowman* one more time my head might implode. But if the next wedding's on

Friday, we need to stake out the Manor ASAP.'

For a few happy moments back there the spectre of Friday's wedding had slipped my mind. I'm just about to curse Rory for bringing me hurtling back to reality when Gracie comes towards us.

She's waggling her snowman at me. 'Snowman's gone down.' From the dark shadows under her eyes, I'm guessing she'll sleep tonight.

I beam at her, willing her to smile back. 'Yes, Gracie, Snowman's gone down the slide a hundred times at least.'

But rather than smiling, her mouth corners droop. 'Snowman's gone. Snowman's gone ...' Her voice gets more urgent, then rises to a shriek as she shakes him at me. 'Snowman's gone! ...'

Rory winces at her howl. 'Christmas, weren't there two of them?' He frowns down at her. 'Where's your *other* snowman, Gracie?'

As a large tear rolls down Gracie's cheek, she points at the cage. 'B-b-balls ...'

Rory rolls his eyes. 'For once I couldn't have put it better myself.'

'Oh my. Is Snowman Two in the ball pit?' Poppy's shaking her head. 'We can't leave him there, he's like part of the family.' Even if she sounds a tad sentimental, we all know what she means.

Rafe's scrunching up his face. 'Can't we just buy another?'

Poppy's eyes widen in shock. 'Please tell me you *didn't* say that.'

Immie's got her hands on her hips. 'Too right. There's only

217

one thing for it. I'm going in.' A minute later, she's horizontal and wriggling through the gap in the netting, swimming her way into the balls. 'Come on, Hols, we'll do a systematic sweep of the cage.'

There are some people you can ignore, but Immie isn't one of them. Next thing I know, I'm diving head-first after her.

'How the heck do the kids do it?' Wading through a sea of plastic balls that comes well up my thighs is harder than you'd imagine.

Immie's sifting through the spheres as if she's doing back skulling, while I'm already on my knees, raking through, like some kind of frenzied mole.

Rory's laughing. 'Shout if you need a poop scoop, Immie.'

Beyond the netting, Poppy turns on Rory. 'Tell me I didn't hear *that*, either.'

'Is this impossible?' Now I'm inside there are so many balls, it's hard to imagine ever finding one small soft toy in here, however systematic our approach is.

Immie shakes her head at me and mutters under her breath. 'About as likely as finding a snowman in hell, I'd say, but given the levels of Poppy's pregnancy hormones, we have to look like we're trying.' She staggers backwards as she comes across a small child, then shouts at Rafe and Rory. 'Come on, you guys. If you want to get home this side of midnight, don't just stand there. You need to get in here.'

They don't need asking twice. 'Chocs away!' 'Tally ho!' As Rafe dives off a platform at the far end, Rory comes sailing down on a zip wire.

Rafe's launching himself as if he's crowd surfing, his dark

cashmere sweater submerging in the mass of brightly coloured plastic. 'How much fun is this?' Talk about men reverting to boys. They just turned the clock back thirty years.

Rory's whooping back. 'Next on my wish list is a massive bouncy castle. A customised Roaring Waves one has to be great for publicity. We could take it down the beach and hire it out for weddings.'

Immie's chiding them. 'Watch out! Don't squash any kids.'

As I notice Snow White on the other side of the netting she's scowling at me as if I'm the Wicked Queen. 'We're looking for the snowman, don't forget.' I shout it mainly for her benefit. Which is just as well as Rafe and Rory have started pelting each other with balls and are completely ignoring me. Luckily the playing children have mostly moved away.

Seeing as I'm hardly getting anywhere with my digging, I stand up and start kicking through the balls, moving towards Immie. 'You'd think a white snowman would be easy to find.'

Immie dips. 'Trumping toad bottoms, dwarves on the warpath!'

I look to where she's nodding and, sure enough, Snow White is marching, with a posse of guys wearing stripey hats, leggings and curly grey beards.

As the piped music choir gets cut off in mid-sentence halfway through 'Silent Night', one of the guys clears his throat and shouts. 'Okay, adults out of the ball cage! That area is for under-tens only.' It's hard to take him seriously when his nose is painted red.

If anyone was going to argue, it would have to be Rory. 'Lighten up, Sneezy, we're only messing around while we look for a lost toy.'

The dwarf puts his hands on his hips and pulls himself up to what has to be a full six foot four. 'Don't push me to bar you, mate. Because I will.'

Rory's voice resonates with disbelief. 'You can't eject *me*, I'm your biggest real-ale supplier.'

The dwarf pulls on his beard and his voice rises to a nasty shout. 'I don't care if you're Santa's main dealer, just get the hell out of my ball pit. NOW!'

'Okay, no need to get your knickerbockers in a twist, we're on our way.' If Rory's conceding defeat, it can only be because he's worried about his beer orders.

You know that reaction as a kid, when getting yelled at automatically makes you run? This is me now. Before I know it, I'm lolloping towards the hole in the netting, sending balls flying in all directions. As I glance over my shoulder, Rory and Rafe are coolly ambling behind me. As I scrabble and scramble, I'm getting more and more frantic, and more and more unbalanced. I'm within a whisker of the gap in the fence when my foot catches, and next thing I know, I'm falling. It's more of a saggy sideways collapse than a heavy fall. But as I twist onto my back, my shoulders sink, and my knees and feet go upwards.

Immie's doubled up. 'Full-blown flight response you had there, Hols. Seeing you plunging under the balls there is *so* funny it's making me wee.'

I'm wailing at her. 'Stop laughing, Immie, and *pull me out*.' But that sets her off again.

'Damsel in distress?' Rory reaches me first, and surprise,

surprise, he's smirking down at me.

As I hiss at him, I'm aware of a crowd of small faces pressed up against the netting. 'Thanks, but I'm absolutely fine. Immie's got this.'

That seems to amuse him even more. 'Sorry, Holly B, Immie's too busy peeing herself. Looks like it's a handsome prince, or nothing.' He half closes one eye. 'Unless you'd prefer an angry dwarf to haul you out, of course?'

I take a few seconds to abandon every last vestige of pride and then I wave my arm in his direction. 'Go on, then.' It comes out very grudgingly. But a moment later it turns to a scream. All I needed was a simple yank to get me onto my feet, but Rory's scooping me up from underneath.

As he strides through the balls, he's clamping me so close to his chest, I get not only the full benefit of the delicious scent of his body spray going right up my nose in a way that's much too swoony for comfort, but also his low laugh resonating through his sternum. 'Who'd have thought I'd have *this* much fun at the Fun Palace?'

I'm talking through gritted teeth, wondering how anyone in such a ragged t-shirt can smell so good. 'Eff off, Rory. And PUT ME DOWN!'

'No need to panic.' He lurches all the way to the edge, then slides me straight through the entrance hole.

There's a thud as I land. 'Lovely, great.' The felt tiles are so rough under my palms, I'm lucky not to have carpet burns. It's hard to scramble to your feet with any dignity at all when there are twenty-odd three and four-year-olds staring down at you.

As Rafe, Rory and Immie arrive beside me and we shuffle like a line of naughty school kids the dwarf is already coming over, pointing at our feet with a horrified look on his face. 'You went in wearing outdoor *shoes?*'

As if the humiliation of me falling over and getting dragged out by Rory isn't enough, now we've got to be told off in front of a crowd of kids. If their wide eyes are anything to go by, they're obviously finding four adults getting ordered out of the play area a lot more riveting than the bouncy castle *or* the singing Santa show.

Rory's nodding at the dwarf's feet. 'Not everyone's lucky enough to have plimsolls with cardboard buckles covered in tin foil, mate. You might like to take this opportunity to change the CD. We could work with Wizard?'

Snow White looks at the Head Dwarf. 'What do you say, Darren? *Now That's What I Call Christmas* would make a change. Those singing seven-year-olds are getting right on my nips.' She barely waits for his nod before she rushes off, and then the music starts up again.

Rory listens to the first couple of bars, then lets out a groan. 'Just my luck to get Mariah frigging Carey.'

I perk up. 'Ooooh, I love this one. *All I want for Christmas is yoooooooooooou.*' Freya and I used to go wild singing along to this in the mirror with our hairbrushes. Although obviously I won't be doing that this year, due to my festive ban.

Rory gives a snort of disgust at me, then turns back to the dwarf. As he gestures towards Gracie he seems to have slipped into courtroom speak. 'We were actually locating a lost toy, like the one the little girl is holding. You might like to keep an eye out for it when you next do a ball wash.'

The dwarf winces. Then he bobs down behind the push-chair. 'There's a snowman here. Is this the one you're looking for?'

There's a ripple along our line. 'Crap ... shit ... jeez ... what the frig?' How the hell did we end up in the ball pit when the snowman was under the pushchair the whole time?

As the dwarf holds out the snowman to Gracie her lips twist. I have to comment, because it's the first time I've seen it. 'That's a lovely smile, Gracie.' It might only be tiny, but it's definitely there, if only fleetingly. 'Are you going to say "thank you" to the dwarf, then?'

Her serious frown's already back as she hugs both snowmen close to her chest. 'Actually he's not a dwarf. 'Cos his beard's falling off.' She wrinkles her nose in distaste. 'And he's not little enough. Or happy, even.'

Rory looks delighted by her candour. 'Okay, how about you say thanks to the big guy in the fake beard, then? And maybe hold onto the snowmen tighter next time.'

She's mumbling, 'Thank you' when I hear a phone ping.

Poppy picks up my bag from the pile and passes it across to me. 'Might as well make the most of the pub's wifi hotspot. It doesn't happen very often round here.'

I'm pleased to have an excuse to retreat from the front line so I can take cover next to Poppy behind the buggy. 'Just an email from Nate and Becky. They're probably sending me their list of groups for the photos.' Hard to believe that at one time I was dreading this list arriving, but now there's a million things to worry about before we even get to it. 'Weird, it looks like she's forgotten the attachment.'

Even as I read the first line of text in the inbox window my throat feels like someone's put a tourniquet around it.

Hi Holly, just to let you know the fab news, Luc's flying in for the wedding.

Poppy's leaning towards me. 'Everything alright there, Hols?'

I open my mouth, but all that comes out is a rasp. 'E-rrr ...' For a few seconds it feels like my heart's dropped through the floor. When it bounces back into place, it's clattering against my ribs so hard I feel like I could run out of the pub, onto the beach and only stop when I reached Australia.

Rory crashes down on the bench next to me and leans in for a look. 'Ewww, is that Luc with a "c" not a "k"? I knew that guy was a no-good poseur.'

Immie's over like a shot. 'The same Luc who thought you were pregnant, but didn't get back to you?'

Poppy scowls at Immie. 'Or even better, the Luc who Hols once went out with but has now moved on from. Are you sure you're okay, Hols? You've gone very pale.'

Rory chimes in. 'What kind of a shit would behave like *that*? Nothing red about those cheeks of yours now, HB. You're whiter than you were on toothpaste day.'

Which is a shame as I'm not going to make the most of it. But just this once, there's something I'm more bothered about than the colour of my face.

'So Luc's coming to the beach wedding after all?' Poppy's probing, very gently.

Immie's not giving up, either. 'Did you two ever have closure? At least you might get a chance for that now. It's very beneficial to have a proper full stop at the end.'

I open the email and skim down it. 'He's flying in ... *in just over a week's time.*' My voice is like sandpaper scraping on wood, but my mind's racing. Not that there's any chance of getting him back at all. But at least I want to give it my best shot. 'How am I ever going to be ready? I need to lose two stone and have a complete make-over.' Luc always preferred me to skip carbs and puddings. How many of those have I eaten in the last year that I wouldn't have had if I'd stayed with him? My mouth's watering at the thought.

Immie's got her 'disgusted of St Aidan' face on. 'You're not seriously wanting him back, are you?'

I ignore the voice in my head yelling 'yes, yes, yes!' and try to steady my voice. 'Totally not.'

Immie shakes her head. 'If you need to show the tosser you've moved on, you could always borrow Rory as your fabulous new "boyfriend".' Her face splits into a grin as she adds the inverted commas with her fingers.

If my stomach was squishing before, this finishes the job. Horrifying doesn't begin to cover it. 'Thanks, but Rory's already got his hands full enough.' Even if Immie's only joking, the old cliché of frying pans and fires springs to mind. I don't want to make a difficult situation horrendous.

Poppy sends me an 'Oh My God' eye roll that moves into a bright smile. 'What we *actually* need to show the world is that you've bounced back as a strong, independent woman, who's got her shit together. Any decent guy will find that *very* attractive.' Her voice is firm and calming. 'There's a lot we can do in a week. We'll make sure you're as prepared as you can be in the time. We'll all help, won't we?'

Rory's rubbing the ragged denim on his thigh. 'Good thinking on that, Pops. You and Immie can concentrate on the pretty stuff and I'll take charge of your motivational development and self-esteem. In ten days, I promise, you'll be so kick-ass the guy won't recognise you. You might want to order that Pocahontas onesie now.'

'What's this about a onesie?' Poppy asks.

I shake my head. 'Believe me, you don't want to know.' Every time I think things can't get any worse, another bomb-shell drops. Pocahontas onesies being the icing on my own personal drip cake of doom.

Immie chuckles. 'Whatever happens with Luc, it can't be any more embarrassing than getting thrown out of a ball pit by a six-foot-four dwarf.'

And then the first bars of Wham! singing *Last Christmas* play out across the bar and I plunge again. Sometime soon I have to reach my proverbial rock bottom.

Chapter 21

Wednesday 13th December
At Brides by the Sea: Harsh words and bulging boxes

There are certain people I meet who I can't help but pre-judge, and Marilyn is one of them. I have to be honest here. Last time we met, Marilyn had barely stormed as far as the White Room and I already wanted to hide. By the time she left the shop after that visit, she'd made it into my 'best avoided forever' box. Which obviously got rapidly revised when I found out I'm taking pictures for an entire day at her son's wedding. But when I saw in the appointments book that she was coming in with her future daughter-in-law, Katie, for a final dress fitting early this morning, I decided the best plan was to stay safely tucked up in bed. But when Poppy rang at seven to tell me Katie wanted me to be there too, to say 'hello' and take a couple of pictures, the only way to combat the bad news was with a stonking breakfast.

Sadly, despite our food science degrees, we can't all whip up the kind of early morning feasts Poppy makes. Which is why it's really lucky there's a bakery a few doors down that sells warm flaky almond croissants and pain au chocolates, from six a.m. onwards. It's amazing how much less intimidated you feel when you've worked your way through a carrier full, eaten the French way. And if my nose stays scarlet until the New Year, after half an hour of serious dipping and slurping over bowlfuls of steaming coffee, I'm just going to have to live with that. The good bit is, that by the time Marilyn gallops into the shop at eight thirty, dragging Katie behind her, I'm feeling well up for the job. Luckily Poppy's there too, with her usual lovely welcome.

'Hello Marilyn … and Katie …' As Marilyn powers straight across to the mother of the bride chair, the hug Poppy gives Katie is so big there has to be some mutual bolstering going on.

After yesterday's promises for motivational training from Rory, I can't help wondering how I'll be handling stuff like this in ten days' time. For now, I'm scuttling behind the desk, thankful I have my camera to hide behind.

Poppy turns her beam in my direction. 'And this is Holly, who *you've* met already, Marilyn. And who will be stepping in to take the wedding pictures.'

'Hi,' I say. I can't help slapping my hand to my hair as I have a sudden flashback to the way Marilyn wrenched out a handful along with the tiara last time she was here. Somehow I manage to move my head rub on into a little wave at Katie and still hold onto the camera. And if Marilyn's looking disbelieving, I completely know the feeling.

She recovers enough to give a little cough. 'Jules already has a list of my stipulations, which no doubt he'll forward to you.' Her words are stiff with disapproval.

Katie's clasping her hands into fists. 'And he also has our list too, which is pretty much the definitive version, if you get my meaning.' Katie's version top trumps Marilyn's in other words.

More fool me for expecting pre-amble. We're obviously going straight into the fighting. 'Lovely, I'll look at them both, and do my best.'

Poppy does one of the most spectacular eyebrow wiggles I've yet seen, so I know there's something mega coming as she turns to Katie. 'Holly's the one who's responsible for all the Best Moments pictures from Nancy and Scott's wedding, which Jules sent to you.'

'Great, so you've seen the mini album.' I'm so surprised I let out a gasp.

Marion shoots upright in her chair. 'You haven't got asthma have you? Or chicken pox? You aren't going to pull out too, are you?' Her eyes narrow as her glare intensifies. 'It's just your nose is very red ...'

Katie and I both clamp our hands over our faces simultaneously, but Katie is first to recover.

'I'm so pleased to meet someone else whose nose suffers in the cold.' When she takes her hand away, her upturned nose is definitely rosy, but on her it looks incredibly cute. 'It's a total nightmare when we ski. It's the one reason I wish we were getting married in summer. And I *loved* your album, by the way.'

When I finally let go of my nose, I'm laughing and picking up my jaw off the floor at the same time. 'Thanks for saying that. Don't worry, any pictures you aren't happy with, we can have a gentle play to reduce the Rudolf effect.'

'Really?' Her eyes are wide with gratitude. 'That's such a weight off my mind. It seemed too girlie to mention to Jules.'

It seems a good time to offer. 'Shall I take a few of you now? I can send them over later to show you how well the re-tint works on noses.'

'Brilliant.' She pulls off her bobble hat and ruffles up her curls.

I zoom in for two close ups. 'Yes, those are fab.' If I didn't know already, I can tell she's going to look amazing in the pictures. Despite the red nose and bitchy mum-in-law. 'Would you like a picture of the two of you while you're here?'

There's a yelp from Marilyn. 'Absolutely not. Have you seen my roots? I'm on my way to have my colours done now.' Someone else clamping their hands over their head here.

'That's fine, we'll concentrate on Katie, then.' I breathe a sigh of relief, then move on to take a few more pictures of Katie's delighted expression when Poppy comes through carrying her dress. And then they head into the fitting room and Poppy whips the grey and white striped curtain closed behind her.

It's not long before the curtain whisks back and I pick up my camera again. 'That was quick ... and the dress is *amazing*.' Even though I've been hanging around the shop for the best part of ten days, I still haven't got used to the transformations. Or how beautiful and individual each bride looks in her dress.

Katie smiles down at the soft gathers of the tulle skirt. 'It's a Sera easy-to-wear and easy-to-get-in-and-out-of special. Very important for a bride like me, who wants to have fun rather than be formal. Anything more complicated and Seth would never manage to take it off.' She laughs as she holds the fabric up to the light. 'There are so many layers, but the top one is studded with tiny gems and miniature snowflakes. And I adore it more every time I see it.'

It's impossible not to be carried along by her practical, down-to-earth approach. As Katie stands and gazes at herself in the mirror, Poppy joins in enthusiastically. 'The top is very simple, with an overlay of the same tiny snowflakes. Then Katie is adding a fluffy jumper and a brightly coloured ski jacket for her outdoor shots.'

Katie's clasping her hands. 'And the six bridesmaids' skirts are in bright purple and blue and yellow tulle short skirts, with contrast jumpers, pink jackets and stripy ski head bands. With bright pearlised stilettos for inside and boots for outside.'

I can feel Marilyn shuddering more with every new colour clash that's mentioned. If Jess were here, I suspect she'd be swooping in with the reviving gin by now.

Poppy sounds truly excited. 'It's the most vibrant wedding we've had yet. It's even brighter than Sera's summer meadow bridesmaids prints.'

Sera, true to form, is hiding in the studio, on call in case of any last-minute problems. It's a kind of tradition with her. She loves designing and making the dresses, but even now she's really successful, she still shies away from meeting the brides who wear them.

Katie's eyes are shining. 'I just *so* want everything to express the kind of out-there, fun couple we are. If my dad hadn't been too ill to go abroad we'd have loved to have got married on the ski slopes, but this is the next best thing. Seth really wants this wedding to pop and I think it will.'

Marilyn rolls her eyes, but there's deep motherly affection in her voice. 'Seth and his popping.' When she leans forward again, her tone is markedly colder. 'So what's happening with the bottom of the dress? I thought the alterations were finished, but it's still much too long.' If Seth's shout-out was all summery, we've just fast forwarded to an arctic winter on this one.

Poppy's awkward customer smile eases across her face. 'Okay, in the business we'd say this hem is breaking on the floor. It's the way Katie wanted it. She'll have to hold up the dress if she goes outside, but it lets her go to higher heels for the times she wears her platforms. She'll try it with those in a second.' At times like these Poppy is so patient.

'Platforms?' Marilyn's yell would be ear-splittingly shrill at any time of day. This early in the morning it's cruelty to thirty-somethings. 'Seth won't be marrying *anyone* wearing *anything* of the kind. I absolutely forbid it.'

Now it's Katie's turn to wince. 'It's Seth who *wants* the platforms, because I was wearing them when we met. He's being a big softy on this one.' She goes into the fitting room, brings out a bag and pulls out a shoe.

'Wow! Electric turquoise! How cool are they?' I'm full of admiration, both for the way she's standing up to Marilyn quietly, yet firmly, every time, and the fact she must be able to walk in six- inch heels.

Katie grins as she rubs at a scuff on the heel. 'Seth says they're my old and my blue all rolled into one.'

Marilyn's eyebrows shoot up at least as high her voice. 'But surely the tiara's your old? And your matching veil will be your new.'

Katie wrinkles her nose. 'Aren't veils what people wear for a joke at hen do's? Seth would die if I turned up in one of those to marry him.' She pauses to drag in a breath. 'And I know you love the diamonds, Marilyn, but Seth says the tiara's *a thousand times* too blingy for the barn.'

Marilyn's nose is quivering. 'Which is exactly why this wedding should be happening in the house not the cowshed. There's still time to change our minds on that.' She raises an eyebrow and eyes Poppy hopefully.

I catch sight of Katie's despairing expression. 'Let's get a picture of you holding the blue shoes. And then I'll take a couple of full length ones, so you get the full effect of the dress.' Although, if the tiara comes out, I'm ready to dive into the kitchen. When I spot Marilyn standing up, I tense. But she's heading for the door, not the desk.

Her bracelets jingle as she glances at her watch. 'So if we're all done here, I must run. Don't want to be late for my colourist. I'll catch you at lunchtime, Katie.' She pauses for long enough to blow Katie a kiss, then she's off.

We all hold our breath as we wait for the shop door to close and watch her car pull away past the window. Then as Poppy and I visibly flop, Katie kicks off her kitten heels.

She grabs the platforms, sits down and begins to do up the straps. 'Right, *and finally* ... Time to check the length with the banned shoes.' When she stands up she's a whole lot taller and she swishes in front of the mirror. 'There, see the way the skirt moves. Isn't it perfect? I'm not being a bridezilla, I just want to wear these shoes.'

'It does look fabulous,' I can't help enthusing too. 'I'll take some full length shots like this.'

Meanwhile Poppy's sympathising with Katie. 'And you're not a bridezilla. But you're still battling Marilyn, then?'

Katie blows out a long sigh as she takes a final look in the mirror. 'It's lovely that she wants to be involved. But last week she changed our veggie buffet to a hog roast, then cancelled the rock band and ordered a singing trio. It's so time-consuming putting the damage right. Worst of all, we never know where she's going to strike next. That's why we're going out to lunch every day. At least that way I get to know which way to leap next.'

Poppy pulls a face. 'Only five more days to keep her under control.'

Katie shakes her head as she makes her way back to the fitting room. 'We're sending her to a spa the day we're setting up. So with luck we've got every area covered now.'

Poppy follows her. 'We'll have the dress steamed and ready for you to pick up on Saturday. Then it's "full steam" ahead for the big day.'

Katie gives a little squeal and laughs at me as she bobs behind the curtain. 'And fingers crossed, there won't be any red noses – or Marilyn-induced disasters.'

I laugh. 'For me *or* you.' But with a mega wedding happening between now and then, my nose is the least of my worries. As for worries about Marilyn, I'll put her in my 'pending' pile. And get her out again on Monday.

Chapter 22

Wednesday 13th December
On the way to Rose Hill Manor: Home truths and car washes

When it comes to our visit to check out the Manor, it actually turns out that the wedding preparations have been under way there all week. So much for Rory and his assumptions that we'll just schmooze our way in any time he chooses. It's a measure of just how gigantic this wedding is that by Wednesday afternoon the place is apparently going to be stuffed full of suppliers shunting stuff around according to a meticulous and complex timetable. Which, when you stop and think about it, is enough to scare the bejeesus out of you. Well, out of me, at least. It obviously helps that Rory's besties with Kip and the gang, who are overseeing the Manor weddings while Bart takes himself off to a safe distance. But it's also a measure of Rory's tenacity and expansive list of connections that he negotiates with everyone concerned and gets us a free pass to look around, no problem.

So I hitch a lift over to Daisy Hill Farm with Lily, who's on her way to check on progress anyway. Which leaves me running from Lily's little pink Fiat halfway up the farm court-yard, across to meet Rory and co in the beer-mobile. When I first clamber up into the front seat, I'm so overwhelmed by the wall of sound, the warmth of the car and the unlikely mix of baby wipes and – according to Immie, who's seen it in the bathroom – Diesel man spray, that at first I don't notice.

'Green Day again?' It's a token protest, seeing the Manor is so close and Teddie's in the back bouncing his fluffy cat contentedly. I'm shouting to be heard over some guy singing about Armageddon flames, of all things, and wondering if this is a prophetic sign of worse to come, when it suddenly hits me the second car seat is empty. 'Where the heck's Gracie?'

Rory's tapping on the steering wheel and he doesn't miss a beat. 'She's with Poppy.' His smile is inscrutable.

I know he's been bumped into giving up his afternoon to help me, but there's no reason at all why Gracie can't fit in with that too. Other than his complete disregard for his duties. Maybe it's because he was so damned enthusiastic about meddling in my life yesterday. Or possibly it's because I was still awake at four this morning, going through every possible scenario of me meeting Luc on the beach. But whatever the reason, my two in the afternoon wafty weariness suddenly turns to tiger wrath. I lean forward, close Green Day down to a whisper. And next thing I know, I've lost it.

'Rory, when the frig are you going to stop dumping on everyone else?' I slam my seatbelt clip into its socket with ten times the force it needs. 'Poppy's knackered, she's way more pregnant than she's admitting, and you're still loading all your shit onto her. It's time you damn well woke up, manned up, and stepped up to your sodding responsibilities.'

Rory stares out across the hedgerows and negotiates the turn into the lane with one hand on the steering wheel. Really? Two hands to bang along to Green Day and one hand to turn the corner? That just about sums it up.

Then he leans and turns the music up a notch and his nose twitches. 'For your information ...' From his smirk, he's about to talk his way out of this. 'Gracie fell asleep on Poppy's sofa earlier and I persuaded Poppy to join her. It's the only way to get Poppy to rest. Otherwise Gracie would be here. Okay?'

That makes me feel slightly small. But I'm still right. 'Fine. You've found an excuse for this particular half hour. But if you actually put your energy into the kids instead of putting every bit into trying to get as far away from them as possible, you all might get something out of it. You might even find you enjoyed your time with them.' When he was useless at the start it was a bit of a laugh. But two weeks on, it's not funny any more.

His lip curls. 'Well, thanks again, Supernanny. No doubt you'll be hoping to rush headlong into having a family when you throw yourself at lover boy next week.'

I'm halfway between stunned and incensed. 'Excuse me? Where does Luc come into this?'

Rory gives a snort. 'You're accusing me of throwing away opportunities, but you're about to do the same. Before you chuck away your chances of a happy life and hurl yourself into oblivion with this Mr Boring of yours for a second time

... remind me, why *do* you want to be with him?' He pauses, then flashes me a sideways glance. 'And I'm not talking swanky flats and furniture here, Berry. I mean the big stuff. Because from where I'm standing, it looks like a complete waste.'

My stomach wilts. If I'd known criticising Rory about the kids was going to end up here, I'd have kept my mouth shut. And strangely enough, I spent a long time in the early hours staring out of the porthole window in the attic bedroom, watching the lights going out across the bay, trying to put my finger on exactly what I do miss about being with Luc. Let's face it, if I'm trying to get back together with him, he's the kind of super-organised person who is quite likely to turn around and grill me about every last reason. I'll need to have my answers fully prepared.

I sigh, stare straight ahead at the potholed tarmac along the single track of the lane and put it out there. 'He made me feel safe?' When I think about everything, that's the bit I miss most. More than the fabulous accommodation and having someone at home to come back to. More even, then being able to say I've got a boyfriend. Or other women's admiring glances when we were together. Even though it's something I got to take for granted when I saw him every day, as guys go he lived up to every tall, dark and handsome cliché. Despite the crumpling effect of work travel, he was always impeccably turned out and pretty enough to make the most of his racks of fabulous suits. I'm kicking myself for making my answer sound like a question when I should be sounding firm and certain.

Rory's puffing out his lips as he takes that in and thinks

about it. 'No, actually, that's wrong.' It took a hell of a lot of frowning for him to get to that. 'Luc makes you feel unchallenged. You interpret that undemanding void you lived in as security, but there's a big difference.'

I stare at him indignantly. 'And how exactly do you claim to be able to see inside my private life?' The back of my neck is prickling. And I can't help noticing that we've slowed from a crawl almost to a halt between the hedges.

Rory pulls a face. 'It's not rocket science, that's what guys like him do. Excuse the cliché, but him grabbing the limelight with his dazzling career provides the perfect shadow for you to hide in. What's worse, that's the way he likes it.'

I give a sniff. 'Now you sound like Immie when she goes all psychological.'

He's completely stopped the car now and he's hanging onto the steering wheel. 'Fine by me. Immie's usually spot-on with her observations. A relationship like that's not really healthy or safe. In the long term, it's pretty damned dysfunctional.'

If my face is puce, for once it's because I'm angry not embarrassed. 'That's damning, considering you've never even met the man.'

He shrugs and puts his hands on his thighs. 'I don't need to meet him. What's more, *I've* known you a lot longer than *he* has.'

I'm shaking my head. 'You can't claim to *know* me. Until last week, you hadn't set eyes on me for *years*.'

The corners of his eyes crinkle as his face breaks into a grin. 'That's the kind of connection we have. All that time apart and I can still see right into your head, just like I could when we were young.'

If my jaw drops, it's because he's just reminded me he's the biggest show off in the area. I'm not letting him get away with that. 'Actually, if we're talking about limelight hoggers, at school you'd do *anything* to get people to notice you. So how are you any different from Luc, then?'

He sounds thoughtful. 'From what you say, with Luc it's all about having an audience to make him feel good.'

'What, and you *don't* show off?' Back in the day, the more the outrage, the better he liked it.

He wrinkles his nose. 'As a teenager I admit my life was a total disaster area, with *everyone* enjoying ringside seats. But I swear, I've never been about grabbing attention. Apart from the business publicity, obviously, which is completely different.'

I have to challenge him here. 'So that time when your dad's brand-new car was lost at sea and it was all over the papers? You parking it on the beach and letting it float away wasn't exactly ticking the no publicity box. So how do you explain that one? Perhaps it's time to tell me now.'

'I knew you were going to drag that up again.' There's a long groan, then he pulls in a breath. 'I told you he deserved it. There's a context. He'd gone off with someone else, my mum was distraught, he was doing his darnedest to avoid paying maintenance. When your dad puts a hatchet through your family, it's bad enough. When he stamps all over it, then decides he wants nothing more to do with you, first it rips your heart out. When you finally get to the part where you're having to sell up and move, it makes you *so* angry you want to find a way of hitting back at him where it hurts most.

Which was exactly why I chose his new Beamer to do it.'

However much he claims things were out in the open back then, the only part of that lot that made the news was the reckless teen and the BMW getting towed back to shore. 'Did it help at all?' Even as I ask, I'm aching inside for that younger, wounded Rory.

He shrugs. 'It was beyond awesome seeing the salt water swirling onto his leather seats. He got the message he was a bastard. That was enough for me.'

I'm still puzzled, though. 'And what about the rest of the car wrecks that had your name on?'

This time his grin is broad, but very guilty. 'One was me recreating the last scene from *Harold and Maud*. The one where the car goes over the cliff and you think Harold's gone with it. Then you realise he's actually jumped out and he's walking off into the distance playing his guitar.' He gives an eye-roll. 'I was filming it, but the camera stopped running.' That sounds about right.

'Jeez, Rory.' Seeing super-confident Rory cringing with embarrassment is a whole new experience for me. I'm ashamed to admit I'm enjoying it. 'And the others?'

He's serious again. 'They were just a crazy, rather lonely sixteen-year-old trying to find some way to amuse himself on Friday nights to dull the pain.' This time there's something so desolate in his voice that my heart is squishing for him.

'I'm sorry you had such a shit time. I can't believe that all anyone saw was the bravado.' However much I want to squeeze his arm, I'm resisting. If I'm thinking I'd like to pat his leg, I'm not actually admitting it, even to myself.

He gives a disgruntled snort. 'Just because I'm a guy, doesn't mean I don't feel stuff.'

I ease my fingers between my thighs and the seat upholstery, and jam my legs down to keep my hands safely out of the way. 'I know that. In some ways my little brothers were a lot softer than my sister and me. You did a great job of hiding it, though.'

He sighs. 'You too. Except you couldn't hide it from *me*. The fact we were both hurting set us apart from other people. That was why we got on so well.'

'What?' I'm not sure I follow him.

'Don't get me wrong. Other people had it tough. Poppy never had a dad and Immie's family were mainly at the Goose and Duck or down the police station. But the two of us started off with happy family units and then they broke. My dad walked out of ours and your sister dying smashed yours to pieces. As we both know, there's nothing quite like the pain from that kind of family fracture.' He's frowning now. 'Every morning after Freya died, I'd get on that school bus and there you'd be, looking so utterly alone and miserable.'

'Who, *me*?' I remember feeling detached, but I wasn't aware I was so pathetic.

'It wasn't the kind of sad you'd get from lost homework, it was more a kind of heart- wrenching desolation you get from being completely crushed inside.' From the way he's screwing his face up, he's struggling to remember. 'I had to try to brighten your day. I couldn't not cheer you up.'

Cheer me up? 'By teasing the living daylights out of me?' My voice is squeaking with amazement.

'I couldn't think what else to do. It was just a way to make you feel better, that's all. It was only because I cared. The same way I still care, which is why I'm helping you out with the weddings.' He shakes his head. 'I can't believe you didn't know all this before?'

And I can't quite believe what he's saying. Or that he's so open, when it comes to stuff like this. 'At least your claims of being able to see into my head are exaggerated,' I say, as he revs the engine.

As he pulls back onto the lane, he turns to look at me again. 'Just promise me you'll be careful, Berry. You're way too special to end up with the wrong guy.'

And for a split-second flash, I suddenly catch what the whole of the rest of the world see in his eyes. They're kind of dark and deep, but unnervingly vulnerable. Both at the same time, that's pretty unusual. The kind of cocoa colour that makes the pit of your stomach melt. If it's on a chocolate cake, obviously. If I never got it before, it's because I was never careless enough to properly look into them. I send a mental note to myself – *definitely do not let this happen again*. Hot syrup in your toes is no state to be in when you're supposed to be getting out of the car approximately zero minutes from now and walking like a sensible person.

'Hey, it's the Manor. We're here.' I know I'm stating the obvious. Twice over. But there are some moments you can't move on from fast enough. And this is one of them.

Chapter 23

Wednesday 13th December
At Rose Hill Manor: Magnetism and stunning views

I peer through the bare branches as we continue down the kind of tree-lined drive you get in films, and I can completely see why people choose to get married at the Manor. When I get as far as the part where I remember that in two days' time I'll be taking pictures of not one wedding here but two, for a second I forget to breathe. There's just a glimpse of the lake, reflecting the grey clouds racing above, then a second later we come to the mellow stone house that's large enough to cause my mouth to drop open. But somehow the irregular windows and a slate roof that's still shining from the last rain shower make it warm and very welcoming. When I finally get my breath back enough to get some words out, it's hard to know what to say.

'It's beautiful. But somehow it looks really different from the photos I've been looking at.' Jules gave me access to his portfolio of Manor weddings so I could check out his favourite and signature views.

Rory laughs. 'That's because they were mostly taken either on sunny days or in deep snow.' He's picking up my confusion. 'No need to look so surprised. Jules knows the value of a well briefed assistant. He sent those pictures to me too.'

I try not to feel put out by this as the tyres crunch through the gravel and we veer round to the front of the house. It's not as if I want ownership of this stand-in photographer role. In fact, the more responsibility that lands on someone else the better. It's just I'd rather it was *anyone* other than Rory I was sharing it with. Talking of whom, he's just ignored all the car parking signs and pulled into a prime spot by the lovely wide front door, which is flanked by two elegantly narrow Christmas trees.

'Shouldn't we be round the side with the rest of the vehicles?' I caught sight of them clustered down in the courtyard by the coach house as we swept in.

'It might have escaped you, but we've got a *baby* on board, HB.' He looks at me as if I'm mad not to get the significance as he jumps down from the car. 'If that doesn't entitle us to priority parking, nothing will. Seeing you're staying at Jess's, we're practically friends and family anyway. Talking of which, how's Uncle Bart's proposal coming along?' Ending his case with a complete flip of subject is what he does.

Given the whole of St Aidan's following events in Klosters on a minute-by-minute basis, I'm not exactly breaking a confidence by updating him. 'Jess came out of the balcony hot tub yesterday evening and found a six foot chocolate fountain installed by the fire. You know how amazing Swiss chocolate is?' I break off to swallow my drool. 'But despite dipping exotic fruit slices in it for an entire evening, she's still ring free.'

Rory laughs. 'If I know Bart, he'll be making her work for her diamonds. That way she'll appreciate it more when she finally gets them.'

This is the difference between lovely, anonymous London and St Aidan. I try not to shudder at the way everyone here not only has an opinion, but feels entirely free to express it. Instead I grab my bags as Rory goes into the back of the beer-mobile and unclips Teddie. 'Not taking him inside in his seat?'

Rory gives a grin. 'I'm actually finding, so long as there's not too much screaming, a man with a baby in his arms gets a universally great reception. You know what I'm like. We might as well turn the negatives into positives.' He slings the nappy bag over his shoulder, pulls Teddie onto his hip and strides the few yards towards the house.

I'm opening and closing my mouth as I run to keep up. 'You're taking the changing stuff too?'

He glances over his shoulder. 'Hell, yes. The more hands-on you look, the better the impact.'

As he opens the door for me, I wander into a fabulous high hallway with the kind of curving staircase I dream of walking down when I'm having a Cinderella moment. Not that I've had many of those in real life. When we went to Luc's smart work's balls, he'd always go on ahead of me to chat with his contacts. Any 'entrances' I made were more me creeping out of the lift on my own, trying not to get lost and accidentally crash into the kitchens. I was more concerned about checking I didn't have my tulle petticoats tucked into my Brazilians than making a big impression.

'Wow.' Two paces into the hall I stop. The half decorated Christmas tree I'm staring up at has to be almost as big as the one at St Pancras. 'Black and white too. That really works.' I'm thinking out loud again. Despite my determination to avoid everything festive, I can't help feeling a little rush of excitement. I'm looking up at two girls in dungarees on high step ladders, hanging baubles and striped bows in the upper branches. By the time I've finished my gasps of awe they're already back at ground level, cooing over Teddie. I try to ignore the 'told you so' grin Rory is giving me over the top of their heads.

As the girls fuss Teddie, Rory plays along until he gets bored. Approximately ten seconds. Then he carries on talking to me. 'So, lots of potential for shots on the stairs. And the brides both arriving together in the same horse drawn cart should be great too, even if there won't be as much snow as there was in Jules's shots of last year's Christmas wedding.' That was when Sera's sister Alice got married in three foot snowdrifts the morning after a blizzard, and needless to say Jules's pictures from that are amazing. 'As for the black and white, they're St Aidan rugby-team colours. Travis and Taylor both play for them. That's how I know them.'

I've a vague recollection of Rory being as outstanding at sport as he was at everything else. Waving silverware over his head up on the school stage. Team captain, collecting trophies in assembly. Probably one more reason they forgave him for the rest. 'Do you still play, then?' I'm not sure I've heard him using rugby as an excuse to dump the kids.

For a second a shadow passes across his face, then he brightens again. 'It's been a while. I'm too busy topping up St Aidan's alcohol supplies these days. Award winning Mad Elf doesn't make itself, you know.' Although, to be picky, there's been precious little evidence of Rory spending time at the brewery these last two weeks, so there has to be a workforce doing it for him. He waves his free hand towards the landing. 'Sophie and Saffy will get ready upstairs. Bridesmaids are in black, by the way, brides in white. Then they'll make the hundred yard journey from the front door to the other side of the house with their dad, driven by Ken and Gary, pulled by Nuttie. There will be more fabulous photo opportunities for you there too.'

'Great.' I'm blinking at how well briefed he is and reminding myself to check out Jules's vantage points when we go back outside. 'Let's hope Ken's feeling less reckless than the day they gave me a lift in the cart, or the brides might end up in the lake.'

Rory ignores that comment and carries on. 'The ceremonies are in the Winter Garden, which due to the sheer number of guests is also going to be used as a bar area later.' He smiles down at the girls as he practically has to wrench Teddie away. 'If you'll excuse us, we need to carry on with our tour.'

We make our way past stacks of chairs and piles of boxes waiting to be unpacked. As we reach some wonderfully airy rooms with French windows looking out across the lake, I can't help comparing. 'Not many living rooms are the size of Luc's loft ... but I reckon these are bigger.'

Rory frowns at me. 'I thought we just agreed you were

going to forget about Luc?'

'What?' Were we even in the same conversation back there? I'm about to ask where the hell he got that impression from when something beyond the torn checks of Rory's threadbare shirt catches my eye. Through some open doors there's a room that makes Luc's flat look doll's house- sized. 'Flaming Ada, is *that* the ... ?'

Rory's voice is calming. 'Okay, Holly Berry, there's no need to hyperventilate. It's only a ballroom. With tables laid out to seat two hundred, for a five-course silver-service meal. And don't worry, the Winter Garden is nothing like as huge.'

Two hundred? Would that be guests? There's a blue linen sofa in front of one of the French windows, and somehow I manage to stagger across and sink down onto it before my jelly legs give way completely.

When my voice comes out, it's a rasp. 'It's *so* much bigger than the Lifeboat Station wedding. And that amazing Christmas tree is only the start. It's all going to be so posh and proper ... and *mahoosive* ...'

As he stoops down and bumps the changing bag down next to me, Rory's voice is low. 'I know it's big and I know it's daunting. But look at it this way. You won't be taking any more pictures than you took at the other wedding. There's potential for fabulous shots wherever you are, here, in or out of the house. I'll line everything up for you, tell you where to be and what to take. All you have to do is look through the viewfinder and click the button.' The resonance of his voice is incredibly soothing. He's almost talked me down here. 'I know it's a double wedding, but ...'

'Aaaaaaaarghhhhh! ...' My howl is because I'd momentarily managed to forget the worst part. And he just reminded me.

There's a scuffling and a crowd of people with inquisitive looks on their faces arrives in the ballroom doorway. 'Everything okay there?'

However wretched I feel, I'm determined that the wedding photographer having a meltdown at the Manor will not be what people are going to be discussing over their cottage pie, sugar snap peas and carrots when they go home this evening.

'Absolutely fine.' I'm lying and croaking at the same time. But the important thing is, I'm holding it together. 'We're just on our way out to get some air ...' I'm bobbing my head so hard at the French windows, trying to get Rory to take the hint, I feel like one of those nodding dogs.

At last he gets it. 'Great. Next job, then.' He sends a smile to the watching hoard. 'We'll get out of your way and check out the views of the lake from the terrace.'

There's a pause, then a hesitant voice. 'Is that a baby you've got there?'

Then another. 'Are you a stay-at-home dad, then?'

Rory looks delighted they've noticed. 'Obviously I'm not a complete stay-at-home person, because I'm out and about, aren't I? And actually I'm the uncle.' He's so pleased, he's almost simpering. 'This is Teddie and if you'd like to meet him, he loves to say "hello".'

If that was meant to be the signal for the crowd to storm forward, it worked. It's more of a stampede than a rush. Don't ask me why one pudgy baby is so much more interesting than setting out a stately home ballroom for a wedding, even if he is beaming around at everyone. Whatever, by the time we push through the doors and back into the cold afternoon, it's a whole lot later. By this time I feel grim rather than desperate. And I'm seeing that what Rory says about the opportunity for fabulous pictures is as true as what he says about the baby thing.

The terrace has lanterns along the edge of the time-worn stone flags and hanging strings of bulbs defining the outdoor areas, which are going to be fabulous at night. I can see by looking in from the outside that the Winter Garden and ballroom have wonderful floor-to-ceiling windows, the stone-work and doorways are lovely, there are gazebos in the distance, and woodland and the drive. And then there's the backdrop of the lake, which makes me go wobbly all over again, but this time in a good way.

Rory's blowing out his cheeks and pulling Teddie's hood up to shelter him from the wind. 'So would you like to try taking a few pictures?'

I pull a face. Somewhere so big, we can't possibly cover every potential shot like we did at Port Giles. Somehow, even trying a few feels like it might jinx me for the real thing. It might be best to come at it completely fresh. 'Thanks. But I think I'd rather just turn up on the day and go for it. So I'm pretty much done here.'

He nods. 'I get that. At least you've got a feel for the place now. We can walk back round to the car the way the carriage is going to drive.' There's a smile playing around his lips. 'You wouldn't happen to be hurrying back because you heard Poppy's got chocolate cake baking?'

I almost melt again. 'She has?' My mouth's already watering. I haven't actually eaten since my croissant-fest when I was getting ready for Marilyn, which feels like days ago now, even if it was only early this morning. 'In that case, maybe we'd better hurry back.'

As we reach the car, Teddie is obviously missing his audience. When Rory slides him into the back of the car he starts to whinge. By the time Rory's lining him up with his car seat, he's screaming and kicking and holding his body rigid.

In mid-struggle Rory suddenly stops and stares back at me over his shoulder. 'Don't have kids with Luc, Holly Berry, have them with me.' He *so* knows how to wind me up. If this is his way of taking my mind off the wedding stress, it isn't going to work. Nothing's going to do that.

His comment's not even worthy of a dismissive snort. 'Eff off, Rory.' I'm careful to avoid meeting his gaze directly.

He's grinning now. 'Our kids would be awesome. We could even train them so we didn't have to put our knees in their stomachs to get their car seat straps done up.' Somewhere along the line, with the whole baby-adoration thing, Rory's definitely lost the plot.

'Sorry to be the one to point this out, but seeing you don't have relationships or girlfriends, you having kids won't actually be happening.' Which reminds me, I need to check out why that is at some point. Although definitely not now. Thank jeez I'm saved that one. However, I realise as I say it that Erin's managed to have children all on her own. Who's to say Rory couldn't find a surrogate or even adopt at some point if he wanted to?

His bottom lip is close to jutting. 'With the kids, though, I really don't mean to be this shit. I thought it would be the one thing I could do. At this rate they'll be home before Gracie's even smiled.' He couldn't sound any more defeated.

He's not wrong about the first bit, but at least I can offer some comfort on the Gracie front. 'She nearly smiled when the big dwarf produced her snowman.'

'Yes, but she didn't really.' He gives a sigh. 'She doesn't even like me. If she doesn't have to hold my hand for health and safety reasons, she won't come anywhere near me.' The look on his face is so genuinely sad, my chest is contracting.

'You could always get an Olaf costume?' That's a joke to cover up the awful sensation of wanting to reach out and pat him again. 'But seriously, Gracie's away from her mum and old enough to know it. She's bound to be unsettled.'

'It still makes me feel like a total failure.' As he gets behind the wheel again, he couldn't look more dejected.

'I'm sorry if I was mean to you before. I just thought if you embraced the kids instead of fighting them, you'd all enjoy it more.'

He smiles wanly. 'You're right, though. I couldn't be any more crap at it. Every single thing they need it's down to me to provide it. It's way more full on than I ever imagined.'

It's way easier to sympathise with him when he's admitting he's finding it tough, than when he's acting like a know-it-all uncle-of-the-year. 'Don't be too hard on yourself. It's a lot to take on two kids when you have no experience. Whatever I say, I'm damned sure I couldn't do it.' I'm racking my brains for something positive to suggest. 'Story-telling might help.

I'll look out for books when I go back to town. Or you might find some ideas on Google.' This time my hands are wedged safely under my bum. And as we pull back out into the lane, I'm poised for his Supernanny snipes.

But he just gives a shrug and a sigh. 'Maybe we'll all feel better after cake in Poppy's kitchen.'

And possibly for the first time ever, I agree with him.

Chapter 24

Wednesday 13th December
In Poppy's kitchen at Daisy Hill farm: Sweet spots and
roast potatoes

'Someone's been busy with the decorations. Did you ever see so many hearts in one place?'

Okay, I know the girl who's banned herself from thinking about Christmas shouldn't be enthusing. But seeing as I love Poppy so much, it's hard not to. Since I was last in the kitchen at Daisy Hill Farm, a whole load of garlands have been strung around the walls, with so many wicker hearts and hessian bows it looks as though someone grabbed the Range's entire seasonal stock.

Poppy laughs. 'Rafe bought this lot to welcome me home last Christmas.' We can take it from this he was ecstatic to see her come back then. But we all knew that already.

Immie's looking proud and she high fives Gracie, who breaks off from her felt tips and colouring for just long enough to oblige. 'Rafe, Gracie and I hung them up this afternoon while Pops was making the cakes for Sophie and Saffy. Seemed like a good idea to make the most of the quiet time before the pre-Christmas storm.' If she's referring to the next two weddings in terms of metaphorical bad weather, I'm with her on that.

I'm hazy about how things work at any wedding, let alone a double one. 'Is each couple having their own cake, then?' There are sponges on cooling trays and wrapped in cling film, lined up all along the granite work surface on the long side of the kitchen. If they're only having one cake between them, it's going to have at least ten tiers.

Poppy smiles. 'They're two sets of twins, but they've got very different tastes. Sophie and Taylor are having plain sponge, covered in buttercream icing, with fruit decoration. And Saffy and Travis have gone for nude chocolate cake, with fresh-cream filling and flowers. Four tiers each.' She's got her feet up on the sofa and she's rubbing her bump. Although she can't have been sitting down for long.

Rory puts Teddie's chair down by the sofa, then goes to inspect the line of cakes. 'Did you mention an extra one?' He's slightly later coming in as he took Teddie back to Home Brew Cottage for a nappy change.

We women all grin at each other, but Immie takes pity on him first. 'Your cake's waiting over by the Aga, next to the pile of plates.' She passes him a knife as she heads for the kettle. 'You do the honours and cut it up and I'll pour the tea.'

You have to have tasted Poppy's chocolate cake to know how delicious it is. This one's got a tiny bit of orange zest in the deep layers of dark-chocolate sponge to remind us about our five a day, and a splash of Cointreau to soften the lashings of pale-chocolate buttercream. At dusk on a windy winter's afternoon, there couldn't be better pick-me-up. As I close my eyes and let the icing melt on my tongue, it transports me to my own personal heaven. I completely forget that Luc's probably packing his suitcase as we chew. That there are still four brides and weddings to negotiate before I can finally get properly stuck into my *Friends* boxed set. And that Rory's given up annoying the hell out of me and started worrying about the kids instead. Although it's not long before the man himself crashes very rudely into my momentary happiness bubble. After two monster slices of cake, Rory's obviously forgotten all about being a down-hearted loser of an uncle and he's back to his high-energy positive self.

'So I was looking on BuzzFeed just now when I was changing Teddie. Apparently you can actually incorporate babies in your home-fitness workouts.'

Immie looks impressed. 'Reading during nappy changes? That's from the advanced course. Sounds like you cracked the multi-tasking thing, then.'

He rubs his forearm, then bends down to where Teddie is sitting in his bouncy chair and holds up his tiny hand to give him a mini high-five. 'Slinging this little guy around all day really tones the muscles. But baby gym takes it one step further.'

I squint at him, because I can't quite believe what I'm hearing. 'Please tell me, you *are* joking?'

'Keep up, Supernanny. *You* were the one who suggested checking out Google. *All* the celebrity dads are using their babies instead of weights. I've seen the pictures. There's exercises for core fitness, upper body, legs and chests. Apparently the kids love it.'

I can't stop myself from stating the obvious. 'But you just stuffed your face with cake, Rory.'

He doesn't flinch. 'Teddie and I will easily work that off later. Although, realistically, running around after these two …' His all-encompassing nod includes Gracie. 'I reckon I burn more calories than a lumberjack. I might need to take some cake with me when we go back to the cottage, just so I don't fade away before morning.'

From the way Immie's eyebrows have shot upwards, she's as appalled as me. 'You can't treat babies like dumbbells. You will be careful not to drop him?'

'Obviously.' Rory rolls his eyes. 'What these famous dads are simply pointing out to the rest of us guys is that parenting doesn't have to be all misery. Approached in the right way, it can be fun too. I might even blog about it. Baby at the Brewery would go down a storm on the Roaring Waves website. I don't know why I didn't think of that angle before.'

'How much longer have you got them for?' Poppy's asked the question we're all thinking as we shake our heads at each other.

Rory wrinkles his nose doubtfully. 'After a bit of a setback post-op, Erin's now recovering well. So only a few more days, I think. Once we're all having a good time, it'll whizz by.'

'So how about Christmas?' Poppy's done it again and put my thoughts into words. Not that I should even be interested. 'Everyone's coming here for a huge Christmas Day feast. We're starting with cocktails in the orangery, then having lunch at a huge table in the drawing room, in front of a roaring log fire, with dancing in the evening. You will come too, won't you, Rory?' The searching stare she gives me tells me she hasn't completely accepted my decision to spend the day in my attic. 'Let's face it, no one who's tasted Rafie's rosemary and goose-fat roasties would refuse *that* invitation.' She gives me another significant frown.

Immie leans back, pats a stomach that's almost as big as Poppy's and groans. 'I'm already dreaming of your flaming plum pudding drenched in rum sauce with a splash of cream. With your Christmas pudding ice cream melting over it.'

Rory pulls down the corners of his mouth. 'Thanks for the kind invite, Pops. You know I'm the biggest fan of Rafe's crispy Maris Pipers. And I'll definitely stay to see Holly through the last of Jules's weddings.'

Poppy ponders. 'That's Seth and Katie's alpine wedding in the barn on Monday. Are you invited to that one too?'

Rory looks like he's racking his brains to consult his mental diary. 'You're right, I think I am. My sixth wedding in 2017. No wonder I can't keep up.' Unbelievably he's snaffling *yet another* slice of chocolate cake, pushing crumbs into his mouth as he carries on. 'But as far as Christmas goes, once I get the kids back to Erin, so long as the warehouses are full enough to keep St Aidan's wine flowing for the full festive season, I promised to head to Bristol to catch up with the old crew over there.' It's exactly the kind of on-the-run, no-commitment arrangement Rory specialises in. So no one looks surprised he hasn't accepted Poppy's invite.

I know the guy drives me round the bend. And admittedly, I'd do anything to avoid being in the same room as him. But suddenly hearing Rory won't be around on Christmas Day leaves me feeling like all my stuffing's dropped out. Which would be really silly at the best of times. Considering I won't even be there myself, it's doubly ridiculous.

'So when are you getting your Christmas tree, Poppy?' Okay. I'm doing my best to avoid trees and Christmas. But I'm blurting out nonsense just to cover up that I'm feeling like shit for no reason. It has to be this damned wedding stress that's making me wobble all over the place.

Poppy gives me yet another stare, which is hard enough to let me know my floppy insides aren't quite as private as I'd like them to be. 'The Aga keeps the kitchen so hot, we're waiting until next week for the tree. This way we'll actually have some needles left on for Christmas.'

Surprisingly Rory's joining in this conversation. 'Did you decide on a blue spruce in the end, Pops?'

The words 'blue spruce' sliding into the conversation oh-so casually almost make me drop my tea mug. 'You can get those around here?' If I sound incredulous, it's only because of the trouble I had sourcing one for Luc's loft apartment last year. It seems strange now to think at the time I couldn't make do with anything less than those gorgeous muted blue-green branches. My elaborate tartan and stag-themed decorations were such an important part of the build-up to our Christmas trip to Luc's parents in Scotland. Although finding a blue spruce big enough was bound to be difficult. There's not much demand for ten foot Christmas trees of any kind in central London. As for getting it up the stairwell, that was another story entirely.

Rory's grinning. 'It's my thank you to Rafe and Poppy for helping me out. Any kind of tree – you name it, I'm your man.' He hesitates for a second, then thinks better of it and continues. 'Well, not *me* exactly. But my mate has the biggest Christmas tree farm in the South West. With hundreds and thousands of trees, you can't go wrong.'

Rory and his endless connections. No surprise there, then. As for me, my plans for a Christmas-free December are slowly being eroded. It's suddenly uncomfortably full of festivity.

When I'm not having a tree at all this year, it's hard to imagine being back in the kind of place where a plain old green tree was entirely out of the question. My boxes of decorations are in piles in that storage unit. It might not just be for this year, either. The way things are going, I can't see what's ever going to change. As I realise I may never get to open them again, the sweet taste of chocolate on my teeth takes on a strangely sour tang. When I get to thinking about how long it took me to tie enough purple and green-checked bows for an entire ten foot tree, my mouth waters even more. I'm remembering haring along Oxford Street in the rain and the dark because I'd run out of ribbon late on a Saturday afternoon, and I wanted to get the tree finished to surprise Luc when he came back from his golfing with the guys. The colours of Poppy's kitchen are blurring in front of my eyes, like the reflections of the festive lights were on the wet pavements that day. There's a strangled ache in my throat and a pool of saliva under my tongue. As my face crumples, I'm looking down, watching a big splash of water spreading out on the rough-hewn wood of the tabletop.

Immie's first to notice. 'Elephant balls, what are those tears doing on your plate? Are you *crying*, Holly?'

I'm wiping my sleeve across my cheek and sniffing at the same time. 'It's only because my stags won't get to come out.' My New Look acrylic sleeve is doing a crap job when it comes to soaking up the damp. I've no idea why I'm sobbing about stag decorations I only got last year. 'And I won't get to see my fairy lights either ...' I'm gulping in air as I snivel.

Immie's on her feet and as her arms close around me, she pulls my nose against her sweatshirt and I'm engulfed in the sweet scent of lily-of-the-valley fabric conditioner. 'Babe, come here, it'll feel better after a nice cup of ... er ...' If she was about to suggest tea, that boat already sailed.

Poppy's flowery apron-covered bump is nudging my elbow. 'Kitchen roll, Hols?'

My nod is as disgustingly feeble as my mouse voice. 'Thanks, Pops ... I'm just missing my cherubs, that's all ... and my knitted Santas might get eaten by mice before I even get to unpack them again ...' I grasp the fistful of paper towel Poppy pushes into my hand. At least my massive nose blow is less wimpish. 'It's why I wanted to stay away from Christmas this year ...'

'How about more chocolate?'

The slice of cake Rory's chopping is the size Freya used to put out for Santa when she'd set her heart on something really humungous. Somehow the size matches the desperation in his eyes. The year she decided she wanted a real-life gypsy caravan, she insisted on leaving an entire quarter of cake, even though we both knew the truth about who Santa was by then. That was the Christmas we realised how good her forward planning was. Ordering ahead for when we could go off on our own as teenagers and be nomads. Afterwards, I don't think my dad ever forgave himself for disappointing her that year. I don't think she really minded getting a garden shed version instead. It even had wheels. My dad's little joke. The only drawback was, they weren't attached, so it wouldn't roll. Not that it mattered at all, seeing she'd neglected to ask for a pony to go with it. It was so much more out there than the art set and sparkly tights I'd asked for. That was the great thing about her. She had the imagination to have really big dreams. So even if she only made it halfway, the results were still pretty spectacular.

I dig up my sleeve, pull out a tissue and scrape it over my eyes. 'Thanks Rory, but I'm good. I've already had two slices.'

If that's a disappointed shrug, he soon turns it into a grin as he whisks the plate away. 'I'll take care of the cake, then. I'm sorry, Panda Eyes, if I'd known you were having crises with Christmas, I'd never have mentioned spruce of any colour. Especially not blue.'

It takes a second to sink in. 'My eyeliner's run?'

He's laughing. 'Only a bit, it's nothing to worry about.' Which obviously means it is.

Although, what's needling me more is him being observant enough to know exactly the words that had set me off. 'I thought we'd agreed before that you *couldn't* see into my head?'

He purses his lips. 'Mostly not. This must have been an

exceptionally transparent exception.' He lifts his eyebrows. 'Anyway, enough about you, Berry. This is way more important. I've found a way to stop Teddie screaming when he has his nappy changed. At least, it worked just before.'

Immie's straight in there. 'Never. This I must see.'

Poppy's laughing. 'Are you sure it's not just a fluke?'

'A one-off accident, perhaps. I was flicking through my YouTube favourites earlier.' Rory looks supremely confident as he slides his iPad out of his windcheater pocket. 'Dad's Rock blog talks about babies having sweet spots. And Teddie's just happens to be Rufus Hound dancing to Cheryl Cole's *Fight For This Love*. Remember the one ... Red Nose Day, 2010?'

Now I'm the one frowning. 'That big guy with splits in his trousers taking the mick out of our Cheryl's soldier dance? Why is *that* in your favourites list?' This guy never ceases to amaze me.

'Because it's funny?' Rory has the decency to look mildly ashamed. 'Teddie's obviously inherited my sense of humour, even if you don't share it.'

'Let's see then ...' Any way of moving on from spruce blues and wet screwed-up hankies, I'll take it.

'Okay.' Rory's holding his iPad in front of Teddie in his bouncing chair. As the first bars strike up and Cheryl begins to sing, there's no reaction at all from Teddie.

Immie's leaning in. 'A bearded guy with lipstick, a red jacket with braid and buttons ... and army boots with a thong sticking out of the top of his low slung trousers? And girls dressed as boys?' She sounds mystified. 'There's a lot of mixed gender messages there.'

Poppy joins her. 'There's plenty of stamping and gyrating and flashing spotlights. From the roaring, the Red Nose crowd like it, even if Teddie's not sure.'

I'm dancing at the side, singing along. 'We're gonna fight, fight, fight, fight, fight for this love, we're gonna fight, fight ...' I catch Rory's smirk. 'What? It's one of my girlie tunes, okay. I'm kind of with Teddie on this. It's just a pity he isn't ...' I'm about to say 'joining in ...' when Teddie gives a yell.

The next moment, he begins to kick. His eyes have gone all starry and big, and he's holding both hands out towards the iPad, opening and closing his fingers.

Poppy and Immie stand back in awe and watch. Meanwhile never being one to sit on the sidelines and miss out on this track, I'm dancing and smiling down at Teddie. As I hold a hand out to Gracie, she carefully puts the top on her felt tip. Then she slips down from the chair, comes and holds my hand and dances too.

Then the music comes to an abrupt stop. In the sudden silence we all stare at each other, surprised smiles on our faces.

'How amazing was that?' Poppy laughs.

'Could two minutes, twenty two seconds of respite be any sweeter?' Rory couldn't be looking more pleased if Bad Ass Santa beer had won a medal for best Christmas ale of the decade. 'That's long enough for anyone to change a baby – even me.'

Immie's puzzling. 'Fascinating to see a baby being so impressed by the tribal beat and warlike imagery.'

We all turn to stare at her together. 'What?'

As Gracie tilts her head at me, her expression is solemn. 'Why have you got black on your eyes?'

'Damn.' I'd almost forgotten. I'm rubbing my lashes, opening my mouth to explain, when Rory gives a shout.

'Everyone ready? One more time!' And then he presses play and a second later we're all dancing again.

Chapter 25

Friday 15th December
At Brides by the Sea: Fur coats and twinkly surprises

'Breakfast, eaten ... batteries, cameras, memory cards, packed ... whistle and bells at the ready?' Rory's standing by the desk in the White Room, ticking items off on his fingers. It's the morning of the double wedding, and if he's eager to be off, it's because he's got to run me over to the Manor, then come back to St Aidan to catch up with the groom's party, who are having breakfast down at the Surf Shack. Since I met Sophie and Saffy yesterday when they came in to pick up their dresses, I'm actually more worried than ever. Ordinary would be easier to cope with. Two gorgeous blondes, with more swishy hair than on the L'Oréal advert, and the longest legs on the beach would be scary at the best of times. When you've got to take their pictures of them both getting married, it's mind blowing.

'All done.' Somehow my heartbeat is too shallow and fast to manage anything more than a whisper. 'Although do we need the bells?' I didn't even think about using them at the

Lifeboat Station. Every ounce of weight we can cut down on counts over a day as long as this one's going to be.

'We'll take them.' That's my protest silently overruled then. 'There's even a dusting of snow back in the village. It couldn't be more perfect. So in that case ...' He looks at his phone to check the time.

I'm willing *anything* to happen to put off the moment when we have to leave for the Manor. So when the shop door slams and the bells on the Christmas tree in the hall jingle I'm giving silent cheers. A second later, as a caped figure powers past the Louis Quatorze chairs so fast the dresses on the rail are flapping in her wake, I make a quick readjustment. That was me wishing for anything. Except *this*.

'Marilyn? Are you here to see Poppy?' If Poppy had suspected a visit from Marilyn, she'd definitely be here. Too late I remember my shop manners. 'And wonderful to see you, obviously.'

'Rory, what a lovely surprise to see my *favourite* boy here.' Marilyn pushes straight past me and practically sweeps her favourite off his feet as she clamps her lips to his cheek. Then she steps back and begins to stroke his hair, her bracelets clinking. 'I hope you're taking good care of that poorly head of yours? And how's your wine business and your lager making? I hear you've created Seth some all of his own?'

Rory finally seizes a gap to reply. 'We're certainly doing Seth and Katie their own extra- special beer labels for the wedding.' Having sprinkled enough sparkle on that, he springs back to a safe distance behind the table and turns to me. 'Seth and I go way back. So how can we help you today, Marilyn?'

If he's stealing my lines, I'm not about to complain.

Marilyn leans in as close as the tabletop will allow, talking in a dramatic, confidential whisper. 'I need to borrow Katie's dress for half an hour, to organise a last minute surprise. There are some darling fur jackets and I want to see which goes best.'

Knowing the unwelcome shocks Marilyn's previous surprises usually turn out to be, I'm hesitating. 'I think I'd need to check that with Sera or Poppy first. And they're not here yet.'

As Marilyn draws in a breath her nostrils flare and her light purr changes to a growl. 'I've already paid for the dress. Personally. *In full*. I fail to see how I need anyone's permission to take it where the hell I want when it's actually my property.' She fumbles in her bag, then slams a piece of paper on the desk. 'Here's the receipt. You can't argue with that.'

Rory's pointing at his phone. 'If we could possibly speed this along? We do have a wedding to get to, Berry.'

As Marilyn butts in, she's stabbing the air with her finger. 'My car's blocking the mews. *No one's* going *anywhere* until I have *my* dress.' No pressure there, then.

'Okay.' Put like that, I'm not sure what else I can do. 'I'll get it now.'

I dash into the room next to the kitchen, where it's hanging in its cover, ready for steaming, and check the label, and that it's the right one.

As I whoosh back into the White Room Marilyn's beatific smile returns. 'Good girl. Well done for that, Berry.'

I have to correct her. 'Sorry, I'm not Berry, I'm Holly.'

She's beaming as she wrenches the hanger out of my hand.

'But Berry suits your rosy complexion and shiny nose *so* much better. Don't worry, I'll have it back in a twinkling.' And a moment later she's stamping out past the Christmas tree, dress bag flying behind her.

As the shop door slams shut, Rory picks up the bags. 'Right. Lights, camera, action?'

I put my hands to my face, cursing myself for skimping on the Red Alert layers. 'Maybe I need more … ?'

He cuts in. 'No time for toothpaste today. Or icing. You're fabulous just as you are. Come on, let's run.'

As the crisp morning breeze off the sea blows into my face as we step out onto the Mews, I can't help smiling when I notice the scarlet lipstick splash smeared across Rory's cheek. Nothing to do with Rory's throwaway compliment either. As far as that goes, he's full of bollocks. End of story. It'll just make a change for me not to have the reddest face in the car for once.

Chapter 26

Friday 15th December
The double wedding at Rose Hill Manor: Zoo animals and cool running

Sophie and Saffy marry Taylor and Travis

Three weddings in, I'm beginning to realise that each one is very different. As I make my way up the wide stairs at the Manor, even though I'm whooping inside because the centimetre of snow is still on the ground outside, my legs are so heavy it feels like it should be the end of the day, not the start. When I reach the first floor bedroom suite where the brides are getting ready, it's mayhem. The tasteful taupe and white decor is obliterated by strewn clothes, far flung suitcases, and more cosmetics and shoes than on the entire ground floor of Johnny Loulou's. But when I look through the viewfinder the mess captures the whole atmosphere of the morning so well, I lose no time in getting to work.

With six bridesmaids, two brides and at least as many again on hair and make-up you'd expect the excited chatter to be loud. When you add in the volume that comes from six empty Champagne bottles, all overlaid with a pounding dance music sound track, it's head splitting. Which reminds me, I never asked which hangover headache Marilyn was talking about when she rubbed Rory's head. But there's no time to think about that now. The good thing is, everyone's so preoccupied with eyeliner and hair tongs, they aren't taking any notice of me or my camera, so I snatch some lovely candid shots.

I'm quickly onto the dresses, shoes and the gorgeous flower posies. Christian Louboutins in the shop make my chest go tight. Coming across them outside the shop, times two, my heart misses a whole series of beats. The white lace and leather platform sandals, with silver threadwork, are Sophie's. Whereas Saffy's are elegant suede courts with diamond strings tracing out flower patterns, and slim heels that are so high they practically reach to heaven. As for the bouquets, the white roses and anemones with black centres, tied with black and white striped bows with trailing ribbon ties are pretty and striking at the same time. And the dresses, although very different, both have Sera's signature details of exquisite beading and the most amazing silk, lace and tulle. Cue more fabulous close-ups.

Even though they're still in their matching flowery silk dressing gowns, the bridesmaids are mostly wearing heels. They're so much taller than me in my leopard print flats, when I look up at the undersides of their perfectly made-up chins I feel like a dumpy elephant who took a wrong turn and ended up in the giraffe enclosure. That would be the young giraffe enclosure, by the way – these twenty-something goddess-girls seem light years younger than me. If I wasn't in such a rush, I'd stop and ask myself, when the hell did I get so old?

Air kisses in the mirror is the closest I can get to the super-glossy Sophie. Saffy, who's a lot less shiny and much more friendly, sends me a smile and a little wave as she peeps out from behind a hairdresser. There's a pile of blonde hair on a pop-up table, which she's somehow weaving into Saffy's own. As if she didn't have enough already. As soon as I'm sure I've taken a good selection of shots, I hurry downstairs, to make the most of the spaces before the guests arrive.

'Rory's completely right when he says that weddings at the Manor are a gift,' I say, as I come across Poppy, setting up her two cakes side by side on matching vintage dressing tables. I stop and watch as she adds the colourful fruit to the perfect ivory stack, with its buttercream smoothed into almost-stripes round the outside, then pounce with my camera.

She looks up as she moves across and scatters icing sugar over the towering chocolate cake, with its bulging cream filling. 'If you'd like a mini cupcake, help yourself from the tin.'

I don't need to be asked twice. 'This is one perk of the job I can live with.' I dive in and in the time it takes her to shake her sugar dust, I wolf down four. Then blame the numbers on the stress adrenalin.

Poppy looks up from arranging flowers on top of Saffy and Travis's cake. Her face breaks into a satisfied grin. 'There you go. I knew you'd start to love weddings if you came to enough of them.'

That makes me wrinkle my nose. 'So long as there are cupcakes, I adore them until the people arrive. Then I'm a lot less enthusiastic.'

Poppy hustles me away. 'Off you go.' She calls over her shoulder as I wander off. 'Don't worry about the kids either. Immie and Gracie were settling down to a *Frozen* fest as I left. Go and have fun with your empty venue. The Winter Garden is astonishing.'

The ceremony room she's talking about is every bit as beautiful as she promised. Poised and waiting, with its rows of chairs, and a snowstorm of rose and gypsophila posies tied to the row ends with black satin ribbons. There are huge glass and stainless steel lanterns with flickering candles and two lots of tables for the register signing, both with the word LOVE in big letters lit up with fairy lights. As I move into the ball-room next door with its fairy light clouds hanging from the high beams, I'm gasping at how pretty it is. There are long tables, and black and white flowers in narrow wooden boxes along the centres, with candles in jars clustered around them. And the black tablecloths, with white damask overlays, look stunning against the silver cutlery and shining glasses.

It's so peaceful as I photograph the table settings with their single white roses, and favour parcels tied with black and white bows, it almost feels like being in the studio at work. There are fifteen blissful minutes when I'm just thinking I might be able to do this, then there's a distant clatter of feet and the sound of laughing men. Next thing I know, a whole load of very familiar wedding suits are bursting in, headed by Taylor and Travis, with Rory coming at the end. I could have done without my stomach lurching at the sight of him in a tux. When I finally wrench my eyes away from him and look past them into the crowded room beyond, it's as if most of the guest list has followed them in from the car park. As I envisage bodies on all the seats, all needing to be captured in pixels, suddenly there doesn't seem to be enough oxygen in the air.

As Rory comes forward, he sweeps me into a squeeze that's as unexpected as it is unwelcome. 'Hey, Holly Berry, just the woman we're looking for. The guys want you to grab a few of their bromance poses out on the jetty. Please don't let them fall in the water. While you do that, I'll go and find the girls' mum, ready for the zipping-up shots.' I should tell him that hugs are off the table, and that anything other than that particular body spray would make life way easier for me. But before I get the chance, he's gone again.

That's the thing I'm getting to know about weddings. There are total mad times, where you get carried along by the whirl of events almost as if you're in a time slip. And then everything stops, and you're suddenly jerked back into real time again. The next time I drop to earth, we've done the brides getting dressed and caught some lovely shots coming down the Cinderella staircase, and we're outside on the drive. Everyone's ready, the guests are all waiting in the Winter Garden. I've taken what feels like a thousand shots of the girls and their dad getting into the very same cart I careered around town on two weeks ago. Only this time it's covered in flowers with the fairy lights. It looks fabulous being driven through a snow whitened landscape by Ken and Gary in their groomsmen suits and sharp overcoats, against the backdrop of the lake and the black and white hills above. Pulled by Nuttie, with bells on his harness, it's completely magical. With their flowing blonde hair and snowy dresses, snuggled in their fur wraps, the brides and their jacketed coachmen couldn't be any more picturesque.

We're within fifty yards of the ceremony when Sophie puts up one lace-gloved hand and makes Gary stop – no easy thing, as I know. Then she jumps down from the cart, with a shout of 'fag break!' Once I've got over the surprise, I hurry across to grab a few 'making it real' shots with Sophie, elbow against the cart in her own personal smoke cloud, while her dad stamps his feet beside her, his breath steaming in the air. Despite the freezing day, I'm making the most of this unscheduled breather, leaning against a tree at the back of the cart, panning round with my viewfinder, when I catch sight of Saffy tiptoeing towards me. As she goes right on past me, I call out to her in a low voice.

'Watch out for the mud, it's wet under the snow over there, Saffy.' It's the first thing I can think of to get her attention. Luckily it stops her.

As she teeters to a halt and stares over her shoulder, there's a glint of desperation in her eyes. 'What?'

'It'd be a shame to get dirt on those lovely Louboutins.' She was pale on the stairs, but now she's ghostly. 'Are you okay, Saffy?' I already know she isn't.

As she stops and turns, her face is haggard. 'Sophie hasn't smoked since she was eighteen, and *she's* the brave one. I've changed my mind. I can't do this. I think I'm going to slip away while I can.'

Exactly what I thought. 'Before you go ...' My heart sinks as I rack my brain for what to say. If I had to choose between a bride with cold feet or a dictator, I'd take the bridezilla every time. 'Just come here and talk to me.' If it takes a runner to recognise a runner, this one's already well on her way. 'So run it past me, remind me why you're making a mistake?'

She's hugging her arms around herself as she hops from foot to foot. 'When I woke up this morning I wasn't sure I could do it. Now I know I can't.'

I'm sure she probably knows this already. 'I once ran away from a wedding related moment, so I might understand.' I'm thinking of all the questions that have flooded through my mind since I ran away from Luc's proposal. 'If you're scared of committing to one person for your whole life, it's completely understandable. It's a huge thing ...' At least it was for me. I might as well bring it out in the open.

She gives a sniff. 'No, it's not that.'

When she doesn't say any more, I prompt her. 'So maybe you don't love Travis? Or you think he doesn't love you enough?' Another crucial one.

Saffy pushes a strand of fair hair off her forehead. 'No, I love him even more now than I ever have, if that's possible. We make a great team. And he'd do *anything* for me.' She gives a sigh. 'I'm just not sure I can do all ... this ...' As she stares down at herself, I completely get where she's coming from. If you're not seeing wedding gear every day, it comes as a complete shock when it's all on at the same time.

'From where I'm standing, so far it's all sounding good.'

Maybe this is a problem we can get over. I push her a bit more. 'So it doesn't scare you to think of waking up next to Travis every day for the rest of your life?' Another from my personal checklist.

A slightly dreamy look crosses her face. 'Not at all.'

I blow out my own mental sigh of relief and go in for the big one. 'And how would you feel if you woke up tomorrow and you realised you and Travis were actually married?'

She purses her lips as she thinks. 'Also okay. Actually, I'd be bloody relieved because it was all over.'

Now we're making progress. 'So it's just the wedding part you're having doubts about, not the marriage itself, or the groom?'

She nods quietly. 'The whole big double wedding was Sophie and Taylor's dream, not mine and Travis's. They're the boss twins. We're here because obviously they couldn't do it without us. I thought it would be fine, but now it's happening, it's just so scary and such a big deal when I'm not that kind of person. All I want to do is run as fast as I can in the opposite direction.' I have a feeling I might have been exactly the same if Freya and I had ever got to do a double wedding ourselves.

I'm not sure how well she'll run in what have to be seven-inch heels. 'So the bit you're dreading isn't the rest of your life, then? It's the day ahead.' To judge by the smoke plumes billowing up from the other side of the cart, whatever Saffy thinks she's not completely alone with the eleventh hour jittering here.

She pushes a slipping diamond clip back into her hair.

'Actually ... it's the next half hour I can't bear to think about.'

'Well done for that, Saffy.' I'm so happy on her behalf, I could almost cry. 'Half an hour is the smallest time to go through to get to the rest of your life on the other side. And I have a feeling you're going to make Travis so happy if you can get through it. Don't think of it all together. Half-minute-size bites are so much easier.'

She's frowning. 'So you're saying to take it a little bit at a time?'

I nod. 'Scared is good, because it means you've thought it through and you're still daring to do it. Tiny steps are what you take to get you there. Break it down and only concentrate on the next thirty seconds. That's the way you'll get through it.' This could be my own mantra for the day.

She lets out a breath. 'I think you might be right.'

I smile reassuringly. 'You're strong enough to do it, Saffy. Because that's what's right for you and Travis.' I wrinkle my nose. 'You two are really lucky to have found each other, you know. Not everyone who gets married is as certain of each other as you two are.' Somehow I feel I'm taking as much from this conversation as Saffy is.

Despite the mud, she rushes across and wrenches me into a hug. 'Omigod, thank you so much for that.' Her fingers squeeze so hard, her stick-on wedding nails go right through the sleeves of my fake-fur jacket. 'I think you just saved the entire double wedding.'

I pull a face. 'I'm not sure I'd go that far. My pleasure anyway.'

'So I guess it's back in the carriage, then?' As she puts her diamond clad toe on the step, she hesitates, and turns to me. 'How the hell do you know all this, Hols?'

I give a shrug and try to look like a wise, but not too ancient, photographer. 'When you go to as many weddings as I do, you get to know when a bride should run and when she should stay.' If I tell her the real truth, about Luc and me, we could be here for hours, and no one wants delays that long. I send her a wink. 'Anyway, I couldn't bear to see you waste those lovely shoes of yours.'

'Sophie?' Saffy's up now and leaning across from the high seat to the other side of the cart. 'Can you please put that effing cigarette out and get the hell up on this cart. Some of us have a wedding to get to.'

Ken leans forward and gets out his phone. 'Any of the brides-to-be like a selfie with the coachman before we set off again? And mind where you're putting your feet, ladies, please. Muddy shoes are usually banned in this cart. We're only making an exception because they're Louboutins.' If they wanted a well-mannered coachman, they should have chosen someone other than Ken. As Sophie climbs up and sticks her head beside his, he gives an impatient cough. 'Holly, we're waiting, can you get this please?'

And okay, I know taking pictures of people taking selfies is way too much. But just this once, I do it anyway. This one's not for Sophie and Taylor, or Saffy and Travis, or Ken, or Gary or Jules. This one's completely for me. It'll go nicely in my best bits frame when I go back to London, next to my own selfie with coachman Santa. To remind me of what has to be my craziest Christmas holiday ever.

Chapter 27

Friday 15th December
The double wedding at Rose Hill Manor: Shouting,
shouting and more shouting

When I suggested Saffy should take the day in thirty second bites, it turns out that's a pretty good strategy. In the end that's how I cope with my own fear too. As the day goes by, I'm picking up that there's a close link between how well the wedding's rolling and how the photography goes too. They're both about close control and impeccable timing. With Kip, Rafe and Lily determinedly on top of the job from the wedding management side, and Rory literally calling the shots from our side, we're nailing this one all the way. What once promised to be the mother of all days, in fact goes like well-oiled, proverbial clockwork.

We have two ceremonies, two happy couples and two confetti shots. Saffy and Travis have theirs on the terrace, while Sophie and Taylor opt for the coach house courtyard. In the end the group shots I've been tearing my hair out over for ten days turn out to be easy as cupcakes. We just keep the groups and swap the couples. And with Rory and twelve groomsmen on hand to call on for rounding up the guests, it's a walk in the park. How did I not think of that before? There's one humungous shot of everyone outside, which I take leaning out of the open landing window, with Kip hanging onto my feet and Rory on crowd control down below.

Then, while all the guests are downing Prosecco like there's no tomorrow, Rory and I and both happy couples go for a walkabout in the grounds, which is blissfully short, because despite three fake-fur jackets between us, everyone's freezing their bums off. Then the party moves onto the main reception and I'm back on fabulously safe ground with the most amazing plated food and some relaxed candid-couple pics. Then hours later, when the meal ends, everyone pours into the Winter Garden bar again to get stuck into the barrels of beer, courtesy of Roaring Waves. Which is the point when everything begins to unravel.

Traditionally speeches take place after the wedding breakfast – or in this case the five-course feast on a theme of Christmas. When I said I'd rather have a bridezilla than a runaway, that was obviously *before* I saw Sophie warming up to her post-wedding breakfast melt-down.

She's tapping her right Christian Louboutin as she looks around the empty ballroom. 'Why the hell has everyone effed off to the effing bar? They should be at the tables for the frigging speeches.' Seems like the twin with the longest eyelashes, the most princessy hair and the brightest lippy also has the shortest fuse. Or possibly she's the most invested. 'It's *my* effing *wedding*, not a sodding rugby club knees-up.'

Kip dashes across at the first agitated murmur and his tone couldn't be any more calming. 'It's the momentary problem of the bar being in the Winter Garden not the ballroom, Sophie. But you really need that extra party space later, with so many evening guests. I'm sure we'll persuade them to come back through as soon as everyone's topped up their glasses.'

Sophie gives a snarl. 'I don't give a damn about later. If the speeches don't happen *immediately* – like, *now* – there isn't going to be a "tonight".'

Jules stresses that as photographers it's our job to record every part of the day as it unfolds. But will Sophie really want to be reminded of looking like Cruella de Vil on a bad day, in mid- tantrum? I'm fiddling with my shutter speed as I agonise, when a scorching glare from Sophie answers my question for me, so I put my lens cap on again.

Her fuming has moved on to a wail. 'How can they be *so* rude ... they've completely wrecked my day ... someone tell them *all* to get back here ... RIGHT NOW!' As she stomps towards the door, I can't help feeling for Bart's polished wood floor getting impaled with every thud of those designer spikes.

Saffy pushes back a stray strand of hair and lets out a sigh. 'Trav and I wanted the speeches before the wedding breakfast, so the speakers would be fresh not wasted.' She's whispering to me, although after Sophie's howls, I'm not sure why. 'Sophie insisted no one was *allowed* to get shit- faced, so speeches later weren't a problem.' Given these are rugby players, with a penchant for drinking each other under prover- bial tables, then puking and starting all over again, you have to wonder where Sophie got her delusions from.

Whatever, Sophie's now storming off in the direction of the bridal suite with a posse of black- clad bridesmaids, followed by a rather worried Taylor, who grabs Kip for his wingman, as all his groomsmen are otherwise occupied.

Travis shrugs at Rory. 'Tits-up was not the plan for this running order.'

Rory has to bear some responsibility seeing as it's his beer they're in the bar drinking en masse. Especially given the groomsmen who should be leaping in to pour proverbial oil on the same kind of troubled waters, are all in the bar necking Santa's Little Helper along with the best of them.

'Great.' Rory says. 'Leave this to me. I'll sort it.' As he marches off to the Winter Garden, Travis pulls his hand out of Saffy's and follows him too.

Saffy gets hold of a bottle of fizz from an ice bucket. 'Do you want a drink while you're waiting?'

I shake my head. 'Better not.' The end of my day is still hours away. After the speeches, so long as we still have brides, that is, there's the cake cutting and then casual bridesmaids' and groomsmen's poses to organise. It's like a record playing in my head. Then the first dance and the disco and band.

Saffy looks around the almost deserted ballroom. 'Sit down and keep me company while we wait. Soph will be down as soon as she's had a chance to cool off.'

I know maybe I should be leaping around, trying to find cute kids hiding under tables or playing in corners. But looking after bride number two seems equally important. 'I'm sure it'll all start up again soon.' I'm trying my best to be reassuring. But seeing as we're the only people here, that might be over optimistic.

I pull up a chair next to Saffy and we sit together, quietly watching the numbers flipping by on our phones. After twenty minutes Saffy sits back and folds her arms. 'The guys are taking a while.' She pulls a face. 'We might need to try out some girl power here. What do you think?'

I grin at the thought. 'I'm up for it, if you are.' Not that we'll get very far. I've a feeling that Saffy's as much of a shade girl as me.

Saffy laughs as if she's read my mind. 'Usually Sophie's the ass-kicker and I'm the one who loves chocolate cake. But today I dared to get married. So maybe I'm on a roll.' She pulls herself up and high-fives me. 'C'm on. Let's go gedd'em.'

From the way she's tottering in her heels, this could be the Champagne talking. But I grab my bag and follow her anyway. As we have to force our way through the crowd by the Winter Garden door to get in, I'm asking myself whatever happened to priority for the bride? I'm shouting at her over my shoulder as I squeeze through the doorway ahead of her. 'This is the place to be, it's heaving.' When we finally emerge into a space, I find I'm staring up into two familiar faces. 'Hey, Ken, and Gary, are you having a good time?' Seeing they're both clasping a Mr and Mrs Roaring Waves bottle in each hand, with a label for each happy couple, I barely need to ask that.

Judging by Gary's beady eyed glance and flaring nostrils, he's after gossip. 'Holly, fab to bump into you again. With all the sagas of chocolate fountains and alpine fondues, you have to update us. Has Jess got her ring yet?'

I know now's not the time to chat, but sometimes it's the

fastest way of moving on. 'Last night Bart popped a cork while they were suspended over a chasm in a cable car, but Jess was still gasping at views, not a Tiffany box.' This was the eight o'clock call that interrupted my bacon sandwich this morning.

Ken's lapping it up. 'All this mountain air, excitement and exercise, she'll come back a changed woman.'

Gary flutters his eyelashes as he looks down at me. 'Talking of changes, whatever you're doing to our cutie-pants Rory, keep up the good work. He's one happy bunny lately.'

I'm blinking at Gary, because I've no idea what he means. 'That must be the children.'

Ken taps his nose. 'Santa knows it's more to do with the little present we delivered to the wedding shop on our first day out with Nuttie and the cart.'

Garry nudges me with his free elbow. 'Look, he's over there, waving at you now.' He gives me a wink and puckers up his lips. 'Isn't he a total dreamboat in a tux?' As we both know to our cost, the transformation is incredible. It's like someone just took my eye mask off, and I can suddenly see Rory, the smoking hot version I've been blocking out all these years. I must say, it's a lot easier as a photographer, when you *don't* want to grab your helper just because his tush looks so edible.

From a distance, Rory's face is all stubble shadows and cheekbones. Then, when his eyes lock onto mine they crinkle. As his face lights up and he pushes back his hair, his smile zings straight across the room and zaps me right in the stomach.

Ken rolls his eyes to the ceiling. 'Eyes off, Mr Naughty,

Rory's all Holly's now. We don't want her getting all prickly and jealous.'

Despite reeling from the shock, I manage a loud squawk of protest. 'Help yourself, guys, he's *nothing* to do with me.' At one time the rush of heat to my cheeks would be entirely about my inability to cope. But this time it's more about fury. At Rory, for daring to go AWOL for the last half hour when he was supposed to be rounding up guests. Then for launching that exocet of a grin. At myself for letting my insides turn to molten treacle, when I haven't even got alcohol as an excuse.

As I look at Saffy beside me, my eyes are flashing. 'Shall we deal with this, now we're here?' Let's face it, no one else is going to get this wedding back on track. This one's down to us.'

She shakes her hair as she gives a shiver of anticipation. 'Over to you, Hols ...'

I've got no idea what she's expecting me to do, but I go for the most powerful tool I have on me. I dip my hand in my bag and close my fingers around the bells. Then I listen to the roar of laughter and chat all around me, drop the bells and grab the whistle. The breath I drag in is so deep, my lungs feel like they're bursting. Then I put it to my lips and blow as long and hard as I can.

The noise is shrill and horribly loud. But the effect is startling. A second later, the silence is huge, gaping and somehow echoing off the high ceiling as I stare at Saffy and hiss, 'Go on, then! ...'

She opens and closes her mouth, and although there's no sound coming out, the way she's blinking at me, eyes wide and desperate, I know what she wants me to do.

I screw up every tiny bit of courage I have. Which, to be honest, isn't a lot. Then, without even thinking what to say, I yell. 'Everyone ... go next door ... it's time for the talking ... thank you, ladies and gentlemen ... very muchly ... please ... now ... hurry ...'

There's exactly the kind of clatter you'd expect from two hundred feet hitting floorboards, and then Rory's sidling towards us, camera and rolled up tie in his hand.

'Thanks very muchly for that, Berry, beautifully done. I was just about to do it myself.' Which has to be a hundred per cent bollocks. So no change there, then.

'Why the hell have you got a bottle of beer in your jacket pocket, Rory?' Thank jeez I'm cross with him. I'd hate to be wondering what the inside of his mouth tastes like if I wasn't. As for eyeing up his Adam's apple and the vulnerable bit of his neck where his shirt buttons end. Well, seeing he's *my* assistant here, that may well count as sexual harassment.

He gives a low laugh. 'Long story. The girls' grandma was feeling queasy and I had to rescue her. Aren't we supposed to be hurrying here?' If his arm's somehow across the small of my back, it's obviously only to speed us along. 'Hey, I forgot to tell you we've found Teddie's other sweet spot. You'll never guess. Go on, have a try ...'

I screw up my face. 'Really, I have no idea.' And neither has he, if he's asking me this now. With St Aidan's wedding of the year about to re-boot, am I likely to have the spare brain capacity?

'Wheatus signing *Teenage Dirt Bag*.' His grin couldn't be

any more delighted as he pulls out his phone. 'Here, I took a video of him watching it.'

The frown I send him is designed to close him down and it works.

'Okay. Sorry, Berry. I know we've got a wedding to go to.' His brow wrinkles and his arm's back again and as he dips down his lips almost brush against my ear. 'Great work back there, by the way. Time for the talking, then?'

Chapter 28

Monday 18th December
At Snowy Pines Christmas Tree Farm: Splashes and wet
hankies

'So we're here for two trees, in any colour but blue,' Rory
says, as he turns off the main road.

I know getting hauled off to buy Christmas trees isn't exactly
in line with my festive boycott. But when Rory waltzed in
shortly after lunch, bringing Poppy to cover at the shop for
a couple of hours, they were both insistent. With two of them
ganging up on me again, it was easier to come than resist. In
a way they were right. After two and a half days solid at the
laptop, sorting the twins' pictures to send off to Jules, I was
more than ready for a break. In the end it was hard to let
them go, because some of the pictures were so pretty it was
hard to believe I'd taken them. But then tomorrow it's Seth
and Katie's ski wedding, and the whole damned business starts
all over again. Three down. I can't believe there are *still* two
to go.

For some reason known only to Rory, who's being bizarrely

secretive this afternoon, he's chosen to approach Snowy Pines Christmas Tree Farm by the private back entrance. If it's a boy-excuse to have fun driving down half a mile of rutted lane, that part's working a treat. Every time the beer-mobile hits a puddle, the mud sluices high up the windows. And every time it happens Gracie and Teddie, encouraged by Rory, scream like banshees.

In fairness, the kids were pretty hyped up before the tidal splashes started, due to the special sing-along soundtrack Rory's made them. All their new favourite songs, plus a few of his own. It's thanks to this gem of a collection we've spent the entire journey shouting along to Slade's *Merry Christmas*, *Karma Chameleon*, *Let It Go*, plus Teddie's YouTube sweet spot favourites.

As we round yet another bend, and the S Club 7 crew burst into *Reach for the Stars*, he takes a moment off from steering wheel tapping and grins across at me. 'Good isn't it? I've put this one on yours too, Berry.'

It would be rude not to ask. 'What the heck are you on about?'

His grin gets even broader. 'My girlie playlist, dedicated especially to you, currently under construction.'

A boy's-eye view of music girls like? I let out a snort. 'You have *way* too much time on your hands, Rory. I can't wait to see what you come up with for that.' Seeing that we've all had to stick our fingers in our ears while Rory insisted on screaming out the high bits in *A Thing Called Love* along with Justin, from the Darkness, I'm really not hopeful about his choices.

Although, you have to give him some credit. If happy kids were what he was aiming for, he's nailed it here with Gracie and Teddie. It's hard to think, sitting in the cosy, baby-wipe-scented fug of the car that a week from now, this will all be over. No more beer-mobile. The kids will be home with Erin. Rory will be in Bristol and then off to his barns. And I'll be thinking about heading back to my skanky flat and London. For some ridiculous reason, that brings on a strange twang in my chest. I ignore it and instead make myself do a mental cheer, complete with fist waving. Why the hell am I feeling like shit and missing the best bit? No more wedding stress, ever. How great will that be?

As we carry on bumping down the lane, the more excited the squeals from Gracie and Teddie, the faster Rory goes. By the time we jump down from the car in a wide yard that's completely rammed with every kind and size of Christmas tree you can imagine, the blue waves on the car are completely obliterated by dripping sludge.

As I take Gracie's hand, I nod at Rory's mud splattered logo. 'If you're hoping for publicity, you might need a hose pipe?'

Rory's already striding across the concrete. 'Nope, today's all about pleasure, not business.' He's got Teddie clamped in the crook of his elbow. 'We'll get the trees first.'

'You want two?' Is that what he said before?

He nods. 'One for Poppy's kitchen, one for Home Brew Cottage, because the way Erin's going, the kids will be here a lot of the week. She's still not well enough to come home yet.' He wiggles his eyebrows at Gracie. 'Gracie and I were hoping you'd help us decorate it later?'

Gracie chimes in. 'With balls ... . and snowmans ... and twinkle lights ...'

Rory looks at her as seriously as she's staring up at him. 'We'll get twinkle lights from the shop later, okay?'

Gracie's voice brightens. 'And soft poop too.'

'Soft poop?' If it's possible to frown and retch at the same time, that's what I'm doing.

Rory pulls a face. 'Soft *scoop* is her euphemism for Häagen Dazs. Keep up, Auntie Hols. Super-appetising, isn't it? This girl has expensive tastes.'

'Moving on before I vom,' I say. 'That tree pile has to be the most massive in the world, ever.'

Rory shakes his head. 'It was way bigger before, this is a huge operation. Only a week before Christmas, these are just the leftovers.' He stares down at Gracie again. 'We need hats too, don't we?'

Gracie nods. 'One for me and one for Hols.'

I'm frowning again. 'Why?'

Rory takes a deep breath. 'To keep your earsies warm. Isn't that what hats do? Unless you're Marilyn and wearing a fascinator, of course.' He pauses to shudder. 'Ten minutes outside at Rose Hill's one thing. All day at a beach wedding, you'll be freezing your butt off. A hat's non-negotiable.'

And then it suddenly hits me. 'Jeez, you guys are talking! How long has this been going on?'

Rory scrunches up his face. 'What *are* you on about? We always talked. But maybe I'm hearing more now.'

A young guy in boots and a Santa hat is coming towards

us. 'Will you be wanting to chop your own tree down, sir?'

Rory pulls a face as he nods down at Teddie. 'Not this time, thanks. We're here to pick up the Roaring Waves order, and visit the, er, livestock?'

The guy gives Rory a wink. Great, gotcha. We've picked out a six footer and a four footer for you, both noble firs. Like you said, nothing blue, nothing spruce. I'll get them tied to your roof rack while you're busy.' He inclines his head. 'The livestock in question are over there. In the field behind the shed.'

'Great.' As Rory sets off at a run, Gracie and I follow at more of a shuffle. As far as I'm concerned, fields mean mud, and livestock's what you don't let your dogs chase. Way less interesting than a shoe cabinet, in other words. I'm guessing from her dragging on my hand that Gracie's with me on this one.

Rory's already behind the shed. 'Hurry up, slow worms, Teddie can see the surprise already, and he's loving it.'

I look down at Gracie. 'There's a surprise?' Maybe he should have said. 'Shall we run?' As she holds her arms up to me, I scoop her into mine. As we hurtle around the corner, I'm completely unprepared for what's there, nuzzling at the straw on the ground. And why the sight of a mother and baby reindeer standing in the corner of a muddy field, munching on a hay bale, should make me cry, I have no idea. But suddenly there are tears streaming down my cheeks.

I give a huge sniff, swallow hard and hide behind Gracie's head. 'Look, Gracie, look, aren't they lovely and brown and shaggy ... and aren't the antlers mahoosive ... ?' If I'm stating the bleeding obvious, it's not only for Gracie's benefit. It's also to distract myself from a sudden urge to fling my arms around Rory and hug him very hard. One hug for this one spectacularly unusual, insightful and awesome act. Not many people would have thought of reindeer, then made them happen. Even if their friend did happen to have a field full.

Gracie blinks and clutches her snowman to her chest as she takes in the dark-brown face and soft eyes of the mother. 'It's like Sven ...'

I'm thrilled she's got the resemblance. 'Yes, it's a reindeer. I've never seen one before either, they're totally amazing.' If anything, I'm even more blown away than Gracie. They're also surprisingly similar to their cartoon counterparts.

Rory's biting his lip, watching her intently. 'It's like Kristoff's reindeer, isn't it?' He's talking about Kristoff like he's one of his drinking buddies.

I frown at him. 'How do you even *know* about Kristoff?' Characters from *Frozen* should be well off Rory's radar. 'And what made you think of coming to see them?'

He answers that with a shake of his head. 'Catch up, HB, *everyone* at Daisy Hill Farm knows Sven, the reindeer with the heart of a Labrador, belongs to Kristoff.' He gives a shrug. 'My mate's had them here for years. But this is the first time I knew anyone who'd appreciate seeing them as much as you and Gracie. Look, they're coming to see you, Gracie.'

'Come on.' I ease Gracie towards the fence, then as I put out my hand, the reindeer comes and sniffs. Close up its nose is velvety and when it lets me touch its neck, the fur is dense and thick enough to bury my hand in.

'Sven's sniffing your fingers, Hols.' As Gracie turns to Rory, her lips twitch and she lets out a laugh. Then her face breaks into the broadest, smiliest smile as her voice rises to an excited squeak. 'Look, he's sniffing Holseses fingers ...'

Rory and I are staring at each other, eyes wide, hardly daring to breathe in case the smile disappears as quickly as it came. But it doesn't. Ten minutes later, her eyes are still shining, even though she's starting to shiver inside her *Frozen* anorak.

I'm fumbling in my pocket for my phone. 'Shall we swap children before we go, then I can take a picture of you and Gracie together?'

Rory smiles. 'Better still, stay as you are. We'll do one with all of us. So long as the photographer doesn't object, and if my arm's long enough.' He laughs. As his temple arrives next to mine, he grabs my phone too. 'Selfie with reindeer. How cool is that?' As he pulls away and passes my phone back again, he gives me a hard stare. 'Everything okay? Your hair's all damp, Berry.'

'Fine.' I'm lying again, but it could be worse. Anything that took his mind off my smudgy eyeliner and red nose has to be good. And at least I know the size of his heart now. Huge doesn't begin to cover it. How the hell did I miss that before?

Another one for the album, then. Although, every time I look at it on the way back home, for some reason it makes me feel like crying all over again.

Chapter 29

Sunday 17th December
In Home Brew Cottage at Daisy Hill Farm: Ski wear and prickly postmen

When we all get back to the farm, Poppy peels off back to her kitchen and as we head off up to Home Brew Cottage to put the tree up, there are girls in padded jackets, neon leggings and dazzlingly stripy leg warmers zooming in all directions. Rory's had time put logs on the wood burner and unload the roof rack, and I've given Teddie a bottle, and they're still running up and down the courtyard, carrying signs of every size from huge to gigantic.

'Eat Sleep Ski ... On Mountain Time ...' Rory's looking up from where he's heaving the Christmas tree bucket into place in the corner of the cottage living room, reading the messages out loud as they pass the cottage window. 'Après ski ... Ski lift this way. Jeez, there's even someone with an *armful* of skis.' It doesn't take a genius to work out they're the final touches going into the barn for Seth and Katie's Alpine Wedding tomorrow.

'Ooooh, Hot Chocolate Bar. That sounds seriously yummy.' As I peep past him I can't help feeling a shimmer of excitement for how much fun it's going to be. Then, looking around the room again and coming back down to earth, I have to ask. 'Have you been tidying up?'

Put it this way. Despite the fact we just came back with most of what was left of the Christmas section at the Happy Dolphin Garden Centre, compared to last time I was here, the devastation is minimal. And in case you're wondering, we got a shedload of baubles and snowflakes and reindeer to hang on the tree. We also found two cuddly reindeer for Gracie and Teddie that are so soft, if I'd had the teensiest space in my suitcase, I'd have bought one for myself to take home too. The only tree toys we didn't manage to find that Gracie wanted were snowmen.

Rory gives a shrug. 'I just got the troops into line, that's all. Made Gracie put her paperwork into piles, taught Teddie to fold his babygrows, stick his bottles in the dishwasher when he's finished with them. That kind of stuff.' His face breaks into a grin. 'Immie and I had a huge push. If we're putting the deccies up, we have to be a *bit* organised.' He stands back to check the tree is level.

'Ready for the twinkle lights, then?' I pull them out of the box and hand them to Gracie, who skips across the room to Rory. 'Somehow I think I'll call fairy lights that forever now.'

As he slings them around the branches, he narrows his eyes. 'I really appreciate you helping, Berry. For someone who's not feeling festive, you ransacked the Christmas aisles pretty effectively.' He nods at the heap of bags on the sofa. 'I'd say you've officially got *all* the decorations there.'

I pull a face. 'Once we decided to go multi-coloured, those end-of-season reductions were so great, we couldn't leave them in the shop.' As I take in Rory standing in his socks, with his threadbare sweater, I'm wishing I'd been spontaneous and given him that one big hug back at the field. At least that would have got it over and done with. Putting it off hasn't made it go away. He's actually starting to look the same kind of edible as he did in his tux. But this time it's less about the sheer phwoar, and more about the softness in his laugh, and the crinkles at the corners of his eyes when he smiles, and just how kind and thoughtful he is. Which is way harder to resist, even when you're sure you don't want it. Not that it's on offer anyway.

He wrinkles his nose. 'Are colour-coded Christmases a girl thing, then?'

I can't help laughing at his bemused expression. 'I used to have different colours every year, but now I've pretty much done every colour at least three times, I throw it all in. Last year I had a Scottish tartan theme for the main space and went wild in the rest of the flat.'

'Keep going. How wild exactly?' Even if he's pushing with a kind of horror-movie fascination, he can't have any idea of quite how much Christmas bling I have.

I get out the box of red, yellow and green baubles and begin handing them to Gracie to hang up. If he's willing me to shock him, I might as well spill. 'Trees in every room, every kind of Christmas light from multi-coloured star chasers to light-up reindeers. Swags, scented pot pourri, lanterns, china, tableware, votive displays. Then there were the angels and my cherub collection.' Due to his jaw already being on his chest, I spare him the bit about the light-up snowmen inflatables tethered on the balcony, and the part where I share that my candle order was big enough for me to keep Yankee Candle in business single handed. 'And this year it's all in boxes.' In an urban locker in Bermondsey. How sad it that? Or should that be, how sad am I?

His frown is horribly sympathetic. 'That's so awful, Berry. If I need a tinsel explosion at the brewery and Huntley and Handsome for next year, you're definitely my woman, then?' He smiles at me. 'It's great you're still celebrating for Freya.'

Something about the way he called me 'his' makes my breath hitch, even though we both know it's only a figure of speech in the middle of a joke. And I definitely know for me that this wedding-frenzy December is an accidental nightmare and not something I'll ever repeat. So when that 'next year' comes, I'll be way off any Cornish radar.

I smile back, liking how effortless it is to talk to him about this, because he remembers. 'Freya and I always loved Christmas. Somehow really going for it is a wonderful way of remembering her. I hand him a box of reindeer. 'Over the years it just got bigger and bigger.'

Decorating a tree in a cosy cottage in front of a log fire is what other people do, not me. No one's ever helped me decorate a tree before. Although I suppose technically I'm the one helping Rory, not the other way around. Even the kids aren't really his. It's as if we've all been accidentally thrown together in the wrong living room, to get a taste of someone else's life.

If it's way too warm and delicious, there's no need to worry. It'll soon be over.

He looks thoughtful. 'A lot of stuff in your life goes back to that, doesn't it?' He takes out a reindeer and dangles it from his finger. 'I suppose if she'd lived to grow up, you and Freya would have been a lot like Sophie and Saffy?' The way he always calls her Freya feels totally natural. Somehow it makes things very easy because he knew her too.

I don't want to be disloyal. 'That's just how it tends to go with sisters. One will be dazzling, out there and confident, like Freya and Sophie, while the other ends up paler and wussier, like Saffy and me.' I don't want to be unfair. 'Although Saffy does know what she wants. She's just more easy going about getting it than Sophie, that's all.'

His nostrils flare as he draws in a breath. 'I hear you stopped her running off too.'

My eyes are popping. 'Who the hell told you that?' As the penny drops, I'm flaring up. 'Ken and Gary? Those two are *so* out of line.'

He ignores that. 'Actually they're very discreet, but they thought I should know. So all I'm pointing out is, you might be quiet, but you're damned good at this wedding stuff. People obviously feel very comfortable with you taking their pictures, and find you very empathetic to have around.' He loops his ribbon over a branch. 'Quieter doesn't necessarily mean less attractive, either. When you look at the photos, even though Sophie's the one with most make-up and more of her boobs out, Saffy's the pretty one.' Sounds like someone's been looking through the files we backed up on his laptop. His lips curl into a smile. 'What's more, a wuss can't shift two hundred people from one room to another in five seconds flat like you did the other day. You were the one with the guts to pull their wedding back from the edge, Berry.'

'I only blew a whistle.' I don't want him overstating this.

He's doing that thing where he twists his lips when he thinks about something hard. 'You saw what was needed and went in to do it. You'd never have done that at the Lifeboat Station. It's good you're improving, because we really need you to be able to kick ass if "the puke" is turning up on Thursday.'

'Sorry?' It's true I'm getting less scared and more confident. It's as if there's so much to face with weddings that I'm fast forwarding through years of fears and coming out the other side feeling like I can do things I couldn't do before. But I've got no idea what the hell he's talking about with the last bit.

Rory's grinning. 'Luc "the puke"? As in your ex. You'll need to be brave with him.'

'Right.' Except it's not. My stomach's cramping every time I think about it. 'He probably won't even turn up.' It's what I'm telling myself to make it through the week. As for the rhyming name, I can already hear Immie saying that's Rory's way of diminishing Luc. I should count myself lucky he's stopped short of derogatory penis comments.

Rory puts down the bauble he's holding and stares at me. 'You *are* going to tell mini-dick where to get off?' Talk about speaking too soon.

I give a private shudder for that bit and hesitate, because I know this needs to sound ballsy. 'Obviously.' It's worth the wait, because when it comes out it's so deep and husky I sound like someone else entirely. Which is kind of good, because I'm not sure I could *personally* say that and actually mean it.

Last night in my dream Luc was walking away and I ran the entire length of St Aidan beach to beg him to take me back. I was within a starfish of catching him when I tripped over a lobster pot. I know it's only a dream. And it's completely ridiculous for so many reasons. As if I'd ever run that far. And anyway, lobster pots are big. You wouldn't fall over them, you'd run around them.

'Phew, right answer.' Rory's shaking his head. 'For a second there you looked like you were wavering. At least you'll be warm now.'

I seize the chance to move this on from talking about Luc. 'Yes, the hats are great. Aren't they Gracie?' So good, we're still wearing them. They're matching, knitted black wool, with reindeer-coloured fake-fur bobbles instead of pompoms. I've got wellies in a bag too. Luckily I persuaded Gracie out of buying the hats with the Happy Dolphin logo. 'And we need to step up the pace here if we're going to finish the tree this side of New Year. "Too many Christmas decorations" said no one ever. But I think we might have over-bought.' I pass another bulging carrier across to Rory.

He puts his hands over his head as he takes it. 'Jeez, we might need the S Club 7 soundtrack to help us along.' He wiggles his eyebrows. 'Only joking. How about you do the reading thing while I finish here?'

I'd almost forgotten the books in my bag. 'I thought you were going to do the stories.'

He gives a shamefaced grin. 'Sorry, HB, I haven't got as far as story-reading on the blogs. It's the same principle as nappy changing, though. Once you've shown me how to do it, I'll be good to go.'

'You're in luck. Seeing as you gave in and bought my favourite strawberry cheesecake poop scoop Häagen Dazs.' I dip into my bag and pull out the books, then make my way across to the sofa. 'So what do you think, Gracie? There's one here about a jolly Christmas postman who delivers letters to Cinderella and the three bears and people like that. How does that sound?'

There's a low laugh from behind the branches. 'Highly entertaining.'

I'm not sure if he's serious or taking the pee here. 'Bought with the adult readers in mind, Rory. It's important *everyone* enjoys these.'

He's straight back from the other side of the tree. 'Hell yes, if Gracie likes them they're likely to be on repeat. Thinking about it, why don't I record my own YouTube versions for her to watch?'

Just when I think he's getting better, he goes right downhill again. I pick Teddie up from where he's lying kicking on the floor, and wedge him cosily in the corner of the sofa. Ignoring Rory, I pick up the book and settle back against the cushions. A moment later Gracie is beside me, snuggled up against my elbow.

The next hour flies by as we search for lost dogs, select suitable pets at the zoo, have tea with tigers, go on bear hunts, zip around with cats in hats and read a whole load of other people's letters. By the time my voice is starting to weaken, Rory's not only put the reindeer on top of the tree – who knew he'd bought an extra one for that job? – but he's also cooked.

'You've made *dinner*?' We've been so engrossed in our reading, that I hadn't realised the extended crashing around the work surfaces had that kind of significance. I'm slightly 'waaaahhhhh' that I've been bumped into anything quite so cosy as dinner with Rory. Then Teddie chucks up all over my leg and reminds me there's no grounds for worry *at all*.

'Marinated herb chicken, halloumi and veggies on skewers, with a tossed green salad and baked potatoes.' Rory seems to be delightfully unaware of how incongruous his teensy Home Brew Cottage *This Kitchen is for Dancing* apron looks on a guy who has to be six two and built.

'Sounds delish.' I've mopped up my leg and for the first time this afternoon, my mouth's watering for the right reason.

Gracie looks across at the open-plan island where he's working. 'Story, Rory?'

I can't resist a grin. 'Hey, Roaring One, it's not just "Luc the puke". You've got a rhyming name too.' Not that I would usually have brought Luc up, but this was too good to miss.

Rory laughs as he pulls out the high chair and throws a handful of cutlery onto the pine table. 'Gory Rory will be Story Rory later. After dinner and before bed. Aren't stories meant to put everyone to sleep?'

Gracie pipes up. 'Not Gory Rory, it's Rory Waves.'

I'm busy smiling at that when it hits me. This is Rory's way of not doing this in front of me. Not that he's the kind of guy who's ever been bothered by an audience. But I under-stand if he wants to read to the kids by himself. So we wolf our mains – and yes, of course he cooks like a demon. If there was ever a day when Rory exposed himself as a keeper for someone, it had to be this one. And Poppy's completely right, as usual. Rory, old and alone, and living above his barrels is a complete waste of the most fantastic guy. Let's face it, how many guys ever take you to see a reindeer, *or* produce a herb marinade? Pulling off both feats within six hours is nothing short of extraordinary. So when we've licked the very last of the Häagen Dazs off our pudding spoons, I jump in with my tactful suggestion.

'Right, I'll clear up, so you three can disappear to bed with your books.'

Rory's wail is at least as loud as Gracie's. 'But we want you to listen and join in too, Berry. We'll do it in here.' He wedges Teddie in the same place on the sofa, flops down next to him and grabs a book. 'Okay, Gracie, which one shall we start with?'

I collect the plates as quietly as I can and hurry around the island. I'm about to open the dishwasher and start popping things in, when something catches my eye. Gracie's up on the sofa. But instead of taking up her usual position, with a good two cushions of clear water between her and Rory, she's moving towards him. I know it sounds like a cliché, but I'm standing, open mouthed, as I watch. Because she still hasn't stopped. And rather than sneaking in beside him, she's carrying on. I can see Rory holding his breath as she clambers across his legs, ducks under his arm, then settles herself down sideways on his knee. As her shoulder comes to rest against his chest, Rory's face slides into the biggest smile ever. He's biting his lip and as I watch him swallow, there are goosebumps on the back of my neck.

'Okay, are you going to choose a book ...'

'I think ...' Gracie fumbles with the pile. 'This one ... *The Holly Postman* ...'

So much for being a photographer. One of the most simple, yet beautiful moments I've witnessed in my life. All the thousands of pounds worth of camera equipment I've got back at the flat. And I'm bobbing down, pretending to pick a mushroom up off the floor, waggling my phone. But when I look at it later I know this one of Rory's best moments yet is too private and precious for my own public collection. This one's going to have to go in the velvet book in the back pocket of my make-up bag. With the picture of Freya and me, helpless with laughter, that was taken the month before she got ill.

Chapter 30

Sunday 17th December
In Home Brew Cottage at Daisy Hill Farm: Postcodes and
dropping stomachs

'**O**kay, Holly Postman ...'

'Rory ...' It's a warning shot across his proverbial bows.
He might have leaped up from his lowest base, what with his
reindeer and his cooking, but one wrong move and he'll be
back down to the bottom faster than you can say 'abseil'.

'What?' His voice is high with mock indignation. 'If you
don't want new nicknames you should be more careful which
books you choose.'

I grit my teeth, because his low laugh has sent a shiver
down my spine. 'This is me, testing out my assertiveness.'

'Great. Well done on that one. Butt-kick noted and
applauded, five stars on Trip Advisor. But really, Holly
Postman's too funny not to use it. So Holly Postman ...'

I give in. 'What?'

He clears his throat. 'Immie popped in while you were in
the bedroom settling Gracie down.'

That doesn't really describe the raucous half hour we just had, although it did end up with her and Teddie sparked out. 'Sorry, I didn't hear her come in.'

'She's really embracing the relaxation thing. She was on her way back from Serene Swimming by Candlelight, but she came to say she and Chas will run you back to town around nine. So you might as well sit down.' His lips are twisting as he nods to the sofa beside him. 'We heard *you,* even if you didn't hear us.'

Quite apart from getting stuck here for longer than I'd intended, as I perch on the edge of the sofa next to him I'm wilting inside. '*Let it go?*' Once we started singing, it was hard to give a damn.

His beam breaks out into a laugh. 'It wasn't like you were singing anything else.' Then without even teasing me, he's suddenly serious again. 'So where had you and Little Richard got to on the kid question? You never actually said. Did someone mention a pregnancy scare?'

It might have come out of nowhere, but I can tell he's not going to back down. Sometimes it's easiest to tell him what he wants to know, and move on. 'We hadn't actually discussed it. But I'm pretty sure kids didn't feature in his future life plans.' The only time he ever mentioned kids was when he was midway into his rather long proposal speech. Before he got to the point where I scuttled across the room and bolted out of the back door and down the long drive out onto the road, his mum had squealed something about grandchildren. But Luc had closed her down with one of those glares of his, then said a family was not on his agenda. 'Why are you asking

309

that now?' At the time I didn't mind, because I'd never seen many kids. Whereas after two weeks of dealing with Gracie and Teddie, I'm starting to feel very differently.

He shrugs. 'If he's on his way back, it's good to keep it real.' His expression is perplexed. 'Not talking to each other's bad enough, but he was denying you kids too?'

There are times when this local right for involvement in people's private business gets way too much. 'And you care about this because?'

He lets out a sigh. 'It seems a pity, that's all. Given how good you are with Gracie and Teddie. You don't want to leave it too late and end up like Immie and Erin.'

Who aren't similar at all. 'Seeing as you're so concerned with fertility issues, what about yours?' I have zero interest in the subject, but it might teach him that being grilled isn't pleasant.

His wince is visible. 'I told you, since the brain injury I don't have relationships. So there definitely won't be any kids for me.'

Shit, and shit again, because whatever he says, he didn't tell me the half of it. 'You hurt your *brain*? That's why Marilyn covered you in lippy? What the hell happened?'

He gives a rueful grin. 'All those wrecked cars when I was a teenager, and the one time I did bash my head, it wasn't me driving.'

'Was it really bad, then?'

He laughs. 'I'm still here, aren't I? Apparently, the coma lasted weeks and when I woke up I couldn't move or remember anything. But the body has an amazing ability to recover.' He gives a grimace. 'After a couple of years of rehab, most things worked again.'

'Crap, Rory. Why didn't you say?'

His brow crinkles. 'Why would I? That's where the YouTube clips are from. The *Fight for this love* clip was the first thing I laughed at, when they were trying to get me to reconnect with my emotions. I keep it on my iPad for old time's sake. It's great it's come in handy again.'

I'm biting my lip because the thought of the most vibrant guy I know cut down and hurting makes my chest ache. 'But you're better now?' He has to be, sitting there like nothing happened.

As he folds his arms, it's as if he's explained this a thousand times before. 'I'm great so long as I don't read too much, or make my brain process too much information at once. I did try going back to my old job, but that wasn't ever going to be a goer.'

'But weren't you a top lawyer?' How awful is this? 'And that's why you can't play sport any more?'

He nods. 'Once I got better, hanging round watching my work friends in Bristol tearing ahead with their careers was the biggest headfuck of all. So I came back here instead and put all my energy into Huntley and Handsome, and then Roaring Waves. The world's definitely a better place now I'm selecting wines and making beer.' It's typical of Rory to pull the best out of the worst.

I'm kicking myself for writing him off as an eternal teenager having a midlife crisis. 'Without your accident, there'd be no Bad Ass Santa and Jess wouldn't have her fabulous Prosecco deal.' I chew on my nail as I puzzle to fit the pieces together. 'But why stop seeing women? I thought all guys in rehab fell in love with their physiotherapists.'

This sigh is the longest. 'Even though I recovered, the trauma meant my brain was extra vulnerable. They couldn't guarantee I wasn't going to have another brain bleed at any moment.' As he turns to look at me, my stomach drops. 'It wasn't fair to lay that one on a partner.'

No wonder Marilyn was rubbing his head. I'm looking at the stubble on his cheeks and the soft brown eyes and the dimples. And his jaw, and the way, even when he isn't smiling, he looks like he is. And thinking about how he might not have been here at all sends my chest into a peculiar kind of spasm. My heart's breaking so much for the way his life's been so screwed up, all I want to do is reach out. Put my hand on his cheek. Run my fingers through his hair, so I can feel the heat of his scalp and know he's alive. I wedge my wrist under my knee, because touching him is the last thing I want to do.

'So Holly Christmas ...'

As he turns to me, I'm close enough to see the flecks in his irises, count the individual eyelashes. As he licks his lip and swallows, I'm watching the column of his neck so closely that somehow I ease the grip on my wrist. A second later, his stubble is rubbing against my palm and my fingertips are tingling as they scrape across his cheekbone. As my fingers entwine in his hair and he slowly leans towards me, his voice is low.

'Good call, Berry ...'

However much I was hyperventilating at weddings, this is

different. The breath I've pulled in is so long, I've stopped breathing altogether and all I can hear is my heart banging against my chest wall. Then the tiniest, most tentative, knock on the door makes me lurch back so hard I almost yank Rory's hair out.

'Shit.' I dive back to the end of the sofa.

'Jeez.' Rory's hand finds mine and just for a second he squeezes, very hard. Then as the door swings open and Poppy tiptoes in he pulls away too.

She's talking in a whisper, so she doesn't disturb the kids. 'Holly, great, you're still here.' She stops as she takes in the tree in the corner. 'Wow, so pretty, cool reindeer.'

Rory hits the ground running. 'All we need now are some snowmen. I thought I'd make some origami ones this evening.'

I'm frowning at him. 'How do you know about origami?' I think we've got away with that. However much he's tugging at my heartstrings, rubbing the face of a guy who doesn't want to date any more isn't great judgement. When it feels that good and I'm actually supposed to be aching for my long-lost ex to turn up, it's bonkers. Marilyn can afford to let her hands wander. But I can't. I need to sit on them more successfully in future.

'It was an obsession when I was nine. Around the same time I got my electric guitar and my first tractor. Leave the snowmen to me, they'll be on the tree by morning.'

Poppy's flapping her hands as she tries to break into the conversation. 'Holly, we need to go to St Aidan.' She stops, then her voice goes higher. 'Like, really really fast, right now.'

I jump up and pull on my jacket. 'Is there a problem?' I let out a gasp. 'Omigod, is the baby coming?' From her agonised grimace, if it's not labour, it has to be something cataclysmic.

She closes her eyes, takes a breath, flaps her fingers in front of her face, and when she looks at me again, her smile's bright and she's got her best customer service voice on. 'At Brides by the Sea, we choose our phrases very carefully at the less-easy times. We have issues, not problems. And never disasters.'

'So?' I rack my brain to find some acceptable vocabulary. 'What's the calamity?'

Her face lapses back into the 'holy crap' expression. 'Bloody Marilyn's chopped the bottom off Katie's wedding dress.' The way she's panting sounds horribly like something off *One Born Every Minute*.

'Are you sure you're not having contractions?'

'Absolutely not.' She breaks off to give a sniff of disgust, then clamps her hand to her bump and squints at me. 'Did you know I was coming? It's just you've already got your hat on.'

How do I explain that one without wasting half an hour? 'Women's intuition?' When she seems to accept that I go on. 'On a scale of one to ten, how bad is it?'

She doesn't have to stop to think. 'Twenty four.'

Ew. 'Twenty four, where bad is *high*?' It's so far off the scale, it's worth clarifying.

'Yeah.' As she nods frantically, her eyes are popping. 'The thing is, Lily's still here working on the barn, Sera's on the night train back from an appointment in London. So that only leaves you and me.' She's back to the mouse squeaks. 'And we have thirteen *tiny* hours to make this okay.'

What is it about weddings? They just keep giving and giving.

Chapter 31

Sunday 17th December
At Brides by the Sea: Shortcuts

By the time we've all got to the shop and Katie's standing in the White Room in her dress and her platforms, Poppy's totally nailed her soothing tones again.

'We're all going to stay super-composed here, Katie. At Brides by the Sea we pride ourselves on delivering happy outcomes. And we're absolutely going to achieve one of those this evening.' She puts a glass of amber liquid on the console table. 'Sip this, it'll help.'

After a mini debate in the kitchen, we decided, with the wedding tomorrow, we'd go for a relaxing Pimms and apple juice Winter Warmer, rather than Jess's usual 'hard times' cocktail of neat gin laced with Rescue Remedy.

Katie's chewing her knuckles and her nose is like a beacon as she stares down at her skirt and mumbles. 'It's too short for the kitten heels, it's not even working with flats.' However much Seth wanted her electric blue platforms at the ceremony, I'm sure he didn't want to see *this* much of them. As the dress is now, after Marilyn's ill-judged, high-speed hacking session on Friday morning, the hem is bobbing around her ankle bone. You don't have to be Yves St Laurent to know it's not a good look.

Poppy's got her inner serene goddess well and truly channelled here. 'So, let's explore the options, very calmly, one by one.' She's sticking up her fingers as she talks. 'Pulling the skirt to sit lower isn't going to work. We definitely don't want to chop another foot off and make it properly short, we agree the ankle skimming isn't working, and adding a longer petticoat looks wrong too.' She pauses and goes again. 'We know all your mini snowflake sequins were specially added. We do have a longer skirt here we could substitute, but it hasn't got snowflakes on it.'

Katie's wail is teensy, but it's still a wail. 'But the snowflakes are what make it m-i-ne.' Her bottom lip is trembling. 'Without them I could be any old bride, but those make me feel like a mountain princess.'

Even as I wave my arm around the long rail of dresses beside me, I know the answer. 'Any of the above?'

This time it's a proper wail. 'Noooooooooooooo!'

Poppy and I are exchanging private despairing grimaces when the shop door slams. As we hold our breaths to listen, there's a loud stomping in the hallway and a familiar booming voice.

'Talk about SOS, What's your Emergency? Don't worry, whatever shitheap you've landed in, I'm here to pull you out.' She gives a cough. 'I've done three meditation classes and a power napping course today. I'm beyond ready to concentrate my mind.'

'Immie.' Poppy's throat cutting signs are going entirely unheeded as Immie bursts through from the hall.

She stands and assesses the damage, with her hands on her hips. 'Rory told me you're up to your armpits in disaster, and trumping toad farts, he's not joking. What the hell happened there, Katie? You look like you've been out limboing with a hedge trimmer.' She's never one to hold back, but we could really do with a less forthright summing up. She couldn't have fitted more banned words into one sentence if she tried.

'I'm so sorry, this is *all* my fault.' I'm looking out at the street lights washing the mews outside with pale light, cringing with guilt.

Poppy turns to me, her voice firm. 'No, Hols, when you let the dress leave the shop you had no idea this was going to happen. We've *all* agreed, there's only one person responsible for this debacle. And that's Marilyn.'

Immie's eyes are wide. '*Marilyn* did *that*? Frig Precisely Peaceful, my inner beauty's going to have to take a running jump. What an elephant-arse bitch queen ... troglodyte mayonnaise ... head slapper ...' She stares round at us, shaking her head. 'Truly, there are no words.'

In some ways, she might have been better to have started with the last bit.

Poppy raises her eyebrows and turns to Katie. 'I'm sorry, I was hoping for more up-beat input there.'

Katie shakes her head. 'Not at all. It's great to hear you telling it how it is, Immie. Actually, it really helps.'

Immie gives her a searching stare. 'You *are* sure you know

what you're getting into, marrying Marilyn's son?'

I'm flashing Poppy a 'what the hell?' look. From my really, really limited experience, I'd say you don't ask a woman that question any time within six months of her wedding, let alone the night before. If there's one thing in life more wobbly than a jelly, it's a bride.

Katie lets out a sigh. 'I do know, and Seth's completely worth it. Coping with his mum is our joint mission in life.'

Immie flops down on the chaise longue. 'Great. Well, in that case, where are we up to?'

Poppy's eyeing her resignedly. 'Okay, telling it like it is, we have thousands of snowflake sequins on the ruined skirt, which all need cutting off and hand-sewing onto the replacement skirt.'

Immie's sitting up. 'Is that all? Why didn't you say that to start with?'

Poppy's looking bemused. 'The first time around, the lady doing the job had the skirt for three weeks. We've got approximately eleven hours. I know you regularly work wonders, Immie, but I think this one's out of your league.'

Immie gives a low laugh. 'Aren't you forgetting about Blue Watch? How many times have they hoicked us all out of the shit?' She's talking about the team of firefighters Chas works with.

Poppy's frowning. 'Well, they saved the day putting up Alice's twiggy ceiling at the Manor last Christmas. And they helped Sera find the missing groom. Then they were like angels with magic wands when we had to move your wedding from the house to the barn at short notice.' She's mixing her metaphors, but we still get what she means. 'I don't see where they can help with this one, though?'

Immie's laughing. 'That's because you don't know about their secret vice. You don't think they spend all those hours on call at work playing snooker, do you? Blue Watch are seriously into needlepoint. But for chrissakes don't go broadcasting it. It's classified information.'

Poppy's looking flabbergasted. 'You mean they can *sew*?'

Immie's looking super-pleased. 'Only like dreams. Give them the needles, the thread and the snowflakes, and set them up at the big bench in Sera's studio. We'll have them working their little tushes off faster than you can say cross stitch. With all of them, they'll piss on this job in no time. There's a load drinking two doors down in the Hungry Shark. I'll get Chas to round them up.'

Poppy's still not convinced. 'They'll work through until morning?'

Immie nods. 'However long it takes. You know Blue Watch. There's nothing they love more than an emergency. Even if there aren't ladders involved, they're genetically programmed to respond to people like us, who are up creeks without paddles.' She opens her bomber jacket and gives a chortle. 'Anyway, it's official – *Firemen can go all night*. It says so on my t-shirt.'

Katie's standing flapping her hands. 'Thank you all *so* much, I don't know who to hug first, everyone's being so amazing.'

'Maybe just hug us altogether?' That's Poppy's cue for a massive group hug. Somehow when people in London do them, they never work as well as the ones here. You've got to admit, people in St Aidan might be hideous for sticking their noses into everyone else's lives. But they know how to come in and haul you out of trouble.

To steal a phrase from Immie ... Festering frog farts, who'd have thought?

Okay, so not only am I going to get to spend the night with a whole load of hot hunky guys in the building, but it looks like we're right on course for a Dress Rescue too. If I'm really lucky, they might even fix the loose button on my jacket. But with a pre-wedding cock-up this enormous, that has to be a good sign for tomorrow. Doesn't it?

Chapter 32

Monday 18th December
At Daisy Hill Farm: Cups and saucers

Katie and Seth's Alpine Wedding

Seeing twelve guys in amongst the fabric rolls and dress-maker's dummies in Sera's studio, with their muscly arms and t-shirts, all poring over a table spread with soft tulle, needles flying, was almost worth the disaster. I admit I sneaked a couple of teensy pics. Obviously for my personal consumption only. Nothing to do with the biceps, simply because of the rarity value. And to remind me, when I look back, just how wild and unbelievable this month in St Aidan was.

Immie and I kept them well supplied with tea and cakes, then when they finished I waved them all off down the mews and locked up. It was some kind of minor feat that by the time I fell into bed at four, when I put my nose to my wrist and sniffed really hard, Rory's scent was still there. Even if I did fall asleep breathing him in, it was still Luc I was chasing after in my dream. He was sailing off out of the harbour on a yacht, and I had to jump in and swim after him. Which was hell, because we all know how much I hate water. By the time Rory waded into my dream to haul me out onto the beach, I'd turned into a mermaid. My mind boggles every time I think of the psychological implications Immie would read into all that.

Then Poppy was back again early to steam the dress and whisk it back over to Katie at the farm. So, apart from feeling like I'd been hit over the head with a hammer due to lack of sleep, by the time Rory arrived to cook breakfast at eight, we were back to business as usual. By making a huge thing of rushing around and giving every detail of last night's drama, I made it deliberately obvious I'd completely forgotten the bit where I ended up yanking Rory's hair out. And I must be making more of this than he is, because he didn't mention it at all either. Not that I gave him any space to get a word in.

Rory drops me off at the farm later as he heads off with my second-best camera to catch up with the guys, who are getting into their ski wear up at the Goose and Duck. As I walk into the rustic shell of the wedding barn, with its lofty ceiling, rough-hewn beams and whitewashed stonework I can see it's the perfect setting for all the props that Poppy, Lily and Katie have added. The wood plank bar, with its *Gluhwein* signs and fairy lights could have been transplanted straight from the inside of a mountain hut. The cosy red tartan armchairs and the cuckoo clock and moose heads are all working their magic as I get out my camera. There are piles of brightly coloured rugs and carefully arranged skis, sledges and ice skates, and festive touches too. A huge tree, with pink lights and multi-coloured bows and cut-out snowflakes. There are wicker wreaths with trailing ribbons hanging from the walls. Outside on the terrace, the open braziers are already alight, radiating their warmth, as the flames roar through huge chunky logs. I know Katie and Seth had been desperately hoping for snow, but after the near miss with the dress, I think they'll be happy enough to settle for a flurry from the snow machine.

The fact that Poppy's putting the final touches of flowers and berries to her four-tier chocolate cake shows that Seth and Katie are standing firm with Marilyn. The fact that her cake is right beside Poppy's shows she still hasn't given up her fight.

I can't help letting out an excited cry when I see the glittery shimmer of icing on Poppy's buttercream-covered tower. 'Awww, the white drip snow looks so amazing on top of the dark chocolate. And the red and yellow, and blue and pink flowers are so zingy. Did the ganache work out okay this time?'

Poppy nods. 'Ganache is much easier to get right when the weather's cold.' She looks at Marilyn's cake. 'Talking of Snow Queens, Marilyn's down in the main house with her own hair and make-up team. They've promised to keep her out of trouble until the groomsmen pick her up later.'

I roll my eyes. 'I'll pop in and take some pictures of her getting ready.' That's definitely one on the lists Jules sent us. 'I'll see Katie and the girls first, though.' Somehow I'm so looking forward to taking pictures of the bridesmaids in their short bright tulle skirts and angora jumpers with all the props, and the guys in their suits and ski jackets, I've actually forgotten to worry.

It seems like last night's predictions for the wedding going well are spot-on. I get some great pre-wedding pictures, including a close-up of the offending blue platforms. Katie's whisper-light white voile skirt looks truly amazing with those hand-sewn snowflake sequins nestling in the gathers. And a lot later on, capturing Katie dodging Marilyn as she pursues her around the place with the tiara and veil turns it into an iconic moment for posterity rather than the almighty show-down it might have been.

As I finally come out of the bride's dressing room, I'm still scraping the tears away from my eyelashes after taking the pictures of Katie with her mum and her very poorly dad. As I hurry into the main part of the barn, it's bursting with excited guests waiting for the ceremony. They're mostly dressed in bright woolly hats and jumpers, all sitting on hay bales, and it couldn't be any more vibrant or photogenic. As Marilyn reappears along with her groomsmen guard, she pauses to take in the full glory of the decorations. She falters for a moment, then makes a beeline for Rory.

If the floral dressing gown she was wearing earlier made me think of the Chelsea Flower Show, the suit she's changed into is like a burst of Kew Gardens on a summer's day. All topped off with a fascinator the size of a flying saucer. She sweeps Rory into a huge embrace, then her lips collide with his face. After an extra-long head pat she pulls away, leaving a slick of orange lipstick that stretches from his chin to his ear. From across the barn, I try to catch his eye as he takes her to her seat – a proper mum-of-the-groom chair that's like a throne beside the straw bales. I'm still pointing to my face as Kip appears, which has to be a sign that Katie is coming any moment. So I dash into position to get the ceremony shots.

Tucked in behind the selfie ski-lift seat, I'm perfectly placed to catch the bridesmaids coming in, then Katie as she walks down the aisle to meet her dad, who is sitting waiting for her at the front. I can't help smiling as the walking in music strikes up. As *I Only Want to be With You* bounces off the stone walls, I jump as someone nudges my elbow.

'This one's on *your* playlist too.' It's Rory, his low murmur rumbling in my ear.

'Great.' Talk about timing. I hiss up at him, 'Why aren't you across the other side of the barn?'

He's grinning down at me. 'Better views over here.'

There's no time to tell him to shut the eff up, because there's a burst of sapphire blue and cerise and yellow, and the bridesmaids are arriving. Then Katie's here, smiling and crying at the same time. As she sways and dances along between the bales I can't help noticing how cute and lovely her rosy nose is. And as she comes to a halt next to Seth and beams up at him, she gives him the briefest flash of turquoise platform from under her hem. Then they both collapse into giggles.

The ceremony is full of all the tears and laughter you would wish for. Hundreds of pictures later, Katie and Seth have read out their very cute promises – which don't mention Marilyn at all – exchanged rings, and had their very first Mr and Mrs snog. The register is signed and then everyone's pulling on their ski jackets, ski hats and mittens, and rushing outside to grab cocktails, under flakes from the snow machine.

Rory's doing up his windcheater as he comes up behind me and we move out together onto the terrace. 'Okay, Hols, all good so far. Rafe and Kip will be pulling the confetti tunnel shot together in about ten minutes. If you want to go in close, I'll get it from further out.' He pushes up his collar and pulls my hat out of his pocket. 'You might need this, there's a bit of a wind getting up. One of Seth's friends is sending a video drone up too, to get a crowd shot from above.'

It might be the fourth time around, but as I pull on my hat I'm still twitching with the pressure to snatch this one-time-only action shot of the bride and groom being showered with confetti. Thanks to Marilyn, the list of groups we have to work through afterwards is endless. But they're mainly a matter of crowd-handling. With every other shot after the next one, there's a chance for a second go. Ten minutes later, my stomach's knotting as I watch the guests being hustled into position. Then as Marilyn comes strutting through, the crowd parts. The cluster of feathery antennae on her head is so expansive it looks like it could be communicating with Houston. If it tones perfectly with the bright pink chaser lights on the terrace, it's definitely accidental.

Then Katie and Seth burst out hand in hand, and there's a cheer, then a blizzard of confetti petals. I'm still madly clicking my shutter when everyone begins to clap. I glance up to see they're all looking upwards, waving and shouting. 'Here comes the video drone!'

Above our heads there's the buzz from the spindly machine as it hovers. Then a ripple of comments. 'How clever is that?

Wave at the spacemen. Don't they bring aircraft down?'

Rory's back at my shoulder. 'Do we take pictures of the drone taking pictures, then?' He frowns at the terrace. 'Jeez, it's flying low.'

I watch as a gust of wind catches it. 'Shit, it's heading towards us. Look out!' I manage a squawk, but it's too little too late. As the mini craft is swooping out of control, my shout turns to a scream. 'Oh My God, it's heading straight for Marilyn!'

It's as if the feathers on her fascinator are pulling it in. It skims across above her, slicing through the quills. Then as the spines tangle in its propellers, it goes into a wobbling spiral and crashes down onto her head.

There's a shrill shriek from Marilyn. Then a roar and everyone rushes forward to help.

Rory's voice is low in my ear. 'Do you believe in karma?'

Someone has to shut him up. 'Behave, Rory.'

There's a smile playing around his lips and his eyes are laughing. 'Right, in that case, you carry on here, I'll go and sort out Marilyn.'

Not that I'd always do what Rory suggests, but this once I do. Twenty minutes later, when Rory comes outside again, I'm back to taking pictures of cherries in pomegranate mimosas, and girls in shorts and neon tights sipping coconut vanilla vodka in milk bottles, through chocolate- wafer straws.

He arrives back with a small group of groomsmen and from the furrows in his forehead, the news isn't good. 'Marilyn needs a couple of stitches. And unfortunately I'm the only sober driver here she's happy to go to St Aidan with. So I'll take care of that, while the rest of the day will carry on as planned.'

'B-b-but ...' I have a feeling my jaw's locked in shock as the realisation sinks in. 'You're leaving me here on my own?'

As he stares into my eyes, he clamps his fingers around my arm. 'I'm sorry, I promise I'll be back as soon as I can. In the meantime, you're in the hands of some dedicated and very capable helpers.' He does a flourish. 'Meet Joel, Jim, Josh and Jack.'

'Four of you?' I recover enough to stammer. 'Hi g-guys.' First firemen, now groomsmen.

Joel's smile is as warm as the hand he's holding out. 'Your wish is our command and all that stuff.'

Jack, the cheeky one, is right behind him. 'On the upside, this might be a great chance to get the job done without any more sabotage from Marilyn.'

'Fire away, then. Who do you want us to round up first?' Josh and Jack are grinning and rubbing their biceps in readiness. And as Rory melts away, I think I hear him saying 'Good luck, Holly Postman, stay nice and brave. You're going to smash this out of the park.'

Chapter 33

Thursday 20th December
At Brides by the Sea: Blowy days and views of shoes

'Cobalt blue and hot pink. Let me guess. It's your Alpine wedding?' It's Jess. She's already made it back from the airport, when most people would still be in baggage handling. And like the super-woman she is, first she whooshed around the entire shop. And now she's peering over my shoulder, checking out the slideshow on my laptop.

There are tingles on my neck as the photos flash onto the screen. But this time around it's more excitement at how well they've turned out than being self-conscious that she's looking at them. 'Just some of Seth and Katie's better pictures. I pinged them off to Jules a few minutes ago.' In the end their pictures are even prettier than I'd dared to hope. And that's despite Marilyn hijacking my trusty assistant. Talk about a handful. Not only did she let him take her to get the dent in her head glued, she also made him detour via Brides by the Sea on the way back, so she could choose a new fascinator.

Jess leans in closer. 'A night-time kiss under the stars, with snow falling, and all those hunky snowboarders in the background. It's making me feel *very* nostalgic.'

I'm smiling because Jess still in holiday mode sounds so dreamy and unlike herself. 'So I take it you had a good time?' If this is what the mountains do for you, maybe we all need a high altitude break. I sneak a look at her left hand. 'No last minute engagement ring, then?'

As she brushes back her windswept bob and finally slips off her fur-trimmed ski parka, I can't help noticing. After two weeks of snow and sun, she's so tanned she's almost turned into Bart. And I'm sure the white snow-goggle effect around her eyes where she's been wearing her sunnies will soon fade. Although after my own recent toothpaste disasters, I'm in no position to criticise.

She gives a husky snort. 'That Bart Penryn is a scoundrel. The places he lured me to with the promise of diamonds.' It's not only her personality that's had a make-over. With her calf-length brown furry boots and black snowflake-print ski pants she's looking more like a lost guest from Monday's wedding than St Aidan's most switched-on bridal-shop owner. 'Last night we sat through an entire ice hockey match and Bart convinced me he was going to do the deed over the loudspeakers.'

I can't help laughing. 'How wild would that have been? Phoebe on *Friends* got proposed to at a football game and hated it, though.' Which reminds me, my boxed set is still waiting for me, unwatched.

Jess nods at me enthusiastically. 'Exactly. That's the silly part. I would have hated it too.' She looks down and scrutinises her bare wedding finger. 'It's years since I had a holiday. Even though I've come home empty-handed, I've still had the *most* wonderful time. Regardless of whether he wants to marry me or not, the man is a legend. He might be a pirate, but he's also proved himself to be a top-quality gentleman. When I stop to think about it, I'm happy to take him just as he is.'

I grin at her. 'That's great news. To be honest, I'm not sure I can take any more weddings.'

For the first time, Jess's eyes pull into focus. 'I've heard you're very good at this, Holly, but now I can see it for myself.' Her voice is suddenly earnest. 'Your photographs have a completely different feel to Jules's. They're much more up-close and relaxed. It's as if you're photographing your friends.'

'I'm fine with the edible ones.' Let's face it, given my day job, those *should* sparkle. 'The rest, not so much.'

Jess's brow furrows. 'Jules thinks you made your brides comfortable because you were a woman. But from the feedback I've had, it's about you being able to reach out and connect with people. That shines through in your work too.'

I let out a groan. 'Feedback?' It sounds like Trip Advisor.

Jess gives a mysterious flutter of her eyelashes. 'Believe me, when brides have fabulous days, they tell me. And between us, Jules wouldn't be sending you hand-tied arrangements if he wasn't delighted with you.' She nods at the bunch of roses and frosted berries on the desk that were delivered to me yesterday. All the way from the flower department in the base-ment. 'And it's all great experience for your beach wedding. By the way, how's that going to work with the wind?'

My gulp's so huge it sounds like it came from Gollum. I

wasn't expecting to leap from Interflora to my most dreaded day ever. As if an outdoor wedding isn't bad enough. With Luc turning up on the same day, my heart feels like it's being freeze dried in my chest. Let's face it, though, if Marilyn can stride back into the wedding in a new hat, after getting bashed on the head by a drone, I can pick myself up here. I make sure my tone is suitably airy.

'Wind's what the beach is all about for Nate and Becky. Extreme surfers like a stiff breeze.' From my porthole window in the bedroom this morning, the sea was slate gray with waves as high as mountains. When Jules's thank you card got whooshed off the windowsill in the draught from the closed window, I missed the significance. If I hadn't been obsessing about Luc, I'd have thought about tomorrow's wedding.

Jess shakes her head. 'You do know it's gale force out there? Our pilot said the wind was so strong, our plane almost ended up back in Switzerland.' She raises an eyebrow. 'Although this does mean your very own Luc will be winging his way across the Atlantic to you faster than ever.' She lets out a low laugh. '*I'm Luc, and I'm coming to get you ...*'

As a bit of sick comes up into my mouth, I'm wishing I hadn't had the seventh maple syrup pancake for breakfast. 'It's *definitely* not like that.' There's no need to ask how she knows he's coming. When she hasn't been busy with proposal outings, she's been on the phone to anyone and everyone in St Aidan. She's probably more tuned into the local grapevine than when she's here at the shop.

Jess beams and peers out beyond the fairy lights and glittery ivy that are trailing across the window. 'Well, here's someone who might put a different slant on Luc's wedding appearance.'

I'm so busy sticking my chin in the air, maintaining my position, I don't get around to glancing at the window. 'Poppy, Immie, Lily, Rafe and Rory are all very clear where I stand on this.' I know my dreams are a bit of a giveaway. But I'm confident that apart from that one wobble with Poppy, my public face has been consistent. It's bad enough Luc turning up, without everyone witnessing me falling flat on my face when he ignores me. Sadly my programme of personal upgrading hasn't got beyond buffing my nails. And with so much wedding stress, my carb boycott lasted approximately five seconds. I've got the whole of this evening to dedicate to beautification. But as yet I have no idea what I'm going to achieve, or how.

Jess looks puzzled. 'What has Poppy got to do with anything? It's Becky who's waving at us from the Mews.'

'Becky?' When I finally swizzle my eyes past the Christmas display, the wild arm movements I catch as she heads for the door look like someone who's drowning rather than waving.

As I hurry out into the hallway, she's already by the Christmas tree, so I go in for my hug and two kisses. 'Lovely to see you. Is everything okay, Becks?' As our cheeks squeeze together, the soaking I get has to be tears rather than sea.

If nothing else, the last two and a half weeks in the wedding shop have sharpened my disaster- management skills. Arriving three hours early, when she's supposed to be out sorting the marquee? Looking like she just surfed through a tidal wave, when she's not even wearing her wet suit? My bride-in-distress alarm bells couldn't be clanging any louder, so I'm keeping it positive here as I drag her into the White Room. 'Sit down. Shall I get you some gin?' I'm racking my brains to remember if there's any cake left in the tins.

Jess steers her onto the chaise. 'Or you could try some schnapps? Raspberry, peach or chocolate? I've got miniatures in my bag. They're great for resuscitating lost mountaineers.'

Becky gives a groan. 'I'm sorry. But alcohol's not going to help here.' For a woman who regularly braves the high seas, her voice is small and very pathetic. 'Our wedding just got blown away.'

'Crap.' Way too major for a cupcake diversion, then. 'What the hell happened?'

She's whimpering into the sleeve of her *Pray for Surf* hoodie. 'We were at our spot down the coast, and the guys left off building the main tent, because the coastguard came to close the beach. And while they were talking, the whole marquee just took off over the sea.' As she shakes her head her eyes are wide with disbelief. 'All that's left of our venue is a few broken poles. And the caterers think their vintage van will end up in the water. So they're pulling out too.'

There's one tiny blissful moment when it feels like the day I've been dreading for the last week is about to melt away. But one look at Becky's anguished face makes me forget that. 'Okay, let's look on the bright side. Your ceremony's at the Town Hall, so that part's still good.'

Her nod escalates into a wail. 'The guys have gone off to look for the canvas, but even if they find it, it's hopeless. How did we ever think a beach wedding with camping would work at Christmas?'

There's no point admitting I've asked myself the same thing. For me, even sleeping in a tent in summer stretches my comfort envelope. Why anyone would want to do it in winter is beyond me. Add in a wedding, and I can't get my head around it at all. 'I know it's all about the sea, Becks. But given the – er – gale difficulties, would you think about moving to a more sheltered location? Somewhere further inland?' As Jess and I exchange glances, it's obvious we're thinking of the same place.

Becky's head shoots up. 'You know somewhere that's available at such short notice?'

I'm treading carefully. 'Daisy Hill Farm, where your parents are staying, has a barn, which I know is still set up from a very relaxed ski wedding on Monday. If you don't mind that it's not at the beach, we could ask about using that?'

I'm expecting reservations. So when she almost knocks me over hugging me I'm not ready for her.

'Yes, yes, yes!'

The only good thing about ending up in a heap halfway along the hall floor, is the view of the Jimmy Choos on the bottom shelf of the shoe cabinet. I'm lying having a quiet swoon at the silver strappy sandals when a close up of Jess's furry snow boot brings me back to earth.

Jess is beaming down at us. 'Surfing and snowboarding are highly interchangeable. They're both about hanging loose.' She sounds like she's the expert on both now. 'Great work, Holly, you handled that like a true pro. In that case there's no time to lose. I'll ring Poppy right away.'

As I see the smile of relief spreading across Becky's face, I wouldn't have it any other way.

Jess hesitates as she turns to leave. 'Just one other thing. While you're down there, Becky, do settle the argument. Luc *is* coming back to see Holly, isn't he?'

Becky grins across at me. 'Of course he is. Everyone knows that. Why else would he be coming?'

For what it's worth, if she'd said that before, I might have been less keen to resurrect her wedding party.

Chapter 34

Friday 22nd December
The Barn at Daisy Hill Farm: My worst day ever

The Snow Surf Board Wedding

The funny thing about dreading something is, it rarely plays out the way it has in your head. At any time in the last week I'd have billed this as the worst day of my life this decade, but it begins with Rory popping in to make his second breakfast, and my first. And I have to admit, smoked salmon and scrambled egg on wholemeal bagels is a great start to any day. Even if he is still making rude remarks about my jim-jams and calling me Champs-Élysées Holly across the little kitchen table, at least it distracts me. Because every time I remember I'll be seeing Luc in barely two hours' time, I shudder so hard I almost drop my coffee cup.

The good news is that as soon as Kip and Rafe gave the go-ahead yesterday, Nate and Becky and their gang transferred their wedding operation seamlessly from the shore to the barn. The immediate clearing up after Monday's wedding had been done, but most of the bigger props were still there to use. So the surfies moved in to festoon the walls with hanging wet suits and surfer t-shirts. The Christmas tree had a whole load of surfboard leashes added, to give a beachy twist to the festive cheer. With surfboards propped up against it, the plank bar was soon looking more surf shack than mountain hideaway. Everyone was so enthusiastic and supportive, that if there had been any more time, I'm sure Rafe would have gone out on his tractor and brought in a beach, like the ones you see in parks in the summer. And once the *Gone Surfing* signs and posters for *Endless Summer* and *Beach Parties* were in place, the transformation was complete.

Immie's found room in the holiday cottages for most of the wedding party, who should have been staying by the beach. A few of the die-hard guests are still pitching low tents in the field behind the wedding barn, sheltered in the lee of the hill. As for the more upmarket guests like Luc, who've booked into the lovely and rather swanky Harbourside Hotel in St Aidan. Well, all they'll have to tweak is their taxi bookings.

As we set off for the farm after breakfast and bump through the lanes to Rose Hill village, the beer-mobile is being buffeted by the gusts from the gale. Because Nate and Becky were never expecting the full 'Jules photographic' works, Rory skips his groomsmen visit and looks in on Gracie and Teddie instead. And I go and take all the girlie pics with Becky, who, unusually for a bride, is already looking relaxed rather than nervous.

As I come back in after photographing her posy of sea holly and dusky blue anemones, she flings her arms around my neck. 'I don't know how I'm ever going to thank you for saving our wedding, Hols.' For the first time this morning she's teary rather than laughing. 'I'll definitely be sprinkling my own special cupid dust on you and Luc later. But if there's anything else I can *ever* do for you, you only have to say.'

It really isn't like me to take people up on their offers. But her make-up looks stunning and her bestie bridesmaid who did it is all ready and sitting with nothing left to do. I peer into a make-up box that's bursting with cosmetics. 'If you really mean that, I'd love a bit of lippy?' Not that I'd usually bother. But seeing I downed tools and came to help here yesterday, the only personal make- over I had time for was couple of coats of black nail varnish.

Becky's back to beaming. 'We can do much better than a smudge of lippy. That's the beauty of having a bridesmaid who works on the Benefit counter.' She turns to the girl by the make-up, who's already put on her bridesmaid's H&M tropical-print maxi dress. 'Bride's request, please Carmel. Make Holly especially lovely. Whatever it takes, she's not going to end the day single.'

I love Becky. Seriously, though, I wish she wouldn't do those winks. But after Carmel's done her stuff, I do feel totally up for whatever's going to be thrown at me.

The rest of the morning is as frantic as any wedding, with the added complication of zooming to a very blustery St Aidan for the ceremony. Running across the Town Hall car park, the wind is so strong it's practically tearing the dresses off the bridesmaids, which in the end leads to some pretty amazing pictures. Not many couples will have wedding albums that look as if they got married in a wind tunnel. And it's so lucky that Becky chose a little boho cotton dress from Topshop. If she'd had pouffy petticoats, I think she might well have taken off.

As we go up the wide steps between the tall columns of the Town Hall portico, the hotel guests file in to join us. Despite choosing upmarket accommodation, they're mostly embracing the casual dress code, wearing shorts and hoodies. A lot of these people are Luc's friends too, but I'm really not prepared for so many enthusiastic hugs and waves. This is the point where I'm literally having kittens. Forget any wedding-stress shutter quake, this is purely down to the thought of bumping into Luc. I'm desperately scanning the horizon, so he doesn't creep up on me unexpectedly. Then just when I feel like I might explode with the toxic mix of fear and anticipation, Nate comes across to where I'm fiddling with my lens cap.

He's looking completely fab in his boarding shorts and Hawaiian shirt, as he leans in to my ear. 'Just to tell you, Luc's been delayed for a couple of hours. At least.'

'Phew to that.' I almost drop my camera with the relief.

The first bars of the Beach Boys' *Good Vibrations* are playing, but he beckons me back. 'Don't worry, Hols, he'll definitely be here at some stage. You two *are* meant to be together.'

'Great.' As I give him a thumbs-up, I'm meaning anything but. 'Good luck, anyway.'

That's my cue to relax and enjoy what I'm doing. There's a short ceremony, where Nate and Becky look every bit as happy and fabulous as they deserve. Unsurprisingly their promises are full of watery jokes about falling off surfboards.

Then we brave the wind and snatch a few shots of everyone with the bay in the background.

As I shout at Rory across the bonnet of the beer-mobile as we run back to the car, my leopard jacket is almost getting carried out to sea and taking me with it. 'I'm truly embracing the moment here, Rory Waves.' And bizarre as it seems, I'm almost sad that I'm doing all these moves for the last time.

'Me too.' He's laughing as he yells back at me.

Somewhere down the line, he must have applied a double dose of Diesel when he was back at Home Brew Cottage, because for a second all I want to do is see how it feels to rub his face. But I slap myself back into line. I crush my fingers so hard under my legs that by the time we get back to Daisy Hill Farm, they're numb. But at least I reckon I'm back in control again.

In tune with the surfie aura, the rest of the day is pretty much a free-for-all party, but Rory and I still work our socks off. After hours of dodging shadows, I'm pretty confident that Luc's a no- show. It's the kind of anticlimax that undoes the knots in my stomach one by one, then leaves me feeling like a popped balloon. By half past nine, I'm also confident I've caught every move a surfer can make to every Beach Boys track and Christmas song in the world.

When Rory comes over, I wave my camera at him. 'I think that's a wrap. Everything okay at the cottage?' While I was capturing the disco jive, he's been back home.

For a second he looks doubtful. 'Erin could be better.' He phones the hospital every evening, but he usually spares us the details, then changes the subject, exactly as he's doing now. His eyes light up again. 'They've just cranked up the snow machine outside. It might be worth a last look.' This is how he's been all day. Steering me round to the action.

I pick up my coat and we weave our way through the bales towards the door. 'A few quick shots and then we'll go.' Despite the lure of snow against starlight, I'm factoring in my lift into town. 'You need to get back to take over from Immie at the cottage.' At this rate it'll be after midnight.

Half an hour later, I've got more blizzard-in-the-dark shots than any bride could wish for. We're working our way back into the barn when it suddenly hits me. 'Rory, why are you wearing my hat?'

He's grinning down as he holds the door open for me. 'No, *you're* wearing your hat. *This* is a matching one I bought yesterday.' He has the decency to look slightly shamefaced.

I pat my head and, sure enough, my hat's there. 'Thanks for pointing that out.' As I notice his guilty shadow flashing across his face, I know I need to push more. 'And why would you do that?'

His smile is unrepentant. 'Corporate identity?' He knows I'm not buying that one. 'Okay, I give in. There's no better wind-up for Luc than us wearing matching hats.'

'What?' My voice is deep with horror. I can't decide if I should be appalled, or *very* appalled.

He's looking exceptionally proud of himself. 'Distracting the opposition's a well-known sporting tactic. Seriously, you need all the help you can get with prick-head. You're dealing with someone who doesn't necessarily have your best interests at heart.'

I'm within a whisker of saying, 'And you do?' But I'm really not going to go there.

His eyebrows knit into a frown. 'Did you once say he looked like the guy out of *What Happens in Vegas*? It's just that I met a dead ringer for Ashton Kutcher going into the toilets earlier. Complete with American twang too. There can't be many of those in Rose Hill.'

The rope in my stomach snaps tight as a tourniquet. 'You mean he's here and you didn't tell me?' My voice is a squeak because I'm so indignant.

Rory's unconcerned. 'It's fine, I'm telling you now, aren't I?'

I'm about to ask what the hell he thinks he's playing at, when I feel a tap on my shoulder on the opposite side from Rory. At first I ignore it, thinking it's Rory messing about. The fourth time it happens, I turn around and the face I'm staring into is familiar and strange all at the same time. I'd know that solid jaw and those deep-set eyes anywhere. It's the smooth-shaven chin that's throwing me.

'Luc? You came after all?' My throat's so dry, it comes out as a croak. If I'm trying to sound attractive and alluring, I stuffed that up straight away. As for my insides, they seem to have disappeared entirely.

He slicks back his hair and gives a sigh. 'I've traipsed the length and breadth of Cornwall looking for a beach wedding.' The smart New Yorker look he's rocking couldn't be further from the laid-back surfer dudes around him. 'Why the hell didn't anyone tell me it had turned into a barn dance?'

'Oh no.' I'm scouring his face to find the humorous twinkle. But he must be hiding it.

'So, great to see you, how have you been?' He's still just as tall and impressive. If we're purely talking 'wow factors', he's still seriously out of my league.

'Well, it's good that you made it eventually.' I'm making an effort to sparkle here, even if he's veered off down the jetlagged and grumpy road and can't get back. Although, unlike Rory – not that I'm comparing – he looks even better when he's moody. 'As for me, I've been here all day taking photos. Becky just said you were the one who suggested me to her. So it's actually all thanks to you I've ended up doing a lot of weddings here.'

'Yeah.' He pulls a face. 'I saw you ordering people around outside before like a pro. When did *you* learn to do *that*?'

I'm liking how intrigued he sounds, so I make a huge effort to look diffident. 'Oh, you know, it's been a busy year.' Or more precisely, eleven months of same old, same old, followed by a crazy three-week learning curve.

As he frowns it only accentuates his strong eyebrows. 'Why the hell are you wearing the Smurf hat?'

This one's easy to answer. 'To keep my earies warm.' Me stealing Gracie's expression was a bad slip. I remember too late that kiddie talk's one of Luc's pet hates. As I see his eyes cloud I decide to push on with introductions. 'So, Rory, this is Luc.' I skip the ex bit, because we all know. 'And, Luc, this is Rory, my fabulous assistant.' I do a little jazz hands wave and laugh to lighten it.

Whenever I've played out this moment in my head – approximately a thousand times a night at a guess – mostly Luc's ignored me. A couple of teensy times I allowed myself to imagine him flinging his arms around me and spinning me around so fast my legs whooshed out. Slightly awkward tension, like now, never crossed my mind.

Luc blinks as he sizes Rory up. 'Hello, Rory. What is this, Smurf Central?' His drawl is every bit as Yankee as Rory said, and makes him seem extra-distant.

I give Rory a nod for the hat recognition. Although, as yet, I'm not feeling the full advantage of the matching heads.

Rory lets out a low laugh and points to a hand painted sign. '*If you're not barefoot you're overdressed.* You might like to take note of that, Luc.' Given Rory and I are currently wrapped in full outdoor wear, referencing the sharp creases in Luc's suit trousers falls slightly flat. In a pot, kettle and black way.

Luc ignores the joke and gives me a puzzled stare. 'Why do you need a helper to take a few snaps of the happy couple?'

If he needs to ask, he doesn't have a clue. But I'm not going to say that.

Rory gives Luc an enthusiastic punch on the arm. 'Anyway, it's great to meet you, Luc. I've heard shedloads about you already. But I'm afraid we'll have to chat another time. I'm leaving and I'm very late already.'

'We are?' I'm turning to Rory, open-mouthed.

'Don't be silly, Berry. You two have a lot of catching up to do. I'm sure you'll be able to share a taxi back to town, so I'll leave you to it.'

As I stare up into Luc's face, my chest clenches. Not that I'm usually tongue-tied with friends, but right now, I can't think of anything at all to say to him. 'Actually, it's been a long day.' I turn to Rory. 'If you're still going to St Aidan, can I grab a lift?'

Rory drags in a breath as he hesitates. 'Only if you're sure that's what you want.'

It's as if someone other than the me who's been aching for this moment for a whole year, is operating my legs and mouth. 'Thanks, I'll come now.' Even as I hear the words, I can't believe I just said them. It's only when I see my own astonishment reflected in Luc's eyes that it clicks. Apart from the day I ran off, I've never actually done anything to surprise him before. If he's been playing this out in his head too, I reckon he's only got as far as the version where I fling myself into his arms and beg him to take me back.

'Er ... okay. We'll do this some other time, then. I'll be in touch very soon, Holly.'

There's something hugely empowering about seeing Luc gobsmacked, even if it is a total accident. Next thing I know, I'm following the back of Rory's battered windcheater towards the hewn-plank exit door. A second later we're being blown down the courtyard and my last ever wedding is over. And so is my long-awaited reunion with Luc.

Chapter 35

Saturday 23rd December
In Poppy's kitchen at Daisy Hill Farm: Making tracks

With Jess back in the shop, after a morning editing pictures and checking my inbox and phone every two minutes, in case Luc finds some signal and decides to get in touch, I decide to hitch a ride out of town with Immie. She's on her way back to the farm after a lunchtime Precisely Peaceful session at the Leisure Centre. Although, judging by the way she's cursing every driver on the bypass, I'm not sure how effective the session's been. She's also really agitated because Poppy's running around when she should be winding down. As for me, as soon as I'm chatting to Gracie and Teddie in Poppy's kitchen, it takes my mind off kicking myself for ducking out with Luc last night. Although Immie, Jess and Poppy are all convinced it was a good move, it was a lot less intentional than they think. But as they say, if he's worth it, I'll be hearing from him. However, once I'm back on my laptop next to Poppy's Aga, and I've eaten my own weight in Christmas pudding muffins, it's much easier to focus. And at least if I'm here, I can make sure Poppy doesn't go dashing out to supervise barn clearing or cottage guests.

Despite being under house arrest, Poppy's up to her elbows in icing sugar, creating an alpine- scene Christmas cake, ready for when everyone descends for Christmas Day on Monday. And along the way I sort out Nate and Becky's mini-album, for what will forever more be known as the Hurricane Wedding. Even though yesterday's ferocious westerly has dropped, it's now turned into an icy blast straight out of the Arctic.

'Looks like we're in for a whiteout,' Rory says, as he calls in later to pick up Gracie and Teddie after dinner. He's just missed out on the most delicious Hunter's Chicken, cooked by Rafe, and turned down a carry-out. 'If you've got a spare half hour later, before Rafe takes you back to town, Holly, there's something for you back at the cottage.' He's trying to sound bright, but a vital part of his happy bunny bounce is missing.

Not only is Rafe a superman in the kitchen, he's also offered to run me home, so that's great. But Rory arriving late for dinner and then turning down food, is unheard of. As for calling me just Holly – when did he ever do that? When I tiptoe into Home Brew Cottage after clearing up dinner, it's unusually quiet. Rory's already sitting on the sofa, laptop open, and as he puts it on the table he nods at the space next to him.

'Am I in time for singing with Gracie?' I've rushed so I'd make it. As I gasp to get my breath back, I'm wondering where his loud boy soundtrack is.

He looks up and blinks absently. 'She's already asleep. Sit down if you can find somewhere.'

I was aching to know what he'd got for me as I came up the courtyard, but his blank stare pushes that out of my mind. Given the easy chairs are covered in clothes piles, I perch on the sofa's edge beside him. 'Is everything okay?' From my personal point of view, it's anything but. I really hadn't expected his lost expression to play this much havoc with my urge to not only to rub his head, but to clutch him to me and hug him hard. If these are the vibes Marilyn picks up from him, I can see why she's so hands-on.

He lets out a long sigh. 'Actually, it couldn't be any less okay. I've just spoken to the hospital. Erin's been fighting off an infection, but it's suddenly spiralled out of control. You know, I'm starting to think they might lose her.'

All the time I've been worrying about Luc getting in contact, his sister has been deteriorating. 'Lose her, as in … ?'

He gives a half-nod and his voice is barely there. 'What am I going to do if she doesn't pull through this, Berry?'

I'm shuddering and staring at the snowmen spinning on the Christmas tree in the warm draught from the fire. 'It's really that bad?'

He closes his eyes for a second. 'They're slamming the antibiotics into her, but she's not responding, so they've just upped the dose. It'll be a few hours before they know if it's working. I'm doing such a bad job of looking after the kids. If they lose her, what the hell am I going to do then?'

It's the first time I've ever heard him sound completely helpless. And as I stare at his haunted expression, what I'm picking up is pure fear. 'Whatever happens, we're all here for you.'

His face creases into an agonised grimace. 'I'm absolutely bricking it here. I've never been so frightened about anything, ever.'

This is the big, huge, lovely guy, who's carried me and hauled me, and looked out for me through the last three weeks. Seeing him crumbling is making my heart ache. 'You're the most fearless guy I know, Rory. If the worst happens, you'll come through it, and make it work, in the same amazing way you have with the rest of your life.' Thinking about his accident, I can't help reaching out and grasping his arm.

He sighs and shakes his head. 'If I could, I'd swap places with Erin. This is just so unfair on Gracie and Teddie.'

I know he means it. 'However scared you feel right now, you'll find a way through. You're every bit good enough for those children. I can't imagine anyone who'd step up and care for them more or better than you. If I was going to die, I can't think of anyone I'd rather look after my kids.' I'm not just saying it. It's true. He might have taken a while to get into his stride, but now he couldn't be trying harder. There's just so much heart there. I can feel his forearm flexing through the soft cotton of his shirtsleeve. 'You know, we'll all be here to help you. We'll find a way to make it work.'

'Thanks, Berry. But you might not be here.' He rakes his fingers through his hair. 'I wanted to talk to you about that too. I finished your playlist.'

'That's why you wanted me to come over tonight?'

He takes a breath. 'That was the excuse. Really I wanted

to talk about ways you might stay on.' He pauses. 'I don't want to come between you and Luc. But I thought if we could work out a workable alternative, at least then you'd have a proper choice when he asks you to go back to him.'

I'm a lot less confident than he is about Luc wanting me back. 'You think I should stay?'

'Everyone does. We can all see you could have a great future here. As Poppy says, there's easily enough work for another photographer. If you don't want to do it on your own, I'll help you. We make a great team. There's nothing I'd like more.'

I have to protest, because the thought of giving up my safe salary and starting a business from scratch makes my heart stop. 'But weddings really aren't my thing.'

His lips give the smallest twist of amusement. 'Are you sure?'

'Actually, you're right. I don't mind them so much when I think of the ways I made a difference to Katie and Becky and Saffy and Sophie and Zoe and Nancy. And how warm I felt inside, when there was even one picture they were delighted with.' However lovely that felt, I'd never dare to make the leap to something so insecure.

Rory gives a nod. 'You're so great with people. You can't tell me you get the same satisfaction from working with plates of sausages, even if you do get awards for it.' He bites his lip. 'When you've found something you're brilliant at, it's a shame not to make a success of it.'

I wrinkle my nose. 'But I'm not that kind of person. Especially not in St Aidan. Freya was the bright star in our family, not me.' The boys have done well, but that's different because they were younger.

He narrows his eyes. 'You know, Berry, as I see it, your whole life you've been hiding behind Freya, even though she's not here any more. The last few weeks, since you've been forced to do the things you were scared of, you've come so far. If only you'll let yourself make the leap, the future could be so exciting.'

I'm agonising. 'Me daring to do stuff would feel too much like I'm trying to be Freya. I'd rather stay just how we were.' I've never thought about it like this before. But now he's mentioned it, I know he's right. The last thing I want to do is take my wonderful sister's place.

He puts his fist to his chin. 'Freya would have wanted you to have the happiest and best time you can. She wouldn't want you to settle for anything less than amazing. She'd want you to fly. I think you owe it to her to go for this.'

'So you're saying I should stay and work with you, as a wedding photographer in St Aidan?' When Poppy mentioned a similar thing the day I second shot with Jules, I was horrified. Tonight, when I'm already feeling a tiny pang that there won't be any more pictures of brides getting ready, it's a lot more tempting.

He nods. 'Surrounded by friends, making the most of all your talents. It's what we all think.'

'Are you ganging up on me here?'

He smiles. 'Poppy, Immie and I did get together on this. You've got some big decisions ahead. You need to find the courage to make the right choices.'

I'm swallowing back the lump in my throat, because he's

worked out what I haven't, in more than twenty years. 'Thanks for that, Rory.'

'Back at you, Holly Postman. No one makes me man up quite like you do.' He's got those thoughtful wrinkles in his forehead again. 'By the way, where do you stand on sledging?' It's random stuff like this that makes him so funny.

I can't help laughing. 'You should know that. Firmly at the bottom of the hill. Every time.'

A smile plays around his lips. 'So you've never felt the thrill of whooshing downhill?' Those crinkles at the edge of his eyes get me just as much now as they always did.

I need to be firm on this. 'Downhill, fast and snow? All three together would be up there with my least favourite experiences of all time.' Not that it's a problem, given snow in Cornwall happens once in a blue moon. Seeing it happened last year, I'm safe. But in case he has other ideas, I need to move this on. 'So when will you have more news from the hospital?'

He pulls a face. 'A few hours, maybe.'

It seems the least I can do. 'Shall I wait with you?'

'I'd like that. If you don't mind.' He pushes himself up and stretches. 'You start on your playlist, and I'll go down and tell Rafe you don't need a lift. No Christmas tunes in there, I promise. You already know the first song.'

'S Club 7?' I'm bracing myself for a punishing couple of hours.

He tugs on his jacket. 'It's a mix. Some to make you happy, some sad ones, some with a message. Some to make you remember us, if you decide not to stay. It's your call to decide which are which.' Then he gets out his phone and adjusts the volume down as the first bars come pounding out of the speakers. 'And Gracie and Teddie will definitely be here for Christmas. So if you've got any brilliant ideas for presents ...' His eyes are still dark with worry, but at least he's lost the hopeless look.

'I'll see what I can think of.' I smile as I wave him out of the door. 'How are you with shopping?'

He rolls his eyes. 'Like everything else – a bit shit.'

* *

Flicking through the playlist, *Fight for this Love*, *Bat out of Hell*, and *Teenage Dirt Bag* all go in the nostalgia pile. *Issues*, *Fix You*, *Wishing and Hoping* and *So Kiss Me*, go in the what the hell? pile. I'm putting *Reach* and *Girls Just Wanna Have Fun* in the happy pile, when he comes back in.

As he throws himself down on the sofa, he looks about as agitated as Immie after she's had half an hour on her *Cool-Head* app. 'Jeez, is this a hell of a night or what?' He blows. 'Poppy's having contractions, so Rafe's taking her into hospital. They were just leaving as I got there.'

'How's Rafe?' This is just what he doesn't need.

'Exactly like a guy who already lost a baby that came early.'

'And Poppy?' I'm wincing and feeling guilty for not making her rest more.

He shakes his head. 'We'll know more later. Right now there's nothing we can do, except hope very hard.' He pores over his laptop. 'Maybe we'll skip *Baby Love* and *Exes and Ohs* and go straight to Radiohead.'

I grit my teeth and stick those tracks firmly in the fun pile. '*No Surprises*?' I smile as the first haunting notes echo across the room. 'It's pretty much my theme tune. I love this track.'

'Me too. It kept me sane in hospital.' He pats his upper arm closest to me. 'Feel free to lean. No strings. It's going to be a long night, that's all.'

Wedged against the solid warmth of his shoulder, with the songs in the background, the hours pass strangely fast. At four a.m. there's a call from the hospital to say Erin's out of danger. At five Rafe rings to say Poppy's not in labour and they'll be home again in the morning. And at six Gracie and Teddie come through and are delighted to find Rory's up before them. And when I wake up even later to find I'm curled up, head in Rory's crotch, under a cashmere throw, he's polite enough to pretend it never happened.

Chapter 36

Sunday 24th December
In Rose Hill village: Gone shopping

'So what colour roses?' Rory's staring at the array of buckets in the village shop. 'Pink?'

'Definitely not, Freya wasn't girlie.' As I look at the blur of colours, I know why I don't usually do this. It's because somehow nothing ever seems beautiful enough. 'I was thinking yellow, but since you found the holly plant, I think the smaller white rosebuds.'

It's only a short walk from the shop to the churchyard, with Gracie hanging onto my hand and skipping, while Rory carries Teddie. Not that I come here often. But I can make my way to the pale headstone by the end wall without even looking.

Rory stoops down and gets the tiny bush out of the bag, and pushes the pot into the ground. 'It's nice to find a holly with so many berries on. Look, Berry, there's still frost on the grass too.'

I take out the roses and bind them with a black and white

ribbon that came from the tree at Sophie and Saffy's wedding. As I bend down and put them beside the pot of holly I'm sniffing away my tears. Then, as I get up, Rory's spare arm comes around me and I bury my face in the soft Diesel-scented folds of his windcheater, and stay there for a long time.

When I finally prise myself away, we walk around the paths between the graves, taking a while to wind our way back to the world outside.

'Are you very sad, Holses?' Gracie's hopping now, pulling on my hand. 'Do you want your mummy?' She stops tugging and begins to rub the sleeve of my furry leopard coat. 'Don't worry, your Feather Christmas presents will make you better.'

The corners of Rory's eyes crinkle as he smiles at me over her head. 'Berry's thinking about someone she loved very much. And promising she's going to be brave from now on.'

Gracie does another lurch forward. 'Brave like you ... going to the shops?'

'Did I say that, Gracie?' He laughs as he holds her spare hand to help her down the worn stone steps that lead back down to the pavement. 'I'll let you know if I'm brave or crazy, once we're back.'

* *

In fact it's hours, and many twinkly shops later, before Rory's satisfied that the pile of carriers in the back of the beer-mobile is huge enough. For a reluctant shopper, he turns out to have a knack for seeing past the tinsel to find perfect gifts. He also manages to dodge to the tills without Gracie noticing what he's carrying. Then we pop into the Fun Palace at the Crab and Pilchard for a late lunch, where Gracie's way more interested in the food than the play area. She demolishes her own pizza on a slate, then works her way through our beer-battered fish and chips too.

And afterwards we go back to Brides by the Sea for our final stop of the day. We're with Sera in her studio, with its lovely brick walls and fabric swatches, measuring Gracie for my own surprise present, when Jess comes rushing up the stairs.

'Lovely, now you're all here, I can tell you about the new plans for Christmas.' Somehow she's purring and beaming both at the same time. 'It's obviously going to be too much for Poppy to entertain at the farm as she is. So it's all settled. Everything's transferring to the Manor. You're all invited, and there's quite enough room for everyone to stay overnight. Lily and Kip will be there. Who knows, we might even persuade Jules to come too.'

However thrilled Jess looks, and however practical this is, I'm still worried. 'How's Poppy taking it?'

Jess pulls the corners of her mouth down. 'She's not happy. But we've all decided it's the best thing for her and the baby. She turns to Rory. 'You and the children *will* come, won't you?'

Rory sends her a grateful grin. 'Thanks, we'd love to. Sorry we're a last-minute addition.'

From the way Jess squeezes his hand, she doesn't mind at all. She goes all twinkly when she looks at Sera too. 'The Manor's the perfect place for you and Johnny to celebrate your first anniversary.' It was this time last year when Sera and Johnny got together at her sister, Alice's massive country-house Christmas wedding.

Sera pushes back her tangle of blonde curls, puts the tape measure back on the bench, and wipes her hands on the back of her ragged denim shorts. 'Thanks, Jess, that couldn't be better. But a whole year? I can't believe it's gone so fast.'

Jess narrows her eyes as she looks at me. 'So, Holly, what's all this nonsense I hear about you spending the day on your own?' She doesn't leave room to explain. 'Bart's orders. Even if we have to drag you, you're coming. We won't take "no" for an answer, okay?' When Jess is this fierce, she's damned scary.

'Okay. Thank you, that'll be brill.' I daren't say anything else. But to my surprise, I find I mean it.

Rory jumps in. 'Seeing we're the early risers, we'll be round to pick you up at ten, Berry. Snow permitting.' He grins at Jess. 'Don't worry, I won't let her wriggle out of it.'

Sera's eyes light up. 'It was *so* beautiful when it snowed for Alice's wedding. Even though it blocked the roads so no one could get there. Is snow on the forecast, then?'

Rory nods. 'It probably *isn't* going to happen. But if it does, Berry, we promise to battle through the drifts to reach you. Although obviously we won't be able to set off until after we've built a snowman.'

Jess's eyes are shining. 'You absolutely *have* to come, Holly. Dress code is anything goes, so long as it includes a Christmas jumper.'

Rory narrows his eyes at me. 'If you haven't got one here, I'll lend you one of mine.'

'Lovely.' Hopefully my enthusiasm hides that he read my thought balloon, yet again.

Jess inclines her head to me. 'By the way, Holly, did Sera tell you Luc popped in looking for you earlier?'

Sera clasps her hand to her mouth. 'Oops! Sorry, Hols.' She's well known for being ditsy, and this is why.

At least her apology gives me the time to cover up that my stomach just plummeted to the basement, then bounced back up again. After waiting all day yesterday, I'd given up hope. All I manage in reply is a gulp.

Jess is chiding me. 'Why on earth didn't you tell us he looks like a film star? Now we've seen him, we completely understand what all the fuss is about. You're a hundred per cent right not to give up on that one, Holly.' Her eyebrows are wiggling excitedly. 'He's at the Harbourside with a group of friends. There's still all the time in the world for him to come good.'

Rory's face falls as he takes hold of Gracie's hand. 'We'd better be off, then. Immie's promised us tea and cake in return for a cuddle with Teddie while I wrap. We can't turn down offers like that.' He lets out a sigh. 'Thanks for all the help, HB. We'll see you first thing, then.'

Whatever hopes Jess had for Luc returning, they come to nothing. I work in the White Room until ten p.m., just in case. As I take a final look down the mews, I'm concentrating so hard that at first I read the flecks falling from the sky as reflections. By the time I've logged them as snowfall, they're already a blizzard.

Chapter 37

Monday 25th December
In the attic flat at Brides by the Sea: Head in the clouds

When I wake on Christmas morning, the bedroom is surprisingly bright. There's so much snow clinging to the glass of the little porthole, I have to open the window and clear it away before I can get a view across the bay. As I brush the ice crystals off the slates and look out across a roofscape of white plains, my insides deflate. Down below the sea and the sky are the same light grey, merging somewhere far in the distance. Out along the bay the people out on early walks with their dogs are battling into the wind, their figures dark against the dazzling white clumps along the sand.

Snow all the way to the edge of the sea? I've never seen that before.

Sticking my feet into my leopard pumps, I whip down the four flights of stairs to the shop. As I peer past the snowy tulle skirts in the window of the White Room, the snow outside in the mews is layered across the cobbles in a thick downy quilt. I know it's hopeless to think Rory can get here with falls like

361

this, but I slide back the lock on the door all the same. I have no idea why the hell I feel this wretched when spending this Christmas day alone is the ideal I've been working towards for months. Then, trying not to notice how eerily quiet it is, I stamp back upstairs and stick some milk in a pan.

PJ's, hot chocolate, cosy duvet. *Friends Season 1* here I come.

Even if I'm looking forward to the day a lot less than I'd imagined, breakfast is shaping up okay. The only way it could be better is if yesterday's doughnuts hadn't gone crusty overnight. If I had to choose again, I'd possibly go for jam rather than custard. But considering how the weather's turned, the twelve pack that felt excessive when I nipped out late on Christmas Eve afternoon seems like startling good judgement this morning.

But when I tuck myself back under the covers and start on my *Friends*-fest, far from me falling out of bed laughing, Jennifer Aniston looks so young, she's making me feel like an OAP. How did I ever think a whole day alone was going to be do-able, let alone fun? Ever since I arrived, I've been busy and surrounded by crowds of people. Somehow, my old hermit routine is a shock I'm not prepared for.

Four episodes in, I press pause and stick my head under the duvet. I'm sniffing and reaching for a tissue when I hear voices.

'Is this Holsie's house? Why are there so many stairs?'

There's a low, familiar laugh. 'Because Berry lives up in the sky.'

'Gracie? Rory?' Mortified doesn't begin to cover that they've caught me crying. But as for them being here, if I'd looked in my doughnut box and found my custard rocks had turned into a Krispy Kreme selection, my stomach wouldn't be whooshing with any more excitement than it is now.

Gracie's eyes are huge as I peep out from under the duvet. 'Does Feather Christmas's reindeers fly up here, Hols?'

Rory's face is split in a grin. 'Holly Christmas! Seeing as this is twenty questions, why are you still in your pyjamas when it's time to go?' His grin slowly turns into a knowing smile. 'Unless your Christmas present to me is asking me to meet you in Paris, via your pyjamas?' Even though we both know it's bull, he never gives up.

I'm trying to shut him up. 'We'll see once Christmas is over.'

'I'll take that as a yes, then?' He doesn't get any less tease-y.

'Ask me again next time you see them.' Obviously there won't be a next time. Part of me is aching inside that he won't be crashing in and waking me up with the smell of cooking bacon. That those pre-wedding breakfasts are over. However seductive Rory's plans sound and however much I man up, with my savings as they are I can't make the figures work. There isn't enough for me to get a business up and running, and eat too. 'But how did you get here? The mews looked impassable. I thought you weren't coming.'

'The main roads are fine.' His brow wrinkles into a frown. 'I promised I'd be here, Berry. If it meant pulling you ten miles on a sledge, I'd still have come to get you.'

Something about the way he looks at me as he says that makes my insides turn all soft. Just for a second I'm regretting that I wasn't out of bed to get a 'Happy Christmas' hug. Although however much I'd like to bury my head in his neck, it's probably best that I didn't, because I might not have wanted to let go. So when Gracie dips around Rory's ragged jeans and holds a furry toy out to me, I'm grateful for the diversion.

When I see what it is, I can't help laughing. 'An Olaf meerkat? Isn't he fab?'

Gracie's beam couldn't be any bigger, although she's still holding snowman tightly too. 'Feather Christmas brought him.'

Rory cuts in. 'I know we're mashing our genres here, but it was your voice in my head telling me he was too cute to leave in the shop.' For a guy who once thought *Frozen* was what peas are, he's caught up fast.

As I smile, I realise what's missing from Rory's hip. 'Where's Teddie?'

'Where do you think? It's hard to prise him away from Immie these days.' He looks at his phone. 'If you'd like to get ready, that would be good. We need to call round by Roaring Waves to get some beer and fizz for Bart and Jess.'

I pick up my best jeans and a Topshop shirt. 'I'll be as quick as I can.'

'Great. Don't forget your wellies.' Just before Rory backs out of the room, he drops a carrier bag onto the bed. 'That's the Christmas jumper I promised you. You put that on and I'll get the Christmas tunes ready.'

I tip it out onto the quilt, but instead of the threadbare Bad Elf Beer hoody I'm expecting, there's a soft, berry-pink sweatshirt with a white-printed caption.

Christmas is too sparkly ... said no one ever...

I'm laughing so hard I can hardly speak. 'Thank you *so* much.' Better still, when I bury my face in it, it smells faintly of Rory. I'm about to dive across for a thank-you hug. But it's too late, he's already closed the door.

Chapter 38

Monday 25th December
Christmas Day at Rose Hill Manor: No surprises

The snow-covered landscape looks magical as we sing along to *Jingle Bell Rock* and *When Santa Got Stuck Up the Chimney* on the road to Rose Hill village. But it's nothing compared with how it looks when we turn down the lane to the Manor and see the gracious stone house with its chimneys and snowy roofs appearing beyond the black and white trees along the drive. The Christmas trees flanking the entrance are covered in snow too, and sparking with twinkling lights, and as we go through the wide front door the warmth hits us. Even though we saw the towering hallway tree reaching for the sky at Sophie and Saffy's wedding, it makes us gasp all over again this time around. Jess and Bart have added several miles of tinsel and a celestial army of cherubs to make it even more Christmassy. Some artfully arranged Swiss sledges and ski boots underneath it add the perfect dollop of festive atmosphere. And from the chatter drifting out into the hall, it sounds as if they've added in extra guests for the pre-lunch drinks party.

As Rory swings in from the car with the first crate of beer, I seize the chance to whisper to him. 'Where are all the pressies?'

He gives the laziest wink. 'They're on their way.'

There's no time to ask more because Jess is welcoming us with air kisses, looking fab in her blue cashmere Klosters Snow Polo jumper and her ski pants and furry boots. She raises an eyebrow and fixes me with that stare of hers. 'Keep your coats with you. I hope you're ready for a day of fabulous surprises.'

'Lovely.' Hopefully there won't be too many like last year's.

Jess is laughing. 'No need to look so scared, Holly. Come in, have some gluhwein and enjoy the ride.'

We move through to the lovely living area, with its comfy linen-covered sofas and wide polished boards. Across the room, Kip and Lily are talking to her mum and her new husband, who are both wearing zingy raspberry exercise wear that matches her lippy. As Bart throws logs onto a blazing fire, Jess ladles warm, spiced wine and hot, spiced apple juice into our glasses. Then we pick up some smoked salmon blinis and while I move on to do the rounds of 'Happy Christmas' hugs and air kisses, Rory goes out for the rest of the beer and fizz.

When I find Poppy over by the doors looking out to the lake, I settle Gracie down on a stool with Meerkat, Snowman and a tray of canapés. Then I give Poppy a special hug, grinning at the *My Little Snowflake* caption on her bump.

'How's that tiny person of yours doing?' Even though we've

chatted on the phone, I haven't actually seen her since she got back from hospital yesterday.

She pulls a face. 'I've pretty much got over having Christmas wrestled away from me. I know Rafe and Jess are only trying to protect us both.' The bump she's patting under the snow-flake is actually huge. 'Whatever it says on my top, there's nothing little about this one. He's run out of space to kick now. They've always been struggling with their dates, but the head's engaged, so he might even be a January baby, not a February one.'

Immie adjusts Teddie on her hip and steps back to get a better view of Poppy's middle. 'Whatever the medics say, you look a lot like I did just before Morgan arrived.' She rakes her fingers through her hair and grimaces in the direction of her chunky six-foot teenager playing on his phone.

I can't help commenting, 'That's a lot less scientific than your usual pronouncements, Immie.'

Immie blows out her cheeks. 'Some things rely more on instinct than science. Birth is one of them.'

Poppy's moving the conversation on with an eyebrow wiggle. 'So, I hear Rory took you for a tour of the brewery, Hols? She flashes a knowing smile. 'Not everyone gets one of those, you know.'

I'm keen not to overplay this. 'We were literally in and out picking up drinks. I had no idea the Roaring Waves name was because it was right by the sea.' The range of barns, clustered by the beach out along the coast road, were truly lovely, and a lot less derelict than Rory had implied.

Immie's come in close. 'It's a great place. But more importantly, did you get a look at the bedroom?'

I'm going to have to fudge this. 'I saw some big shiny tanks and a marketing suite. And a bit of the house that was way tidier than Home Brew Cottage.' I know my cheeks are scarlet. When I accidentally caught a glimpse of a monumental wooden bed, I shot back out to the beer-mobile.

Immie's lips are twitching. 'Bound to be tidier without the gruesome twosome messing it up. Everyone in St Aidan knows about the bed. It's the only furniture in the room, with a view straight out to sea. Most importantly, though, there's no curtains.'

Even I can't keep a straight face at that level of local knowledge. 'Thanks for that. On a need- to-know basis, I don't need to know any of that.'

Immie beckons us in closer. 'On another subject entirely …' She fishes in her pocket.

My sigh of relief for that lasts until I see what's in her hand. 'Immie, what the heck?'

Immie gives a chortle. 'Keep your tinsel on. Haven't you seen a urine sample before?'

Poppy sends me a long-suffering glance over the pot of wee in Immie's hand. 'And you're waving it around because?'

Immie's face crumples. 'This is my fourteenth alcohol-free day. As far as the baby-making goes, I've been super-chilled and we've been bonking like rabbits.' She breaks off to point to her red sweatshirt. '*I keep calm, I'm in love with a firefighter*. I'm totally what it says on the tin, thanks to my classes and my chillaxing apps.'

I'm puzzling. 'So where does the wee come in? You need

to be careful it doesn't get mixed up with the apple juice.'

Now it's Immie's turn to look despairing. 'With so much Christmas booze on offer, I might just crack. Which is where you two come in.' She rams the sample into my hand, then pulls a box out of her pocket and shoves that at me too.

I let out a shriek as I look down at the wee and the box. 'A pregnancy test?'

'Keep it down. I don't want the whole world to know.' If Immie's looking daggers at me, it's way too late. She hisses at us, 'If I say the word to you and Pops, I want you to do a test for me and tell me it's negative. And that'll be the go-ahead for me to have whatever drink I'm craving.'

Poppy's voice is sympathetic. 'Any reason why you can't do it yourself?

Immie blows up at her nonexistent fringe. 'To be honest, I've done so many tests the last few months, seeing another negative would wreck my Christmas. I know it's a big ask to get friends to put your pee on the stick for you. But I thought you two wouldn't mind. It's only for use in the direst emergency. We all know it'll be negative. But this way I don't have to look at it.' She scans our faces.

I open my shoulder bag and push the sample and test in. 'Great. Say the word and we'll be in the cloakroom.'

Poppy's eyeing Bart as he comes across the room, balancing a tray of steaming glasses. 'More drinks, ladies? Jess has told me to make sure everyone has a full glass.'

I take some gluhwein and turn to look out across the lake to the snowy hills beyond. I'm just bending down to check on Gracie, when there's a squawk from Immie.

'Hang on to your thong, Hols, Jess is waving and it looks like she wants you.'

Poppy's blinking. 'Christmas crackers, is that *Luc* she's got there?'

The lurch my heart makes is so big, it practically jumps out of my chest and lands on the terrace outside. 'It can't be.' Despite throwing down a huge slug of gluhwein, my mouth's dry.

Immie's voice is a low growl. 'Elephant bollocks, it sodding is. The *Ashton Kutcher* is sailing this way. With Jess at the helm and Rory following close behind.'

I give another gulp. 'He met her at the shop. She's probably just invited him over for drinks.'

Poppy sounds perplexed. 'For someone only out for a drink he's looking very focused. He's heading over here like a guided missile, but twice as fast.'

I let out a little moan. 'I'd hoped for a catch up over coffee …'

Immie's voice is gruff. 'A cream tea would definitely have maxed out the food-intimacy connection.'

I can't help smiling at that. 'Hot chocolate at the Surf Shack, I'd melt faster than you can say "Christmas muffins".' Although that would hardly fit with Luc's carb ban.

Beyond the sofas, Jess is somehow propelling Luc toward us, clinking a glass at the same time and shouting for everyone to be quiet. If I wasn't bricking it, I'd be in awe of her multitasking skill. I clench my bum really tight in the hope it'll help me drop the inches I've gained since last December.

As everyone goes quiet, there's a terrible sense of déjà vu.

As Luc comes to a halt a few feet in front of me and starts to clap his hands, it's like I've lived this before. I know exactly what I've got to do. I'm edging backwards towards the double doors to the garden. Behind my back, I locate the handle. When I push, I feel the door spring ajar. I'm just about ready to run for my life, when I look up and Rory catches my eye. You know when people talk about communicating without words and it sounds like crap. But there's something in his gaze that freezes me to the spot. I'm not taking the easy way out any more, am I? This time, I'm not going to run. I'm going to stay and tough out whatever's going down here.

As Jess clears her throat the look on her face is as delighted as mine is horrified.

'Everyone. Please. Luc wants to say a few very important words to our very own, and very special, Holly.'

As Luc towers in front of me, in his sharp dark-grey suit and pristine white shirt, I can see why Jess is bowled over. All the way from America. All the way to Rose Hill Manor. Exactly a year to the second, practically, since ... well, since last year. Somehow, now I'm staring up at him, my crazy heartbeat is getting more sensible again.

'Hi again, Luc.' I smile at him, because if nothing else, his timing is impeccable.

He clears his throat and looks around to check he's got everyone's attention before he begins. 'Holly. Last year, I asked you to marry me, and at the time, due to – er – extraneous circumstances, you didn't give me a proper answer. And I left for New York, thinking our relationship was over.'

The American twang is a shock all over again. And this is

how Luc is. If there's an audience, he'll always go out of his way to bring them up to speed first, before he gets to the point. He's already lost Immie with his preamble, because she's rolling her eyes. Extraneous circumstances? He pauses for long enough for me to think that's a bit of a strange way of describing what happened and I catch Rory sighing too, over Luc's shoulder.

Luc clears his throat again. 'However ...' He lets that very big word hang for a while. So long, in fact, I'm wondering if he's forgotten what comes next in his head. Then he kicks off again. 'However, during the year, I had time to reflect. And I decided that maybe my future was not in New York after all, but in London. With Holly.'

There's another pause. Possibly to give me time to work out if this is about me or the job. Because, from where I'm standing, it's not at all clear where he's going with this.

'So, in short ...'

Which it isn't at all, but whatever. Immie's not the only one yawning. He's pretty much lost me too. I think I must miss the next bit because I'm so busy frowning, looking out at the hills. But when I look back round, my eyes almost pop out of their sockets, because he's scrambling onto the floor. Then he pulls a chunky pale-blue box out of his pocket. As he shows it around the room, his flourish reminds me of a magician with an eye on the Oscars. Then Jess hisses the word 'Tiffany' so loud the cows at Poppy's farm probably heard her. There's a rumble that goes all around the room. Realistically, stunned silences *never* happen here, because everyone's always got too much to say.

There's no need for Jess to get overexcited. Even if it's a prettier box this time, it's still going to be his grandmother's ring inside. Then, as he flips back the lid and does another whole-room show-off, the sparkle is so totally dazzling even I do a kind of croak in my throat.

As he looks up at me from where he's scrunched up on one knee, the expression on his face is so earnest that, for a nanosecond, my heart squishes. Then my gaze moves on to his navy silk tie. And the slight graze on his neck where he's shaved too closely. I can only think Americans don't approve of designer stubble. Not that I'm shallow, but he looked so much better 'with' than 'without'. All this time, despite the bling in the box, his lips haven't deviated from their straight line. When the main words finally come out, they're low and quite growly, 'Holly, will you marry me?'

I'm opening and closing my mouth, and it's nothing to do with my shock at the new ring. 'I'm sorry, Luc, but ...'

That's as far as I get. Then Jess swoops in and grabs the box from Luc. 'Holly, remember what you told me?' She beams down at Luc. 'Thank you, Luc, Holly is truly delighted, she *especially* loves your ring. This heartbroken girl has waited patiently for you all year. Please bear with us, she'll be accepting very shortly.' In one movement, she rams the ring onto my finger, then powers me backwards onto the sofa. As I land against the kind of luxurious feather cushions that hug you right back when you fall on them, someone's clearing their throat.

'Holly Berry, you can't throw your life away, don't marry him,' It's Rory. Every bit of colour has drained from his cheeks, but he's still just as chilled, leaning with his shoulder on the wall, arms folded. 'He doesn't love you ...'

Rory's voice has kickstarted my heart again. There's a glorious moment when it dawns on me what he's about to say. There can only be one reason why he's joining in here. I'm thinking, *yes, yes, yes, I love you too, Rory Bad-Ass Sanderson, how the hell did I not see that before?* And Rory standing up here now to tell everyone Luc doesn't love me, but he does, is the most romantic thing I can think of in the world. So romantic, my mouth goes all sour, because I might just be going to cry. Smiling across the room at Rory and sniffing hard as he finishes his sentence, I'm already anticipating how amazing it's going to be to snog him.

I'm aching to hear the words. 'He doesn't love you, Berry ...' *I do...*

Except it isn't that. Rory's voice carries across the room, and it couldn't be louder, or clearer. 'He doesn't love *you*, Berry ... the only person Luc loves is *himself*!'

I'm squirming inside for having got that so wrong.

As Rory's words bounce off the white walls, Luc is looking up, scratching his head. 'Who's this Berry, anyway?'

As the murmuring around the room gets louder, Immie's frowning and growling at me. 'Stuff Jess! You *can't* marry a guy who didn't even bother to get in touch when you told him you might be pregnant!' Except in the end it's indignant and horribly loud. There's a ripple of gasps around the room, then the roar of excited chatter.

Let's face it, this is St Aidan. Everybody cares enough to wade in when you're at the checkout buying cereal. Getting proposed to, the discussions may take all day. I smile at Gracie, who slides off her pouffe and comes to nestle against my knee.

She wrinkles her nose. 'Is this Luc the p ...

Happily, I cut her off before she gets to the 'puke' bit. 'Yes, this is Luc, and he's come all the way from America.' I'm sounding like a song. 'Luc, this is Gracie.'

As Gracie puts her hand up to wave, Luc backs away as much as a man on one knee can and pulls a face. 'I've consolidated a lot the last year, Holly. We're world leaders in Sound Operating Environments now and I'm currently screaming up the ladder.'

'Great.' It's so absurd, what he's saying, that my lips are twitching. 'I hope you've attached your safety harness?'

He squints at me. 'What?'

Our old conversations are all coming back. 'Site regs when working at a height. Don't you have to clip on above two metres?' He talks the talk, I make the jokes.

His face is still blank. 'Shall we get on with this, Hols?'

As I stare around the room, everyone's talking so hard it's as if they've forgotten we're here. It's very like the night we had to force everyone back into Sophie and Saffy's reception. As I catch Luc's eye again, I give an apologetic shrug. Then I dip my hand into my bag and the first thing I pull out is Immie's wee pot. Which was well worth it, if only for the look of disgust on Luc's face. Second time lucky, I pull out the whistle. Two sharp blasts later, the room is ours. Almost.

I'm just psyching myself up to speak when a loud voice from the back breaks the silence. 'I heard Holly talk Saffy into getting married when she was ready to run off. She'll know her own mind here. Be quiet and let her speak.'

Good point well made, about letting me get a word in. But I'm gobsmacked that he's been so indiscreet. 'That was supposed to be a secret, Gary.'

Ken joins in. 'We're backing Team Rory!' With comments like that they're completely living up to their matching *Bad Elf* jumpers too.

I glare at them both, then take a moment to focus on the dazzle coming off my hand. It's so much more than I'd ever hoped for. I've spent an entire year aching not to be on my own. Luc taking me back at any point would have been beyond my wildest dreams. Yet now I'm staring down at this startling row of diamonds, in just the kind of simple and classy white-gold setting I'd have chosen myself, it couldn't feel more wrong.

'Okay.' As I take a deep breath, I'm taking it for granted that everyone wants to hear this. 'As some of you already know, this time last year when Luc proposed to me, it's no secret that I ran away. Then, by the time I was ready to say yes, he'd changed his mind.'

Immie interjects loudly. '*And* buggered off to America. Don't forget that bit. As dickheads go, they don't come any bigger.'

I pause for a moment, then start again. 'It's true what Jess said. I cried for an entire eleven months.' I pull a face at her. 'And then I came here. And for the last few weeks, I've done a lot of things I'd never have done by choice. But somewhere along the line that's made me into a different person. It's showed me I'm capable of a lot more than I thought.' Even as I'm speaking, I know the Holly who came off the train would never have dared to do this. Although admittedly, I'm still a long way from coming out with the kind of slick performance and fancy words Luc uses.

Poppy flops down beside me and punches my arm. 'Go Holly!'

I glare across at Gary and Ken. 'And it definitely isn't about teams, okay?' It's somehow very important to make that clear. 'This is *only* about Luc and me. And Luc, you're a great guy. For four years, you were solid and certain. But I think what I took from you was security rather than love. Somehow we collided and we stuck together, when maybe we shouldn't have. I was your happy accident, who all your friends thought was ditsy. And you were my comfortable option. However hard we work at this, we're never going to make it more than that.'

Luc's blinking up at me, as if he's been struck dumb.

I look across at Gary. 'I think I finally began to understand the day I talked to the bride Gary mentioned. I was taking pictures at her wedding when she had a wobble and I helped her sort out why. Her reluctance was all about little things. But she showed me what it was like to be crazily in love with the man she was going to marry. So in love she couldn't imagine a day waking up without him. The kind of love where all that mattered was that they were together. Enough love to see them through the bad times, as well as the good times.' I turn to Luc. 'When I ran away last Christmas, Luc, at the time I didn't have a clue why it had happened. But now I know, it wasn't because I was shocked or because I was scared.'

As I look between the faces, I see Rory, back by the wall, nodding gently as he listens. Of all the things I've done since I've been here, he's pushed me the hardest. But he's also been there supporting me, every inch of the way. I can't actually believe I'm daring to stand here saying this to everyone. And without Rory's help, I never would have been.

I take another breath and look back to Luc. 'I now see, if we'd truly loved each other, I wouldn't have had misgivings when you asked me to marry you last Christmas. And you wouldn't have been able to leave me in the way you did. So I've finally worked it out – my instincts were good that day. I ran because we didn't have the kind of love we needed to carry us through. I ran because deep down I knew what you were asking was wrong for both of us.'

Luc's still down on the floor, resting his elbow on his one knee, propping his chin on his hand. For the first time in our entire relationship, I've got his undivided attention. And, blow me down, as they say in the States, but he's actually *listening* to me too.

As I've no idea how long this state of bliss will last, I press on. 'So that's why I'm just as certain I should be saying "thanks, but no thanks" this time around. I'm very touched that you've come back. It means everything that you've asked me to marry you a second time. And I'm truly sorry I can't accept. But at least it's given me a chance to explain. And this way we can say a proper "goodbye" too. Believe me, you're a fabulous man. Just not the right one for me. And I'm certain there will be some very lucky woman out there, who will make you a lot happier than I ever could.'

I've pretty much said it all. I'm wavering, wondering what the hell to do, apart from giving the ring back, obviously. Next thing, I find myself getting up. I've tugged the ring off my finger and I'm stepping forward, holding it out for him to take, my arms open. And I've completely forgotten that Luc's not *ever* a huggy person. And *definitely* not in public. As he scrambles to his feet, I can't help noticing how obsessively shiny his shoes are. But that's not my problem any more. He's also totally overdone the expensive-smelling and rather spicy cologne in his collar region, so even from two feet away, my eyes are starting to stream. But whatever, the hug we both participate in feels more spontaneous and heartfelt than any he's ever given me. As my cheek is rammed against his lapel, the tears I'm sniffing away are mostly allergic. If there's a tiny twist in my heart and a lump in my throat, they're for all the things we couldn't give each other.

Then everyone starts to clap and cheer. And strangely, it feels like it couldn't have been any louder if we'd just got engaged.

Chapter 39

Monday 25th December
Christmas Day at Rose Hill Manor: Swishy tails and special deliveries

As expected, turning down a proposal, in public, in Rose Hill isn't without fallout. I get enough hugs, well wishes and advice in the next hour to last at least until the mince pies come out a lot later this afternoon. By midday, when a lot of the guests are peeling off back to their own Christmas lunches, I'm pretty much over the shock of getting engaged then unengaged all inside ten minutes. I'm catching a quiet moment by the French window when Rory sidles up with Gracie for his own debriefing.

'Well done for that one, Berry.' As he pulls me towards him with his one spare arm, there's a waft of delicious Diesel mixed with Rory's own particular guy smell, and a crush so hard I can hear his heart hammering against his chest wall. He frowns down at me. 'Are you okay? Have you survived the mass concern and love?'

I nod. 'I even had a hug from Jules. He's very brave to come out when he's still blotchy.' For someone as appearance-orientated as Jules, a face that's all red must be a nightmare.

Rory laughs. 'There's barely an inch of face showing between the top of his scarf and his Santa hat. And that's covered in concealer.' He looks down at Gracie.

'So how about these presents?'

Gracie's bottom lip wobbles. 'P-p'raps them's at Mummy's house.'

I'm about to tear into him for being mean, when he scoops her into his arms. 'Can you hear anything, Berry Christmas?'

Gracie gets in before me. 'Jungle bells ... I can hear jungle bells ...'

Immie arrives, beaming, Teddie on her hip, and throws down an armful of coats and boots. 'I think they're all here.' As Rory lets Gracie down, Immie zips her into her anorak. 'Come on, Hols, time to put your leopard on.'

I pull on my hat and my wellies, and help Gracie into hers. 'What's going on?'

Immie chortles. 'This is Rory's surprise. You can't help but love this one.' She points to the window. 'Look outside, Gracie. See who's coming.' As she opens the door there's a gust of icy air and the sound of bells coming closer. 'This is going to be so ace.'

We stumble out onto the terrace just in time to see a cart zooming towards us. As Nuttie the pony tosses his head as he trots, the bells on his harness are ringing and snow is flying up off the cart wheels. White fairy lights, winding right across the cart, are twinkling and sparkling against the snow. And sitting high on the front of the cart is...

'Santa! ...' Gracie's scream of excitement echoes across the snow. 'It's Feather Christmas Santa ... he's bringing my presents!'

It's amazing how fast kids pick up on this stuff. She's already spotted the huge hessian sack in the back. And unlike the time I hitched a lift with Santa and his overfriendly elf, this time the presents are real.

Rory's busy with the disclaimers. 'Right, Santa's had to come on his cart, with his pony, because you're the last person he's visiting, and his reindeer are too tired to pull his sleigh.' He swipes his hand across his forehead under his hat. 'And this is for one time only. Every other Christmas, Santa will be coming when you're asleep, okay?'

But Gracie isn't listening. She's already rushing across the snow to where the cart has pulled to a halt at the edge of where the lawn should be.

Rory hurries after her and hands her up to sit between Santa and Elf. He pushes me up onto the cart too, then springs up beside me. Somehow I can't say anything, because when I look at Gracie's face, literally shining with happiness, there's this huge lump in my throat that won't let the words out. After a huge nose blow, I manage to whisper to Rory, 'You've smashed this one, Sanderson.' I'm familiar with the routine now, so I grin at Ken and Gary. 'Isn't this where we all go in for a selfie with Santa?'

Ken laughs at me. 'Christmas Crackers, you're right.' He looks down his nose at me. 'You wouldn't have been getting one of these either, if you hadn't chosen Rory.' He shakes his head. 'There's enough sizzle between you two to cook a turkey.'

He pauses as a doubtful look passes across his face. 'You do know he doesn't have curtains in his bedroom?'

I'm shaking my head in despair. 'Yes. Immie already told me.'

Ken's nostrils flare. 'You can't pass over an Adonis like him purely for lack of soft furnishings. The fabric shop in town has a lady who'll run up anything you want. You might as well get matching cushions and a valance too while you're at it.'

Sometimes it's hard to remember – they're like this because they care. 'Thanks, I'll bear that in mind, Ken. Shall we have that selfie, now?' Although in some ways I'm grateful. Not so much for the interference. But at least it's distracted me from my uncontrollable blubbing.

'Okay, first we'll do a circuit of the house, then the selfies.' When Santa tells you what's happening, you go with it.

Everyone who can fit on clambers aboard. The air is cold against our cheeks as we fly up the drive. I'm rammed up against Rory, and with the snorting of the pony, and the flying snow, I know it's a once in a lifetime event. Rory's right to tell Gracie she'll probably never get her presents personally delivered by Santa in the snow, ever again. And my heart's bursting in my chest that Rory's made it happen for her now.

'Selfie time.'

I should have realised, when it comes to selfies with Santa, Ken likes to call the shots. Then Rory produces a pillowcase out of his windcheater pocket, and Gracie holds it open, while Santa fills it with her presents, and I take pictures of her expression. Delighted doesn't begin to cover it. Then, last thing,

Rory produces a carrot for Gracie to feed to Nuttie. Truly, this man has every aspect covered here. Then we all clamber down again and Chas and Rafe take the rest of the presents from Santa's sack. Then we all stand and wave as he drives away, and when his bells are just a jingle in the distance, we all walk back towards the house.

Another selfie? I get as far as thinking this one's what I'd like to wake up to every day on my bedside table. Then I remember that table's three hundred miles away and my stomach wilts.

Chapter 40

Monday 25th December
Christmas Day at Rose Hill Manor: Bubbly and ripping
yarns

'Okay, presents by the fire?'
Back inside the house, the adoring way Rory's
looking down at Gracie would turn anyone's toes to syrup.

We all take up places on the sofas and watch as Rory's
meticulous wrapping is torn to shreds in seconds. It's no time
at all before Gracie and Teddie are sitting surrounded by piles
of toys and what looks like the entire contents of a paper-
recycling factory.

Rory's startled expression is priceless. 'What happened
there? Fifteen hours' work destroyed in three minutes flat.'

Immie laughs. 'That's kids and Christmas, Rory Waves. If
it means we can move on to lunch, don't knock it. And what
a great idea to have Johnny, Rafe, Kip and Chas in charge in
the kitchen.'

Gracie brings me the dress I got Sera to make for her. 'It's
an *Anna* dress.' That's Anna, the heroine of *Frozen*.

'Would you like to put it on?' I'm grinning at Sera, who worked so hard to make it yesterday evening. The long silky blue and purple dirndl style dress look exactly like it does on screen. 'It's so pretty, I think I'd like one of these too.'

Rory laughs. 'Wait and see what's in your parcels, Snow Berry. There might be something in there you like even better.'

But before we get to the adult presents, there's the small matter of lunch, which is served at a long table in the Winter Garden, where the windows are so large, it almost feels like we're dining outside in the snow.

The guys have excelled themselves in the kitchen and Bart's in charge of the wine, which changes with every course. With Brie and cranberry quiches, fried ravioli, meatballs and stuffed mushrooms, the starters are a meal in themselves. There's pork, turkey, ham and nut roast for the main course, with all the trimmings. Buttered carrots, purple mashed potato, snap peas, stuffings, stuffing balls, sauces, Yorkshire puddings, Rafie's roasties and lashings of gravy.

'Are we eating Immie and Chas's piggy ring bearers here?' Rory asks. Their wedding was one of his forty, so he knows all about the runaway porkers.

'Definitely not,' Rafe laughs. 'Everyone who comes to the farm wants to see those bad boys.'

By the time we get to the Christmas pudding and rum sauce, with Poppy's speciality Christmas pudding ice cream melting over it, we're more than full. But we soldier on valiantly to tackle a cheeseboard the size of a snooker table, then move on to coffee and liqueurs, and chocolates.

We're sipping coffee with chocolate and praline overtones,

surrounded by gilded plates of truffles when Jess looks over at me.

'Well, there's still one more teensy surprise left. Another one for you, Holly.'

Rory sends me a grin over the top of Gracie's head. 'Hopefully this one's better than the first.'

Jess sends me a sideways glance. 'Not many people would have been strong enough to refuse that ring, but whatever. I'm assured there's a lot I've missed out on in Switzerland after all.' She draws herself up in her seat. 'This is more professional than personal. When Jules became ill, we were all aware that without a photographer, a wedding might as well not happen. Without one all our reputations would have been at risk, and without a doubt, all our businesses would have suffered. But you pulled out your cameras and stepped into the breach, Holly, and saved the day for all of us. We all know it wasn't easy for you, but you came through amazingly. So, well, we're all of the same opinion – you absolutely *have* to stay on and be part of the team.'

Usually I'd be scarlet by this point. But I'm actually so gobsmacked, I feel as if all the blood has drained from my face. Rory saying it privately is one thing, a big announcement like this is making me feel as though my spine has been surgically removed. I'm actually sniffing into my hanky again and the fairy lights that are strung across the ceiling and along the windows are blurry through my tears.

Jess smiles. 'I know you're having quite an emotional day. But to show how much we appreciate what you've done, we'd like to offer you the studio rent-free for a couple of years. Or as long as it takes for you to get a business going. We'd like you to install yourself there and use it. And Jules,' She beams across at the figure who's now added reflective sunnies to his Santa hat and scarf combo. 'Jules will be on hand to either share, or help, or join in, in whatever way he can.'

'Absolutely.' Jules puts his thumbs up. It's strange, but losing his fabulous complexion seems to have temporarily taken away his normal personality too.

Jess carries on. 'The attic flat is yours as long as you need it, too. We're all determined to work with you to make this happen, Holly. All you have to do is say the word when you're ready. And, unlike this morning, I'm not pressuring you for an answer. Take however long you need. But please, please, please choose Brides by the Sea. Because now you've given us a taste of your magic, we really can't do without you.'

Poppy comes over and gives me a squeeze, and Lily and Sera, then Immie, get up too. 'Okay, group hug.' I'm damp, and sniffy and slobbery, but the hug is so warm and long and lovely that at the end of it I feel better rather than worse.

Okay. Well at least feeling like a wrung-out dishcloth is a great excuse to tuck into a white chocolate and raspberry truffle with my coffee.

Rory stands up. 'Great, thanks for that, Jess. Is this a good time to move on to the grown-ups' presents? Shall I play Santa?'

I see Gary lurch across the table to object. Then he remembers he left his Santa persona with his Santa suit, and sits down again.

For someone who isn't supposed to be participating in

Christmas this year, my stack of presents is mahoosive.

Rory leans over and picks a packet out of my pile. 'Okay, this one first, it's for you and Gracie to open together.'

Gracie doesn't mess about, but then as the paper comes off, I understand what I'm looking at and she doesn't. 'Oh my, how awesome. Me and Gracie got matching *Wonder Woman* pyjamas, from Rory.' Yet again my voice is all high and squealy.

Rory raises an eyebrow and laughs. 'Glad you like them. I left the onesie in the shop in the end. But you can always have that for your birthday.'

Poppy's looking at me, one eye half-closed. 'What's that about onesies again?'

I close my eyes and shake my head. 'Trust me, it's best not to know.'

Gracie's already onto my next present, which turns out to be a Happy Dolphin Garden Centre reindeer like the one we bought her and Teddie. I turn to Rory. 'Bought on the same day we did the tree?'

He's frowning. 'Obviously. You looked like you were about to cry when you had to leave the shop without one.'

Immie laughs at him. 'When you get kids of your own they'll have you wrapped around their little finger, Rory Waves.'

I'm kind of holding my breath waiting for his 'no kids' speech, but somehow it never comes.

Then Rory opens the cashmere sweater and shirt I've bought him, and likes them so much he insists on putting them on. Although, I admit, having to cope with a flash of his gorgeous pecs and torso was something I'd overlooked when I chose the present. I've just opened some Snowberry nail varnish – just Rory's joke, apparently – when there's a howl from across the table.

When we peer past the candles in mason jars and paper piles to see what all the fuss is about, the duck egg blue of the box Jess is holding looks very familiar.

Her howl's subsided and her voice has gone all peculiar and small. 'Bart, you bought me Tiffany earrings? Do you know how long it is since anyone bought me jewellery?'

Bart's sitting next to her, looking very pleased with himself. 'Well, the first day we met, you told me you always bought your own. But as we know, every Cornish pirate needs rings in their ears.' He gives a sniff. 'Well, open the box. See how you like them.'

Jess does as she's told, but when the box springs open, she looks puzzled. 'But there's only one? So it really *is* a pirate earring?'

Bart gives a whoop, then his face creases up in laughter. 'Pass it here, it's actually upside down in the box, I'll show you how to put it on.'

'Okay.' Jess is blinking in confusion as she passes over the box. 'Whoever knew Tiffany did earrings for pirates. Whatever next?'

As Bart takes out the piece, he holds it up and it flashes in the light.

'Oh my.' I'm murmuring under my breath to Rory. 'That's not an earring.'

Bart looks at Jess. 'Give me your hand.'

'My *what?*' Jess hesitates.

'Your hand, Jess. Your left hand.' A second later Bart's dropped down on his knee beside her. And he's still laughing. 'Jess, only you could spend three solid weeks searching for an engagement ring in every chocolate fountain in Switzerland, and miss it when it finally arrives in Christmas gift wrap. That's why I love you. That's why I want to grow old with you. Make me the happiest man in Cornwall. Please, Jess, will you marry me?' The next instant, he slides the ring onto her finger.

It's a good thing he's not waiting for an answer, because she's still opening and closing her mouth minutes later as she wipes her eyes on her serviette and stares down at her finger and sniffs. 'Thank Christmas I anticipated an emotional day and put my waterproof mascara on.' She's almost growling at him. 'Come here, you old pirate. Of course I'll marry you. So long as you promise to behave, of course.'

Bart's laugh is very low and his eyes flash. 'You'll have to make me.' He stands up and dips in for a kiss. Then he rubs his hands 'Great work, me hearties, this calls for a toast. I've got the best champagne on ice. And how about elderflower fizz for the alcohol-free?'

We all file round the table, and wow, Jess's treasure is worth inspecting. It's a glorious solitaire, with smaller diamonds embedded in the ring all the way around. For someone who's always leading the way, Jess has gone remarkably quiet. But we all go in for squeezes and pecks on the cheek anyway.

Now it's Immie's turn to growl. 'I thought I'd hold out at least until the Christmas Pudding Martinis.' She lets out a long groan. 'Elderflower fizz or vintage champagne?' She bites her lip. 'Okay, Hols and Pops. It's official! I've cracked. Off to the cloakrooms and give me the go-ahead. For one day only I'm back on the bevvy.'

I pick up my bag and Poppy and I make our way out to the loo, which is so posh it has its own liquid soap dispenser.

'Jeez,' I say, as I get one of the test sticks out and dip it into Immie's pee. 'This toilet is bigger than my entire London flat.'

Poppy laughs. 'Yet another reason you should move back here. Just saying.' She takes the box from me, reads it, then pops the stick back in the box and puts it back in my bag. 'Early detection. That's good. Immie only wants to know if it's positive. It'll be ready in three minutes. Shall we help Bart in with the glasses while it's cooking?'

We're so busy delivering ice buckets and dodging popping corks, by the time I creep into my seat and get to peep at the stick in the bag, most people are sitting with full glasses in their hands.

'What are you doing, Berry?' Rory's looking at me over Gracie's head again.

I'm peering at the stick, looking for the line in the little perspex windows. When I see which window the line is in, I don't know what to do. 'Pops, quick, can you come here a minute?' She diverts from where she's walking back to her seat. 'Can you look at this?'

Her face comes over my shoulder. 'Oh shit.' She's looking at me with wide eyes. 'Do you think it's real?'

We're agonising. When we said we'd do this we assumed it

would be negative. Staring at a test stick that says *positive*, how do we break it to Chas and Immie? We don't want to get their hopes up if it's wrong.

'Immie ...' As I call her she's waving her champagne. 'We've got a bit of a situation with the stick. You might need to come over for a look.'

As her chair scrapes back, she passes Teddie over to Morgan, who's sitting next to her, then she bustles over. 'Don't tell me another one of those toad-arse tests hasn't worked. Where the hell will that leave me?'

I'm trying to put her right. 'No, there's definitely a line.'

Immie's voice is a whisper as she squints at the stick I'm holding. 'Ass hats, badger bottoms and toad bollocks.' As her fist goes to her mouth, tears begin spurting out of her eyes. 'Chas ... Chas ... I'm not sure ... but I think we might be ...'

Chas ambles over frowning, looking especially snazzy in his *I'm having a meltdown* fleece with the picture of a collapsing snowman. It takes Immie a while to make him understand, because her voice has disappeared and there are rivers of tears flooding down her cheeks. But when he does finally get what's happened, he sweeps her into his arms.

I watch as he hugs her. 'I'm *so* happy for you.' She might put the pregnancy success down to the Serendipity classes and alcohol-free beer, but I'm sure it's got much more to do with the hours she's spent cuddling Teddie. Whatever the reason, it's still the best Christmas present ever.

After a whole lot more hugs, Jess and Bart's engagement toast is postponed for long enough for Immie to go and pee on the second stick, just to make sure. But this next test says the same as the first. If I know Immie, she'll have another hundred sticks back at the farm and she'll use every one in the next few days. But for now, she's swooningly happy to swap her glass of vintage bubbly for elderflower fizz.

Immie wandering back from the cloakroom punching the air is the signal for the toasts to get underway again. As the gentle late afternoon sunlight floods into the Winter Garden and illuminates the bubbles rising in the golden champagne, we stand and hold up our glasses.

Kip leads the first toast. 'To Jess and Uncle Bart, all the good luck and love in the world for your engagement.'

There's a chinking of glasses all around the table and everyone takes a slug.

Then Bart takes over. 'And to Immie and Chas, huge congratulations for your wonderful pregnancy news.' There's more gulping and some refilling of glasses.

Then Jess lifts her glass. 'Firstly, thank you to my wonderful fiancé, Bart, for making me the happiest woman in Cornwall, if not the world. You managed to surprise me yet again. And thank you to everyone at Daisy Hill Farm and Rose Hill Manor for two years of the most fabulous weddings.' She's beaming round at us all now. 'When I began Brides by the Sea all those years ago I had no idea it would grow to this, or change so many of our lives so much.'

Poppy and Rafe, and Sera and Johnny, and Lily and Kip, and Jess and Bart are all nudging each other and smiling at this point. Although, really, it's not just couples that have sprung up around Brides by the Sea. Under Jess's watchful eye, every one of us has had our talents nurtured, and have been pushed into more and better things than we ever thought possible.

Jess is purring now. 'Together we make the most fantastic team. It's not only because of the amazingly talented individuals here in this room. It's also because we really are like one big family. So this is for all of you. It's for all the wedding days we've made fabulous, and for all next year's weddings too. May every one be spectacular!'

From the special nod she gives to Bart, she's thinking about their very own wedding there. And what an amazing day that will be when it happens. As for me, even before Rory catches my eye and gives me a significant nod at the part where Jess talks about the team, I already know how lucky I feel to be included here and how much I want to be part of this.

'So please raise your glasses ...'

We're all doing as she asks, but as the glasses rise a sudden wail breaks the momentary lull.

'Waaaaaaaaahhhhh ...'

Rafe jumps forward. 'Pops, are you okay?'

As Poppy puts her glass down on the table and looks down at the floor, her face crumples. 'Actually, I'm sorry to interrupt the toasts, but please do you have a mop?' She hugs her bump miserably. 'This is *so* embarrassing. But I think my waters just broke.'

Chapter 41

Monday 25th December
Christmas Day at Rose Hill Manor: Going downhill fast

So Poppy and Rafe leave the rest of us to finish the champagne and head off to hospital. Later, when Teddie, Immie and then Gracie fall asleep in a pile on one of the sofas, Rory suggests a walk in the snow before tea. It's another one of those moments when my feet overrule my sensible self. Even though I'd much rather be curled up toasting my toes, watching the logs shifting on the fire, I'm out in the hall. Worse still, I'm being bullied into some salopettes and a ski jacket from Jess's collection, which is now huge enough to take up an entire wall in the downstairs boot room. Before I know it, there's an arctic blast whistling across the bit of my face between my hat and collar. And I'm stomping along in my wellies and snow socks beside Rory, who's dragging one of the huge toboggans from under the tree behind him.

As we round the bottom of the lake, scramble over a fence and start to climb up the sloping field on the other side, he finally slows down enough for me to start reflecting on all the excitement. 'Snow, Santa arriving, two proposals, an unexpected pregnancy announcement, then Poppy going into labour. This has to go down as one of the most dramatic Christmas Days ever, doesn't it?'

'All the more reason to finish off with some sledging, Snow Berry.' He couldn't sound any more enthusiastic.

Although it should be dark, there's a half moon illuminating the lightly scudding night clouds, and the white folds of snow are shining where the moonlight catches them. Being the boy that he is, Rory's stuffed his pockets with head torches and goggles, but it's so bright so far that we haven't needed them. It should take ages and a ton of effort for someone as unfit as me and stuffed full of Christmas dinner, to climb a hill this steep. But somehow my legs are flying.

As we get two-thirds of the way to the top, Rory stops and turns to look down. 'This should do it. The ride down will be well worth the climb, I promise.'

The kick in the stomach I get from his grin turns to an anxious pang. 'But what about your head? If you can't play rugby, should you be hurtling downhill at a hundred miles an hour?'

He gives my elbow a nudge. 'We're talking about a baby slope here, not the Olympic bobsleigh team. That's why I brought the slow toboggan. I know you won't want to go down too fast.'

'Me?' I blink at him, because I couldn't have made it clearer. I'm only here for the walk. 'What part of "I watch, I don't sledge" did you not get?'

His expression is so eager and hopeful. 'But you're doing

all the scary stuff now. Every time you've dared to put your-self out there, hasn't it been worth it?'

It's not helpful that my stomach's squishing again at the hollows in his cheekbones. 'I really appreciate you helping me understand about Freya.' This isn't only to get out of sledging. I want to thank him.

He pulls down the corners of his mouth. 'When you lose someone, especially when you're young, it can take years to work through the grief.'

It's nice he understands. 'It's funny. You don't ever get over it. You just learn to live with how things are. But I'm really glad you knew her too.'

'So am I.' He nods. 'It's the same with heartbreak and life-changing events. There's no easy fix. You have to do the time.'

I wrinkle my nose. Not that I want to keep going on about him, but I want to make it clear. 'I think I'm completely over my break-up now. There really was no connection with Luc any more. But I'm glad he came back, because it let me understand what went wrong. And made me feel stronger too.'

For a moment he looks very grave. 'I didn't want to cause complications there. That's why I've stayed back. Just so you know.'

I'm frowning. And shriveling inside all over again for thinking he was going to say he loved me when Luc was here. How the hell did I think that? He couldn't have been clearer about why he won't ever commit, and I need to respect that. But if I loved him before, I love him even more for making Gracie's Christmas so magical. That's what's amazing about Rory. He's so good at knowing what will make things wonderful. Then he makes them happen. There really aren't many people who can do that. I don't know which would be harder. Living near him and not being able to have him, or living far away and not seeing him at all.

His lips twist into a smile again. 'So how about this hill? If you can brazen it out to get St Aidan's wedding of the year back on track, five seconds' whizzing on a sledge will be a piece of cake. Shall we give it a go? There's nothing better. The icy air whooshing past you, rolling off into the snow at the bottom.'

'Stop, that's enough!'

'But if you're serious about pushing yourself, you've got to try it once.' He lines up the sledge and sits down on it. Then he nods at the gap between his legs. 'Tuck in in front of me. You never know, you might even like it.'

I let out a long sigh. 'Okay.' It's another time when my head is yelling 'no', and my mouth's saying the opposite. But there might never be another chance to know what it feels like to have his arms around me. Some obscure part of my brain must have done the maths. *Five seconds of sheer terror is a small price to pay for the thrill of being jammed between Rory Sanderson's thighs.* There's simply no other reason my back would be wedged against his chest, my eyes welded closed.

His face is so close his stubble almost brushes my cheek as he leans forward. 'Are you okay?'

'Of course I'm bloody not, I'm about to hurtle downhill!'

'Ready, Berry?'

It has to be said. 'If we wait till next Christmas I'll never be ready.'

'Point taken. We might as well be off, then.' He's lifting his heels off the floor. 'Un, deux, trois, here we go.'

He was right about the rush of air. As we bump and pick up speed, there are ice chips too. The only way to cope is to fill my lungs to bursting and let out the loudest scream I can. There's a few seconds of zooming, then we're down, and we slow and shudder to a halt a few yards from the fence.

Rory's laughing as hard as I was screaming. 'Not so bad was it?'

I'm not going to agree. 'Ten times worse.'

He's leaping to his feet. 'I'm risking my eardrums here. Another run?'

I'm missing the warmth of his body already, so I'm off up the hill again. 'Maybe one more.'

Five runs later and this time we've almost climbed all the way up to the summit.

My cheeks are burning from the effort. I let out a groan. 'I'll be such a Rudolf by the time I get back to the Manor.'

His voice is all protest. 'But I love your red cheeks and nose as much as I love you. I thought you knew that?'

'Bollocks.' He never gives up on winding me up. Really, however determinedly single they are, anyone who says that should have a hug. Although, given what the dark look in his eyes is doing to my insides, it's probably a good thing he's already stooping down by the sledge.

He's looking up at me from where he's crouching. 'Okay, I reckon we're ready for the advanced moves. I'll lie on my stomach and you lie on top of me. It's closer to the ground, so we'll be more aerodynamic.' Those are the worst reasons I've ever heard for a guy getting a woman to jump on top of him. But, due to this being Rory, he's getting away with it.

This is more precarious, but what the hell? It's also way more bumpy, and longer, and the snow spray is hitting me in the face. But this time my eyes are open and instead of hating the rush, my heart is racing with the thrill. When we trundle to a halt and I bump off into the snow at the bottom, I'm starting to get the plus side of salopettes too. As I roll over onto my back and look up at the stars through the gaps between the clouds, Rory's rolling too. A moment later, his body bumps into the space next to mine. And next thing he's propping himself up on his elbow, looking down at me.

'So you risked the hill.' His face breaks into a grin. It's a statement, rather than a question. 'Now you passed that first test, there's something else.'

I'm shaking my head, staring up at him. 'If you'd told me this at the start, I'd happily have skipped straight to step two.'

'That's not how it works.' He laughs, then he goes all serious again. 'You see, however hard I've worked to get back on track after my head injury, there's always been a part of every day when I'd have swapped back to my old life before the accident, if only someone had given me the chance.'

'Awww, Rory.'

He's biting his lip. 'Then after years of living with those regrets, things have suddenly changed. Since you've been here, I don't feel that any more.' He gives a sniff. 'Having you around makes me really happy. I never dreamed I'd ever get to say this. But being with you, as I am, is a life I'm completely happy with. It's the only life I want.' His voice is low as he slides his fingers between mine. 'I don't want you to leave. I want you to stay here and live your life with me. I want us to be together.'

Looking up at his beautiful face, knowing he feels like that, I'm crying, and I can't stop. 'I think it's the life I want too. When I first thought about staying, it seemed impossible. Now everyone's offering so much help. But most of all, every time I think about heading back to London, I can't imagine not being with you every day.' I'm smiling up at him, wondering why he's holding back. 'Isn't this the point where you come in and snog me?'

He laughs. 'I haven't finished yet, but seeing as you've asked.'

As he dips down and his mouth slides onto mine, it hits me that this is the kind of kiss I've been waiting for forever. Light, delicious. With a touch of mocha. Like there's a mass choir singing in my body. When he gently pulls away after a kiss that's longer and sweeter than any I could even have dreamed of, all I want is more.

His grin is shamefaced. 'Sorry, I didn't mean to do that yet. You see, for the best part of ten years I've been resigned to being alone because my head injury was so unstable. I assumed if I didn't date, I wouldn't fall in love. I never thought as far as what to do if love came out of nowhere and zapped me, like it has done with you. But do you think you have enough courage to take me on, complete with my uncertainty?'

I let out a sigh. 'It's a good thing you showed me how to be brave.' I think for a second. 'Although, I'm not sure I'd have had a choice, even if I wasn't. I love you, Rory. I love you because you've got the biggest heart of anyone I've ever met. And the most enthusiasm. And the most courage. And all that's quite apart from being the most beautiful guy in the world, inside and out.' I stop and wrinkle my nose. 'From what I've seen so far, anyway.'

He laughs and pulls on his zip. 'I'm happy to show you the rest. Just say the word.'

Now it's my turn to laugh. 'I made a good choice of present, I already got a flash of torso.' When I put my hand up to rest on his cheek, just because I can, my fingers tingle. 'The thing is, you understand me better than anyone else I've ever known, and you know how to make me the best person I can be. But I love you exactly as you are. Whatever uncertainty your life holds, I'm ready to take that on, because that's how big my love for you is. Even if it's only a day, I'll have to be the one to have that day with you.'

He lets out a sigh. 'Every year that goes by, it's a sign that my head has healed better than they'd ever hoped. But I'll never be as good as I was before. That's the other thing. Until the kids came to stay, I had no idea I'd want my own.'

My eyes are wide, but I'm teasing. 'You're seeing past all those dawn starts, wall-to-wall Disney films and nappy changes?'

He shrugs. 'It's made me know for definite that I want that with you. To have our own family at the Roaring Waves Barn.'

I bite my lip. 'There might be a problem there.'

His brow knits in a worried frown. 'What's that?'

I shrug. 'More than one person has warned me about the curtains.' I keep a straight face for as long as I can, then my smile breaks through. 'Or the lack of them.'

'Any more cracks like that and you may have to have snow down your neck.' He laughs. 'Actually I think I've always loved you. All those days I asked you out on the school bus, I was longing for you to say yes, even if I was years ahead of you.'

I put my hands to my cheeks. 'You gave me goosebumps and hot flushes every time I saw you. Back then, and after twenty years.' I laugh. For the time being I'll keep it to myself how devastated I was when I first saw the baby seats in the beer-mobile. 'And today, when you stood up to tell me Luc didn't love me, I was desperate for you to tell me you did. I knew at that moment that I loved you. But I thought I wasn't going to be able to have you.'

He's laughing again. 'You've no idea how hard it was not to say I did.' He frowns again. 'I've been thinking. We could call your photography business Mr and Mrs – couples getting married, being photographed by a couple. It works, doesn't it?'

'What?' I take a second to grasp that he's hinting at us being Mr and Mrs. Then I change my tone. '*What?*'

He's looking slightly ashamed. 'I'm sorry if it sounds like the third proposal of the day. But I already know it's what I'll want whenever you're ready. It's the same as already knowing I want to have kids with you. That's what comes of falling in love when you're as ancient as me.' He's laughing now. 'I've had long enough to know exactly what I want when I find it. And that happens to be you.'

My smile's so wide, I feel as if my face might split. 'Bloody hell, Rory Waves. You don't mess about, do you?'

He laughs. 'I never have. I'm very organised, when I know what I want. There's another thing, Berry.' He's pulling something out of his pocket. 'I brought mistletoe. And this time I'm not letting you get away.'

I'm teasing him again. 'If you're sure we've covered everything?'

'Absolutely.' He's holding up the berries as his mouth crashes onto mine.

It's a long time later when we brush ourselves down and head back for mince pies and Christmas cake.

Rory's hanging onto my hand very tightly as we stagger through the snow together. 'If we ever tell our kids we had our first kiss in a snowdrift, they probably won't believe us.'

I laugh. 'And we probably won't say it was so good we were still there an hour later.'

He tilts his head to watch me. 'If you want me to miss out the bit about you getting engaged to someone else on the same day as me, you're going to have to promise to cover the whole of the Roaring Waves barn in twinkle lights next December.' He laughs. 'And promise to love me forever, too.'

I'm laughing at him as well. 'I think I can deliver on both those promises. So long as you snog me again, right now.'

He's dropping the sledge rope and pulling me into his arms again. 'Funny, you're usually way more cake-orientated.'

By the time we get back to the Manor, it's so late Poppy's Christmas cake has already been demolished. We tiptoe back in, hoping no one will notice how long we've been away. But when Immie notices my hand in Rory's she starts to clap. And in the end the roar is loud enough to make the bells on the tree in the hallway jangle.

There's a lesson for everyone there. If you want to keep things quiet, don't fall in love at a Christmas party anywhere near St Aidan.

Chapter 42

P.S.

Poppy and Rafe's son, Gabe, arrives safely just before lunch on Boxing Day, weighing in at a healthy six pounds two. We're all still at the Manor and toast his arrival with Rory's special alcohol-free Rockdance beer, so Chas and Immie won't feel left out. Rory's promised to name next year's Christmas brew after him. So long as he's as angelic as his name. Although Immie's pointing out that he might need to make two festive brews, because of course, by next Christmas her and Chas's baby will be here too.

Erin comes out of hospital just after New Year, and Rory and I take Gracie and Teddie for the kind of reunion that's so happy, however many hankies you have, it isn't enough. I have a feeling we'll always see a lot of each other.

When we go back to St Aidan without the children, we finally get to try out Rory's very own bedroom at the Roaring Waves Barns. I'm able to assure the community, via Immie, that whatever people think, the 'no curtains' thing isn't a problem. Due to the window height in relation to the sea, any passing fishermen will be too far away to focus. Put it this way – we won't be rushing out for blinds any time soon.

With my job in London, the company are happy to swap my notice period for guarantees of freelance work. So, Jules and I move the photo business straight into the studio at Brides by the Sea, and it's lovely working with all my friends and being part of the team. If the early bookings are anything to go by, there will be enough weddings and more to share between us.

Some time towards the end of January, we make the trek to London to pack up my room and bring all my boxes back from the storage unit. Rory's delighted to make some orders while the beer-mobile is parked in Bermondsey. He also claims to be looking forward to having the Roaring Waves Barns and Huntley and Handsome festooned with as many decorations as I can throw at him when next December comes.

And, yes, it might sound like we've moved in together very quickly. But some kinds of love are so crazy that when you finally realise you've fallen into them, you can't bear the thought of not waking up next to each other every single day. That's definitely how it is for Rory and me. He's still drives me mad calling me Holly Postman and Berry Berry Pink Cheeks. But when I think of being with Rory every day for the rest of our lives … well, somehow, that doesn't seem long enough.

Some Delicious Recipes from *Christmas Promises at the Little Wedding Shop...*

In *Christmas Promises at the Little Wedding Shop*, Holly loves dipping in to Poppy's baking. I'm really lucky because my son's girlfriend, Caroline Tranter, is a fabulous baker, and she's recreated some of Poppy's recipes in real life. (Caroline's from Bakewell, which is such a perfect place for a cake maker to live, she almost needs a book of her own!) If you'd like fully illustrated, step by step recipes, look out for mouth-watering blog posts around publication time. We've included the recipes here too, in case you'd like to try them for yourselves at home.

Here's Poppy's recipe for her chocolate orange cake, as designed by Caroline Tranter. This is the cake they are all enjoying the afternoon Holly gets upset remembering the ten-foot-tall Christmas Tree she bought for Luc's flat the year before. It's also the cake that's so delicious Rory won't stop eating it. When you taste it you'll realise why.

Poppy's Festive Chocolate Orange Cake

Makes 1 7inch Cake
Preparation Time: 15 Minutes
Cooking Time: 20- 25 Minutes

Ingredients
Sponge:
- 150g Unsalted Butter
- 150g Caster Sugar
- 150g Self Raising Flour, Sieved
- 3 Eggs
- 1tsp. Baking Powder
- 30g Cocoa Powder, Sieved
- Zest of two large oranges (put a side a tsp. for the topping)
- Juice of one and a half large oranges

Chocolate Orange and Cointreau Buttercream:

- 150g Butter
- 400g Icing Sugar, Sieved
- 40g Cocoa Powder, Sieved
- Juice of half an orange
- 3 tsp. Cointreau
- 1tsp Orange Essence

Topping:
- 50g Dark Chocolate, Melted
- Edible Silver Glitter (optional)

Method

1. Preheat the oven to 170°C Fan/ Gas Mark 3/ 190°C Electric. Line and grease two 7 inch tins.

2. **To make the sponge:** With an electric or hand whisk, beat together the butter and sugar in a large bowl until light and fluffy.

3. Into the same bowl add the flour, eggs, baking powder, cocoa powder, orange zest and juice. Whisk the ingredients until fully combined.

4. Divide the cake mixture equally into the two tins and bake in the centre of the oven for 20-25 minutes. The sponge will come away from the edges of the tin slightly when fully cooked. Once cooked, remove the cakes from the oven and leave on a wire rack to cool.

5. **To make the buttercream:** Add all the ingredients to a large bowl and with an electric or hand whisk, whisk the ingredients together until fully combined and light and creamy. This will take a few minutes. (Note: For a more intense Cointreau flavour add an extra 2-4tsp. with the addition of 20g of icing sugar to thicken the buttercream).

6. **Assembly of the cake:** Place a nozzle of choice into a piping bag (This recipe used a Wilton 2D) and spoon all of the buttercream into the piping bag.

7. Take the cakes out of the tins and remove the baking paper. Place one sponge onto a plate or cake board and pipe rosettes on the surface of the cake, filling in any gaps with small piping's of butter cream.

8. Place the second sponge on top of the first sponge and sandwich together. Cover the top of the sponge with the melted dark chocolate and leave to set.

9. Once the chocolate has set, pipe rosettes around the outside edge of the cake.

10. Finally, sprinkle edible glitter and orange zest over the top of the cake.

Poppy's Christmas Pudding Muffins pop up throughout the book. And Caroline Tranter has perfected these. They're actually amazingly chocolatey, but are iced to look like Christmas puddings. If you choose to use chocolate chunks instead of chips, the effect is awesome. Again, they might need to come with a warning. It's hard not to eat too many!!

Poppy's (Chocolate!) Christmas Pudding Muffins

Makes 11 Large Muffins
Preparation Time: 15 Minutes
Cooking Time: 20 Minutes

Jane Linfoot

Ingredients
Muffin Mixture:
- 250g Self-raising flour, sieved
- 200g Caster sugar
- 150g Dark chocolate chips (alternatively cut a dark chocolate bar into small pieces)
- 50g Cocoa powder
- 1 tsp. Baking powder
- 1 tsp. Vanilla extract
- 1 Medium egg
- 200ml Semi skimmed milk
- 120ml Vegetable or sunflower oil

Decoration:
- 150g Icing Sugar, Sieved
- 3 tsp. cold water
- Red coloured ready to roll icing, rolled into 22 berry sized balls
- Holly leaves, washed
- Silver edible glitter

Method
1. Preheat the oven to 200°C Fan / Gas mark 7/ 220°C Electric. Line a muffin tray with 11 paper cases.

2. **To make the muffins:** In a large bowl combine and mix the flour, sugar, chocolate chips, cocoa powder and baking powder until equally distributed.

3. In a separate bowl whisk together the vanilla extract, egg, milk and oil until fully combined.

4. Pour the oil mixture into the flour mix and fully combine the ingredients to form a thick consistency.

5. Spoon heaped tablespoons into each muffin case around ¾ full. Bake the muffins in the middle of the oven for 20 minutes until a skewer or toothpick inserted into the centre comes out clean. Once cooked, remove from the oven and leave the muffins in the tin to completely cool down.

6. **To decorate:** In a bowl, combine the icing sugar and water to form a very thick paste. Spoon a teaspoon of icing onto the centre of each muffin and then spread it out to direct the icing to drop down the muffins.

7. Place two red icing balls onto the centre of the white icing while it is still wet, as this acts as a glue to secure the balls in place.

8. Finally, place a piece of holly leaf on each muffin and sprinkle over the glitter.

Note: Alternatively if you do not have access to holly leaves, or wish to use an edible decoration, using green ready to roll icing and a holly cutter to form leaves works just as well.

Even though they're not strictly festive, I loved the idea of seaside cupcakes. So Poppy gets to make some for the surfie wedding, and Holly and Gracie both love them. Caroline's recipe has shells moulded from icing, highlighted with gold spray, with crushed biscuits for the sand. And they look and taste amazing.

Poppy's Sea Side Cupcakes

Makes 11 Large Cupcakes
Preparation Time: 15 Minutes
Cooking Time: 20 Minutes

Ingredients
Cupcake Mixture:
- 3 Eggs
- 150g Self raising flour, sieved
- 150g Caster sugar
- 150g Unsalted butter
- 1 tsp. Baking powder

Buttercream:
- 250g Butter, room temperature
- 400g Icing sugar, sieved
- Blue food colouring

Shells:
- Ready to roll white icing
- Silicon shell mould

414

- Icing sugar, enough to coat the silicon mould
- Gold glitter spray

Decoration:
- Silver sugar balls
- 4 digestive biscuits

Method

1. Preheat the oven to 170°C Fan/ Gas Mark 5/ 190°C Electric. Line a deep cake tin with large cupcake cases.

2. **To make the cupcakes:** Combine the eggs, flour, sugar, butter and baking powder in a large bowl and with a hand or electric whisk, whisk the ingredients for a few minutes until light and creamy.

3. Spoon the mixture equally into the cupcake cases and then place the cupcakes in the centre of the oven for 25 minutes. The cupcakes are done once a skewer or toothpick inserted into the centre comes out clean.

4. **To make the buttercream:** Using a wooden spoon, cream together the butter and icing sugar until combined. Add a drop of food colouring and then whisk until light, creamy and a pale blue colour.

5. **To make the shells:** Coat the silicon mould with icing sugar and tap off the excess. Insert the ready to roll icing into the mould and press out onto a plate. Repeat this until

there is around 30-35 shells, depending on how many shells you want on each cupcake. Lightly spray the gold glitter over the shells and then leave them in the fridge to harden.

6. **Assembly of the cupcakes:** In a bowl, finely crush the digestive biscuits with the end of a rolling pin and place to the side.

7. Spoon a teaspoon of butter icing onto each cupcake and spread evenly over the top of the cupcakes. Press the biscuits crumbs into the butter icing and tap off the excess.

8. Place the remaining butter icing into a piping bag with a nozzle of your choice and pipe tall swirls onto each cupcake. (Note: This recipe uses a Wilton 2D nozzle).

9. Finally, lightly press the shells and silver sugar balls into the butter icing.

A huge thank you to Caroline Tranter for all her help with this.

Favourite Cocktails from *Christmas Promises at the Little Wedding Shop*

In case you'd like to try a taste of Brides by the Sea at home, it's become a bit of a tradition to include a few recipes at the end of the book. So here's how to make some of the fab drinks featured in the book. Don't stress too much about the quantities. At Brides by the Sea it's much more about sloshing it in and having a good time. As Jess would say, LET THE FUN BEGIN...

POMEGRANATE MIMOSAS a.k.a. TICKLED PINK

A perfect combination of sweet and tart, these ruby red mimosas make a fabulous festive drink with a delightfully humourous alternative name.

120cc of sweetened pomegranate juice
1 bottle of champagne, chilled
Pomegranate seeds to garnish, (or lime slices work well too if you prefer)

Perfect served in champagne flutes. Put a dash of chilled pomegranate juice in a glass and top up with champagne. Float the pomegranate seeds (or lime slices) on top, and you're ready to go.

CHRISTMOSAS

2 Granny Smiths Apples, cored and chopped
1 cup of whole fresh cranberries
1 cup of green grapes, cut in half
1 cup of pomegranate seeds
1 cup of chilled sparkling grape juice
(1 cup equals 30cc)
1 bottle of chilled champagne (prosecco or cava also work well and can be used instead)

Mix the prepared fruit together a bowl. When you're ready to serve, add the sparkling grape juice and the champagne. Ladle into wide stemmed glasses, and enjoy!

CHAMPAGNE MARGARITAS

Adding champagne is a great way to give your standard margaritas a festive boost.

15cc (half a cup) fresh lime juice
30cc (one cup) tequila
15cc (half cup) Cointreau or orange liqueur
1 bottle champagne
Lime wedges and salt for glass rims

Place all the liquid ingredients in a large jug or pitcher and stir well to mix. Choosing champagne flutes, run a lime wedge around the rim of each glass, and dip into salt. Fill the glasses, and garnish with lime slices. These are delish. Stair climbing may be difficult after too many!

COCONUT AND VANILLA MILK BOTTLE COCKTAILS

These fun cocktails were served at the ski themed wedding in the book. Their creamy blend of coconut, vanilla vodka and warming nutmeg make them a perfect choice for Christmas parties too. For extra fun, serve in mini milk bottles.

100cc vanilla vodka
160cc coconut cream
1 tablespoon crème de cacao
Half a teaspoon of finely grated nutmeg
2 chocolate wafer straws to serve

Put a few ice cubes in a cocktail shaker. Add the vanilla vodka, crème de cacao, coconut cream and grated nutmeg. Shake, and strain into two mini milk bottles. Serve with a rolled chocolate wafer in each.

Cheers!

Love Jane xx

Acknowledgements

A big thank you ...

To my wonderful editor Charlotte Ledger, who becomes more talented, brilliant, supportive and lovely with every book we work on together. This series belongs to both of us, and I've had the best time writing these four books. To Kimberley Young and the team at HarperCollins, for the fabulous covers, and all round expertise and support. To my lovely agent, Amanda Preston, for being generous, wise, helpful and fun, and adding so much energy, support and inspiration.

To Debbie Johnson and Zara Stoneley, and my brilliant writing friends across the world. To the fabulous book bloggers, who spread the word.

A special shout out and thank you to the most fabulous wedding related people we've met over the last couple of years ... To Emily Bridal of Sheffield, whose shop and dresses are simply fab. Emily came up with the most amazing wedding dresses for both my girls. I literally get tears in my eyes every time I think of how beautiful she made them as brides. To

Jenn Edwards and Natalie Manlove, and the Jenn Edwards Wedding Hair and Make-up Team, who travel nationwide, making women into the most beautiful versions of themselves. Jenn and Natty gave me hair and make-up that made me feel like Sera on the day of Alice's wedding. I so love it when real life and fiction get mixed up. To Melanie Brunt from Drop Dead Gorgeous Sheffield for fab nail and beauty treatments and expertise. I'll remember my bright pink gel nails forever. Thanks, and huge admiration go to brave and super-talented photographers Jon Dennis from S6 Photography, Sally from Sally T Photography, and Hannah from CameraHannah. Coming on to the sweet part, thanks to Ashleigh Marsh at Oh No! Delicious, for cakes so astonishing they take your breath away. And thanks to amazing cake baker, Caroline Tranter for bringing the cakes in the books to life, designing the recipes, and for letting us use her fab pictures. To High Street Bride guru, Samantha Birch for sharing her insider knowledge. To Losehill House Hotel, near Edale, and West Mill, in Derby, for two wedding days that could not have been more wonderful. Two very different venues, both spectacular, each perfect in their own way.

Big hugs, to India and Richard, for their amazing wedding, which is where this series began. And more hugs and good luck to Anna and Jamie whose very own Sequins and Snowflakes wedding in February was the happiest of days … complete with surprise snow the day before that almost sent this mother-of-the-bride over the edge. To my entire family, for cheering me on all the way. To my wonderful dad, and my lovely mum, who has been so courageous since she's been on her own. To Max for being the man about our house, and bringing me cake. To Caroline for the cake. And big love to my own hero, Phil ... You know all the down sides of living with a writer, and still hang on in there every day. Thank you for never letting me give up.

Coming soon from Jane Linfoot

A brand-new series!
More Cornwall
More delicious bakes
More romance…

The Little Cornish Kitchen

Jane Linfoot